# WIT AND

# *Prattles*

## NANCY MARTIN-YOUNG

**World Castle Publishing, LLC**
Pensacola, Florida
Copyright © Nancy Martin-Young 2021
Hardback ISBN: 9781955086073
Paperback ISBN: 9781955086080
eBook ISBN: 9781955086097
First Edition World Castle Publishing, LLC, August 3, 2021
http://www.worldcastlepublishing.com
**Licensing Notes**
Cover: Karen Fuller
Editor: Maxine Bringenberg

# Preface

*Wit and Prattles* owes its inception to Jane Austen. The broad strokes of Charlotte Jennings and Thomas Palmer came from her pen. In *Sense and Sensibility*, the Palmers are mere minor characters who encounter the Dashwoods late in the novel. Ebullient Mrs. Palmer contrasts with sober, judgmental Elinor Dashwood, while dour Mr. Palmer is a foil for the overly romantic and impulsive Marianne.

So, dear reader, allow me some license. Charlotte and Thomas do not fit the mold of wallpaper historical romances. While she *is* plucky and skirts the edge of propriety, she is in no way a modern heroine. And while he fits the taciturn alpha male model, he's much more. And both are firmly rooted in their time and place.

Their evolving relationship is the heart of this story.

Austen herself describes the couple this way: "Mrs. Palmer was several years younger than Lady Middleton, and totally unlike her in every respect. She was short and plump, had a very pretty face, and the finest expression of good humour in it that could possibly be. Her manners were by no means so elegant as her sister's, but they were much more prepossessing. She came in with a smile, smiled all the time of her visit, except when she laughed, and smiled when she went away. Her husband was a grave looking young man of five or six and twenty, with an air of more fashion and sense than his wife, but of less willingness to please or be pleased."

I'm fascinated by odd couples who, against all odds, make a relationship work. *Sense and Sensibility* is essentially a novel about odd couples. As I reread the book a few years ago, I found myself speculating on the Palmers' backstory and what their relationship was like behind closed doors. Austen offers hints at their depth. Despite his reticence, Mr. Palmer attends to his guests, loves his son, and protects his family. I suspect he also loves his wife.

Mrs. Palmer and her mother, Mrs. Jennings, are the kindest characters in the novel, a virtue I admire above all others. The Jennings women alone remain constant. As Kathleen Anderson and Jordan Kidd explain in "Mrs. Jennings and Mrs. Palmer: The Path to Self -Determination in Austen's *Sense and Sensibility*" (*Persuasions* 30: 135-48), those two ladies are "the only characters to remain happy of their own accord throughout the novel" (147).

Happiness is a choice. In fact, that's one of the major themes of *Wit and Prattles*. Mr. Palmer must learn that wit is no license for cruelty, and much sense hides in seeming prattles.

Of all times, now is the age that needs this message.

Thank you for reading.
Nancy Martin-Young
(writing in other genres as Nancy Young)

# *Chapter One*

London's Argyle Room offended Thomas Palmer on every level, from its presumptuous Corinthian pillars to its garish gilt lamps. The ground-floor rooms were particularly distasteful in their excess, with scarlet draperies in one and an out-of-place green trellis in the next. In the ballroom where he eventually found himself, he discovered more scarlet, more brass, and more pillars. He longed for the open simplicity of Cleveland and the cold cliffs of Somerset.

Above the orchestra, a motto proclaimed, "*Sollicitae jucunda oblivia vitae.*" "Forgetting troubles," as it ordered, was laughable in the stifling atmosphere. Sweat trickled down his neck and soaked his cravat, its intricate folds now limp. The ball was officially a crush, with barely space to squeeze from potted plant to punch bowl.

In such a crowd, he couldn't distinguish one young miss from the next, much less arrange for introductions to those potential brides on his mother's list. All the females before him were equally well groomed and fashionable: depressingly fresh from the schoolroom with their hair crimped, their gowns pressed and beribboned, and their dancing shoes unscuffed. Remembering his duty, he bowed and smiled as often as he could force himself to and, after introductions, partnered a succession of young misses, some pretty, some shy, all polite and predictable. And all deadly dull.

His brother Henry had long ago abandoned him in favor of a cluster of young blades already dipping deep in drink. Thomas eyed them with envy. His mouth felt dry as sawdust. The struggle to keep up inane conversations made his head ache. He'd been hard put not to bolt on at least three occasions when the female jabbering became too much to bear.

Close quarters made his heart pound.

Yet escape was out of the question. He needed funds. He had to forget his last unfortunate foray into the marriage mart. In the years since his humiliation, he'd armed himself with a thick skin. No young miss would slash his pride again. This time, he'd succeed in securing his future and the future of Cleveland.

Resolute, Thomas set about locating another marriage prospect in the melee, this one the niece of a baronet. As he escorted the well-connected but dour Miss Askew to the refreshment table, he cast about for something, anything, to say. "May I get you a glass of punch?"

"Please," she answered, inclining her head. It was a surprisingly big head, he thought, especially since it balanced on a remarkably thin neck.

He downed a quick glass before returning with one for the lady. "Will you be staying in town after the season is over, Miss Askew?" Travel seemed a safe enough topic, unlikely to inspire uncomfortable confidences or batting eyelids.

"My brother and I plan to stop at Bath. Is Cleveland far from there?" Her immense forehead wrinkled in a most unattractive way.

Thomas had a dark vision of the heavy-headed Miss Askew and her flinty-eyed brother dropping by his estate for tea. "Quite far. At least a day's journey," he lied. "Miserable this time of year, with the threat of rain." He felt immense relief when Miss Askew coughed and excused herself, leaving Thomas momentarily freed from the ordeal of carrying on polite conversation.

But duty still had him shackled. He must press on.

The stuffiness of the room led him to ask the lovely but limpid Miss Anne Ludford if she'd care to step into the lobby. She perked up quite astonishingly at the suggestion. He grew increasingly uncomfortable as she batted her pale brown eyes at him and tossed her brown ringlets, and hung on his words as if everything he said bore the wisdom of Solomon. Thomas doubted she'd have demurred if he'd suggested slicing a baby in two.

For several embarrassing minutes, he deflected her attempts at further intimacy by leaning away as she leaned forward. After an interminable period, her clinging arm nearly threatened to restrict his blood flow. With a grimace, he finally scraped her off and returned her to her chaperone. Miss Ludford's name fell to the bottom of the list.

No clinging vines for him.

As he tried to recall the next name on the list of potential life partners, his attention flickered to the dance floor, where, besides the pool of hopefuls, a few more mature ladies of stature danced with their husbands.

It was no wonder his eyes sought and found *her*, taller than most of the ingénues whirling about, her perfect head held up, a coronet of gold hair coiled high, and an unmistakable air of poise and grace wrapped like a mantle about her. Mary Jennings, now Lady Middleton, and out of his reach forever.

When the set ended, a muscle twitched in his jaw as he watched Sir John Middleton escort his lady through the crowd. Mary floated like a goddess in her blue gown, like Venus on a cloud, while her husband trod upon the polished floor like a crude, aging Vulcan.

Thomas allowed himself to be carried by the tide of guests away from the refreshments table and through the crowd, his focus entirely on Lady Middleton's retreating back. Even her spine was elegant—straight, unbending, and untouchable. Unable to look away, he shadowed the couple, who finally paused at the edge of the ballroom to chat with a group seated there. Thomas hadn't drawn within a dozen feet of them before a voice screeched, "Why, look who's here, upon my word! If it isn't Mr. Palmer, as distinguished as ever!"

He stiffened, recognizing that grating voice and braying laugh. Mrs. Jennings waved vigorously in his direction, her squat figure joggling. Thomas would have veered away, but Lady Middleton turned to stand by her mother's side, flanked by her thickset husband. A young woman of perhaps eighteen sat next to Mrs. Jennings, whose laughter grew louder as he approached.

He bowed to her, cringing all the while and bracing himself for the assault he knew to expect. "How do you do, Mrs. Jennings?"

"Exceedingly well, Mr. Palmer. Delightful to see you again! Don't often come across you in town these days. Been much too long since you graced our drawing room. Why, you used to call every day! It's high time you showed yourself at one of these to-dos and gave the young ladies something to swoon about. Don't you agree, Mary, dear?"

When he bowed over Lady Middleton's hand, the pallor of her perfect complexion grew whiter still, though the impression was fleeting. She looked up, and he noted her eyes exactly matched the color of her gown. "A pleasure," he murmured, proud his firm voice revealed nothing, though his knees felt unsteady.

Her voice was equally neutral and steady in response.

Sir John, however, bellowed his welcome as he reached out his hand. "Palmer, isn't it? Believe we met years back. Duck hunting, I think. Good to see you."

"You also remember my sister, Mr. Palmer?" Mary asked with, he thought, a hint of trepidation. "This is Charlotte."

Little Lottie. She'd been a plump and giggly girl, all bouncy curls and non-stop chatter, frisking about the house like a roly-poly puppy. Seven years later, she was still plump and bouncy, her yellow ringlets barely checked by fluttering pink ribbons, and her giggles not suppressed at all. Charlotte. He bowed.

"Do you dance, Mr. Palmer?" Mrs. Jennings asked as she fanned herself. "Much too hot for me. I fear my dancing days are over. But you young people have more energy. And dancing's the very best way for couples to get to know each other. My Lottie dearly loves to dance, don't you, my dear?"

Her Lottie, rather than blush with embarrassment at so bold a hint, laughed merrily and nodded. Then she turned the full force of her round blue eyes on Thomas, widened her smile, and said, "Yes, I do so love to dance, Mama. If I could, I think I'd dance until my slippers were worn through." The girl continued to look directly into his eyes until Thomas was forced to look away. His gaze inevitably drifted to Lady Middleton, whose expression altered minutely as she spoke. "I cannot imagine exerting oneself to such an extent, Charlotte. I much prefer to dance in moderation."

"Mr. Palmer," her sister said, with what he thought might be a teasing twinkle, "we haven't yet heard *your* opinion of dancing." Her extraordinary eyes widened.

Thomas knew he was left with no choice whatsoever. He would not shirk a gentleman's duty. If he didn't ask her to dance, the minx might ask him.

While he hesitated, the girl took a step closer, subjecting him to more of her unsettling stare. "In case you wondered, I happen to have this dance open."

Struck speechless for a moment at her forwardness, he eventually managed to reply, "May I have the pleasure, Miss Jennings?"

"Of course!"

Her laugh trilled for a full five seconds. Thomas knew it was five because he counted the duration beneath his breath. As he led her to her place for the country dance, he noticed her hands were small, and the skin above her glove was soft; indeed, he soon discovered, all of Miss Charlotte Jennings was soft: her hair when it brushed against his chin, her arm, her body beneath the white silk and excessive ruffles of her gown.

"Tell me the truth, sir. Did you truly want to dance, or were you tricked?" Her question drew all eyes to her as they progressed down the line. "Not that I mind either way," she continued. "I really do love to dance. How vexing it is to wait for the chance."

"A gentleman has the advantage," he agreed cautiously. "He is at liberty to choose a partner, while a lady may choose only to accept or decline."

His comment earned yet another laugh from the girl. "What, pray, is the difference? The lady still holds the power of yes or no."

Thomas couldn't think of a polite answer, but no matter, since Miss Jennings had more to say on the subject.

"A lady may choose to be noticed or hide herself if she wants to avoid a partner. If she can't hide, she can claim a cramp, or thirst, or weariness, or simply give up on all dancing for the evening. But a man has an *obligation* to dance, especially when there are fewer men than ladies present."

Thomas was overly acquainted with obligation. He was distracted from his own because the hops required by the country dance made the parts of her exposed by her square-cut bodice jiggle to an alarming extent, riveting him to the possibility her softest curves might escape their confines. Since they'd only just begun the first dance of two in the set, he faced a suspenseful half-hour.

"Is this not a wonderful ball, Mr. Palmer?" she asked when the form reunited them. "Have you ever seen such a refined company?" Further observations proved Miss Jennings liked everybody effusively. She also liked the music, the refreshments, the flowers, and the fine weather, finding every possible opportunity to share her opinions when she wasn't laughing or dancing away from him.

Mr. Palmer made no comment.

"I do so love the plumes some ladies are wearing. Don't you agree? I saw a feather palatine earlier. The fashion makes them look like exotic birds, don't you think?" Charlotte looked down at her silk gown. "Ruffles flutter nicely too. They make me feel like a bird taking wing. Do you like them? Madame Roussard assures me that three rows are even better than the two rows I saw in a design in *Ackermann's*. My sister disagrees. She always cautions me not to overdo." She frowned at the thought. "It's true that no one was wearing more than one row of ruffles at the last ball."

Thomas sensed the beginning of another headache as he struggled to keep up with her twittering. "Will a blanket response suffice, Miss Jennings, or should I answer each question in order?"

He was spared her answer when the steps of the dance drew him away from her. It was some minutes before he was brought face to face with her again. She raised one eyebrow as he took her hand. "You are so droll, Mr. Palmer. I do believe I have never met a man so amusing."

The pounding in his head now exceeded the pounding of the dancers' feet. "You should expand your acquaintance," he replied, then regretted it since his remark elicited a peal of laughter. Nothing he said seemed to quench her humor. It was really quite remarkable.

# Chapter Two

Charlotte had not forgotten how gloriously tall he was, nor had she forgotten the lean handsomeness of his face. And now he had appeared at the perfect moment. The London season might be drawing to a close, but not her options. All thoughts of other suitors faded. Mr. Thomas Palmer was exactly the kind of man she dreamed of; in fact, he *was* the man she had dreamed of since she'd been in the schoolroom and he'd been courting her sister.

She used to watch him arrive at their townhouse on Berkeley Street, his height and his aristocratic bearing unmistakable. She'd peer down from an upstairs window and admire the thick waves of his brown hair. And if she hurried, she could skid into the entrance hall in time to admire his eyes, a fascinating color somewhere between brown and green. The intensity of his stare as he looked down at her made her heart beat even faster. Everything about Mr. Palmer, from his impeccably tailored coat to the mirror shine of his Hessian boots, was fashionable and immaculate, then and now. He represented the epitome of gentlemanliness. Or perhaps not the epitome, since Mr. Brummell was rumored to be in attendance this evening, but near-epitome.

And here was the near-epitome leading her through the country dance, his head bent over *her*, his warm hand at her back eliciting the most delicious of shivers. She could bask in happiness at this very moment — if only he would stop glancing at the seats where her mother and sister conversed. Charlotte's brow puckered. By all accounts, he'd been terribly disappointed when her sister married another. *That* was in the past. Now was *her* chance. She must make an effort to draw him out. If she could keep him talking, his attention would remain on her.

"Have you been hiding yourself, sir?" she asked when the steps brought him close again. "I am sure I would have seen you at the balls or card parties or concerts if you had been in the vicinity."

"I've only recently arrived in town."

*Six words this time. An improvement of sorts.* His last answer had included only five and had bordered on rudeness. "What brought you here so late in the season? Surely it can't be for the entertainment. This ball is the last big event of the year. Several families have already left town for their country houses. Are you here for business, perhaps? Business goes on regardless, does it not?"

"Do you require an answer, or would you prefer to supply your own, Miss Jennings?"

Her eyes widened at the curtness of his response. A retort nearly escaped her lips, but she bit down on it. Far better to deflect his string of negatives with her own positives. Honey sweetened vinegar. She *must* keep him talking. "Oh, you are being witty! I had forgotten that about you."

"You remember me from all those years ago?" At last, Mr. Palmer's full attention was on her.

Charlotte nodded, relishing his unwavering regard. He was so *very* handsome. Sometimes a gentleman seen at a distance did not have the same charm at arm's length. With Mr. Palmer, proximity only increased his appeal. And that appeal had not diminished with time. He was a man in his prime now, with the most distinguished crease between his brows, as if he pondered great matters of state.

"I remember everything about your visits," she blurted

out. His gaze sharpened, causing Charlotte to misstep briefly. What was she thinking? She sounded like a ninny. His closeness drove all caution from her and made her so nervous that she giggled far too often. He probably didn't remember *her*, after all. He hadn't actually said he did when Mary had introduced him.

"I'm flattered," he said, his words flavored with irony. "I seem to recall as a child, you were often underfoot."

*A child?* Was that how he saw her still? She strained to stand taller. "So you *do* remember me. I'm glad. I think to be forgotten would be the very worst, don't you agree?"

"To be forgotten would be preferable than to be remembered with disdain," he answered as he led her down the line in a promenade.

His remark stung. Though the effort cost her, Charlotte's smile didn't waver. She still had his attention. She resolved to keep the upper hand. "I shan't forget this dance," she said. "I can't remember when I have laughed at anyone so much." Laughter was better than tears, she knew. Laughter held power.

"Is that a compliment, Miss Jennings? If so, again, I'm flattered."

"As you should be, sir," she said as the dance carried her away from him. The very wide smile remained on her face as she held her hands out to the next man in the line, causing him to stumble a bit before taking up the steps. An hour before, Charlotte had danced the second set with this gentleman, a younger son of some minor peer, and while his dancing skills were not the best, he had been an excellent listener. If he had not held up his half of their conversation, perhaps he was overheated. It had been a vigorous dance.

Not every gentleman could keep up with her.

Mr. Palmer's new partner in the set seemed quite subdued, hardly a rival. Why, the Ludford girl barely said more than a sentence at a time! And her steps, while correct, lacked liveliness. Her coiled brown hair didn't bounce even during the turns. Her profile, however, was flawless. Charlotte bit her lip.

When the form returned her to Mr. Palmer's side, Charlotte

cast about for anything to draw his attention back. "I do believe I have never been to such a well-attended ball, Mr. Palmer. I see Lord Alvanley and Mr. Pierrepont, and there's Lady Worcester. All of London must be here!"

"Surely not. I see no sign of my solicitor, for instance," he said, looking about the room.

"Perhaps not all," she agreed, ignoring his attempt to undercut her. "I also see no sign of the urchins who were begging coins outside, poor things." At that, she did not smile.

"Town is full of rabble," Mr. Palmer replied. "I much prefer the country. There are far fewer people to trip over there."

She had to laugh. Really, Mr. Palmer worked hard at being contrary. He truly was the most amusing man. And when she stood this close, she could appreciate the cleft in his chin, the breadth of his shoulders, and the power of his thighs, details that had escaped her notice when she was a girl.

His manners, though, did not live up to his appearance. Curt manners were indeed a flaw. But she would not give up on him. He was young, single, fit, a man of means, and obviously in the market. Since this was the end of her last season, she had few options. She could overlook a few flaws. If she concentrated, Charlotte could surmise any number of explanations for Mr. Palmer's boorish behavior. Perhaps he was unused to company, after so long an absence from society? Following Mary's engagement, Mr. Palmer had fled town. His father had died as well, hadn't he? The period of mourning and the demands of an estate must have kept him away.

Shyness might explain his reluctance to join in the conversation for the rest of the set. Shyness would also explain why he persisted in looking over her head to scan the assembly. That was certainly a better reason than the one she suspected might be true. She resolved to double her efforts to put him at his ease.

"Tell me about your home, Mr. Palmer," she said when they were again face to face. "It's in Somerset, is it not? Not so very far from Bath. Mama and I visited Bath last year. It was immensely diverting. Have you seen the Assembly Rooms there? They're magnificent." It was a testament to her health that she could keep talking while executing a series of complicated movements.

"I visit Bath as infrequently as possible."

"Oh. You did say you prefer the country. Is your home by the sea? I don't believe Mary ever mentioned it. I've never been to the sea. Is it quite overwhelming? It's so very vast, after all."

"And so very wet."

She would *not* rise to his bait. "Do describe it, Mr. Palmer. Please." And willed him to answer.

"Yes, Cleveland is near the sea. The north wind blows ocean spray across the lea, and from the hill on the estate, one can hear the waves crash and smell the salt air. It is invariably damp and cold." For an eternity, he pinned her eyes with his. "The seaside is an unforgiving landscape, Miss Jennings, all rocks and stunted trees. Nothing whatsoever like the refinement of Bath."

"Such a place would transport the senses to a higher plane. How perfectly invigorating it must be!" Remembering a sublime painting she'd seen of a storm-dashed sea and rocky coast, she took a deep breath, imagining her lungs filling with fresh salt air. When her bodice consequently dipped lower, she was gratified at having secured Mr. Palmer's complete attention at last. She pressed home her advantage. "To see the coast, Mr. Palmer! To feel the surge of the waves and be stroked by the potent force of a sea wind. How exhilarating! How I should love to experience it!" Charlotte grew quite warm at the idea of experiencing such a place with *him*; she could feel a blush rising from her bosom and up her neck to heat her cheeks. Mr. Palmer's gaze remained steadily on her, and she thought she detected a rise in his temperature too.

She pondered the renewed possibility of making his home hers.

But the dance drew all too soon to its end, and Mr. Palmer led her back to her seat. How she wished he would reserve the supper dance with her, which no one had yet claimed. Then they could share a table, and she could command his full attention and quiz him further about the seaside and his home there. She would even be content to watch him eat. His teeth were so very white, and his mouth both firm and well-shaped. As a girl, she had hoped her first kiss might be from his mouth instead of the rather slobbery one she'd endured from the youngest son of a viscount. *He'd* tasted of brandy.

She wondered what a kiss from Mr. Palmer would taste like. And when she considered his wit, she wondered about the sharpness of his teeth.

~*~

"Ah, here you are, back again," Mrs. Jennings greeted them as Mr. Palmer returned Charlotte to her side with a bow. "You were without a doubt the most attractive couple on the floor. Don't you agree, Mary?"

Lady Middleton's expression might have put off a more reticent sister, but Charlotte was made of sterner stuff than most fishwives. "Mr. Palmer's a divine dancer, Mama. You already knew that, Mary, having danced with him during your own season *all* those years ago." Before her sister could object, Charlotte continued. "We had the most delightful chat. Mr. Palmer was telling me about the wonders of the seaside, a sight not to be missed, I'm sure. The scenery must be breathtaking." And she took another deep breath at the thought, hoping to again draw Mr. Palmer's eyes her way.

Lady Middleton's eyebrows rose two notches. "Indeed. I never heard Somerset offered much in the way of natural beauty."

Mr. Palmer smiled slowly. "Somerset is no London," he agreed. "Here, beauty is everywhere I look."

Charlotte smiled back, but when she gauged that the gentleman's attention was still on her sister, her smile drooped. "But I thought you preferred the country to the town. I'm sure I heard you say so."

"I was thinking of a much more cultured beauty, one which doesn't fade with the seasons," Mr. Palmer replied, still looking at Lady Middleton. "Such beauty is more often found in town."

"What pretty words!" Mrs. Jennings said. "Though I think you mean more than just the beauty of our parks, don't you, Mr. Palmer?" A delicate flush painted Lady Middleton's cheeks, and Charlotte's smile faded further. Surely Mr. Palmer wasn't flirting. After all, Mary was a married woman and a mother!

Charlotte stepped closer, putting herself between him and Mary. "Mama and I love to walk in the park. And the gardens there are so lovely in spring and summer. The view of the Serpentine is especially nice. Do you ever walk there, Mr. Palmer?"

"No."

She was not to be put off by a single syllable. "Why ever not? I could understand if the weather had been unpleasant, but it's been quite cool this summer, don't you think? And one sees everybody at the park. Even Mary walks there on occasion when she is in town. Her house is in Conduit Street, you know, very close."

Lady Middleton acknowledged that was so. "As a matter of fact, I plan to take the children for an outing on the morrow if the weather is fair," she admitted. "The fresh air will do them good. Too much time indoors isn't healthy for them."

Charlotte's spirits rebounded at the prospect of an afternoon stroll on Mr. Palmer's arm with all of London society watching and noting what a lovely couple they made. "Oh, yes, please! We must make an outing of it! Do join us, Mr. Palmer! You simply must."

"Perhaps I will," he said, his eyes on Mary. "Good evening, ladies."

With a slight bow, Mr. Palmer took his leave. As Charlotte watched his back disappear into the throng, her perpetual smile faded entirely away as she plotted. *It's only a matter of time and good planning. I'll bring him up to snuff by the end of the year. Thomas Palmer is my best chance at future happiness.*

~*~

"Wondered where you'd got to, Tom," Henry said as he elbowed his way past a prodigious palm. "The carriage has been brought 'round."

Henry's eyes were bloodshot, and he listed heavily to the left, but Thomas was too weary to call him out over it. "The best news I've heard all evening," he said instead. Given his intense dislike of closed carriages, that said much about the evening. If he had to lead one more vacuous partner out onto the crowded dance floor, he might start to howl, which would undoubtedly disrupt the merriment around him and ruin his chances forever of finding a suitable wife. Never had the quiet of his solitary room in Hanover Square held more appeal.

"Saw you dancing with at least four very acceptable-looking ladies," Henry continued. "Mother would be proud."

"I managed introductions to six on her list. And one who was not, thankfully."

"Any who might suit?"

"Almost all." Thomas grimaced at the thought.

"Shouldn't you be pleased, then?"

"How do you know I'm not pleased?"

"You hardly look like a man on the brink of matrimonial bliss." Henry gestured to the room. "There are any number of possibilities here besides those on Mother's infernal list of 'suitable young ladies of good family.' Some of them must appeal to you."

"I'll allow most are tolerable until they open their mouths. Then they either simper or mumble in monosyllables."

Henry leaned against the wall, smirking. "Being pleasant and sociable for an entire evening must have exhausted you."

Thomas smiled slightly. "You know me too well." He rubbed a hand over his face. "I admit I'm out of my depth. I thought it would just be a matter of picking one from the fold."

Henry laughed. "Like spring lambs? How were their teeth?"

"Only one smiled enough for me to determine, and she is totally unsuitable."

"Not fluffy, sweet, and amiable?" Henry teased.

"Extremely," his brother said. After a pause, he added, "I spoke to Lady Middleton."

Henry stopped leaning against the wall. "Did you, now? Is she as graceful and refined as ever?"

"Perhaps even more so, though I can't say the same for her sister. Dancing with *her* was like being tethered to a whirligig." Over Henry's shoulder, Thomas watched Miss Charlotte Jennings skim about the room beside her mother, both of them twirling first this way and then that as they greeted acquaintances, nodded, and waved. They looked like spinning tops escaped from the toy box. The two stopped next to every widow and wallflower on their circuit, paying equal attention to all, whether they possessed title and property or not. It was really quite curious. Miss Jennings' smile never faltered despite the smoking candles and stifling heat. Rather than wilting in company, she bloomed, eyes bright, cheeks rosy.

When Thomas offered no further comment, Henry cleared his throat. "Since you've exhausted the supply of eligibles, we're off then?"

Thomas nodded, still staring at Miss Jennings, then shook his head. The season may be over, but London still held possibilities, and Thomas Palmer, Esq., was a patient, determined man.

# Chapter Three

Charlotte Jennings was running out of patience. A day of fog and downpours had dampened her mood. All morning she'd waited for Mr. Palmer's calling card. All afternoon, she'd willed the steady rain to relent. All season long, she had accepted every invitation and attended every ball, supper, card party, and musicale. Ahead of her stretched months of trailing after her mother, sitting with wilting dowagers over tea, visiting Barton Park, and perhaps taking the waters at Bath. In ten years, she'd be a confirmed spinster. In twenty, her dear mama might be gone, and then where would she be? Living with Mary, who would daily point out her shortcomings and never let her forget her dependence? Showering all the love she'd garnered for future children on her nieces and nephews?

She must do something.

Yet here in the bedroom she'd slept in since she left the nursery, all she could do was fume. The rose silk walls felt more like a prison than a refuge. Memories of the night before trapped her further. Particularly, Mrs. Jennings' comments at the close of the ball still rankled. As Charlotte readied herself for bed, she mulled over the exchange.

"I don't know what I'll do if I can't find a match for my

Lottie," her mother had said to her friend, raising her voice so she could be heard over the orchestra. "Lord knows I need someone to take the girl off my hands. Why, her sister was snatched up within weeks of her first season."

Mrs. Tharrington had looked over her stooped shoulder to study Charlotte, who had pretended an intense interest in a potted fern. "She seems cheery enough. Pretty too. Can't imagine why she didn't take."

"I've asked myself the same question. She filled her dance cards at the start, but now that we're at the end, two seasons, mind you, only one or two prospects are still in the running."

"Good possibilities?"

"I have great hopes for the one," Mrs. Jennings had said. "A title. But I mustn't say more." She'd leaned closer to the hunched figure beside her before adding, "He may be a bit older, but I don't count that as a drawback. Why, Sir John is a score older than my Mary, and look at them!"

Charlotte closed her eyes, trying in vain to shut out the galling memory.

It was true. She had met dozens of suitors, many of whom she found amusing and some of whom she found attractive. It was *not* true that she had only two in the offing. Why, last week, she had met the very handsome Mr. Tierney, whose smooth manners were all that was agreeable. He'd been deliciously brazen in asking for an introduction to her at a card party and later had pursued her at the Courtnays' ball. She felt certain he was interested in her. But Mama had pulled her away before she could learn much about him. She'd no chance to accept his pressing invitation to walk about the gardens in the dark, where she was sure to have learned more, especially the kind of knowledge that her mother least wanted her to have.

Charlotte had had enough of propriety. Current circumstances called for drastic action if she were to avoid being put on a shelf.

Sadly, most gentlemen wanted only to talk. Men's topics were nothing like that of women's circles, full of weddings and bonnets and births and billet-doux. With effort, though, she managed to discover *something* of interest in nearly all her potential partners. Two nights ago, a gentleman from Staffordshire had astounded her with his startling description of how a bolt of lightning had killed an entire herd of deer in his park. Then there was the bucktoothed gentleman who had been able to carry on a discussion of nothing but horses' gait and breeding for over an hour. The breeding part, in particular, Charlotte found enlightening.

Most eligible of the marriage prospects, according to her mother and sister, was the dapper Lord Dysart. Charlotte made an effort to recall his virtues. He was exactly her height, so she did not have to look up at all, saving her neck from strain. True, he had lacked the stamina to dance much, whether because of his age or his girth, she wasn't sure, but he'd been generous in his compliments and had loaded her plate and his with every sort of delicacy from the refreshment table. He did not gamble or take snuff. A life with him would be comfortable. Undoubtedly, it would be preferable to hanging about her mother's neck like a millstone.

Last summer, she had held out hope for a taller prospect, a colonel from Devonshire — so rigid and formal he'd been! Since he lived at Delaford, quite near the Middleton estate, Charlotte had encountered him now and then at Barton Park. At assemblies, he'd danced as if he were out on a march. She suspected he was older — but not as old as Lord Dysart. The colonel's dashing appearance in his uniform, with gold braid hung about the shoulders of his red coat and a line of medals decorating his chest, was all that was pleasing. She'd thought perhaps something might grow between them, but he had returned to his country estate without even an invitation to visit him there.

The colonel had been deliciously towering, nearly as tall as — .

But Charlotte wouldn't think of him. No, wishing for *him* was a path to disappointment. He had not called or left his card. So be it. She was determined to be happy with whoever she was paired with, no matter the circumstances.

Her resolve lasted less than a minute. The sun might yet shine on her. It was still possible that *he* might walk on the morrow. She would make sure that *she* would be out if she had to drag her mother all the way to Hyde Park. Charlotte plumped her pillow and smiled. She fell asleep imagining her arm tucked under Mr. Palmer's as they strolled about.

# Chapter Four

If a gentleman wanted to flaunt his high-stepping horse or his well-sprung phaeton, Hyde Park was the place to prance about. Thomas knew this, though he'd never been inclined to prance. He was even less inclined to stroll along crowded paths and exchange pleasantries with those who *were* so inclined. And yet, here he was, strolling along the grassy walkway and ruining the polish on his boots while fashionable London trotted by on Rotten Row.

Mary was nowhere in sight.

Underfoot, however, were two fair-haired imps racing around and producing enough noise for six. He guessed them to be young, certainly still in the nursery, which was where they should be instead of screaming and tearing about a public park. Where was their nurse? Idly he watched the children's antics while taking care not to muddy himself. He'd dressed with care for this occasion, hoping to impress in a new, perfectly fitted blue coat. So far, his beige pantaloons remained uncreased. He'd like to keep them that way.

Now the scamps—little boys—had darted toward the low fence at the edge of the wide carriage path. Any moment and their keeper would call them back. But as he scanned the green,

Thomas saw no other adults in the immediate vicinity. Far to his right, Rotten Row curved around a grove of trees, and beyond it was only the shallow lake. Why were the little hellions untethered and unattended? Like romping pups, they circled and tumbled, their play taking them ever closer to the carriage path and danger.

Any minute now, someone *must* come running after them. Yes, any second.

The morning's bleak drizzle had given way to a watery sun that cast weak shadows this late in the day. Thomas's own shade looked solitary and stiff as he stared at the damp ground, wondering if he had somehow misinterpreted Lady Middleton's invitation to walk if the weather suited.

Why did he seek her company? Nothing could come of their reacquaintance but a renewed reminder of what he'd lost. He should turn his attention elsewhere. Perhaps if he started toward Kensington Gardens, he might catch a glimpse of Mrs. Jennings and Miss Charlotte. Mary's sister at least had the virtue of being unmarried. He crossed the green, carefully avoiding the slickest spots and steering away from the noisy boys, all the while scanning the area for a group of ladies, including Mary — yes, graceful Mary, strolling along the footpath, a parasol shading her perfect complexion, her eyes demurely cast down, her hand resting lightly on his arm as he'd escorted her through the park all those years ago.

But Mary was nowhere in sight this afternoon.

Above the boys' clamor, Thomas gradually became aware of the distant pounding of hooves, a clear signal for him to step far away. He looked back at the children. Young though they seemed, the boys must know the risk of running where sporting fellows routinely raced. The scamps would stop or change course. Their instincts for self-preservation would prevail.

But the boys continued to tumble about, intent upon their play.

Rounding the curve by the trees about a hundred yards to his right, a curricle nearly pitched on its side, then righted, pulled by massive matched bays barely controlled by the idiot holding the reins. Thomas couldn't hear his own voice shouting over the rattle of the carriage, the jangle of the harnesses, and the hammering of hooves. Onward the driver raced at top speed, heedless of what may lie ahead.

*The boys did not change course.* They jumped over the wooden fence and kept running.

"Damnation!" Thomas veered back toward the gravel path.

The oblivious driver flicked his whip, urging the horses on. Thomas picked up his pace, first loping, then slipping and sprinting through the grass and mud, not daring to look to the right, his focus on the little boys still running heedlessly toward those deadly hooves. His stomach churned at the thought.

"Stop! Boys, stop!" They ignored him, recklessly running forward. Thomas knew in a matter of seconds he'd see their small bodies trampled and crushed beneath the flailing hooves and murderous wheels—unless he reached them in time. *If* he could reach them. Summoning powers he'd never called on, he ordered his thighs to pump, his arms to stretch, his back to brace. The horses were mere yards away, so close he could smell their sweat. With a groan, he lunged and grabbed, hauling a boy under each arm, then falling and rolling with them over and over on the sharp stones and bark while the yoked bays thundered past, hooves spitting gravel, wheels rumbling. The very ground beneath them shook.

The driver never looked down.

Above Thomas, heavy clouds stalled. This time, the carriage had not tilted. No one had been crushed. History had not been repeated. Once his breathing slowed, and the thump of his heart quieted, he became acutely aware of the dampness seeping into his coat and the gravel digging into his backside. He was likewise aware of the small, squiggling bodies beside him. *Alive*, thank God. He sat up. "All right, are you?" He had no idea what he might do if they'd been injured in the fall.

But the boys were apparently unhurt. Two pairs of round blue eyes stared at him for a moment, time enough for him to notice their blond curls and round faces resembled those pictures of chubby cherubs hanging about so many London drawing rooms. But these boys were no angels. Even after their brush with death, they had the temerity to *laugh*. Ignoring him, they rolled away and over each other, tussling in the mud. Then, with nary a "thank you," they bounded to their feet and ran across the path toward the wood.

"You cork-brained little hellions!" Thomas shouted after them, hands still trembling slightly. "Your mother ought never to have let you out of leading strings!" After they disappeared into a thicket, he hoped never to see the miserable scamps again.

Thomas stood slowly, straightened his coat, and frowned at his boots. He must return to his townhouse. Imagine meeting Mary now, with grass in his hair, mud smearing his wobbling knees, and a streak of blood running down one stinging cheek. Farley, his valet, would likely click his tongue when he saw the state of the new blue coat.

~*~

"I was sure he'd be there today!" Charlotte wanted to stamp her foot in frustration. After all her prodding and planning—cajoling her mother, convincing her sister by expounding on the staleness of nursery air, retrimming her best bonnet for the occasion—Mr. Palmer had still not appeared. She was tempted to kick one of the Chinese urns Mary had set about the entryway of her London home.

"He did say 'perhaps,' Lottie," her sister admonished. "That's hardly a commitment. And it *has* been wet." Despite her measured words, Mary looked disappointed. Charlotte was sure of it, and the possibility worried her further.

"Do you think he's still in town, Mama?"

Mrs. Jennings cocked her head. "So that's the way of it, is it, lovey? Well, if ye want to see the man, I think the best way is to invite him to the house."

"Oh, Mama, could we? How soon?" The thought of Mr. Palmer seated next to her in their own drawing room, inches from her on the settee, his arm brushing hers, brought a blush and a smile to Charlotte's face. "I suppose this evening's out of the question, but tomorrow? Could we ask him for tomorrow? To tea?"

"Really, Lottie, restrain yourself, I beg you," Mary said. "The invitation would be for tea, nothing more." Charlotte thought her sister looked cross and secretly relished the fact.

"Company for tea is always welcome," their mother declared stoutly. "Goodness knows any decent company's scarce this time of year. Mr. Palmer still cuts a fine figure. I miss seeing him about. You'll come too, won't you, Mary? And bring the children?"

Charlotte's smile dimmed, but she resolved not to allow her sister's presence or the distraction of her nieces and nephews to taint the pleasant expectation of Mr. Palmer's visit.

# Chapter Five

Thomas read the note twice, at first in surprise and then in befuddlement. What had prompted the invitation? Certainly, nothing he'd done could have encouraged this level of interaction with the Jennings ladies. And after their failure to appear at the park, such an invitation was unexpected. Not a word of explanation?

Henry's entrance into the drawing room disrupted Thomas's brooding.

"What has you in such a brown study? Or should I say black?" Henry's voice was still blurred with sleep, though the hour was long past noon. Without answering, Thomas handed him the invitation, then waited for his brother's eyes to focus.

"Don't laugh," Thomas warned. "If you laugh, I shall have to hit you."

"I take it you plan to refuse?" Henry asked, failing to hide a grin. "Because of your dignity's recent plunge in the mud?"

Thomas regretted anew telling Henry about the previous day's disaster. He should have known the teasing would be unbearable. "I can't imagine accepting." The prospect of politely sipping tea while Mrs. Jennings violated every rule of etiquette and Charlotte discovered new ways to lower his comfort level made him blanch. An entire hour sitting thigh to thigh with the outrageous Miss Jennings would strain his limited tolerance for company. Come to think of it, though—not once in the time he'd spent close by her had he felt at all cramped or closed in.

"The family is well connected, you know. Besides the Middletons, I mean. They have friends in Parliament, which should interest you. And Mr. Jennings left a sizable fortune, even if he was a cit. Enough funds to bring a few titles sniffing about the daughters. The younger girl's dowry is more than generous, I hear."

"If the dowry exceeded ten thousand pounds, it wouldn't equal the cost of spending a lifetime with Charlotte Jennings."

Henry laughed. "It's only tea, you know. No one expects you to do more than make polite conversation and drink out of a cup." He paused before adding, "I wonder if Lady Middleton will be there."

~*~

Mr. Palmer had accepted the invitation, and at the appointed hour the next day, he arrived at the Jennings' house near Portman Square. From her bedroom window, Charlotte watched him pause at the gate before mounting the front steps. With eager hands, she smoothed the sunny ribbons on her favorite sprigged muslin gown, delighting in the way the tiny yellow flowers twined about, making her feel like a walking garden. She hoped Mr. Palmer was fond of flowers. Surely he was. Who didn't like flowers?

Today, he would notice how very mature she'd become, no longer a silly young miss, but a lady. Instead of running down the stairs like a hoyden and skidding to a stop at his feet, Charlotte willed herself to descend the broad staircase slowly, elegantly, her head held high, her hand clammy on the polished railing. Her countenance was all that was reserved and dignified. But when she stole a glance down, Mr. Palmer wasn't watching her regal descent with awe and admiration. Instead, he was peering into the drawing room, which he entered after leaving his hat and cane with the footman, never having noticed her at all. Neither did Mr. Palmer look at her as she hovered by the door, uncertain now, for he had already seated himself in an armchair, ruining her hope of sharing a seat with him.

"How hale and hearty you look, Mr. Palmer," Mrs. Jennings was saying. "So pleased you could join us for tea. Did you walk? Didn't hear a carriage. Hanover Square's not so very far, is it? And a fine afternoon for a walk, much better than earlier in the week, which was quite damp, I must say. I'm not surprised we didn't see you at the park."

"I am sorry I missed you and your daughters," he replied.

"Ah, here's one of them now! Do come sit down, my dear. Expect my other daughter will be along shortly."

Charlotte's tentative smile froze when Mr. Palmer's expression faded from eager to disappointed as she entered. He did rise but offered only the slightest bow. He must not think her worthy of a deeper one! Schooling her features into as much of a haughty expression as she could manage, Charlotte held her head higher as she greeted him coolly with the merest curtsy. "How good to see you again, Mr. Palmer. I trust you are well."

"Why ever do you have your nose stuck up in the air like that, my girl?" her mother exclaimed. "Something wrong with your neck?"

"No, Mama. Certainly not." Charlotte's cheeks grew hot. The blush only deepened as she observed Mr. Palmer's pained expression.

"I'm quite well, thank you, Miss Jennings," he said. As he turned his head, his cheek became fully visible.

Charlotte gasped. "Oh, but you are not! Your face!" She abandoned all thought of cool reserve as she studied him.

"I beg your pardon?" Mr. Palmer quickly swiveled his head.

"You've injured yourself." She started to reach out to the jagged cut on his cheek, but Mr. Palmer backed away.

"I assure you, Miss Jennings, I am fine. It is the merest of cuts. A trifle. Nothing to be concerned about." He seemed to grow inches taller as he spoke.

Before Charlotte could inquire further, they were

interrupted by a chorus of high voices and scrabbles from the hallway. When the footman opened the door, the noise level exploded. "Lady Middleton," the servant shouted above the din. Two yellow-haired, round-faced boys raced in, followed by a wispy-haired tot who toddled with determination in their wake. After them came a nursemaid carrying a bald, solemn-eyed baby. Last of all, Mary herself swept in, attired in a fashionable walking dress of a muted dark pink, its front embroidered with a curved design that emphasized a graceful figure. The plume on her bonnet fluttered fully eight inches high. Charlotte sighed, reminded of how short and plump she herself was in comparison. Looking down, she smoothed the yellow ribbons on her dress, which now seemed hopelessly girlish.

Mr. Palmer bowed slowly. Did Mary falter when she saw him? And did he look stricken when he saw her and the children?

Charlotte's stomach hurt.

After a momentary pause to exchange greetings, Mary's attention returned to her offspring. "John! William! Do get down from there, darlings. You might fall and hurt yourselves." Ignoring their mother, the boys continued to scale the settee, nearly upsetting the tea table.

~*~

There could be no doubt about it, Thomas thought. These were the very same boys. The world could not hold more than two like them. How long before they exposed yesterday's humiliating tumble in the mud? He no longer had an appetite for tea, which Mrs. Jennings was already pouring.

"Sit down, Mr. Palmer. Boys, if you sit nicely, you shall have some cakes. Mary, I think they've grown since yesterday! And look at Annamaria walking! I declare they are all far more advanced than Mrs. Courtnay's grandchildren. I am the proudest grandmother in town."

Thomas kept silent as the tea was passed and the children's accomplishments enumerated. Charlotte, too, remained blessedly silent.

"But Mr. Palmer has not formally met our angels," Mrs.

Jennings exclaimed. "Come boys, climb down from there and make your bows to Mr. Palmer."

Thomas waited for the inevitable as Mary's sons, eyeing the cakes, came closer. "This is my eldest, John, and his brother William," Mary said, a fond smile softening her features. "And here is Annamaria. Do take your thumb from your mouth, my pet!" Mary laughed lightly. "The baby's watching it all, it seems. Boys, bow like you've been taught."

John and William stood staring up at Mr. Palmer. He met their gaze, unflinching, all the while preparing to explain to the family why he had wrestled Mary's darlings to the ground in the park and failed to mention it. Anticipating the humiliation of having to describe the entire ignominious episode made his jaw twinge.

As the silence grew long, the boys began to fidget, one scratching his neck and the other twisting a button on his jacket. Thomas raised an eyebrow. The standoff continued. One boy, the elder, turned red but continued to stare, though the younger inched closer to his mother.

At last, Thomas broke the silence. "Pleased to meet you, young gentlemen." The boys' mouths opened in unison, but no polite response came forth.

"Bow, darlings," their mother prodded.

Thomas smiled coldly as the boys whispered to each other, their eyes remaining on him. They were probably plotting how to most disgrace him. After a nod or two and some elbowing, they made the slightest of bows. Before anyone had a chance to react, each turned with glee and grabbed a cake from the tray before they darted around the nursemaid, nearly knocking her down, then bounded through the door, their giggles echoing about the marble hall.

Thomas's taut jaw dropped.

"Boys, no!" their mother scolded, still anchored to her spot by the toddler at her side.

Mrs. Jennings shook her head at the sound of a crash from the hall. "William, stop!" she called. "John, come back at once!

Lottie, catch them, can't you?"

Charlotte leapt to her feet in pursuit of the escapees, whose whoops and hollers echoed as they scaled the stairs with their aunt in rollicking pursuit.

There was no time for a sense of relief. To Thomas's chagrin, the infant in the nursemaid's arms began to wail, forcing the girl to exit the drawing room in order to quiet the babe. Throwing her hands in the air, Mrs. Jennings bustled past to add to the melee.

"They do love a game of chase," Mary noted. "Lottie will corner them soon enough."

As the noise diminished, Thomas found himself alone with Mary and the chubby, pink-cheeked toddler at her side, who looked up at him with interest and smiled before returning her thumb to her mouth. "She looks like you," he said. "Your daughter. Same hair. Same eyes."

Lady Mary smiled warmly. "Thank you. Annamaria favors me more than she does my husband. My sister looked much like her when she was a baby." Her gaze remained on her daughter's face as if it were some treasure map she needed to commit to memory. Thomas felt all but forgotten.

"You enjoy motherhood?" Improbable, but possible, he thought.

Her expression grew fierce. "It's everything to me."

"Everything? What of your music? Surely you still play."

The incomparable Mary Jennings had been renowned for her virtuosity at the keyboard. She knew dozens of pieces by heart and had often been pressed to play at social gatherings. Sitting tranquilly at the instrument, she'd drawn all eyes to her, then commanded continued attention from the opening chords. Her slender fingers flashed over the keys. Her touch was light and fluid, and the music floated about the room as if it had taken on a life of its own.

Now her features drew into a mask, shutting him out completely. "I have too much else to attend to now."

Thomas would have pressed for her reasons, but the return of Charlotte and Mrs. Jennings, and the ensuing noise, prevented him.

"What a merry chase!" Mrs. Jennings puffed. "They had us upstairs and down, Mr. Palmer! Who knew little legs could move so fast!" She mopped her brow with a flimsy handkerchief while Charlotte plopped onto the divan. The girl's cheeks glowed red from the exertion, Thomas noted, and her eyes shone. The activity had loosened a mass of riotous curls to bob about her shoulders.

"Where are they now, then?" Mary asked her as she seated herself in the armchair he'd vacated.

"I took them up to the old nursery," Charlotte said. "They're happily tossing balls and chucking blocks. The nursemaid said she'd check on them as soon as the baby's settled."

"Shall we have our tea?" her mother asked. "I'll ring for a fresh pot. This one must be cold." She gestured to the divan. "Here, Mr. Palmer, come sit back down and tell me your impressions of the ball. I daresay I saw you dancing with no fewer than ten young ladies, not to mention our Charlotte. She's quite a good dancer, don't you think? Years of lessons, of course, and then the whole season long, never without a partner. You were lucky to find a space on her dance card."

Mr. Palmer sat and ran a finger around his collar, which had grown tight. "Indeed," was the only response he could muster.

Mrs. Jennings did not let a mere lack of response silence her. "Doesn't our little Lottie dance charmingly? Her dancing master was most impressed by how very tireless she is. She has as much energy as three girls, don't you agree?"

Though Mr. Palmer made an effort not to look at Charlotte, his eyes betrayed him. She sat very still next to him, eyes modestly downcast. "Very energetic, Mrs. Jennings," he said, hoping the answer would be enough to satisfy the woman so she would drop the subject. When Charlotte looked up quickly, he looked away, vastly uncomfortable without knowing precisely why.

"Just don't see the appeal in these languid, droopy young things," Mrs. Jennings continued. "They look as if they'll faint away any second. Not like my girls. Strong stock there."

"Really, Mother," Lady Middleton interrupted. "We are not cattle. And women have always been the weaker sex."

"Nothing weak about it," Mrs. Jennings sniffed. "Like to see the man who can run a household, raise babies, and please a husband."

Mr. Palmer cleared his throat. "Rest assured, no man cares to try."

Charlotte shifted in her seat. "But Mr. Palmer, how is an unmarried lady to channel her energies now that the season is over?"

The pert set of her mouth when she posed her question made Thomas blink. She was too innocent to be implying something inappropriate, wasn't she? And yet, the teasing look she gave him made him wonder.

"Whatever shall we do with no more balls?" Mrs. Jennings agreed. "The summer goes so slowly when everyone leaves town."

Charlotte leaned forward, hands clasped. "Mary, you must press Sir John to fill the gap by hosting us all at Barton Park. Wouldn't it be a nice break from all those hunting parties? And you know how you love to entertain. I'm sure Mr. Palmer would enjoy himself."

Mary frowned, then glanced at Thomas.

"I'll bring the matter up with Sir John," she said, and when at last she smiled at him, Thomas no longer felt the sting in his cheek.

# Chapter Six

Most who traveled to Somerset after the London season went no farther than Bath, so the road to Cleveland was clear save for farm wagons and an occasional horseman. After the close air of London, Thomas could finally breathe again. Salt marsh was like a tonic, banishing the cloying scent of drawing rooms and city gardens. And here in open country, at least when the rain stopped, he could see again, see broad vistas of green hills, ditches dotted with willows, and distant cliffs beyond which lay shingle and bay and open sky.

In London, the sky had been a low gray roof ready to fall and pin him to the ground.

After two days' travel, he looked forward to the comforts of his own home, though perhaps not to the comforts of his family. Ahead, Cleveland Park offered familiarity and predictability. As the sun set behind the manor house, its balanced façade of hamstone ashlar seemed to soak in the golden light. Thomas paused at the bend in the drive to admire the sight before shaking his head at such fancy.

It was merely a house, after all. And yet, the solid pillars flanking the wide entryway promised stability. The arched cornices that interrupted the firm line of the slate roof, however, looked like eyebrows raised in speculation.

Shaking his head at the bilious yellow silk with which his mother had recently — and to his mind, unnecessarily — decorated the walls, he made his way into the drawing room. His aunt, uncannily like a crow in her stark black gown, welcomed him from her accustomed seat, where she sat reading.

"And how was the trip? Did you manage to cut a suitable bride from the string?" She set down her magazine and gave him her full, unnerving attention.

"Really, Georgina, comparing ladies to ponies does neither of us any credit." He bent over and kissed her cool cheek.

"I take it the answer is no."

He stifled a sigh. "Didn't Henry entertain you and Mother with an account of every excruciating minute at that confounded ball? He must have been home for days now."

"Henry's observation was from a distance. I prefer a first-hand account."

This time, Thomas did sigh as he settled in his favorite armchair, stretching his boots out in front of him, wondering if they needed polishing. "Too many guests in too small a space. Too confining. London, in general, has far too many people."

"You have to pick only one." Georgina nodded at the magazine by her side. "There's always Bath, you know. The Assembly Rooms there are quite airy."

"But the people are just as solid. Half of London society will pack themselves into the tearooms this month, while the other half floats away in Brighton." He scowled at the thought of escorting someone like the heavy-headed Miss Askew to a tearoom in Bath. But for some reason, he pictured himself instead escorting Miss Charlotte Jennings to tea, sitting next to her at one of those uncomfortably small tables and watching her lift a cup to her pink lips. The image brought a smile to his own mouth. She would probably gobble the cakes just like her nephews and comment at length on every tablecloth and china plate. She *had* said she'd been to Bath, hadn't she?

Thomas's daydream ended abruptly when the drawing room door banged open, admitting a disheveled Henry, who stumbled through the doorway without the benefit of footman or manners. "Welcome home, dear brother," he slurred as he crossed the room and held out a hand in greeting. "Trust the rest of your time in London was unpleasant?" He crossed to the sideboard and helped himself to port, though dinner was still more than an hour away.

Thomas frowned. He would have to discuss the state of the wine cellar with Mr. Nash. How much would it cost to replenish the stock? "I had more than my fill of suitable young ladies."

"Ah, but their charms outweigh their shortcomings," Henry said, raising his glass. "Don't you agree, Georgina?"

With eyes like ice, his aunt looked steadily up at him as if memorizing every flaw.

Henry remained undaunted. "You and Miss Walker seemed quite happy in each other's company last Sunday when you went off arm in arm through the hedges after church," he added. "If you were a man, you could be hung, you know. Perhaps I had better become a barrister, just in case."

When she finally answered, her tone was steely. "You're too foxed to know what you're saying."

Henry belched, and Thomas reevaluated the pleasures of homecoming. "Enough, Henry. You're a grown man and should act as such." He stood and placed himself between Henry and the decanter.

Henry belched again. "Don't be pompous."

Thomas rubbed his temple. "It's high time you secured an occupation other than drinking."

"Hear, hear," his aunt echoed.

"Ah, yes. Here it comes." At that, Henry drank deeply.

"You seem unfit for the life of a clergyman."

Henry sputtered.

"Nor can I see you as a clerk. And I shudder at the thought of setting you up as bailiff here." Squaring his shoulders, Thomas studied the portraits above the mantelpiece, portraits of relatives he'd never met. They looked down their high-bridged noses at him, their dark hair, piercing stares, and discontented expressions much like his own. What might they say as they contemplated this fair-haired descendant who frittered away his time at clubs and stables and returned home only to refill his pockets and his stomach? "Given your morals, the only occupation remaining open to you may be the law."

Henry stalled with his glass partway to his mouth. "I was joking."

"No one laughed," Aunt Georgina said.

"Of course, setting you up as a barrister will further strain our funds. Then there's the cost of canvassing the neighborhood for the upcoming Parliamentary election. And with so many rents unpaid, my failure to find a wealthy wife puts us in a bad way."

"In my experience, dear brother, wealthy, well-bred ladies prefer wealthier men or men with titles. Or, if they can get them, men with both blunt in the pocket and a crest on the carriage."

Thomas stiffened. "You needn't remind me." He hid his hands behind his back to hide his clenched fists. He'd lost Mary Jennings to a Devonshire man old enough to be her father but who had the luck to inherit a baronry.

"You're too particular," Henry said, carefully enunciating the words. "The selection in London seemed more than ad… adequate to me."

"I take it you have your own list of qualifications for the honor of marrying you, Thomas?" Georgina's smile looked dangerously sardonic.

Thomas shared his list with caution. "Accomplished, certainly, with a thorough knowledge of the female arts, but also a lady whose station befits her position as a future politician's wife."

"A paragon, I take it." Georgina nodded. "Just as I'd expect of you."

Henry sank into an armchair. "Still pining after the exquisite Mary?"

Thomas glanced toward the terrace, where a cool breeze from the open door chilled the room. "As you know, my fondness for her was mere youthful folly."

"She fit the type, though — you'll admit that."

On this matter, Thomas refused to comment. The sense of loss lingered the way a broken bone might ache in bad weather.

But Henry wasn't ready to relinquish the subject. "If *I* were in the market for a wife — which, thank God, I am not — " and here he raised his now half-full glass — "I'd want someone sweet-natured and healthy, with a decent bloodline."

Thomas raised his brows. "Your ideal spouse bears a striking resemblance to my horse."

"Well, you know my fondness for a good mare. A man could do worse than to pick a wife with as much care as he'd choose his mount. After all, he'll be mounting *her* the rest of his life."

"No need to speak quite so baldly," Thomas observed, glancing at his aunt. "And given your habits in town, I expect *you* are more selective in choosing a tailor than in choosing more gentle company."

Henry's shrug had changed little since their schoolroom days. "When the occasion offers a variety of choices, I feel obligated to taste as many dishes as are offered, at least while they're in season."

"'Gluttony kills more than the sword.' We both had to memorize that one, remember? After you stole a batch of jam tartlets from the kitchen."

Georgina shook her head at the two of them.

"You paid the price for me more than once." Henry's grin showed no hint of shame.

All looked up at a voice in the hallway. "Ah, Thomas. Home at last." Both men stood as their mother entered the drawing room, arrayed like a peacock in blue, an arresting contrast to her sister-in-law. Mrs. Sophia Palmer relied on dress and décor to set her apart from the taint of rural humanity. She believed herself too good to mingle with most of the neighborhood, even though her forebearers on her mother's side were drapers. Passing years had left little mark on her, though she often alluded to her delicate constitution and palpitating heart. Thomas privately thought his father's death had been partly an escape from her complaints.

"Have you heard the latest?" she greeted him. "Old Mrs. Norris has finally passed. She must be ninety. And the rector of Swinnerton lost his youngest daughter in a most gruesome way while they were visiting Bath to take the waters. The child's clothes caught fire while her mother left her alone in the parlor with the older girl. Both caught the flame, though the older survives."

Thomas lost his appetite for dinner. "Wherever do you gather such news, Mother?"

"Georgina has been reading me the obituaries in *The Gentleman's Magazine*." His mother turned her stony gaze on Henry, who immediately squelched his snicker.

Thomas reseated himself next to his mother and steeled himself for the possibility of more grisly conversation. No wasting disease, gruesome accident, or loathsome act escaped Sophia Palmer's attention. Perhaps had she spent more time in town, she would have discovered a plentiful supply of death, decay, and misery, but life at Cleveland proved disappointing and dull: the tenants were invariably healthy, and accidents exceedingly rare.

"Was there no pleasanter news to be found?" Thomas asked his aunt.

"I read a quite spirited piece on Horace and Catius, though the extended discussion of wine grew tiresome." His aunt's love of classical literature was well known and largely tolerated; labeling her a bluestocking saved the family from dwelling on other reasons she steadfastly refused to marry. And so the conversation turned to philosophy, which was altogether a more congenial topic than roasted children.

"There is, of course, a distinct difference between hedonism, which Horace rejects, and true epicureanism," Georgina observed, though no one had introduced an argument to the contrary.

"Much to be said for both, I'd say," said Henry. "*Carpe diem* and so on."

His mother sniffed. "I suppose I should be glad you

absorbed something from your education, Henry, though that particular phrase is hardly one by which you should live your life."

Thomas was glad his mother's knowledge of Latin and Greek was thin, in case Henry, in his cups, offered mottos other than the one from Horace, perhaps even something coarse from Catullus.

"Henry says you've yet to find a suitable match. I can't believe none of those on my list would have you."

"I wonder," Georgina said, "does Thomas *desire* a wife or merely *need* one?"

Thomas raised a brow. "I beg your pardon?"

"The latter implies a sense of urgency," Georgina continued. "One *needs* a wife to stave off unpleasant consequences, while one *desires* a wife for quite other reasons." She paused, and the silence in the room grew uncomfortable.

"I both *need* a wife *and* desire one," Thomas said, his voice echoing off the walls with the force of his frustration.

"For what purpose?" His aunt's voice held neither approval nor censure.

"Really, Georgina, that's hardly the question—," Mrs. Palmer began.

"It's a very reasonable question," Georgina countered.

"Absolutely," Henry added. "If a man is in the market for a horse, whether he chooses a draught horse or a high-stepping beauty depends upon his purpose. If he plans to ride it, he doesn't want a swaybacked nag."

Thomas shook his head. "Again with the horses."

"We're not discussing livestock, Henry. And keep a civil tongue in your head," his mother snapped. She was not so easily rendered speechless. "I am relieved to know I have a chance to see you wed before I leave this plane, Thomas. I don't have much time left, you know. Not that you'd miss me."

Thomas looked to the ceiling. Sophia Palmer had been warning the family of her imminent demise for years. He remained silent as she described her latest symptoms, which took away any remaining vestiges of appetite. At last, her recital drew to a close, and he could complete his answer.

"I assure you, dear Aunt, that I *desire* a wife for much the same reason all men marry."

As the family members at last rose to dress for dinner, Thomas allowed himself to imagine a future life at Cleveland, a tranquil, well-ordered life with a compliant, comely girl who would add some much-needed normality to the household. And some relief in his bed.

~*~

Not surprisingly, dinner was a tense affair, with Georgina cutting her meat with a marked ferocity while Henry slouched over his food and Mrs. Palmer demanded a full account of whom Thomas had met.

"Only six? And not one worth a second look?" Sophia Palmer plucked at her neckline. "You did look at them, didn't you, Thomas?"

Knowing his meat would grow cold, Thomas set down his knife. "Certainly. Otherwise, I'd have trod upon their feet."

"Don't be impertinent. Not one? I find that hard to believe. They were all eminently suitable." She paused to sip her wine. "Can you at least describe what they were wearing? Is the Egyptian style quite passé?"

"How should I know whether people are still wearing the Egyptian style? There seemed to be a number of ruffles. You've already pointed out I can't tell a walking dress from an opera dress. You'd do better to ask Henry."

"Henry had even less to say on the subject than you do. Surely you paid *some* attention to those young ladies you danced with. Try, will you? *Ackermann's Repository* showed only one gown, and it had a dreadful square bodice that would be totally unsuitable for me." At that, Mrs. Palmer tugged at the lace fichu that covered any flesh her own neckline might have bared. "Why the magazines must put so many pages of drivel in is beyond me. Scientific tables. Articles on architecture. Poetry, for heaven's sake. Whoever reads poetry?"

"The article on Vienna was most informative," Georgina said, for once laying down her knife. "And *I* read poetry, though the selection in *Ackermann's* is disappointing. Singsong treacle about the joys of spring and such. Give me a good Grecian ode any day."

Thomas recalled that his aunt was especially fond of the lyrics of Sappho, yet another poet whose works failed to appear on his tutor's syllabus. He himself had been more drawn to the epics, preferring the heroic glories of the *Iliad* to the sighing and yearning of the odes.

Mrs. Palmer was not to be distracted. "The sketch of the green spencer was more illuminating than any other pages, thank you. Did you see any like it in town, Thomas?"

"I didn't notice any great quantity of green," he said, unsure of what a spencer might be. "As far as gowns, I recall seeing a white one at the ball, with a ridiculous number of pink ribbons hanging off it. And Lady Middleton wore something blue with rather puffy sleeves."

"Lady Middleton has a sister, does she not? A younger sister?"

Thomas admitted that was true.

"They are all in good health, I trust?"

Thomas agreed that they seemed healthy.

"And what of this sister?" his mother pressed on like a hound on a scent trail. "I believe their father left the daughters a tidy sum. After all, the older girl married quite well. Did you not meet the girl?"

To that, Thomas gave no reply and fervently hoped that Henry might be struck dumb.

"I must say," his brother began, "Thomas cut quite the figure on the floor. You should have seen him, Mother, gamboling about with one particularly energetic girl. Didn't know he had it in him. What was the girl's name again, old boy?"

"Miss Charlotte Jennings."

Thomas tuned out his mother's continued discussion of the Middleton family fortunes, devoutly wishing he had never traveled to London in the first place. If only one could place an ad in *Ackermann's* for a wealthy wife of the appropriate age and status, a quiet, retiring sort of woman not given to conversation or social gatherings.

"I've heard that the grounds of Barton Park surpass most in Devonshire," his mother was saying. "And Lady Middleton is said to set an elegant table."

"The hunting's reputed to be superb," Henry said.

"Met him at a hunt," Thomas mumbled. "Years ago."

"Sir John is supposed to be quite the sportsman. His house parties are legendary. Picnics, games, hunts—all manner of fun. Grouse should be ready about now, come to think of it."

Since Thomas's idea of fun rarely involved interacting with other people, he merely nodded. However, when the expected invitation to a house party arrived a week later, he found himself unable to refuse, given the pressure from his mother to further his acquaintance with Miss Jennings. "The invitation includes you too," he told Henry. "No accounting for taste."

"Inviting *you* to a social occasion shows a remarkable lack of sense if you ask me," his brother shot back. "If you go, you definitely need me along. Otherwise, you'll have to face a house full of females by yourself. And talk to them too."

And so, as August brought the sun out, it shined upon Mr. Palmer and Mr. Henry Palmer on the road to Barton Park.

# Chapter Seven

The chaise passed through the village of Barton, a hamlet tucked into the hills rather like a dog tucked into a pile of blankets. Thomas's stomach started to tighten. Barton Park must be ahead. By the time the wheels sped past a sprawling farm, he felt positively nauseated.

"Whatever is the matter?" Henry asked. He looked the soul of contentment as he leaned against the padded seat.

"I can barely breathe in this tight space. We should have taken the horses." Traveling eighty miles in a closed carriage was enough to drive him to the brink. Thomas wiped his forehead and focused on the sturdy brown cows that roamed the green valley freely, with nothing required of them but to chew their cuds in peace. Would that he could be a bull in that pasture instead of finding himself a mere mile or two from the dreaded confinement of a country house party.

"Ah, here at last!" his brother said, stretching to see out the window as the post boy turned the horses down a wide lane, bordered by tall trees and affording occasional views of the far-reaching hills and valleys of Devonshire. "Weeks of country life! Hunting, shooting, fishing, riding. And nothing expected of us but to be diverting. Let us hope the food is as good as rumor has it, and the other guests are all charming females."

"Do you think there will be a lot of them?" Thomas weighed the possibilities. Several eligible ladies would increase his chances of singling out a good one, but the idea of a throng of guests sent a new pang to his stomach. And the thought of seeing Mary — Lady Middleton — at home with her husband and children surrounding her gave him a fierce cramp.

"The Middletons are known for large gatherings, old boy. Most people would be looking forward to the benefits of a well-appointed estate and a congenial host whose only desire is their comfort and happiness. Come now, buck up. We're almost there. A few weeks, and you'll find yourself back in Cleveland with a bride in tow."

~*~

Charlotte watched from her vantage point in the upper level of the grand hall, squinting into the slanting sunlight for the silhouette of riders or the cloud of dust from a carriage that would herald the Palmers' arrival. All morning she had rehearsed what she would say to Mr. Palmer. She had even practiced in front of a mirror, trying various inflections and tilts of the head. She'd gotten it exactly right: an artful tilt to the left and a superior smile that would astound him with its sophistication. This time, he'd be captivated.

Her plotting didn't end with the greeting, however. It extended to planned chance meetings, arranged seating, and clever ways to be paired with him at the many amusements always available at her sister's country estate. Charlotte's current favorite daydream was of her seated at Mary's abandoned pianoforte, playing and singing like a nightingale while Thomas leaned over her to turn her pages. He'd brush her shoulder as he reached past her and be dumbstruck by the sensation. The mere thought of such a moment sent a thrill through her, chilling her while leaving her curiously warm.

Such plotting was essential, for to her dismay, the recent guests at Barton Park included the refined Miss Ludford, who was everything Charlotte was not. Miss Ludford's glossy brown locks turned Charlotte's colorless and dull, and her dainty figure left Charlotte feeling like a dumpy country milkmaid. Without saying a word, Miss Ludford drew the attention of every gentleman in the room. Charlotte fervently wished that Sir John knew only women who were knock-kneed and homely, then was immediately ashamed of the impulse.

"He's here at last!" she called to her mother.

"Don't just stand there, girl!" Mrs. Jennings laughed. "You've been spying out these front windows all afternoon. Get yourself down to the door! They can't admire your pretty face if they don't see it."

Charlotte needed no further encouragement. Gathering her skirt high, she turned from the window toward the short flight of steps that descended at a right angle to the landing. Her haste sent her skidding on the polished marble floor, so she was forced to grab onto the curved stone balustrade to stop herself from hurling headlong down the next flight of wide marble steps to land at the feet of the new arrivals.

Unaware of Charlotte's near tumble, the Middletons greeted the Palmers in the vast vaulted hall below. "Welcome, gentlemen. Welcome!" boomed Sir John.

Charlotte stalled at the landing, wavering a dozen feet in front of a niche that housed a marble Aphrodite, its form discreetly robed except for the shapely legs. Charlotte quickly dropped her own skirt to avoid appearing in a similar state of undress.

"Welcome to Barton Park," Sir John repeated to the Palmers, pumping each gentleman's hand. "Lady Middleton and I very much hope that you enjoy your stay. Isn't that right, my dear?"

At his side, Lady Middleton looked up the stairs at the sounds of Charlotte's scuffles. She gently shook her head before returning attention to her guests to echo her husband's greetings, though with less enthusiasm. As Mr. Palmer and his brother thanked their host and hostess and all proceeded up the main stairs, Charlotte held back on the landing, suddenly unsure of herself. The greeting she'd practiced depended on Mr. Palmer's first looking at her. And he looked only at her sister, as before.

Charlotte bit her lip, uncertain how to go on.

Upon reaching the wide landing, Sir John glanced over to see that Charlotte stood a few feet in front of him. Winking at her, he motioned her to join him. "Has your brother met Lady Middleton's sister, sir? Mr. Henry Palmer, Miss Charlotte Jennings. A more sweet-tempered young miss you'll never find."

Henry scaled the remaining stairs and paused in front of her. Charlotte made her curtsy to the younger gentleman, who seemed to her to be a fairer, less serious version of his older brother. "A pleasure, Miss Jennings," he said as he bent over her hand, adding, "I was struck at first sight by the similarity between you and the sculpture behind you. Up close, I see the resemblance even more clearly." He held her hand a fraction too long, and her palm grew damp.

"I'm very pleased to make your acquaintance as well," she said, slipping her hand from his while looking over his shoulder at his brother.

To her frustration, Thomas remained stoic, stationary, and silent. She'd be forced to speak to him first, which was not part of her plan. And since he remained two steps below her, the practiced tilt of the head was useless. They stood eye to eye.

"How nice to see you once more, Mr. Palmer," she said. The singularity of his gaze rooted her to her spot.

"Good day, Miss Jennings," he answered with a slight quirk to his lips. "May I pass?"

She stepped aside, heat flooding her cheeks. Thomas strode past her to join his brother in the upper hall, where Mrs. Jennings greeted them, further delaying their progress.

"And how was your trip, Mr. Palmer? Your estate is nearly a day's journey from here, I believe. Not too tiring, I hope? Sir John has a great number of activities planned for your stay, you know, so it simply won't do for you to be tired. All the young ladies would be exceedingly disappointed to be denied your company." Mrs. Jennings nodded at Charlotte, who had mounted the remaining flight of steps to join the rest of the group. "Isn't that right, my love?"

Charlotte covered her lingering embarrassment with a toss of her head. "Of course, Mama," she replied. "Cards and picnics are so much better with a group! So many activities are — battledore and shuttlecock, dancing, though that really only requires two. Now that I think of it, two can also enjoy many pleasant activities together." At last, she employed the artful tilt of her head she'd practiced. "Don't you agree, Mr. Palmer?"

At that, Mr. Palmer coughed.

Lady Middleton's tight-lipped smile cut Charlotte's musings. "Gentlemen, you'll be shown to your rooms," the lady said, nodding to the wide archway to the left of the statue. "Right this way."

Only then did Charlotte recall Mr. Henry Palmer's comment regarding Aphrodite. How much of her exposed legs had he seen? And, more importantly, had Thomas seen them too? And if so, what had he thought of them?

# Chapter Eight

"Lottie, could I have a moment, please? There's something I'd like to speak to you about." Mary's request sounded more like a command.

Charlotte's mind leapt to a dozen topics that Mary might consider urgent enough to discuss this late in the day. Something about the children? Which gown to wear to dinner? The evening's guest list? How many card tables might be needed?

"Come into my dressing room," her sister said, nodding at her door. "We shan't be overheard there."

So she was to be scolded. Oh, not severely—Mary was never harsh, though she could be sharp. Her mouth was set in a thin line, leading Charlotte to expect the keen side of her sister's tongue over whatever the current offense was.

Mary motioned for her to seat herself on the chair in front of the vanity, then stood behind her, their eyes meeting in the mirror. Charlotte studied the reflection. Their coloring matched and the straight line of the nose, but those similarities made the difference in stature and expression more pronounced. Charlotte tried not to squirm during the cool inspection.

As Mary lifted one thin hand to Charlotte's curls, the older sister's arched brows drew together, etching a barely perceptible crease in the marble forehead. "Can your maid not manage to dress your hair better than this? You're too old now to let it go wild."

"Susan does the best she can," Charlotte answered, her own hand tucking the escaped curls back in their ribbons. "It looks well enough at the start of the day, I think." And yet, as she gazed in the mirror, the contrast between her own rumpled appearance and Mary's perfect grooming stared her in the face. She tried to smile but failed at the first attempt and so tried again.

"Surely Mother can find you a better lady's maid, even if the French ones are hard to come by these days."

"Oh, we couldn't replace poor Susan. Her father died in Spain. She's her mother's only support now, and *her* with two boys still at home."

"The welfare of servants is not your concern, Lottie."

"Fine. If my hair is all you wanted to see me about, I'd best get back to my room to see if I can make it more acceptable."

"Stay seated, please. It's not only your wild hair that needs attention. It's your behavior."

Now Charlotte's brows drew together. "Mother hasn't said anything to me."

"That doesn't surprise me," Mary said wryly. "But now you are in my home, and I must ask you to restrain yourself. You smile too much. You laugh too loudly. You chatter incessantly. And you show far too much of your feelings. Oh, don't look at me like that. You know full well what I'm talking about."

Charlotte turned to face her sister, raising her chin to look up at her. "Are you telling me not to be happy?"

"Don't twist my words. Surely you realize that when you smile at a gentleman, you are inviting attentions that no decent young lady should encourage."

Charlotte kept her chin high. "I intend nothing indecent."

"I know you don't. But the effect is the same. A true lady is known by the elegance of her manners, by the dignity of her posture, by the refinement of her attire. In short, she declares herself a gentlewoman in hundreds of inexpressible ways that come to her as naturally as breathing."

"I can't be you, Mary. There's no sense in trying. I can only be me." Their eyes locked before Mary looked away.

"I love you, Lottie. I want only what's best for you."

"I want that too," Charlotte replied. "I only wish you'd leave me to it."

Later, a maid delivered a book from Mary. The title alone was enough to make Charlotte's shoulders slump: *The Mirror of the Graces.*

~*~

That evening's dinner proved vexing indeed, for the new arrivals were seated with Mary while Charlotte sat lower. Her spirits had been likewise lowered since her sister's lecture, so she was resolved to speak only when spoken to at dinner. She would deport herself with "the chastened dignity of a vestal," like the ideal female described in the grace and deportment book Mary had sent her. This night, at least, her behavior would be utterly above reproach. That intention lasted through the first course as Charlotte silently watched Mr. Palmer and Mary converse.

Sir John presided over the other end, however, and his good humor soon elevated her own. "If the weather holds tomorrow," he announced, "we should form an al-fresco party. Explore the countryside. Ancient standing stones not far from here. Sheep. Good views."

Charlotte's spirits rallied, along with her tongue. "A delightful plan!" Mary's book advocated "gentle and daily exercise in the open air" for growth and vigor. That advice, at least, Charlotte was happy to embrace. Mr. Palmer probably took exercise *very* regularly, given his physique. As Sir John outlined the next day's itinerary, she pondered how to insert herself into whatever carriage carried Mr. Palmer and secure him as her walking partner. Leaning on his arm, she would stroll through waves of wildflowers under the benevolent Devon sky. That night, she fell asleep imagining it.

And yet, when the party set out the following day, Mr. Palmer was not among them. He had elected to stay behind with his brother to try their luck in the fishpond, which Sir John had promised was stocked.

Charlotte's disappointment in the outing lasted only briefly, for the day was fine and the company merry, a very pleasant party comprised of several young people, some from neighboring families and the rest, guests at Barton Park. She was happy to discover some acquaintances among the new guests, in particular the handsome Mr. Tierney, whom she'd met in town during the season.

Despite Mr. Palmer's absence, Charlotte enjoyed herself immensely. Without thought to rank, the party dispersed into smaller groups of three or four, picking their way across the stone-strewn moors, then wandering a grassy path to the summit of a nearby hill. By afternoon, the sun grew hot, and the party sought relief in the shade of a massive oak. There they lounged and admired the view spread out before them, sweet meadows and deep, shadowy gorges. The outing had been most refreshing, arousing their appetites. The cold chicken and joint of ham tasted all the better for eating it out of doors.

Sated, Charlotte took off her hat and stretched her hands above her head. "I could live here all summer long!"

Mr. Tierney leaned back on one elbow and regarded her steadily. "But where would you sleep? The hills grow cold at night."

Something about Mr. Tierney's bearing reminded her of a leopard she'd once seen at the menagerie at the Exeter Exchange. Perhaps it was the way he looked at her, almost as if she were some delectable morsel. The thought gave her a tantalizing shiver.

"I'd spend my days in the sunshine and store up warmth for the night ahead," she laughed, and he laughed with her. His attention was refreshing and flattering, though she knew her mother would not approve. That fact added to his appeal. He was nothing like Mr. Palmer. But Mr. Palmer still dominated her thoughts.

~*~

The group returned soon after, and Charlotte resolved to

try anew to secure a position at Mr. Palmer's side. That evening at dinner, however, she found herself again at the far end of the table, across from the Gilberts, who lived in the village. She sat between Mr. Henry Palmer and the somewhat deaf Mr. Browne, the local rector, whose family had been invited to even the numbers. The clergyman's sole interests seemed to be birding and the sermons of Claudius Buchanon. Unfortunately, Charlotte was thwarted in her attempts to talk with Mr. Henry Palmer instead since *he* was deep in conversation with the rector's daughter.

Charlotte was thus reduced to nodding pleasantly as Mr. Browne expounded on the villainy of keeping songbirds as pets. "Now, you might think that these birds ought to be happy. After all, they live in a pretty cage, enjoy regular meals and shelter from storms and predators," he said, slicing a bite of pheasant. "But a cage is still a cage, Miss Jennings, no matter how pretty it seems. Beasts of the air should be free to fly and sing from the treetops."

"I'm sure you must be right, sir," Charlotte said absently as she strained to hear crumbs of conversation from the other end of the table, where Thomas sat to Mary's right. On Charlotte's other side, Mr. Henry Palmer's conversation was easily audible, especially now that he and Miss Jane Browne had sunk their teeth into two ends of a conversational bone.

"You must admit that Bath has many more amusements to offer, Miss Browne."

"I admit nothing of the kind, Mr. Palmer. Bath is dull. Too many entertainments involve sitting and *doing* very little. The most popular seem to revolve around watching *other* people do something—dance, sing, perform a play. I much prefer rural pursuits. You must admit that the country offers more opportunities to participate in life."

When Henry smiled, Charlotte found herself wondering if Thomas would look as charming if his mouth ever turned up in such delight. A smile was a wonderful thing. The thought of Thomas's mouth distracted her for a moment, so she was slow in catching the next threads of conversation.

"Our dear Lord has a special fondness for birds, you

know," Mr. Browne was saying. "Did you know that nearly three hundred verses in the Bible mention them? Starting with Genesis—."

"You sound like my brother," Henry continued. "He'd bury himself at Cleveland if he weren't so set on a seat in the House of Commons."

"And yet in Leviticus, some of our feathered friends are called an abomination, not to be eaten. Vultures—I suppose one can't be surprised at listing them, and owls too."

"I venture that I am very much like your brother," Miss Browne declared. "He sounds like a man of good sense."

"And eagles, ravens, kites…hawks, as well." The rector warmed to his subject.

"Thomas would undoubtedly think that was a compliment." His brother grinned.

"All birds of prey, you see. But in Matthew, our Lord counsels the disciples to be harmless as doves. Very worthy birds, doves are."

"And you do not?" Miss Browne's voice rose a notch.

"I value good humor above good sense." Henry Palmer leaned back in his chair.

"Then you are remarkably lacking in the virtue your brother possesses in abundance."

"And you in humor."

"It was a dove Noah sent out to check the flood waters. Doves are a universal symbol of peace, you know, Miss Jennings."

It could not be said that peace reigned to Charlotte's right, since Mr. Henry Palmer and Miss Browne held their tongues only to better fuel their glowers. Miss Browne, whom Charlotte had not before considered a serious rival, looked lit up from within. She reminded Charlotte of a painting she'd seen at an exhibition, a figure representing Tragedy, her profile perfectly hewn, her back straight, her gaze unflinching.

Since Mr. Browne took a break from cataloguing birds to sip from his wine glass, Charlotte was free to peer down the table at Thomas Palmer. Mary must be punishing her to seat him so far away. The lovely Miss Ludford, in a pale yellow gown that set off her hair, was turned toward Mr. Palmer, so Charlotte could see only her unblemished shoulder and part of her face. She sat in the easy attitude *The Mirror of the Graces* prescribed for sylphlike figures. Charlotte felt her own shoulders stoop.

Miss Ludford's smooth brown tresses had been gathered at her crown, allowing only a few well-behaved curls to cluster near her ear. Charlotte's own ringlets were already escaping, despite Susan's renewed effort to contain them. Provence rosebuds, which Mary's book declared appropriate adornment for women in their "blooming years," now tangled and drooped in Charlotte's curls.

If only it were possible to change places with Miss Ludford entirely! Charlotte clutched her napkin in frustration.

But Mary's annoying book warned that evil temper is a more terrible enemy to female beauty than smallpox. Charlotte took a deep breath and banished any distressing thoughts that might carve dreaded grooves in her forehead. Two more breaths and a bite of salmon set her to rights again. There was still the dessert course, but afterwards, she might manage to secure a place next to Mr. Palmer for the evening. Spirits renewed, she turned to the rector. "Do tell me more about your favorite sermon, sir."

~*~

"Could you tear yourself away from the gentlemen for just a moment, Mr. Palmer?" Lady Middleton said softly as the other ladies rose, leaving the men to their port.

Thomas looked up in surprise. "Certainly." He glanced at the end of the table, where Sir John was laughing with Henry and Tierney. They wouldn't miss him. Still puzzled, he followed her into the hallway and through a set of double doors into an empty room. The windows on this side of the house faced west. In the golden light, Mary looked insubstantial, her edges blurred, her face in shadow as she paused with her back to the setting sun.

"I wanted to speak to you alone, away from the others. You see, this is a matter of some delicacy."

Thomas waited, now doubly confused. What could she

possibly need to discuss away from the others? He reminded himself that he was an honorable gentleman, that she was a married lady, that Sir John was his host, and that if they ever came to blows, the man outweighed him by at least a stone.

"I'm at your service, ma'am," he said at last.

"I've come to you because we once were rather close. I feel I can trust you."

"Absolutely." Again he waited.

"This is much more difficult to say than I thought."

Thomas took a step closer. "There is nothing you cannot say to me."

"I feel I must apologize."

At this, Thomas stepped back. "Whatever for?"

"My sister. Her behavior is most distressing. I try to curb it, but she cannot be contained. I hear she was lolling about on the grass this afternoon without a hat. And you saw her indiscretion when you first arrived. I still blush when I remember it."

Unbidden, a vision of Miss Jennings intruded. When he'd arrived at Barton Park, she'd nearly tripped down the stairs. Her dress had been hiked up to her knees—very pretty knees, pink and dimpled above her white stockings, which were gartered low. Several seconds passed before Thomas could think of something to say. If he agreed with Mary, he would be insulting her sister. If he disagreed, he would be insulting *her*, his hostess. At last, he settled on a neutral response.

"How can I help you?"

"I knew you would understand. You were always so solid and dependable. Like the brother I once had."

*Solid and dependable. Like a brother.* Thomas bristled. A brother? She'd effectively doused any lingering hopes, though he still guarded the last scrap of his infatuation. "You may rely on me," he said, bowing stiffly and wondering how many days he would have to stay in residence before he and Henry could return home.

"I knew I could. If you could keep an eye on Lottie for me—I try, but there are the children to look after and the household to run. Mother's no help at all; in fact, she encourages the wild behavior, and I'm at wit's end!"

"You want me to spy on your sister?" Unthinkable. Surely she wouldn't ask such a thing.

"Oh, la! Spy is such an ugly word. But if you could watch out for her, perhaps step in to prevent her from making such a cake of herself in front of the other guests, then I'd be most grateful."

Thomas knew now that her gratitude would be merely that, with no promise of more. The knowledge sat uneasily in him, like underdone pork. "I'll do my best to save your sister from herself," he said and so resigned himself to playing nursemaid to a headstrong young miss.

~*~

At last, the ladies rejoined the men for cards. Unfortunately, Charlotte was late catching up with the rest of the group. She had been listening at length to Mrs. Browne's extended description of the proper way to prune summer roses. Unwilling to interrupt the lady, she'd sat nodding and smiling as the other women left.

Finally freed from deadheading spent blossoms, Charlotte paused at a cracked doorway, a perfect vantage point for observing guests in the drawing room without being obvious. Thomas Palmer sat on the far side of the room near a set of French doors, his back to the windows overlooking the terrace. He looked especially dashing in a yellow waistcoat. When she entered, he glanced up only briefly, then studied his cards.

He was partnered with Miss Ludford. Charlotte pouted. They were a well-matched pair, much like the ceramic figurines her mother set about the morning room at home, or rather — at this she laughed to herself — like a pair of chestnut horses set before a royal carriage. Delighting in the image, she imagined Miss Ludford with a feedbag of oats. This time, she laughed aloud. The sound attracted the attention of a group seated nearby. One gentleman, in particular, smiled back at her and then joined her, the very agreeable Mr. Tierney.

"You're looking especially fine this evening, Miss Jennings.

Though I still treasure the image of you from our picnic. You reclined on the hillside like some pagan nymph." He stood so close she could feel his breath on her forehead. About him hung the faint odor of anise. She wrinkled her nose and stepped back, astonished but attracted by his forwardness.

He was nothing like Mr. Palmer, always the picture of refinement. Mr. Tierney was dressed in the pink of fashion this evening: his square-cut tailcoat fit superbly, his collar points reached his cheekbones, and his cravat had been meticulously arranged in a waterfall. He'd combed his black mane just so to frame his face. If his silvery eyes were unsettling, she resolved not to notice. Perhaps they did not affect her in quite the same way as Mr. Palmer's eyes, but at least he was looking at her.

"Thank you, sir." She made sure that she did *not* smile at him, in case Mary was watching. As he gently led her past the card players, she nodded in greeting to the group. No one nodded back. The game would likely last for hours. Charlotte's plan had been scuttled for the evening.

Distracted by her disappointment, at first, she failed to register that Mr. Tierney had maneuvered the two of them through the open doors and out onto the terrace. The night was dark. The only light shone from inside. A sudden gust from the garden rustled her dress, blowing it flat against her body. Her escort looked down at her for a moment before returning his gaze to her face. "Your delicate gown highlights the purity of your complexion," he said.

The skin on her bare arms tingled. Though she'd been out for two seasons, that comment rattled her. No other gentleman had ever ventured to say anything so personal. While there was nothing objectionable in the words, the way he'd said them made her face hot, despite the wind. She sensed that it was her form, not her skin color, that he had studied. She took a shaky breath. As wrong as it was, his attention soothed an ache right below her breast.

Out here near the garden, a trellis of vines and flowers screened them from the guests inside. They were alone, with no chaperone in sight. Mary's earlier lecture pricked at Charlotte's conscience. But what harm could come to her when a roomful of people sat only a few feet away?

Would Mr. Tierney take her hand? Mary's book had cautioned that when a man who was not privileged to claim it attempted to take a lady's hand, she should withdraw it immediately.

As if prompted by her thoughts, Mr. Tierney reached for her. But he did not reach for her hand. Charlotte froze. For a fateful moment, she thought that Mr. Tierney would lay his hand where his eyes again rested. Whether she was relieved or disappointed when he let it drop, she did not know. She did know that if *Mr. Palmer's* hand had reached her way, she would have grasped it in turn. And if *he* dared lift it to rest on any part of her, she—heavens, she didn't quite know what, but she'd certainly feel differently than she did at the moment. And yet, Mr. Palmer remained inside, immersed in his cards and his partner.

"You flatter me, sir," Charlotte replied, voice wobbling. *I should not be out here alone with him.* But she made no effort to return to the safety of the drawing room. The thrill of the moment canceled out all caution. Mr. Tierney stepped still closer, forcing her to retreat into a shadowed corner. Her back was now pressed against the trellis, and Mr. Tierney stood close, too close, blocking her escape.

"It's not flattery if I speak the truth."

"I suspect you have honed that compliment with many a young lady for it to have reached its current level of charm."

"You find me charming, do you? Then we are in agreement," he answered, leaning forward until Charlotte could feel the lapels of his coat brush against her. "For I find you utterly delicious. I'm wondering if you taste as sweet as you look." And he bent his head down, not to her lips, but lower.

It was a step too far. Charlotte's eyes narrowed. He'd shocked her. The sensations his touch aroused and the way he'd said those words made her glimpse something dark, something forbidden and dangerous. "I'm not edible, sir," she replied loudly, pushing him away. "And I certainly am not inviting you to taste," she said louder still.

~*~

At that, Thomas looked up from his cards. Whatever was the chit up to now?

He couldn't hear the answer from Miss Jennings' companion. Tierney. It could be no other. Henry was over by the pianoforte arguing with the earnest Miss Browne. Her father, Miss Ludford's father, and Sir John were also on the other side of the drawing room, not that any of them were likely to be importuning the troublesome Miss Jennings.

*Damn that promise to Mary.* He hadn't expected to have to act on it so soon.

Tierney was a rake, a fact generally known at Mr. Palmer's club, though perhaps not known to the gentry at large, or Sir John would not have invited the man here. When Thomas looked out the window, he saw a trellis shake and bend outward. "If you'll excuse me," he said, jumping to his feet and crossing the room without looking at Miss Ludford. He was through the doors and on the terrace in twelve strides.

The sight before him resembled one of Cruikshank's seamier etchings. Tierney had backed the girl into the latticework. Her hair had come loose, and her flimsy white gown had slipped off one shoulder. A rope of vine had etched a green stripe across what little of her bodice still covered her.

Before Thomas could act, however, little Charlotte Jennings shoved the cad hard with both hands, then hauled off and punched him in the nose. Thomas stood rooted in the spot. The girl had an impressive right hook. "I say," he began but then could think of nothing *to* say.

Tierney looked up. The oath that poured from his mouth was totally unsuitable for the ears of a lady. "You're not needed here, Palmer," the miscreant snarled. "Miss Jennings and I were about to take a turn around the garden."

"We were not!" The girl struggled to free herself from the greenery and latticework.

"Miss Jennings," Thomas replied, "since you appear to be tangled in that vine, I think you have communed enough with nature. And you, sir, will want to change your neckcloth."

"What the devil?" Tierney said, wiping his nose with his hand. He stared in disbelief at the smears of red staining it and his snowy cravat. "*She* did this?"

"As I said, Tierney, you'll want a fresh one."

"By Jove!" Mr. Henry Palmer interjected from the doorway, "Do you require assistance?" Behind him, Miss Browne, Miss Ludford, and Sir John peered out at the compromising scene.

"Quite all right, nothing to be concerned about," Mr. Tierney snuffled, catching the red drips with his cupped hand. "A nosebleed, that's all."

"Wasn't talking to you," Henry said.

Thomas looked at the incomparable Miss Jennings, who was hurriedly adjusting her dress after extricating herself from the trellis. A dead leaf still clung to her curls. "I believe someone should escort Miss Jennings to her room," he said.

# Chapter Nine

She'd been sent to her room like a naughty child. Charlotte kicked at the edge of the rose-colored coverlet, tangling the fabric between her legs and almost tripping in the process. Even the bedcovers warred against her. The quantity of pastels about the room did nothing to calm her. She willed the walls to turn red.

Her cheeks burned along with her mood as she remembered all those eyes upon her, watching as she fought her way out of the trellis and tugged her bodice back in place as best she could. The onlookers' expressions had ranged from shocked to amused. Miss Ludford's could only be described as smug.

But Thomas Palmer's face had been carved in stone as he stared at that awful Mr. Tierney. Charlotte wanted to die. He'd seen her punch a man. Mr. Palmer would never think of her as anything but tainted now. Mary had made that very clear when she had practically dragged her up the stairs.

"Two seasons and no engagement. And tonight, you nearly ruined your last chance for a decent match," she'd hissed. "Whatever were you thinking?"

"I wasn't thinking he'd back me into a trellis."

"Now is not the time for levity."

Several retorts had sprung to Charlotte's tongue, but in the end, she'd merely hung her head. There was nothing remotely funny about the incident.

"Lord Dysart is due to arrive at the end of the week," Mary had continued. "We must hope none of the guests reveal your indiscretion. The Brownes, I think, are above gossip, and Mr. Henry Palmer seems uninterested. Miss Ludford has a clear field to Mr. Palmer, so it's not to her benefit to shift attention to you. Lord Dysart may be none the wiser."

Charlotte did not find that thought as comforting as Mary did. Lord Dysart was pleasant, but he could hardly hold a candle to Mr. Palmer. And now Miss Ludford had *him* to herself.

Alone in her room once more, Charlotte kicked the covers harder. If only she could turn back time and avoid Mr. Tierney altogether. She couldn't forget the way Mr. Palmer had stared as she tried to pull her dress up over her shoulder. He'd stood stiff as a poker. Was he utterly disgusted by the sight of her in a state of *dishabille*? No, not disgusted. She shook her head, remembering. Riveted. Heavens, no wonder. He'd seen everything. Her reputation was as stained as her dress. Would she ever regain his respect?

Tears pricked her eyes, and her lower lip trembled. Her perfect plans were for naught. He'd never want her now. It was marry Lord Dysart or resolve herself to living forever with her mother.

Startled by a soft knock on the door, she barely had time to turn before her mother entered. "Oh, my dear Lottie! My poor, dear darling girl! Now, now, my pet. You're all right. Don't cry, now. This will pass." Mrs. Jennings folded her daughter in her arms, muffling Charlotte's attempts to answer.

"He'll never look at me the same way again."

"Mr. Tierney? Certainly not, and thank goodness for that. He's been sent packing. No worry there. None of the other gentlemen think the less of you, I'm sure. You did nothing wrong, child. Well, except for letting him escort you outside alone. Now, now. No sense in making a fuss. You merely got yourself stuck to a trellis. You're not the first girl to get in a tangle on a terrace. Could happen to anyone."

"But Mary said—."

"Don't worry your pretty head about what your sister said. And forget about Mr. Tierney. Look at the bright side! Who came to your rescue, after all? Mr. Palmer! Think on that, my girl! If you had seen the look on his face as he followed Mr. Tierney into the hallway, you'd stop fretting this minute! Why, I'm quite sure Mr. Palmer is more than half in love with you already. He must be, else why would he have acted so?"

Charlotte's spirits rose to new levels. True, *she* had been the one to smack Tierney, but no one but the three of them knew that. And Mr. Palmer *had* rushed to her aid, at least a bit.

~*~

Morning was such a hopeful time of day. Charlotte set about making new plans as soon as she opened her eyes. She must push her advantage now that Mr. Palmer had demonstrated his possible *tendre* for her. He needed only a nudge or two or three to bring him up to the mark.

Her plan for today would let him rescue her for real. Somehow, she would entice him down to the fishpond. Then, situating herself at the brink of the steep bank, she would feign distress, and Mr. Palmer could rush to her rescue. He would snatch her from the brink of peril and enfold her swooning self in his strong arms. Then he would sweep her off her feet and carry her all the way back to Barton Park. It would be only a matter of time before he declared himself.

Such an occasion called for her very best day dress, she thought as she hummed to herself. "The green and white one, please," she directed her maid. The white cotton gown with the pleated bodice and puffed sleeves was innocent but beguiling. Delicate tendrils of ivy had been embroidered on the gossamer fabric. Susan tied the green sash, then tugged and brushed Charlotte's hair until she achieved a style they both approved of: the strands in front parted in the middle, leaving a few yellow tendrils free to spring about her cheeks, and the rest brushed smooth at the crown and bound with a gold band, allowing a cascade of curls to coil down her back. Charlotte gave a satisfied nod. She looked years older and inches taller this way, to be sure.

~*~

*Good God, the girl is covered in vines again.* She looked absurd in the thin gown, like some forest sprite. One would think she'd distance herself from all greenery for the time being. Thomas closed his eyes and wondered what great sin he'd committed to be saddled with the protection of this little ninny. *Sin.* The word conjured a vision of milk-white skin. He swallowed twice and opened his eyes to watch Miss Jennings pause at the doorway to the dining room. The culprit glided in as if the night's excitement had never happened.

"Good morning, gentlemen," she said, punctuating the greeting with a smile so sunny Thomas was tempted to shade his eyes.

He rose to his feet. "Good morning, Miss Jennings." His voice sounded strained.

"Ah, Miss Jennings," Henry said as he helped himself to a slice of spiced bread from the sideboard. "I trust you are rested? No ill effects?"

"I'm quite well, thank you," she said, piling her own plate with an assortment of sweets and sitting down next to Thomas. "How could I not be, on such a glorious morning?"

Thomas could think of at least two reasons that she might be less than well — one being the possible soreness of her knuckles — but since she seemed determined to remain cheerful, he kept them to himself. The quiet lasted a few minutes since Miss Jennings' mouth was full.

How was he to make good on his promise to Lady Middleton? He couldn't follow the girl about all day. There must be some entertainment planned that would keep her in check and allow *him* to keep watch without drawing any undue attention. The very last thing he wanted was for anyone but Lady Middleton to become aware that he was spying upon silly Lottie Jennings.

Feeling his way into his new role, he asked, with caution, "What activities have you planned to fill these glorious hours,

Miss Jennings?"

If he had thought her previous smile too sunny, the one that broke out in response to his question was blinding. "How kind of you to ask, Mr. Palmer! Miss Browne and I thought we might take our sketchbooks and paints down to the pond. Some charming wildflowers bloom along the bank, flowering rush and fennel. And daisies. I so love daisies. Perhaps you noticed them since you seem to enjoy fishing there."

"As a matter of fact, my brother and I had just now decided to fish there again today," Thomas said, pointedly ignoring Henry's startled expression. "It would be our pleasure to accompany you once you've breakfasted."

"I shan't keep you waiting," Miss Jennings replied, nearly leaping from her chair, though her meal was only half finished.

Thomas chewed his roll with all the enthusiasm of a highwayman facing the gallows.

"Spirited, isn't she?" Henry observed, smirking. "Since when have you had this mad desire to fish? One would think you're angling for something other than a trout."

"We can't hide indoors."

"I know you prefer the open air, but I had no idea your interest lay in that particular direction."

Thomas scowled.

Even the weather was against him, for the sun shone relentlessly, providing not even the hint of rain to ruin the outing. At least he was saved the trouble of conversing when Miss Jennings rejoined them since she kept up a constant commentary as they walked.

"An enchanting spot, is it not? The pond is so clear that it looks like there's an entire upside-down world in its depths. Oh, and the colors! I've never seen the sky so blue. That willow is a lovely light green, and the dear daisies nod their heads when the wind blows, and oh! There by that clump of cattails. The ducks! I must draw them!" She set about her sketching as soon as she settled herself on the blanket Thomas had carried for her.

"With all the scenery about you, you choose a fat white

duck as your subject?" One duck seemed unusually cooperative, waddling up the bank with intermittent quacks before settling on a tuft of grass only a few feet from them. Thomas watched as Charlotte sketched the round shape and added what looked like a smile to the beak. She had taken quite a lot of license with her drawing, from what he could see.

"I draw them for my nephews and niece. Do you not like ducks, Mr. Palmer?" She tossed the bird a bit of a roll she took from her reticule and giggled as the bird caught and swallowed it.

"On the contrary. Well dressed, they are delicious."

At that, Charlotte set down her sketch pad and shook her head slowly. "A man who cannot see the merits in a fat white duck is narrow-minded indeed." Her expression grew uncommonly solemn as she tilted her head back and studied his face. "I may have misjudged you, Mr. Palmer."

Could she be serious? And the worst of it was that he felt vaguely disappointed that she disapproved of him. Since he could think of no answer to such a comment, he bowed slightly and walked away without a word.

Several yards away, Miss Browne had settled herself on a folding stool under the willow. The contrast between the two females couldn't be more pronounced. Nary a breeze stirred Miss Browne's bonnet ribbons, and not a crease marred her simple white dress and blue apron as she leaned toward her easel. Miss Jennings squabbled and rustled about on her blanket like one of the ducks she prized, while Miss Browne had all the grace and dignity of a swan.

"Now there's a female who would never grate on the nerves," he said to Henry, who was baiting his line on the bank nearby.

"Miss Browne? Hah! Don't be fooled. I'll admit that on the outside, she seems all that's cool and serene. But her tongue has a bite. I still bear the scar from our last conversation."

"You? I thought you impervious to such wounds."

"Only because the kinds of company I keep have softer

tongues."

Thomas laughed. "Still, I'll risk an approach. Perhaps her tongue-lashing was reserved for you alone."

Thomas picked his way carefully between the rushes and stooped beneath the willow canes to enter Miss Browne's shady open-air studio. Her painting proved as serene as the lady: a wash of blues and greens faithfully rendered the pond and plants. When he drew closer to study the painting in progress, however, he noticed an odd addition to the bucolic scene.

"Is that a snake?" At first glance, he'd thought the brown shape painted in the corner was a fallen branch, but on closer inspection, the branch appeared to have a faint stripe and a pointed head. An adder.

Miss Browne looked over her shoulder, brush still in hand. "Absolutely."

He studied the grass and pond before him. "But I see no such threat here."

"I suspect there's a serpent in every garden, Mr. Palmer. Even if we don't see it."

"That's rather a bleak view of the world, isn't it?"

"Realistic," she corrected without smiling. "One should always see the world as it is, not as one wishes it to be."

Thomas was unaccustomed to encountering a philosophy so in tune with his own. Usually, he found himself defending his rational approach to life and its disappointments. "One should accept what cannot be changed," he replied. "And yet one has a duty to improve one's condition, and the world's, when one can."

Miss Browne lifted her chin, so her bonnet no longer shaded her face. Her hair was pale and smooth, as controlled as her features. She studied *him* much as Thomas had studied the adder. "You sound like a politician, Mr. Palmer."

"In fact, I hope to secure a seat in the House of Commons."

Even as he said it, he explored the notion that Miss Browne would make an observant, practical, uncomplicated partner in life, despite her lack of fortune. The idea took hold. Why not? She was accessible, as well as presentable and intelligent. His brother seemed to enjoy her company. At Cleveland, she would bring a calming presence to his household. She would never surprise him. Although he had not yet seen her smile, that point should not be held against her. He was sure her teeth were as straight as her gaze.

"And what think you of the Irish corn trade?" she asked, still studying him.

"I beg your pardon?

"Do you favor changing the Corn Laws?"

"I have not yet formed an opinion on the matter." Thomas glanced over at Henry, who was barely concealing a grin. "Do you follow politics, Miss Browne?"

"Ladies have as much at stake as gentlemen in political matters, sir."

"My own aunt has much the same opinion," he replied. Georgina might meet her match in the unflappable Miss Browne. No harsh breeze would ruffle this swan's feathers. She radiated strength and dignity, though the fowl was also known for its a fierce temperament.

It seemed that choosing a wife meant identifying which particular variety of suffering he would most readily sacrifice himself for. The thought brought him full circle to Miss Jennings. Where had she got to? He looked around. *There* she was, by the edge of the pond, gazing at the ducks. He frowned. She was leaning rather precariously.

Before he could examine the impulse, he hurried toward her. "Be careful, Miss Jennings. You're too close to the verge," he said, holding out his hand.

The look she gave him stopped him short. What on earth was the matter with the girl? Instead of accepting his aid, she advanced another step, perilously close to the edge of the very steep bank. The very *slippery* bank. She discovered how slippery when she started to skid.

"Help, Mr. Palmer! Save me!"

Thomas darted forward and reached for her. Miss Jennings

grabbed at him, but before he could tug her to safety, his boot caught on an outcropping of rock. For a moment, they balanced at the brink. Then gravity did its work. Down Thomas fell on the relentless stone, while, arms flailing, Miss Jennings plunged down the steep slope. Recent rains had eroded the dirt into the slickest of mud, speeding her descent. Thorn bushes snatched at her as she slid, snagging at her limbs and tangling in her garments.

He'd never known a female to have so much trouble with vegetation. *Trouble.* That word should be stitched across her skirts. Though he could feel the bruises already blooming, Thomas knew his duty. He rose gingerly and slipped down the bank, avoiding the worst of the bushes. At the bottom, Miss Jennings crouched amid a swarm of prickers. He was sorely tempted, for a moment, to leave her there.

"Oh, Mr. Palmer!"

She did look pitiful. The more she tried to extricate herself, the more embedded the thorns became until her thin gown risked being torn to shreds. One thorn had scarred a red trail down her arm, and Thomas felt a pang at the offense. He dragged his mud-spattered self to her side as swiftly as he could and reached out to pull the barbs from the fabric.

"Really, there's no need. I shall get myself loose in a moment, I'm sure." Yet the more she fussed with the mess, the more entangled it all became.

"Dash it, Miss Jennings, stop pulling! You're making it worse. Here now, turn back this way. Better. Now I can see what's what. I think we can salvage the dress if you'll stay still for one blasted minute." He was forced to step closer since the gown was now wrapped quite tightly about her. Her form felt uncommonly yielding when he put his arms around her. The curls atop her head tickled his chin. "Stop shaking. I've almost got it." He leaned still closer. "Oh, the devil take it." His foot slipped again on the muddy bank, and he sat down hard. The commotion sent the watching ducks into a fit of quacking.

His knee stung like the dickens, his backside ached, and slime and bird droppings encrusted every inch of his once-pristine buckskin breeches. The last time he'd been similarly soiled, he had been rescuing two other Jennings relatives. If he spent much more time with this family, his valet would quit. Yet Charlotte Jennings required assistance. He cautiously heaved himself to his feet, wincing.

"Oh, Mr. Palmer! Are you hurt? No, please don't trouble yourself further. I think I almost have it. There!" With a deft twist, she freed the yards of fabric from the bush. A single thorny branch still clung. Both of them stared down at it. Then Charlotte began to shake anew.

Any second she'd be bursting into tears. Who could blame her? Thomas looked in desperation for Henry, who had abandoned his fishing rod to join Miss Browne under the willow tree. They'd been no help, absorbed in each other. Nothing would stop Miss Jennings' imminent bawling. And it *was* imminent. Her shoulders quaked. Her neck reddened. Her mouth opened wide, and…she *laughed*.

Thomas stared in amazement. The girl was mad.

"Mr. Palmer, if you could see your face! And look!" She raised her skirt with the thorny stem dangling from it. "Do…do y'suppose that people will think it's part of the embroidery? I'm afraid I don't know the proper etiquette for a moment like this. *The Mirror of the Graces* offers no advice for this situation." Then she sobered and let the dress fall. "I'd be forever grateful if you didn't mention this episode to my sister."

"As you wish, Miss Jennings." He almost wished the smile back on her face. It was as if a cloud had passed in front of the sun.

He quite forgot about his knee.

# Chapter Ten

While the two couples headed up the path from the pond, so many thoughts swirled about in Charlotte's mind that her brain was in danger of spinning out of her head. Yet she couldn't concentrate on any single thought because Mr. Palmer limped next to her, occasionally leaning on her and bumping her side as she carried her blanket and sketchbook. His strides were uneven, so she had to adjust her own. Every few minutes, she assessed his progress, biting her lip at the beads of sweat dotting his forehead and the thin line of his mouth.

He suffered all this pain for her. True, he hadn't *said* he cared. He hadn't actually said anything at all since they began to walk back from the pond. But Thomas Palmer was a man of few words. And actions counted more than words anyway, didn't they? He had twice rescued her now, once (nearly) from Mr. Tierney, and this time, from the muddy slope and dratted bush. Her plan had worked at first. When she leaned over the bank, Mr. Palmer's attention had rested fully upon her, not Miss Browne. Such an opportunity was not to be wasted. It was a simple matter to feign distress.

She had not counted on *real* distress, however.

Mr. Palmer never suspected the truth, not even when she'd had a fit of giggles over the ruse. She did not feel like laughing now as he stumbled along.

He *must* care, at least a little. Why else would he follow her on her outing and leap to her side to help her, scaring the ducks and nearly falling into the pond in the process? He'd been a perfect gentleman, though he'd had to stand very close indeed as he tried to pick out the thorns. She'd loved the feel of his arms wrapped about her, his hard chest at her back, his breath warm on her neck. Just the scent of him, sweat and earth, made her woozy.

She could disregard his antipathy toward ducks.

Miss Browne and Mr. Henry Palmer had been most solicitous of Charlotte's plight, but when reassured that she was fine, they'd resumed their focus on each other, never noticing Mr. Palmer's injuries. On the path ahead of her, the two engaged in a lively discussion, though Charlotte could not quite make out the words. The gentleman seemed highly amused by something the lady was saying, while *she* looked anything but pleased. Charlotte wondered why they continued to seek each other out since they obviously had little in common. Yet when the path forked, Henry Palmer continued walking with the lady toward the gate instead of continuing on to the manor house.

Charlotte and Thomas took the other fork. No other houseguests wandered about the gardens. No rivals could distract him. She had him to herself entirely. Getting him alone, out of sight of the house, was ever so much better than being seated next to him in company. "I must thank you, Mr. Palmer, for all your assistance today. Why, had you not saved me, I might still be stuck in that bush. You risked all to rescue me." That should be enough to prompt a declaration of some sort.

Mr. Palmer frowned. "If you had squealed more loudly, I'm sure Miss Browne and my brother would have come to your aid."

"But you stepped in so quickly!"

He grimaced when she grasped his arm. "Please, Miss Jennings. There's no need to say more."

Obviously, the man needed more prompting. "But I would

have been hopelessly tangled up had you not appeared just when you did. Why, my gown might have been torn to ribbons! I could have been stuck there on the bank, cold and naked and helpless." At that, Charlotte turned the full force of her bright blue eyes on him, willing him to envision the sight, or at least to say *something* gallant.

Mr. Palmer raised one eyebrow. "It would be my pleasure to rescue you under those circumstances, Miss Jennings."

She did not look away. "Not only *your* pleasure, Mr. Palmer," she whispered.

"Yet it's highly unlikely that you'll find yourself in such circumstances again."

"Must you always look on the dark side, Mr. Palmer?" The man was infuriating.

"I beg your pardon?"

"Could you not once look on the lighter side of things?"

"There's a happy side to being tangled up?"

"There is, depending upon with whom one is tangled."

But Mr. Palmer's gaze shifted to the gravel drive. "I say, is that a carriage up ahead? Is Lady Middleton expecting other guests?"

Charlotte could see a trail of dust. Far ahead, a black Berline carriage rolled past the twin elk statues that marked the courtyard entry to Barton Park. Only one other guest was expected.

Lord Dysart had arrived.

~*~

The trying morning was about to become an even more trying afternoon. After changing his clothes, Thomas wanted nothing more than to retreat — to the garden, to a nearby tavern, to some secluded grove in the park. Unfortunately, as a guest, he must observe conventions. It would not do to avoid the baron. Any man with an eye to Parliament knew the importance of connections. Lord Dysart had influence at court. His reach was long, despite his height. That height seemed no impediment, judging from the way he was fawning about Miss Jennings as the party gathered for tea on the terrace. Dysart's bow was so low that he nearly bumped her midsection, and Thomas could swear that he took a gander at her body on his way down and up.

Of course, the innocent Miss Jennings was totally oblivious to the danger, probably blinded by the title, as her sister had been by Sir John's. It was mere days since that cad Tierney had tried to lure the girl into the hedges, and yet she allowed this undersized peer to court her openly. For courting, it undoubtedly was.

Look at the way Dysart threw back his head and laughed at whatever she was saying. Irritating. And look at the smile she bestowed on him in response! Much too forward. Thomas refused to step closer so that he could eavesdrop on their conversation. But when he casually walked past them, he overheard a bit of her simpering and his gallantry.

"I must say, Miss Jennings, your description of the duck's reaction is priceless! I haven't laughed so much in weeks, not since you left London. Town is much duller without you."

The twit should be able to see through such idle flattery. Nothing sincere in the least! If she had a speck of sense, she'd walk away.

And yet, she continued to smile. "You're kind to say so, my lord." For a moment, she looked up and met Thomas's eyes before returning her attention to Dysart. "And may I say that Barton Park is more lively now that you have come to stay? You've saved us from falling asleep from boredom and inaction, like one of those enchanted castles one finds in fairy tales."

"If this were a fairy tale, then I think you would be the sleeping princess waiting to be awakened by a kiss." Dysart's rubbery lips practically drooled as he spoke.

The bounder! Thomas could listen no longer, despite his promise to keep an eye on the girl. There were limits to being solid and dependable, and he was feeling anything but *brotherly* toward the insufferable Miss Jennings. Let her walk this thorny path to perdition on her own. He'd had enough.

A cup of lukewarm tea and a tasteless biscuit sustained him well enough. It was hours until dinner, and no activities had been planned other than to mingle. Looking about for something, anything, to keep his attention away from the ridiculous behavior of his charge, he drifted toward the divan where Henry sat with Sir John.

"Ah, Thomas, do join us," Henry invited. "Our host was just telling me of his plans for a musical evening. He's hired five professionals from the village. Should be quite a night."

"Just so," Sir John agreed. "Got to keep things lively, don't you know? Can't have guests just sitting about. Young bloods need activity. Nothing like song and dance to add some spice to a party."

Although dancing appalled him and his knee still hurt, Thomas was curious about the possibility of music. "Will Lady Middleton play?"

"Got a hired man for that," Sir John said carelessly. "Some of the guests are bound to perform, though. Young ladies like to show off what they can do. Sing. Plunk at an instrument. Heard one of them practicing this morning. Charlotte, I believe. Or perhaps it was Miss Ludford. Sweet voice." He looked pointedly at Thomas.

"If there's to be dancing, will there be other guests besides the present company?" Henry asked with a studied nonchalance.

"Invited some of the neighbors. Should be plenty of partners to go around." Sir John winked.

"Will the Brownes be attending, by any chance?" Henry's offhand question caught his brother's attention.

"They will, as will most of the families in Barton. M'wife's already deep into the planning. Nothing she likes better than to supervise a big fete."

"She used to play beautifully," Thomas said quietly.

"She don't anymore," her husband replied.

~*~

Charlotte's plan to spark jealousy in Mr. Palmer seemed to have fizzled, but a new one was in the offing. There was to be a musical evening! Charlotte practically danced about her room at the thought. Such evenings offered any number of chances to pair off once the rugs were rolled back and the bows rosined. This opportunity must be executed perfectly. Dutifully, she consulted *The Mirror of the Graces*, determined to avoid any more pratfalls. Several pages were devoted to the management of one's person in the exercise of accomplishments.

Dancing, it seemed, was "the singular accomplishment best calculated to display the female form in all its elegance." It allowed a lady to display her fine figure and graceful carriage to the appreciative eye. Besides a mastery of the steps, the book stressed that a lady must at all costs avoid an awkward stiffness of the upper body and neck. That was new. Her dance instructor had been most strict in reminding her to stand straight. Instead, apparently, she must deport herself in "graceful undulation." Charlotte raised her arms, stretched her neck, and practiced the desired movement in the mirror. The look was certainly fluid. She'd never seen anything quite like it at the London balls, and with good reason. Still, it might catch Thomas's eye.

A brief knock on the door announced the arrival of Lady Mary, who entered and stopped short. Looking up, Charlotte smiled but did not stop her practice.

"Whatever are you doing?" Mary demanded after a brief silence.

"Undulating," Charlotte answered, enjoying the chance to tease.

"Whatever for?"

Charlotte turned to face her stuffy sister. "Because elegant motion of the feet is only half the art of dancing."

"Exactly what art are you applying?" Mary demanded, hands on hips.

"The art of 'conspicuous elegance.' I am also practicing fluttering my lashes to convey my modesty."

"Where did you hear such nonsense?"

"In the book you gave me."

Mary sank on the bed. "Lottie, elegance isn't something you don like a gown. It's an attitude that comes from within. And modesty comes more from covering up than displaying something." She sighed. "I fear I've done you a grave disservice in giving you this manual. I intended you to absorb the spirit of the instruction, not follow it like a primer. A lady does not undulate, at least not in the way you are doing it."

"You, I suppose, are the great authority on all things elegant."

"As you are the authority on impertinence. Really, Lottie, you try my patience. I'm simply attempting to help you and Mama. It's her dearest wish to see you settled, with a home and family of your own. And since you failed to secure a match in London, we both had hopes that you would find a suitable choice here." She paused delicately before adding, "Lord Dysart traveled all the way to Barton Park for a reason, you know. I doubt it was only to shoot a few birds."

Lord Dysart *had* been attentive since his arrival. He'd been quick to appear at her elbow whenever she ventured downstairs. When they spoke, he made a point of mentioning his country estate in Surrey and his other holdings to the north. Charlotte knew that a future with him would be secure, much as a handsomely fashioned birdcage was a pleasant abode for a songbird. "What if I prefer another gentleman?" Lottie lifted her chin, daring her sister to answer.

Mary laughed. "Is there another here that would have you? Have I somehow missed a suitor among the guests?"

"There's Mr. Palmer."

Mary stopped laughing. "Mr. Henry Palmer is far too young and unstable to be a good husband. In a few years, perhaps, his prospects will be better. I cannot imagine that our mother would approve of him now."

"It's Mr. Thomas Palmer I speak of, and you know it," Charlotte said softly. "He was once considered suitable enough for you."

"Mr. Thomas Palmer is not suitable for you, however," Mary said curtly. "Imagine you shut up in that rustic house by the sea. Besides, he has no title. And though he hopes to join Parliament, he hasn't won the seat yet. Lord Dysart is a far better choice."

"Lord Dysart is a very nice gentleman," Charlotte said. "I find no fault in him. He is kind and amusing and would be a good husband."

"I'm relieved to hear that you are open to reason."

"But I *can* imagine myself as Mrs. Palmer," Charlotte replied.

~*~

By midmorning, Thomas Palmer had finished his breakfast and was considering the possibility of calling on Miss Browne while Miss Jennings was occupied when Lady Middleton entered the dining room. After nodding to the other guests still lingering over their buttered rolls, she leaned over to him. "May I have a word with you, Mr. Palmer?"

This was becoming a habit. Folding his napkin, Thomas agreed and followed his hostess into the corridor. "How may I be of service?" he asked reluctantly. The lady's last request had seriously curtailed his ability to woo a wife. Miss Browne so far remained aloof, and he had not yet summoned the courage to approach the ladies visiting Barton Park with whom he was not yet acquainted. At this rate, he'd be stuck in Devonshire for weeks. He *must* return to Cleveland with a suitable wife. His family's wellbeing and his political future depended upon it.

"I wanted to thank you privately for your diligent care of my sister. I now realize what an imposition it was and sincerely apologize. Since Lord Dysart has arrived, I'm sure that Charlotte will be quite adequately supervised and have no further opportunities to—well, misstep, shall we say?"

"Miss Jennings is adventurous, but I doubt that she intentionally missteps. Rather, her feet are prone to finding ways to trip." Thomas smiled slightly at the memory of Charlotte tied up in thorns—and the feel of her in his arms.

Lady Middleton's expression hardened. "Please do not feel compelled to continue at your post, Mr. Palmer. I have trespassed on your goodwill long enough."

His brows knit together. "You wish me to stop my

surveillance, then?"

"Just so."

With the freedom to look and go wherever he chose, Thomas felt oddly static. Fishing without Miss Jennings at her sketchpad now failed to lure him. And putting Dysart on guard duty was tantamount to setting a wolf in front of a cut of veal.

The later arrival of a letter from his mother further depressed his spirits.

*My dear Thomas,*

*I was glad to read you arrived safely. I trust that this letter finds you well, and Henry. Your aunt remains in annoyingly good health here, which I suspect she flaunts. She attributes her state to her frequent walks in the country. As you know, the delicate nature of my own health means such rigors are out of the question.*

*You will have seen in the papers that Dr. Leeds has died, a great loss to his family. His passing was a mercy since the man had been in a miserable state of health for some time with a weeping growth that he could barely cover with a patch. I believe you met his eldest son in Bath. He was about to marry a girl not worth two shillings. Now they'll have to put it off, but perhaps the time of mourning will allow him to reassess his poor choice.*

*By now, I expect that you and Henry have examined any number of eligible young ladies. I pray that you find among them a suitable match — a meek, pious, biddable young woman with a comfortable fortune.*

*Your loving mother*

Meek, pious, biddable, and rich. Thomas found the list as constricting as his over-starched cravat. He considered again the ladies currently gathered at Barton Park. Miss Ludford came closest to fulfilling his mother's requirements. He reassessed his original opinion of the girl. From his seat in the drawing room, he could watch her in conversation with Lord Dysart.

Meek? She kept her head bowed demurely. Pious? Of that, Thomas couldn't be certain, but she did wear a cross on a chain about her neck. Biddable? Most certainly. She'd followed his every lead at cards. And rich? Ludford's income was rumored to be over £5,000. The girl's marriage settlement would be generous. Thomas could overlook her damp tendency to hang on his arm. Miss Anne Ludford was entirely suitable — nothing like Charlotte Jennings.

Thomas had a sudden urge to break something.

# Chapter Eleven

The approaching musical evening absorbed all Mary's attention, which left Charlotte to her own devices. Yet for the next three days, Sir John kept Mr. Palmer fully occupied from morn till dusk. Charlotte suspected Mary had a hand in that plan.

She whispered as much to her mother one afternoon as they sat with the ladies. "She's made sure he's anywhere I'm not. The men hunt grouse from first light till night, Mama, even when the sky empties buckets on their heads."

"Men are hunters, dear. Most are anyway, unless they're mollies. The poor dears need to stomp about in the forest and bring back their trophies."

"Why do they turn to nature for the sole purpose of killing? Given the energy they put into shooting them, it's a wonder any birds remain in the entire county."

"Be that as it may, you might remember that Mr. Palmer ain't the only eligible gentleman at Barton Park."

"What does it matter if all day long, none of them ever come inside?"

And so Charlotte sat with the ladies working on her drawing, adding new ribbon to a bonnet, nodding and smiling and fidgeting in her seat. Gossip and news remained their sole entertainments when the gentlemen were out.

"Have you heard Dashwood died? Sussex family?" Mrs. Jennings inquired one afternoon when the rain had finally stopped. While several ladies murmured, she continued. "Left his widow—second wife, that was—and three daughters at the mercy of the son by the first wife. Young Dashwood's married now, with a son of his own. *His* wife used to be Fanny Ferrars. Ill-tempered sort, that one. Grasping. Wouldn't be surprised if she was behind ousting the lot of them. I believe Mr. Palmer once knew her well." Mrs. Jennings pursed her lips.

Charlotte dropped her drawing pencil. "Mama, I'm quite sure Mr. Palmer would have nothing to do with a cold-hearted woman. He is the soul of generosity."

At that, the ladies laughed.

"Mr. Palmer is the soul of *reticence*," one lady observed. "Why, last week I was seated with him at whist, and he scarce said a word. Not even when he and his partner won the rubber."

Miss Ludford colored at that comment. "Mr. Palmer is quite skilled at cards," she said so softly that only Charlotte heard her.

"Mr. Palmer is observant." Charlotte nodded. "It's no wonder he wins at cards." She glanced at Miss Ludford, who had been his whist partner. The lady swallowed but made no further comment.

"*Lord Dysart* has winning ways," Mrs. Jennings said with a broad wink. "He's certainly taken with you, Lottie. Couldn't take his eyes off you at breakfast. Am I not right?"

Most of the ladies nodded and twittered in agreement.

"Won't be long until I have more little grandchildren running about," she added, much to Charlotte's discomfort.

"Really, Mama—."

But Mrs. Jennings had more news to share. "And have you heard that Lady Caroline Capel now has another? I believe that's her third boy."

"Third of twelve." All the ladies looked down.

The talk of motherhood made Charlotte even more frustrated with her current impasse. She left the ladies to their gossip and sought the nursery at the top of the house. It was an airy, open space, full of joy and noise. A wooden hobby horse, toy soldiers, blocks, balls, pull-toys, kites, sticks, and string littered the floor, and a row of chipped china dolls watched from their shelf.

The harried nursery maid was more than glad to give up her rambunctious charges to their aunt, who was just as grateful to escape the confines of the drawing room for the freedom of the park. John and William raced ahead, with Charlotte and Annamaria following, to chase about the wet fields, stalk butterflies, skip rocks, and finally rest on a garden bench and listen as Charlotte read aloud.

When they returned to the top of the house, she entertained them with made-up stories of Penelope Pond Duck, drawing picture after picture of watery adventures for them. To Charlotte, descending later from the nursery to join the world of restrictions and expectations felt like donning a harness. Not even the hoped-for pleasure of Mr. Palmer's company could release the tightness of her chest as she returned to the world of adults to dress for dinner.

Each evening, Mary arranged seating and entertainments that continued to divide Charlotte from her quarry. No matter how she maneuvered, she could not manage to be seated elsewhere. When the men did join the ladies, she and Mr. Palmer were assigned to separate teams at pantomimes and on opposite sides of the room for bouts-rime. She did her best to make him look at her, but his eyes often strayed to Miss Ludford.

The situation was most unsatisfactory. But Charlotte always made the best of any situation. She had another option. Night after night, while she watched Mr. Palmer with Miss Ludford, she nodded and smiled at Lord Dysart, who remained at her side. He fetched her tea, escorted her from one room to the next, and bid her good night with all sincerity.

He had begun to take on a distinct air of ownership.

~*~

Thomas had all but determined to make Miss Ludford his

bride. Each evening, he observed her during the entertainments. In everything, she behaved impeccably. Her verses at bouts-rime were simple and predictable, never naughty. If her performance in pantomimes lacked luster, it never lacked decorum. Certainly, she was a stark contrast to the boisterous Miss Jennings, whose antics left half the room laughing and the other half scandalized.

"What are you looking so blue-deviled about?" Henry asked him one night as they stood on the terrace after an especially lively session of pantomimes.

"I have to reach a decision. We can't stay at Barton Park forever, much as you'd like to hang about," Thomas replied. "In a week, two at the most, I have to be back to canvass for votes among the potwallopers."

"The what?"

"The voters. To vote in the borough, a man needs only a chimney and hearth to stir a pot in."

Henry laughed. "I can just see you shooing pigs and chickens as you knock on cottage doors."

Thomas was not amused. "More likely, as I dole out the best ale at the tavern." He thought of the cost of that ale. "It's time to act."

"You've narrowed your choice."

Thomas nodded. "I believe so." He pictured himself proposing to Miss Ludford. She would tremble and look up at him with her wet brown eyes.

Henry's eyes narrowed. "Not—."

"No. Miss Browne is not the one." He opened his mouth to announce he'd selected Miss Ludford to be his wife. He couldn't bring himself to say her name. "I'll let you know when I declare my intentions."

But when? Thomas thought ahead to when an announcement might be made. The upcoming musical should provide the right atmosphere for a proposal.

~*~

At last, the musical night arrived. Charlotte waited impatiently for the opportunities it offered. As the moon rose, her hopes also rose for a chance to shed Lord Dysart for good and engage Mr. Palmer's attention—perhaps for a lifetime. Surely Mary could not keep the two of them apart in a roomful of guests!

In the music room, silver and crystal gleamed. Floors glowed with polish. Dozens of beeswax candles flickered in the breeze from the open doors, their light intensified by the glow of gilt mirrors. The air was heavy with wax and roses. At one end of the room, the hired musicians tuned their strings and flute. Nearly forty guests greeted their host and hostess, then milled about, conversing and finding their seats to enjoy the performances.

Charlotte scanned the room but saw no sign of Mr. Palmer, although his brother was in attendance, absorbed in conversation with Miss Browne. The lady looked *different* this evening, dressed in a simple gray gown that moved with her, softening her angularity. Even the planes of her face seemed gentler. And Mr. Henry Palmer never took his eyes off her. How very unexpected. More expected was the fact that Lord Dysart nodded at Charlotte from across the room. Reluctantly she nodded back, though she felt like a puppet on a string. Soon, however, taller men came between them, and she could no longer see him in the crowd.

Sir John had decreed that the guests were to perform before the dancing commenced, and Mary had cautioned her to observe decorum during the recital segment. Mary herself would not participate. "Remember, Lottie," she'd said, "try to maintain a serious but ladylike countenance. And take care in the song you choose. None of those overly amorous ones that I sometimes hear at the London assemblies."

"I promise to do my best to choose as forlorn a song as possible. Rest assured, I'll be mindful of the occasion and of your refined sensibilities."

Mary looked sharply at her. "I don't appreciate your mockery."

"And I, your lectures." She sighed. "Come now, Mary. Can you not enjoy the evening you've worked so long to arrange? I, for one, plan to enjoy it immensely."

Mary raised her brows. "That's what worries me most."

~*~

At the piano, Miss Ludford leaned over a pile of sheet music. Clad in a peach gown with a gauze overdress embroidered in whitework, she looked truly stunning, except for the furrowed brow. Charlotte glanced down at her own grass-green gown and felt like a frog. "Good evening, Miss Ludford," she said, her voice as taut as piano wire.

"Good evening, Miss Jennings. Are you also searching for a song?" Miss Ludford continued leafing through the stack, discarding sheet after sheet.

"I have one since we're required to sing for our supper. Have you not yet chosen one?" Charlotte couldn't imagine waiting so long.

The lady reddened. "I'm afraid I put the task off, hoping to avoid it entirely. But my mother insists I participate." She lowered her voice. "To tell you the truth, Miss Jennings, I'm not used to singing and playing in front of anyone but close family." Her hands visibly shook as she reached for another sheet.

Charlotte took pity on her, despite her beauty. Miss Ludford seemed quite distraught. "Have *you* a certain piece in mind? Could I help you look for it?" For the lady was flipping through the stack at a rapid and increasingly agitated pace.

"Something short and simple." She paused, her hand on an Irish air.

Although Charlotte had dutifully practiced a piece that Mary would applaud, she had no great need to perform it. And poor Miss Ludford seemed desperate indeed, no longer a scheming rival at all. "Would you consider a duet? I see here a copy of 'Robin Adair.'"

"I confess that the idea of performing at all terrifies me," Miss Ludford said with a strained smile. "There is such a very large company. I'm sure to shame my family. You would be doing me a great service if you would share the song."

Charlotte felt a pang at such obvious signs of distress. To be frightened of company was such an odd notion. The girls of her acquaintance were eager to display their talents. Poor Miss

Ludford, to suffer where others rejoiced. "In that case, let's support each other. Do you take the lower or the upper range?"

"The lower, I think, to stand out less."

"I shall do my best to overshadow you, then," Charlotte said, gathering up the music. "Would you like me to play? Then you might hide behind the instrument."

Miss Ludford's smile widened. "Thank you. I'll not forget this kindness."

Once the remaining guests had been seated, Sir John welcomed the assembly and, one by one, introduced those who were to perform. The first musician Charlotte recognized as one of the guests who had been on the picnic. She was a willowy lass who played a haunting melody on the harp, which looked in imminent danger of crushing her. Then one of Sir John's neighbors launched into a jaunty rendition of "The Husband's Return." The lyrics undoubtedly had Mary frowning. Even Charlotte blushed at the third verse. Too soon, the song ended to much enthusiastic clapping and a few shouts. Miss Browne came next, playing a stately Bach sarabande on the pianoforte with such dignity, precision, and restraint that the composer himself would have applauded. Charlotte was quite sure Mary approved in that case.

At last, Sir John announced the duet. Charlotte nodded to her companion, who approached the front with less enthusiasm than a schoolboy facing the rod. Charlotte seated herself at the instrument, remembering to keep her back straight, for Mary was seated in the first row next to their mother.

Taking a deep breath, Charlotte played the opening chords, nodding to Miss Ludford. The first line, however, Charlotte had to herself, so she projected her soprano to fill the room. Miss Ludford's soft alto entered on the second but could barely be heard through the rest of the verse. Charlotte smiled encouragement during the piano bridge, and by the second verse, their tones matched in volume. The assembly, she saw, listened politely, and some even nodded in time to the music. Lord Dysart, seated near the front, regarded the performance with great concentration.

By the third verse, Charlotte found Mr. Palmer standing at the back of the room, looking ever so handsome in his evening coat. He was undoubtedly the tallest man in the gathering. His attention seemed entirely on her and on Miss Ludford. Charlotte's fingers stumbled on the keys, eliciting a worried look from her partner in song. Charlotte ignored her. Mr. Palmer was *watching*. But so was Mary.

One verse to go. Charlotte knew she stood on another verge. Destiny hinged on this very moment. Did she dare? Two futures beckoned. One offered a safe, gentle, and yes, amiable life as Lady Dysart, with multiple estates and multiple offspring. Her life would be full, smooth, and predictable. Her mother and sister would approve.

The other choice offered a leap into something risky and irresistible. Charlotte's heart beat faster. Miss Ludford sang on. Lord Dysart nodded in time to the music. Mary leaned forward. Their attention drove Charlotte to a decision. She looked up, away from the music. Instead, she trained her eyes on the tall figure at the back of the room and swelled her voice with the final verse so that the clear tones quite eclipsed those of Miss Ludford: "Yet he I love so well, still in my heart shall dwell. I can ne'er forget Robin Adair." She barely heard the applause when the song was done. She saw only *him*.

# Chapter Twelve

The girl had been staring at him. Thomas looked about to see if anyone else had noticed. Lord Dysart turned around to glare, but no one else seemed to have noted that Charlotte Jennings had been singing to him. *To him.* What madcap impulse had pushed her to such outrageous lengths?

Miss Ludford had scurried off from behind the piano before he could approach her. No matter. He would follow her and secure a dance. Or two dances? That would make his intentions clear.

Mercifully, Henry was still occupied with the proper and appropriate Miss Browne, whose performance had riveted his brother, much to Thomas's own amusement. Now *there* was an odd pairing. In the times when he himself had sought Miss Browne out, she had rebuffed him. Thomas wasn't sure she welcomed Henry's attentions either. She gave none of the female signals that indicated interest: no flutter of fan or eyelashes, no high-pitched giggles at every witticism. But his brother wasn't easily discouraged. Even now, Henry was bending over her, and Thomas could swear that she was smiling back.

As Charlotte Jennings was smiling. And she was smiling right at *him*. Thomas cleared his throat. Though Lady Middleton had assured him that he might relinquish his spying duties now that Lord Dysart had arrived, each evening, Thomas had kept an eye on his charge from a distance. And from a distance, he had watched that oily Dysart fuss and flatter. The baron had probably already secured two dances, though the musicians had yet to strike up a tune.

Thomas frowned. He needed air.

All around him, he felt hemmed in by country neighbors who mixed with London guests. It was easy to distinguish among the ladies. The ostrich feathers, pearls, and silk proclaimed town polish, as did a more reserved manner. The Middletons' gentry neighbors, in contrast, were free with their laughter and more relaxed in their attire. Thomas forced himself to note the outfits, for he knew he would be writing such details to his mother.

To his left, a group of young bucks fresh from London were intent on assessing the company. One red-faced youth with ginger hair spoke loudly enough to be overheard easily. "The tall, spare one seems a bit standoffish, don't you think? Reminds me of my sister's governess."

"The dark-haired one who was singing the Irish air, she's a beauty," said his friend, raising a quizzing glass with as much ostentation as a rake at White's. "Could be Aphrodite herself, I'd say."

Thomas scowled. The fop was talking of his possible future wife. The mention of Aphrodite unexpectedly called a vision of another young lady to mind, one who had paused, skirts lifted, before the goddess's statue when he'd arrived at Barton Park.

"The little one in green's pretty enough," the ginger-haired blade replied. "Seems a good-humored sort."

Thomas followed the direction of that gentleman's gaze and found it resting on Miss Jennings. A stab of annoyance caught him between the shoulders. Miss Jennings was bouncing about, speaking to first this person and then that one, so that it was no wonder she'd drawn the attention of all the young men in the room. Those gawkers would be seeking an introduction any minute.

It was not so easy as Lady Middleton imagined to

relinquish his charge. He crossed the room to intercept the object of their attention.

"Good evening, Miss Jennings." Up close, he saw that strands of her hair had been twined with ribbons and small blue flowers, and her eyes sparkled in the candlelight. The tension in him relaxed when she smiled at *him*. He forgot entirely about Miss Ludford.

"Good evening, Mr. Palmer." Even her curtsy bounced.

"May I congratulate you on your fine performance?"

"Did you really think it was fine?" Her round eyes grew rounder. "We had not practiced, you know. I do think Miss Ludford knew the song, for everyone knows 'Robin Adair,' don't you think?"

"Undoubtedly." Though the piece was not the sort often heard at Cleveland. At the mention of Miss Ludford, he looked about the room but did not see her.

"Will you be dancing this evening?" the little goose before him asked. He thought he detected a flutter in her lashes.

"It would be expected. As I recall, you yourself dearly love to dance, Miss Jennings."

"You remembered! I'm flattered, Mr. Palmer. As *I* recall, you do not." Her smile bordered on pertness.

"Is your dance card quite filled already?" Thomas couldn't imagine what had prompted him to ask. He needed to secure his dances with his intended. But he waited impatiently for Miss Jennings to answer.

"I believe I have a few open," she said, eyes dancing already. "Why do you ask?"

He cleared his throat. The room had grown damned hot. "Would you do me the honor of saving one for me?"

Now he'd done it.

"I shall save you the best. There's to be a *waltz* at the end," she replied, to his dismay.

Thomas bowed and retreated in search of punch, wondering what had come over him. Miss Jennings had been right. He hated dancing, even when he knew the steps. He couldn't remember ever actually dancing the waltz in public. He'd rarely seen it at Almack's, though he remembered it at smaller balls in town. He was surprised that Lady Middleton allowed it at Barton Park. But Sir John was ever eager to entertain the young people who were his guests, and the thrill of a waltz was sure to amuse. Still, it was a very unsettling kind of dance, all swirling and familiar clasping.

And why was he contemplating a dance with Miss Jennings? He should be pursuing Miss Ludford before her dance card filled up.

"Lost in thought, dear brother?" Henry's drawl caught Thomas by surprise.

"Not lost, but at sea. Tell me, do you know how to waltz?"

~*~

He'd approached her! Sought her out! And, wonder of wonders, she and Mr. Palmer were to dance a waltz together! That he would grasp her about the waist and turn her about made Charlotte giddy. Most of the complaints about the risqué dance had died down in society, though a few stodgy matrons still sniffed about the degrees of familiarity it encouraged.

But familiarity was precisely what Charlotte sought. Now to plan the next step for after the music died. *One must go after one's happiness.* Tonight, she was determined to have her way with Mr. Palmer.

~*~

Fortified by his brother's encouragement and aware of his social responsibilities, Thomas faced the rest of the evening with fatalism, if not pleasure. Having succeeded in securing a place on Miss Ludford's card, he led her to the floor for the Devonshire Minuet, an out-of-fashion dance that that allowed him time to worry about the waltz looming at the evening's close. The formality of the dance kept him at a fair distance from his partner, and the mincing steps he was forced to perform made conversation difficult. He noticed, however, that Miss Jennings chatted away with the ginger-haired fellow who'd admired her earlier. He nearly missed a turn as he watched her smile and twirl.

At last, the tedious set was finished. With a bow, he relinquished Miss Ludford to Lord Dysart for the next set and stood as far from the milling dancers as he could to watch the company prancing about. When he could stand no more, he retreated to breathe the cool air outside on the terrace. Against the wall, the fateful lattice still hung slightly askew.

"Hiding, Thomas?" Henry clapped him on the back. "Want to go over the waltz steps before you're in for it?"

"I'd be grateful if you could prevent me from looking an absolute fool."

"Remember, the dance speeds up," Henry said, watching Thomas as he tried to execute a pirouette to the count of three. "You look stiff as a soldier. Come, loosen your shoulders. There, that's better."

"I need a drink," Thomas said.

"Ah, the power of wine to bolster flagging spirits." Henry struck a pose, hand raised. "*Wine can of their wits the wise beguile, make the sage frolic, and the serious smile.*"

"Homer, isn't it?" Thomas wished he were safely ensconced in Cleveland's library with a book instead of facing the ordeals ahead—a waltz, then a proposal to Miss Ludford. In the midst of his musings, he was struck by the clarity of Henry's speech. "I don't believe I've seen *you* take a drink all night."

"Miss Browne doesn't approve," his brother said lightly. "She's another female around whom it's best to keep one's wits."

Thomas needed all of his wits, not only to get through the dance but to survive the set with Miss Jennings smiling up at him. He'd watched her with any number of men. Dysart had led her out, and one of the clusters of young men from London had partnered her for a cotillion. Perhaps she'd be too worn out by the time the last dance was announced.

It was announced all too soon. He found his final partner by the refreshment table, looking disappointedly animated, not tired in the least. In fact, she seemed ready to bound onto the floor when she saw him. The fabric of her gown, no doubt dampened by her exercise, clung quite distractingly to her form, and the curls had worked their way free of their ribbons and now sprung about her cheeks with each shake of her head.

He bowed. She curtsied. The music swelled. And so they danced. Thomas managed through the slow part without disgracing himself, even during the pirouettes. But when the tempo changed, it was time to adjust the hand hold.

Miss Jennings stepped closer, very much closer, and he detected the scent of honeysuckle. She looked up and rested both her hands on his shoulders. There was nothing he could do but place his own about her waist—a small waist, he found, though the cut of the gown had disguised it and the damp cloth only hinted. With his hands placed so, he could feel *through* the fine cotton of her gown to the flesh beneath, feel it quite distinctly. And if that sensation were not enough to send him reeling, next the steps called for him to move his feet in *between* hers in an uncomfortable parody of the act he could not stop thinking about.

The room was too close. The girl was too close. He turned, as the music bid, bending to the side into the swoop the form required. The bend brought her even closer, so he could see the pulse in her neck, the fine texture of her skin. The sweet scent of honeysuckle nearly overcame him, and coupled with the turns, made him lightheaded. His only support was this girl.

"I am so happy that Sir John ordered a waltz. Mary was against it, you know. She thinks it unseemly. But there was a waltz at Lady Caroline Barnham's ball. I think it's becoming quite accepted in town."

Thomas watched her lips, so remarkably soft and pink but constantly moving. As the music's tempo and volume increased, so did their turns about the floor. Even his partner had to conserve her breath and spoke no more about the wonders of the waltz. Thomas started to perspire.

Eons passed before the music slowed again, and he could relax into a dignified promenade, releasing his hold on Miss Jennings as they marched side by side for the final movement. With the last chord and final bow, he was finished. He thought he knew how Nelson felt after Trafalgar. Adding to the victory, Miss Jennings remained solemn and quiet next to him. A second glance at her, however, had him bending over her once more.

"You look unwell, Miss Jennings. Is something amiss?" He had to bend very close in order to hear her reply.

"Do you think that perhaps you could escort me out? I have a stitch in my side," his partner whispered. Her smooth shoulders quivered as she held a hand to her ribcage.

"Of course." He offered her his arm, upon which she leaned. "Come, it will be cooler and more private in the drawing room." Walking slowly, he led the way across the entry hall and to the empty room. "Will you sit while I fetch you some punch?"

"Oh, please don't leave me." She grasped his hand when he tried to back away. "Really, I'll be fine in a few minutes." He was relieved to see the color still shone on her cheeks. After a moment, she stood straighter and favored him with that familiar smile. "Thank you, Mr. Palmer. It's vastly cooler and quieter here. Not that I wasn't enjoying the dancing, mind you. I don't think I've enjoyed a dance as much in my entire life." She squeezed the hand she still held. "Tell me, did you not enjoy it too? At least a little?"

Her lips drew Thomas closer. Thomas forced himself to look away.

"It was most pleasant."

"I read that waltzing is a promoter of vigorous health. The dance is so very intimate, is it not? Not only because the partners have the chance to talk, but they also enjoy so many opportunities to move together…and to touch."

Thomas felt a rush of heat. He had to silence her before she said more. "Do you never stop chattering?"

At that, she glared. "I can't leave the conversation up to you, can I? *You* dole out each word as if it's some precious gem you can't bear to part with!"

Thomas suppressed a smile as the lass stamped her foot. The kid slipper made the merest slapping sound on the parquet floor.

His mockery incensed her further. Charlotte's voice climbed two notes as she planted herself solidly in front of him. "That's exactly what you are, Mr. Palmer. A word miser. I can see you hunched in some corner with your pitiful pile of words, rubbing your hands over them and clutching them to your breast."

"I most assuredly do not clutch them to my breast." As he glanced down at her, his smile widened. A silence built between them, and Thomas stopped smiling.

"What do you clutch, then?" Charlotte looked up. The dare sparked in her eyes as she stared at him, lips parted.

Thomas chose not to resist this time. Thoughts of Miss Ludford faded. He pulled Charlotte to him, then bent his head, planted his lips on hers, and kissed her soundly.

He meant it to be a quieting kiss, one designed to shut her up completely. It didn't. As he ran his hand down her yielding back, she made little mewling noises. The sound deepened his efforts, and she wound her arms around his neck and kissed him back with surprising force.

Thomas felt it down to his toes, though the impact was hardest in his groin, a fact she surely must be aware of since she plastered herself to him, her plump breasts pressing against the buttons on his waistcoat so firmly he was certain she'd have circles imprinted on her tender skin—very tender skin, smooth and flawless, and tinged a pale pink like the roses arranged in the urn by the door. An image flashed of him kissing those imprints, moving his lips between her round breasts and trailing lower.

His lips and hands had begun to recreate that vision when everything ground to a halt.

"Look at the lovebirds! Just as I suspected! I knew you two would make a match! Didn't I say so?" Framed by the doorway, Mrs. Jennings clapped her hands together. "What an adorable couple you make! Oh, don't look so red-faced, Mr. Palmer. It was only a matter of time before you gave in and admitted you'd fallen in love. Charlotte, I'm so happy for you! Wait until I tell Mary!"

~*~

It was inevitable, Thomas supposed. He'd kissed the girl — well, to be honest, more than kissed — and had been caught at it. His previous plan to address Miss Ludford withered on the vine. How could he propose to that lady when Mrs. Jennings had caught him *in flagrante* with her daughter? So be it. Forget Miss Ludford. He'd never relished the idea of a lifetime with a timid mouse anyway. Miss Charlotte Jennings was the proper class, with the proper education and accomplishments, the proper upbringing and connections. Her father had made a fortune in trade. She was happy and desirable, if also flighty and talkative. Those deficiencies would doubtless improve with marriage. In time, she would become as admirable a matron as her sister.

Yes, he would settle on her.

The only proper course of action now was to make a declaration. Mrs. Jennings would offer no objection to his pressing his suit. In fact, she was so delighted when he approached her, she had to sit and fan herself.

When he confessed his intentions to Henry later on in the library, his brother's reaction was less enthusiastic.

"You've *what*?" Henry nearly dropped the glass in his hand. "Miss Jennings? I thought you disliked the girl. 'Annoying little twit' were your very words."

"I'll thank you not to repeat things I may have uttered in the past. Miss Jennings is my intended, your future sister."

Henry gaped. "You're serious! You're really going to take the plunge with her. Shackle yourself to little Miss Giggles." At Thomas's glower, Henry held up his hand. "I meant nothing by it. She's a cheerful enough lass."

"Cleveland will benefit from a dose of her lightness to banish the gloom. Between Mother's imagined ailments and Aunt Georgina's grim commentaries, there's a perpetual pall about the place."

Henry clapped his brother on the shoulder. "If I didn't know better, I'd think you'd fallen for her. Wouldn't blame you. Sweet little poppet. Not a mean bone in her body."

"There's more to Charlotte than meets the eye," Thomas agreed.

"Generous settlement. Pretty face. And a more than passable figure. More than a handful, I'd say!"

"That's my future wife you're talking of," Thomas pointed out calmly. "If you ever repeat such an insult, I shall lay you flat."

Henry held up his hands. "Good God, man, I'm not Tierney, you know. I'm only teasing you."

"Don't." Thomas was unsettled by the cold rush of anger that surged in response to Henry's offhand remark. He'd been the target of Henry's jibes for years but hadn't felt the urge to actually punch him since they were boys.

Henry eyed him warily. "Didn't mean to upset you, Tom. Charlotte's a jolly good girl for all her indiscretions. You're right; she should brighten up life at Cleveland considerably. I'm already contemplating pitting her against Aunt Georgina."

"Not a fair fight. Charlotte would win every round," Thomas said, finally unclenching his fist.

"It was enough, you know, for you to choose anyone other than Miss Browne. The two of you are cut from the same cloth. Prickly. Stiff-necked. Best leave *her* to me." Henry laughed at his brother's sour expression. "I must say, Miss Jennings is an improvement over Miss Ludford. With that one, you'd be bored in a fortnight."

"My present contentment would be less with such partners," Thomas agreed. "Miss Ludford's head is empty, and Miss Browne's, all too full." At this moment, his future with Charlotte looked as rosy as the sunset beyond the window.

"And you *are* totally satisfied with your present choice? You had hoped for another once."

There may have been a slight softening to Thomas's expression as he considered his answer. He knew his future bride was neither sophisticated nor elegant. But Charlotte had assets. Her dowry was generous, as was her spirit. With her connections, she would likely improve his standing in society. And the girl was plump in a pleasing sort of way. Her manners were lively.

She smiled always; in fact, she was a veritable fount of good humor, he mused, scowling slightly. Or rather, his face fell into the pattern that his entire five and twenty years had etched upon it.

"She's nothing like Lady Middleton. I grant you that. But I'll wager she's made of stronger stuff. I believe that Napoleon's army could march to the front door, and Lottie Jennings would smile at the novelty and invite them in for tea." Thomas was not sure if this trait in a spouse were admirable, but it was undeniably amiable. And as his family life had been less than that, he hoped for better for his own children.

"How ever does she put up with *you*?"

Thomas walked to the window before answering. "She thinks I'm droll."

Behind him, Henry snickered. "That's one way to put it, I suppose. Not the word I'd use. Now crusty, crabbed — I can think of plenty that fit you better. If you're truly set on asking her, you'd best bring something to sweeten the offer. Token of affection." He smiled at the blank look on his brother's face. "Nothing fancy. Some flowers would do it."

Come dusk, Thomas thought, he would lead his intended down the sloping lawn, away from the house, to trace the winding paths past shrubberies and stands of fir and ash until they reached the folly. There under its domed roof, they might peer between the columns and watch the sun fade against the hill. And there in that lofty refuge, he'd ask her to be his wife. The idea was not at all displeasing. She would gladly accept. Then he'd press his lips again to his Charlotte's soft, sweet mouth and his hands to the plump flesh to sample the fullness of what waited for him in entirety once they were wed. He felt a corresponding fullness rise below his waistcoat at the prospect.

And if perchance she became entangled in the rose bushes that bordered the garden path, he'd have the pleasure of rescuing her once again. In the meantime, he needed to find some flowers.

# Chapter Thirteen

Finally! After long, frustrating months of plotting and fretting, Charlotte had triumphed. Thomas Palmer had, at last, demonstrated his feelings! It had been a close call. She'd nearly lost her temper the night before when, after their heavenly waltz and his solicitous behavior over her feigned cramp, he'd failed to speak.

But actions *did* speak louder than words.

Charlotte had relived the kiss they shared a dozen times. Such a kiss signaled intent. Even Mary's fusty book had said so. "Only to kindred or to one soon to be a husband, for them alone is reserved the delicate press of lips." Not that Thomas Palmer's kisses had been delicate. She had been totally unprepared for what had transpired in the empty room. Who could have guessed the power of lips meeting lips?

She'd hoped his kiss would be better than the wet smack she'd once endured behind a potted palm. But comparing Thomas's kiss to that one would be like comparing a thunderstorm to a sprinkle. Thomas had pulled her close, closer even than he had by the pond, and had pressed his mouth to hers with such insistence that her own lips had opened. He had *tasted* her. The sensation had pushed her off balance, so she had held on to him to try to find it again. Now the urge to taste *him* persisted so that she couldn't wait until he returned.

Susan relayed his invitation to join him for a walk, and Charlotte's feet barely touched the stairs as she hurried to join Thomas in the twilight. This was the moment she'd dreamed of ever since she'd spied on him from the top of the stairs in her home in Berkeley Street. At last, he was waiting for *her*. She ignored the twinge of guilt for not checking with her mother or Mary first before leaving the house.

Nothing would keep her from him.

He stood on the entryway landing next to the statue, looking like a Greek god himself. His back and his expression were unbending, but in one stiff hand, he clutched a bunch of daisies, some with the earth still clinging to the roots. They were the most flawless flowers Charlotte had ever seen.

"Thank you. They're lovely," she said, cradling the bouquet on one arm.

The evening was warm and still, so she didn't need a shawl. The lawn and wood were bathed in that golden light one sees late in the day, the kind of light found in French landscape paintings. Charlotte breathed deeply, wanting to drink in the air and make this perfect evening a part of her. When Thomas, instead of offering her his arm, took her hand in his, she knew a level of bliss that rivalled the treetops. His hand was so big that her own was lost in it, and his grip was firm, as it had been when he'd danced with her.

He said nothing while they followed the path down the hill and then up the stone steps to the folly that capped the rise. In the slanted light of the setting sun, its marble glowed warmly. Charlotte knew the view from this height must be breathtaking, but her eyes could look nowhere but at Mr. Palmer. *He* looked uncomfortable, almost ill. Could he possibly be nervous? He must know that she cared for him.

"I have already spoken to your mother, who has consented to allow me to talk with you," he said. He cleared his throat before continuing.

Charlotte knew that hearts did not actually burst with happiness, but her own swelled so with joy that she wondered if hers might be the exception.

He cleared his throat again. "Miss Jennings, would you consent to be my wife?"

Charlotte opened her mouth, but could not answer. That was it? No sweet words? No declaration of love or even affection? Nothing to indicate the state of his heart? *No bending whatsoever?*

Surely he didn't expect her to say yes without some declaration of devotion. She plucked at the daisies in her hand as she crafted a response designed to elicit the desired result. "I'm very much aware of the honor, Mr. Palmer. But—could I hear more about the sentiment before I answer?"

"Sentiment? I've said I wish to marry you." His brows drew together. "Is that not sufficient?"

Charlotte reached up and placed her hand on his cheek. "I didn't mean to offend you, Thomas. But please, I'd very much like to hear more." Smiling now, she waited, her eyes never leaving his face. It was such a handsome face.

Thomas began to pace. "My prospects are good. I believe we should get on well enough together. Although you are young, that need not be a drawback. Saplings can be coaxed to bend in any shape, and I find you suited to my needs."

Charlotte laughed. "Oh, Mr. Palmer, you are so amusing. You woo a lady by comparing her to a tree? And I hardly like the idea of being bent. Come now, try again. You cannot reasonably expect me to feel flattered by such a comparison, though I'm glad you think we shall suit."

He halted the pacing, and though he remained motionless, Charlotte felt him withdraw. "I beg your pardon. If a marriage based on reasonable precepts is so abhorrent to you, I will retract my proposal and return you to your mother at once."

Could he be serious? Did he not realize how much she loved him? "In no way do I find the thought of marrying you abhorrent. Quite the contrary." Was he really taking back his proposal? She wrung the daisies until they were limp.

Mr. Palmer watched her mouth, then stirred to speak again. "I am a man of reason, Miss Jennings. I offer you a marriage of reason."

"Reason? Is that all?" A chill made Charlotte wrap her arms around herself, crushing the daisies. This was not at all the proposal she'd imagined.

"Your future will be secure, as will the future of our children."

Charlotte blushed at that. "I should like to have children," she said carefully. "And a happy home." The future beckoned, but she needed proof that their own happiness was assured. "I agree, sir, that a marriage of reason sounds practical. Sensible. Safe. Dependable." She took a breath and willed herself to finish. "I hope that you'll agree that it can also be empty and even cruel if there is nothing more." The daisies dropped to the ground.

"I shall do my best to make sure it is neither." He smiled, reaching for her, but Charlotte held back.

"Will we be happy?" She tried to see the answer in his eyes, but the light had faded.

"I cannot answer that. I hope so." He closed the distance between them and took her hands in his. His hands were warm. "It *is* yes, then?"

"How could you think otherwise?" She forgot her fears in the heat of his kiss.

~*~

Mrs. Jennings was nearly overcome with excitement at their announcement. "My youngest is to be married! Did you hear? Both my girls settled! I could tell that Lottie had set her cap for the gentleman. Mr. Palmer is such a handsome man! So tall! So distinguished! And a future in Parliament! They shall live close by in London, and I can divide my time between Devon and Somerset when they are not. Is it not wonderful!? Of course, we have to meet the family and post the banns. So much to do!"

She flitted from guest to guest, scattering her enthusiasm like a farmer scatters seeds. Sir John called to toast the upcoming nuptials, and the guests at Barton Park were quick to raise their glasses and wish the happy couple joy. Even Lord Dysart congratulated them, though not heartily. If Mr. Palmer looked less than elated, Charlotte was determined not to notice.

Later that evening, the Jennings females gathered in Mary's private sitting room, far from the rest of the revelers who remained about in the other wing of the house.

Mary stood before the empty fireplace. "Honestly, Mother, do you really think they will suit? Lord Dysart seemed much more genial." Her words fell like icicles in the chilly room, made chillier still by the blue wall hangings. "Mr. Palmer is a very reserved gentleman, after all."

"He is not always so," Charlotte protested. "In fact, at times, he can be quite …uninhibited."

Their mother laughed.

Mary did not. "A virtuous lady does not encourage a gentleman to be free with his attentions, even if that gentleman is her betrothed. Please tell me that you haven't encouraged him, Lottie! After all I've tried to teach you!"

"All men require a little encouragement to come up to scratch," their mother said. "Sir John needed a little push, as I recall."

Mary frowned. "Good sense and principle are what *hold* a husband. Lottie would do well to remember that." She smoothed her skirt. "But since you've accepted him, the deed is done. You could have done worse. He has some good qualities, I suppose," she continued in her litany of faint praise. "He is only a little older than you. His hair is dark and thick and unlikely to fall out, and he is not fat."

Charlotte blushed as she admitted her Thomas had a particularly fine form.

"Aye, and I daresay he's right fond of yours too, my girl," said Mrs. Jennings with a pronounced wink.

Charlotte grew warm as she remembered their time in the folly. Thomas had held her closer than ever before and put his hands in places that made her twitch and moan. Soon, her curiosity had overcome her shyness, and she'd ventured to touch

Thomas, exploring his hardness, at least until he'd grabbed her arms and warned her to stop.

But she'd entirely lost the direction of the family conversation.

Mary had chosen to ignore her mother's interruption. "I will say that Mr. Palmer is well respected, a man of sense who knows his duty. But I wonder, Charlotte, whether he will be an easy man to live with."

"Of his good sense, I have no doubt. My Thomas conducts himself and his affairs with the utmost care and tact. He is... thoughtful, so he is perhaps overly careful in offering praise and somewhat eager to offer his opinion. I must say, though, his perception in matters of politics is matched only by the keenness of his words. He never fails to hit the mark when he speaks." She laughed. "He has built such a wall about himself, you understand, but I see through it to his tender and generous heart. We shall be so very happy." And she wanted to believe that.

"I fear that you are woefully unprepared for the trials ahead of you," her sister said.

"Hardly trials, Mary! Joys." Charlotte stood and took her sister's hand in hers. "You must wish me joy. You see, I crave what you already have: civility, affection, comfort, a family."

Mary shuttered her expression and withdrew her hands from Lottie's grasp. "You have no experience of what goes on between a man and a woman. A wife's duty is...perhaps distasteful, but it is a necessary part of the compact. And it brings its reward in time. My own life would be empty were it not for John, William, Annamaria, and the baby. Children are such a comfort."

"True enough, my girl," their mother nodded. "Lord knows, I love mine. But there's comfort to be found in a husband too. More than comfort, I'd say. Especially with such a finely made man as Mr. Palmer."

Remembering the feel of Mr. Palmer's finer parts, Charlotte blushed again. She could hardly wait to discover what more awaited beyond the comfort.

~*~

"So." Lady Middleton's eyes were cold as she stood in the doorway to Charlotte's room two hours later. "I'm not finished with you. There are things I need to say that I can't say in front of Mother." She shut the door behind herself and walked unsteadily to the center of the chamber. "It's not too late, you know. No settlement has been made yet. This was hastily done. You can still back out."

Charlotte stared up at her. "But I said yes!"

Mary threw up her hands. "What were you thinking, Lottie? Did I not warn you to consider your future?"

Charlotte detected the sweetness of brandy fumes, though her sister remained a few feet away. "That's precisely what I did," Charlotte replied warily, standing her ground, her back to the window. "And my future is with Mr. Palmer."

"The man I refused? My *cast-off*? I can't fathom it. He's beneath you. Oh, Lottie, you could have done so much better!" Mary veered across the room and planted herself before her sister, so close her spittle struck Charlotte's forehead as the railing continued. "Spurning Dysart! A reckless act. You could have had ten thousand a year. Likely more. An estate in Surrey. His manor house south of Richmond is among the finest in England. You could have been Lady Dysart." She threw up her arms again, barely missing her sister. "Mrs. Palmer of Cleveland. What a waste."

Charlotte stepped back until she could feel the cold glass on her shoulders. "A title is no guarantee of happiness."

Her sister's lips thinned. "Marriage is not a guarantee of happiness either."

"Are you not happy, Mary?"

Her gilded sister looked tarnished, all traces of elegance gone. Her proud carriage had collapsed, her gown was wrinkled, and her eyes were red.

Lady Middleton turned away from the scrutiny to gaze out at the carefully laid-out gardens below, sharply drawn in the moonlight. Measuring each word as if she were doling out guineas, she answered softly, "I am content." She drew herself upright and reordered her perfect features into their customary mask. If her next words slurred slightly, they were still intelligible. "I have my children and the house. Sir John is kind and generous. I could not wish for more." She turned too rapidly, nearly losing her footing. "I wished the same for you."

Charlotte reached out a gentle hand to steady her sister. "But I want more."

Mary's mask cracked briefly before the features smoothed once again. "I hope you don't live to regret that, Lottie."

After Mary left the room, Charlotte leaned her forehead against the cool glass of the window and watched her breath haze the pane. She wiped it clear with her hand.

# Chapter Fourteen

The approach to Cleveland looked the same as it had when Thomas left, its long gravel drive raked smooth, the fir, mountain-ash, and acacia tall and full, the firm stone façade unchanged. Yet all had changed for Thomas, including the level of noise inside his carriage. Mrs. Jennings and his future wife had not stopped talking since they entered Somerset.

"What an extensive pleasure ground you have, Mr. Palmer!" Mrs. Jennings said. "And your house is nicely situated on the rise of the hill. Such a pleasant prospect! And so many windows! It is a very modern house, is it not? Not one of your dreary old castles."

"Cleveland is relatively new if one compares it to some of the ancient fortresses in the countryside. The estate has no colorful history, but the halls are far less drafty."

"I wouldn't say it lacks color," Henry added as he roused himself from dozing. "Wait until you meet our aunt."

Thomas ignored him and instead turned his attention to Charlotte, who had leaned out the window nearly far enough to tumble from it. He reached to tug her arm, panic tightening his grip. He closed his eyes to the fleeting memories that made his breath short. It would not do to show his disproportionate reaction. "I beg you, take a care lest you fall. I've promised my mother to deliver you safely." In truth, his mother *was* impatient to examine his chosen bride face to face, a fact that had left him with more than a little trepidation.

Charlotte was not quite the paragon his mother expected.

She drew her head back in, bumping her bonnet. Eyes shining, she looked over her shoulder at Thomas. "Your description didn't nearly do Cleveland justice. It's so stately!" Resting her arm on the window's edge, she gazed out from the relative safety of the carriage interior. "What wonderful stone, the very color of honey! How it gleams! And such tall windows, like a wall of glass. It must be full of sun inside." She turned back to him. "Oh, Mr. Palmer, we shall be so happy here!"

Thomas looked at Charlotte, her face aglow, her bonnet tilted over one eye. There was not the slightest artifice in the girl. He slowly rubbed the center of his chest, which felt tight, though the rest of him experienced a general lightness he could not name. He found himself smiling back, despite the uncomfortable closeness of the carriage.

That bemused smile persisted as the carriage rolled up the drive. A groom ran to hold the horses, and Thomas directed two footmen to unload the luggage, then turned to hand the ladies down. His smile lasted until he and Henry escorted the guests into the Grand Hall, a dreary, ostentatious room designed to intimidate visitors. The combined effect of ancestral portraits, including his mother's, plus the living presence of his mother and aunt, would have silenced lesser women than the Jennings pair.

Undaunted, however, their exclamations echoed about the chamber before they were even introduced. Not a foot of space escaped their notice: the vast height of the ceiling, the skilled hand of the portrait artists, the richness of the walnut paneling, the majesty of the carved archways and pediments—even the shine on the floor earned a remark.

His mother had posed herself near the massive fireplace beneath her own portrait. Though it was early for dinner, she had already dressed for it in a gold gown that would not have looked out of place on a duchess. Aunt Georgina, in her customary black, stood like a sentinel next to a carved highboy on the other side of the fireplace. Neither woman smiled as the guests moved forward.

Thomas cleared his throat to draw their attention from the wainscoting to the ladies of the house. "Mother, may I present Mrs. Jennings and my fiancée, Miss Jennings? Ladies, my mother, Mrs. Palmer. And this is my aunt, Miss Georgina Palmer."

As the ladies made their curtseys, Thomas skewered Henry with a look that kept him from retreating. Their aunt seemed to be dissecting the arrivals as if they were some new species of bug. Their mother's back grew stiffer by the second. So far, things were progressing much as Thomas had expected.

"Such a great pleasure to meet you at last, Mrs. Palmer!" Mrs. Jennings said as soon as she surfaced from her curtsey. "I believe Mr. Jennings knew your grandfather. A draper on Pall Mall, wasn't he? They shared a love of cards, too."

Mrs. Palmer paled and reached a hand up to her neck. Mrs. Jennings' faux pas in acknowledging the family's link to trade was perhaps forgivable, and the lady could not have known how much the family fortunes had suffered because of the love of cards.

Thomas hastened to change the subject while his mother recalled her manners. "Miss Jennings has been very much looking forward to meeting you, Mother," he prodded.

Mrs. Palmer was too well-bred to ignore the jab from her son. "I wish you much happiness," she replied, voice faint. "It's my pleasure to meet you both. Welcome to Cleveland." She inclined her head with more dignity than warmth.

Thomas watched Charlotte's expression shift from excitement to puzzlement to disappointment, as if his mother had dashed water on her instead of delivering a half-hearted greeting. An awkward silence reigned before she found her response. "Mrs. Palmer, I'm so glad to finally meet you. I hope that we will soon learn to love each other."

Mrs. Palmer mustered a weak smile but said no more.

Charlotte began to giggle nervously. Thomas looked beseechingly to his aunt, not knowing what else to do.

Aunt Georgina stepped into the gap and linked arms with Mrs. Jennings and her daughter. "My nephew's letter writing leaves much to be desired. I look forward to getting to know more about you. I trust your trip was uneventful?"

That question unleashed a stream of descriptions regarding the wonders of the Somerset countryside, the comfort of the well-sprung carriage, the fineness of the weather for travel, and the pleasure of good company. As mother and daughter interrupted each other, Aunt Georgina's eyebrows arched higher. Behind him, Thomas could hear a muffled snicker from Henry. Their mother remained silent.

At last, the travelogue came to an end. Thomas took it upon himself to suggest the ladies might like to be shown to their rooms and rest before dinner, and soon the room emptied of all but his aunt and himself.

"So you've settled on the little chatterbox."

"If you mean Miss Charlotte Jennings, then yes." He worked to keep his voice steady. "She comes from a decent family with advantageous connections and a generous dowry. She will be an entirely suitable bride."

"Or the closest you could come, I imagine."

"I beg your pardon?"

"Don't pretend with me, Thomas. I find it tiresome. You've chosen little Charlotte because you can't have her sister. She's a rounder, bubblier version of Mary Jennings at that age. No, don't try to deny it. I know something of thwarted desire."

Thomas scowled. "We will not speak of these things, Georgina."

Her laugh rang hollow. "That should be the Palmer family motto. Much better than the one we have. Yes, it fits. *Ne loquaris.* Speak not. Do you never feel the urge to shout? To scream until the sound echoes from the rafters?"

"No. Never."

~*~

Charlotte wanted to shout with joy. She didn't know where to look next as she and her mother followed the housekeeper up the stairs and down a long hall to their chambers. At each window, Charlotte paused to glance at Cleveland's grounds. Everywhere were clues to the life her Thomas led. Outside were broad lawns where he and Henry might have raced, trimmed hedges perfect for hide-and-seek, a fountain for wading, and trees for climbing. Inside they were led past rooms where her future husband ate and slept—chambers they would soon share. Her heart beat faster at the thought, and another nervous giggle spilled out, causing her mother to glance over as they stood alone in the chamber designated for Charlotte.

"It is quite an estate, is it not? You should congratulate yourself, Lottie, on finding yourself such a fine husband. Why, look at this tapestry! And the hangings on the bed. Must have been imported. I wonder how many servants are employed. You'll live comfortably here, girl. Maybe it's not as fancy as Mary's estate, but it's well enough. And you'll have plenty of company with his mother and brother and aunt, and your children, in time."

Charlotte reddened anew. "Do you think his family likes me, Mama? His mother said little." Any impulse to giggle faded away. "And his aunt seems so severe."

"What's not to like? You are a very pretty girl, sweet as a day in May." She patted her daughter's cheek. "He's lucky to have you if you ask me. Don't you fret another minute about it, love. Give them all a chance to know you. Then they can't help but love you as Mr. Palmer does."

Charlotte clasped her hands together. "Do you truly think Thomas cares for me?" At times—like when he kissed her—she was sure he loved her. But at other times....

"What kind of question is that?" When Charlotte only bit her lip, her mother continued. "Of course he loves you, pet. Can't I see it every time he looks at you? Never took his eyes off you from Devonshire to Somerset. Remember how concerned he was that you might fall out of the carriage? And the proud way he introduced you to his mother? Like he was presenting a great prize. And that's what you are, dearie. A prize. Mark my words, Mr. Palmer adores you."

Charlotte wanted to believe her. "But he's never said so."

"Men don't say it, as a rule. Not much for flowery words. They show it instead. I saw the two of you together, remember. Nothing indifferent in that embrace. And didn't he ask you to marry him right after?"

Charlotte was glad to be convinced. Yes, Thomas loved her. His family would grow to love her. Once his mother got to know her better, she would welcome her as a daughter. All was sunny in her world. She steadfastly refused to let her niggling doubts spoil her happiness. *She was loved.* She held tight to that thought, which buoyed her up until she descended to join the family below.

If ever there were a space not conducive to conversation, Charlotte concluded it was the drawing room at Cleveland. The yellow wall covering cast a jaundiced light on the hostesses. The chairs must have belonged to some previous generation, for they were remarkably heavy and unyielding. Charlotte found herself shifting from side to side, trying to find a comfortable position against the upright seat. No other guests had joined the company, so the distances between the ladies and gentlemen stretched as wide as the River Frome. It took a concerted effort on her mother's part to keep a conversation going, but Mrs. Jennings was fit for the challenge.

"And how can it be that you have remained single for so long, Miss Palmer? I would have thought your handsome face would have attracted any number of men over the years. Is it the fact you're so far in the country? Perhaps the isolation has limited your advantages? Surely you had a come-out in London at one time? Some girls don't 'take' that first season, but tastes change, and given a generous enough settlement and a pretty enough face, most find a match eventually." She nodded toward the happy couple.

Charlotte studied Thomas's aunt as Mrs. Jennings interrogated. There was little soft about Georgina Palmer, though her figure was womanly and her features pleasing if inspected one by one. She was not yet truly old, probably no more than ten years older than her nephew. Charlotte puzzled over the enigma. Miss Palmer's dark eyes were wide and intelligent, her nose straight, her mouth well defined and firm, much like Thomas's own. The entirety, however, was too sharp and off-putting to be labeled as anything as simple as pretty.

Miss Palmer's tongue was forthright as her gaze. "Most find a match who desire one, Mrs. Jennings," she said, then said no more.

Mr. Henry Palmer looked from his aunt to his brother. "Miss Jennings has certainly been successful," he said smoothly. "Not all are inclined toward marriage, however."

Miss Palmer, in turn, rested her hand on his arm for a moment before returning to her stoic posture. Mrs. Palmer's hand went to her throat and stayed there. But Charlotte was forced to divert her attention from the confusing scene, for her beloved was speaking.

"My own match having been secured, I can testify that such matches can be found," he said.

Charlotte waited for Thomas to add to the statement, perhaps expounding on the perfect nature of the match or his happiness in having found it, but her mother interrupted before he'd finished the last word.

"Are they not the most congenial match imaginable? A match made in heaven, it is!" she declared. "I cannot tell you, Mrs. Palmer, how very delighted I am to have Mr. Palmer as a son at last. I'd thought perhaps at first that Mary would have him. Didn't see that Lottie had set her cap for him when she was but a wee lass. I am the happiest creature alive to have both daughters settled. Such a life my girl will have! Once Mr. Palmer takes his seat in Parliament, they'll live in London, to be sure, and we can see each other daily. When they leave town, I'll very much enjoy my visits here."

The shock of hearing her mother remind everyone that he had first chosen Mary kept Charlotte silent in her seat. Across from her, she saw that her mother's words had had a similar effect on Mrs. Palmer. The lady looked positively gray. She had pressed her lips together in a line so thin no spoon could wrest it open, had there been tea in the offing this close to dinner.

When it became obvious that Mrs. Palmer would not respond, Thomas stepped into the breach. "Cleveland's doors remain always open to you," he said, his eyes on his mother, who looked down. He leaned over to speak to her, too softly for Charlotte to overhear.

"I feel a bit indisposed, I'm afraid," Mrs. Palmer said weakly. "I believe I'll rest before dinner. Please forgive me," she added, nodding to her guests, who were left sitting, mouths agape.

~*~

Out of hearing of the Jennings women, Thomas cornered Henry. "What the devil has gotten into Mother? I've never seen her rude."

Henry laughed. "You've never seen her with someone like Mrs. Jennings, I'll wager. The woman is a gabster. Mother can stand only so many assaults to her sense of propriety. Didn't help when the lady started quizzing Aunt Georgina either. Not something one wants to get out, you know."

Thomas knew. If local gossips got wind of his aunt's sojourns into the bushes with a certain young lady from the village, his chances for a seat in the House of Commons would be dashed. But despite the indelicacy of the subject, it was unlike his mother to retreat with such incivility. "I shall have a talk with her."

"With Georgina?"

"No point in that. No, with Mother. These pretended bouts of illness have gone on far too long. The slight to my future mother-in-law is unforgivable. And I won't have her using her feigned ill health to manipulate me the way she did Father. If you would make my excuses to the ladies—tell them I shall see them at dinner."

And so Thomas turned to seek his mother and secure her

promise to behave in a more civil manner to his future bride and mother-in-law. He planned his speech as he strode down the long gallery, up the curving stairs, and down the wide corridor to her rooms. He paused before her door, hesitated, knocked, then knocked again.

She did not bid him enter.

Well, he couldn't intrude without an invitation, could he? She was resting. She might even take a tray in her room if she felt put out enough. Once when his father's friends had overstayed their welcome, she'd taken all her meals in there for three days in a row. Thomas straightened his shoulders. He'd come back when she'd had a chance to recover from what she undoubtedly thought of as a bout of vulgarity. And Mother felt the same way about vulgarity that most people felt about the great pox.

From within his mother's chamber, he heard a loud thump, followed by a prolonged crash. "Mother? Mother, are you all right?" The noise signaled trouble of the most serious kind. Even at her most irate, the great-granddaughter of the seventh Duke of Somerset would never throw things. Had she tripped over that ridiculously long gold train?

Thomas put his ear to the door. No answer. Was she hurt? Dread made him cold all over. "Mother, can you hear me?" Still no reply. Thomas rattled the doorknob, which turned easily in his hands. The heavy door swung inward, revealing a sight that was to haunt him for months.

# Chapter Fifteen

Laid out in the drawing room, Mrs. Sophia Palmer looked more at ease than she had at any time since her husband died. Her brow was smooth, and her lips turned up slightly at the corner. Thomas suspected the smile was due more to rictus than to any peace she had found in the afterlife. The funeral had better be soon. Though a profusion of flowers surrounded her, the whiff of decay lingered. He'd have to order the coffin lid fastened before her features showed signs of corruption.

Aunt Georgina sat motionless at Sophia Palmer's head, as she had since dawn. It was she, not an undertaker or a servant, who had washed the body and wound the woman in a woolen shroud, observing the letter of the old law. His aunt had also cut locks of Sophia's hair. These she'd plaited into keepsakes for him and for Henry.

Georgina had no need to order mourning clothes; she still wore the black she had donned when their father died. Ignoring all protests, she had insisted she would attend the funeral, scoffing at the custom barring women from attendance.

Thomas tugged at the black cravat that made swallowing difficult. He himself had written the letters informing friends and relatives of the death. Black sealing wax had dripped onto his writing desk. He had not scraped it off. For years he'd ignored his mother's complaints—clear warning signs, he could see now. And his choice of wife had been the spear that stopped his mother's heart. Now he couldn't fathom how he was to go on with his engagement, given his role in her death.

His choice of bride may indeed have killed Sophia Palmer.

Charlotte and *her* mother remained in residence, though he had not joined them for meals. He had no appetite, and he had much to occupy his time. There was so much to arrange, and so many details remained to be managed. For days he'd been walking about in a stupor, shifting from one task to the next by rote, walling away his grief until the funeral ordeal was over.

*Sophia Palmer should not be dead.* She should be alive to see him married, to see Henry married, to dandle her grandchildren on her knee. She should be present when he was sworn into Parliament.

If only he'd delayed bringing Charlotte to Cleveland.

If only he'd never set eyes on the girl, his mother would still be alive.

Gradually he became aware of someone standing behind him. Henry. His brother had been noticeably withdrawn since Thomas had come down the stairs three nights earlier, shouting for someone to fetch a doctor, even though one look at his mother had been enough to show him she was past saving. Her mottled skin, the bluish tinge to her nose, the staring eyes and lack of breath all bespoke her demise long before the doctor declared it.

"Come away, Tom. Standing here won't make a difference. She's past knowing." Sophia Palmer's death had altered Henry, as well. Dark circles shadowed his eyes, and his voice sounded muted and hollow in the echoing hall.

Thomas hadn't seen his brother take a drink in days. He himself had finished half the decanter of brandy before noon. "I should have paid more attention when she said she was feeling ill. I should have called for the doctor then." He rubbed his face with both hands, trying to erase the image of his mother slumped on her bedroom floor. "And God forgive me, here's the worst of it. I'm almost relieved she's gone."

The two stared in uncomfortable silence.

At last, Georgina cleared her throat. "She could be difficult.

You should not blame yourself."

"You couldn't have known this time was different," Henry added. "No one thought anything of her complaints. Not Uncle Tharp, who certainly knows his family's history. Not even our aunt."

At that, Georgina's head came up sharply. "Sophia knew she was gravely ill. The doctor warned her time and time again. Why do you think she obsessed about every death? She's been preparing for this for years." She looked back at her sister-in-law. "I wonder what she thinks of it now."

~*~

The ceaseless tolling of the village church bell made Charlotte's head hurt. Mrs. Jennings stood close by her daughter's side in the dark at the edge of the drive as they watched the procession of mourners pass. First came the family, including an uncle from Bath and, shockingly, Miss Palmer, seated upright in an open carriage behind the coffin. Next came friends and distant relatives who had been able to reach the ceremony in time, followed by a long line of local mourners carrying torches, many of them Cleveland's servants in black hat bands, and some of them hirelings to mend the show of respect.

By now, the head of the procession must have reached the lynch-gate at the church. The service would be hard on Miss Palmer and on Thomas, and the burial even harder. Charlotte was glad females were not expected to tax their sensibilities by attending. Even though she had known Mrs. Palmer for only a few hours, she mourned her. The trappings of death drew out memories. While the pain of her father's passing had dulled with time, the current circumstances restored the loss, so it felt as sharp as the edge of a graveyard shovel.

Her mother had sent to Mary to borrow the necessary bombazine and crape, but soon the ladies must meet with a dressmaker to arrange for an appropriate wardrobe. They would need to wear the dreary clothes for six months. That span of time would take them through the holidays and nearly to spring. And it would be *at least* that long before she and Thomas could marry.

*Six months! A lifetime!* But poor Mrs. Palmer had no life now. "Mama," Charlotte whispered, drawing closer, "I've had the most unsettling thought. Could it be that one Mrs. Palmer had to die before another could take her place? Would God be that cruel?"

"Upon my word, child, what a question! There are living mothers-in-law all over England!" Mrs. Jennings drew her daughter close. "Mrs. Palmer's time had come. That's all there is to it. At least the poor soul lived to see how well settled her son would be. Mark my words, she died happy knowing he had chosen you as his wife."

"How long should we stay on at Cleveland, do you think? They wouldn't expect us to quit right away, would they? And yet we can't remain indefinitely."

Mrs. Jennings tilted her head. "We shall stay as long as we can provide comfort and sympathy, my dear. Surely your presence is a balm to Mr. Palmer's spirit. It would be heartless to take that from him in his time of need."

"He hasn't spoken more than a dozen words to me since she died," Charlotte said, shivering. The shawl she'd hastily grabbed did little to keep out the cold.

"Mr. Palmer is a man of few words. That don't mean he's a man of few feelings. To think otherwise would be a mistake, lovey. Wait it out. He'll come to you in his own time."

Charlotte chewed her lip until it stung. "I hope so."

Yet he did not come. Charlotte waited out the night hours in her room, listening to the mantel clock's strike. From an upstairs window, she watched the funeral party return. From the stairs, she saw Thomas, Georgina, and Henry pause in the entry, then glimpsed the men turn toward the library. Much later, through her cracked door, she spied Henry walking down the hall toward his chamber. He'd left Thomas alone.

*He should not be left alone at a time like this!* A son's grief for his mother must be profound indeed. Her own grief at the loss of her father remained a heavy weight. And poor Thomas was an orphan now that Mrs. Palmer was laid in the grave. A chill ran along Charlotte's spine at the memory of stiff Sophia Palmer laid out for eternity. She hadn't looked peaceful. Far from it. Did the uneasy dead visit the living? If Charlotte were to take the candle and venture down the stairs, would she encounter a ghostly Mrs. Palmer in her shroud, graveyard earth still clinging to it?

Charlotte fervently wished she had never read *The Mysteries of Udolpho*.

But Thomas remained downstairs in the library, solitary and comfortless. Surely it was her duty as his future wife to go to him and provide what comfort she could. Grasping the silver chamber-stick, she shielded the flame with her hand as she inched down the echoing hall, looming shadows stalking her. She kept her eyes ahead, her focus on Thomas.

When the draft from the stairwell nearly blew out the flickering candle, she stopped to listen, eyes closed to better tune her ears for what she thought she'd heard. No, she certainly did *not* hear the soft squelch of bare feet on the stone steps behind her, nor did she detect the faint whiff of rot. Nonsense. That rustling was merely drapery, or perhaps the movement of her own gown, not the swish of funeral raiments. Firmly she shut out the image of a pale Mrs. Palmer floating behind her, bringing the cold wind of the cemetery with her. No decaying hand reached out to glide a nail across the nape of her neck. The tingle between Charlotte's shoulders was mere imagination. Cleveland was no moldering castle in Italy. No veiled figures lurked here.

Only a few steps more, then across the Great Hall. Cold sweat broke out on her forehead, and her hand trembled as she clutched the wavering candlestick. Neither the living nor the dead watched as Charlotte lifted her skirt in her free hand, sped down the last few stairs, and ran the remaining distance before bursting through the carved double doors into the library.

This room, too, was dark. Her candle had gone out.

Faint moonlight filtered through the tall leaden windows. Step by step, Charlotte sidled past bookshelves and tables, tripping over clawfoot legs as she advanced into the heart of the library. It was as if the darkness closed in around her, muffling sounds until all she could hear was her own breathing.

Still, she threaded her way forward, bumping her toes, cheered by a faint glow in the center of the room. She had found him, her poor, grieving fiancé. Only a dozen more steps. Then she would hold his head to her bosom and comfort him while he wept. In gratitude, he would fold her into his arms and kiss her the way he had at Barton Park.

Seven steps. Thomas slumped before her in a massive leather chair pulled up to the empty fireplace. Its yawning white mouth gaped like the entrance to an ancient tomb. On the table beside him, a single candle cast more shadows than light on his features.

He did not look at her.

Charlotte rubbed her arms. "You must be cold, with no fire," she said gently.

When he did look up, his eyes were as cold and empty as the hearth. "What the devil are you doing here?"

She startled at the curse. "I worried about you." Hands shaking, she lit her candlestick from his and set it on the table next to an empty decanter. When she knelt at his feet, the cold marble seeped through the thin muslin of her gown, chilling her to the core. "I didn't want you to be alone."

He looked down at her with a bitter laugh. "I am poor company this evening."

"I prefer your company to all others," she replied, laying a hand on his arm.

"Do you indeed?"

Charlotte was startled again, this time by his rough hands as they hauled her onto his thighs. This close, she could smell the cloying odor of brandy and musk. Thomas's cheek was rough with stubble as it scraped against her own. His fingers pressed at her sides so that breathing pained her.

"What comforts are you prepared to offer, Lottie?" His breath on her neck was hot, and one hand now rested below her breast, his thumb stroking its underside.

Charlotte shivered.

"*You* are the one who's cold." He ran his hand slowly up and down her ribs.

She pressed her lips together to stifle a giggle at the ticklish feeling. "No. Not cold." How could she be, with his hand on her?

"Frightened, then? You should be. This is no place for you tonight." And yet, he did not release her. His smile reminded her fleetingly of Mrs. Palmer's dead grin.

Charlotte refused to give in to her uneasiness. *This* was her place. She had braved the shadows to offer comfort, and comfort him she would. With renewed determination, she settled herself into his lap, despite the uncomfortable hardness of it, and gazed straight into Thomas's slitted eyes. "My place is with you, my love. Always."

"You may learn to regret that," he muttered, still holding her, though his grip relented. More confident now, she relaxed into his arms and rested her head against his shoulder, burying her face in his neck.

If only he would kiss her. Then they might comfort each other.

But something in the distance had caught his attention, something above the library door. Charlotte again thought of the faint rustling she'd heard behind her. Was Thomas now staring at some dreadful apparition? She turned, eyes wide.

There was nothing there but the doorway.

"Tell me, Lottie, can you read Latin?" He nodded at the words carved over the lintel, faintly visible in the weak light.

Charlotte squinted to make out the dim letters outlined in gold. "*Hoc age*. I'm afraid I don't know what it means or where it comes from."

"Our family motto. Loosely translated, it means 'do it'—rather forcefully, in fact. The words were uttered before a Roman priest raised the sword for a sacrifice. Chaerea shouted it before stabbing Caligula. Did your education include mention of Caligula?"

Charlotte shook her head. "My education ran more to stitching landscapes in silk."

"My innocent lamb." He moved his hand higher. Charlotte gasped. "Are you a willing sacrifice, Lottie?"

"I don't understand." The sensation of his hand on her breast shocked her. What he was doing was most improper. They were not yet wed. She should stand up. She should go. But she could not bear to leave him alone in the cold and dark. "I want to understand you, Thomas." Plucking her courage, she brushed her lips against his.

Thomas sat stiff, his chest and thighs as unyielding as stone. Charlotte pressed her mouth against his, willing him to respond, to once again become the man she knew.

He moved his lips.

But this kiss was different from the last—more insistent, and yes, frightening. More a plunder than a kiss, the sensation left her breathless and confused. Charlotte finally lifted her head, but she could do nothing but study his face, searching for any trace of tenderness, any remnant of her beloved in the stranger who held her. His complexion looked ashen in the moonlight. Worst were his eyes: the whites were shot with blood, and the pupils nearly eclipsed the irises.

"Don't look at me like that," he said. "You kissed *me*, remember. Will you punch me now, as you did Tierney?"

She shook her head. "I came only to comfort you in your time of grief."

"What did you think to offer? A cool hand on my fevered brow? A cup of tea? Some empty words?" His tone had turned as bitter as his laugh.

Charlotte bit her lip, chillingly aware of the extreme lateness of the hour and their distance from the sleeping household. "What comfort would you have, then?" she whispered, bracing for the answer and readying herself to do whatever he asked.

But no answer came. Instead, Thomas pulled her to him, pressing his hot forehead to her breast. His grip on her ribs grew fierce, but this time she felt less pain than pity. With a tentative hand, she smoothed the wild hair from his temple. The dark strands tangled in her fingers like a snare. For an eternity of seconds, Charlotte held still, afraid that even exhaling would break the balance.

"How much are you offering?"

Her nerves drew tight and thin. Their future might well hinge on this moment. Then the unthinkable happened.

She could feel it starting, swelling inside of her despite every panicked effort to tamp it down. She snatched her hand from his hair to stifle her mouth, but the sound surged, irrepressible. When she tried to swallow it, it escaped in spurts.

Charlotte began to giggle.

The sound trilled high and echoed off the walls. Her shoulders shook. At last, she tried to muffle the giggles with a cough, but the damage had been done.

Thomas glared.

"I'm truly not laughing at you," she choked. "I'm sorry. Sometimes I just can't help it."

He said nothing.

"It's been my curse ever since I was a little girl. Whenever I'm nervous — ."

He stood abruptly, setting her an arm's length from him. "Go to bed, Charlotte."

"But — ."

"Go. Before I change my mind."

Hand to her mouth, she ran from the room.

~*~

Thomas watched her retreat, willing his pulse to stop hammering and the pressure in his loins to abate. He'd lost his mind. *Hoc age* be damned! Why, he'd nearly taken his bride-to-be on the library floor, with his mother barely in the ground three hours. No amount of drink could explain such abysmal behavior. And rather than be appalled, Charlotte had *laughed* at him! If he didn't get the girl out of the house soon, there was no telling what he might do before they could be decently wed.

Bed her.

Or strangle her.

# Chapter Sixteen

Charlotte refused, absolutely refused to dwell on hurt feelings and embarrassment. There was no profit in misery. The world had enough of that, she was sure, what with so much war. True, her beloved had sent the Jennings ladies back to London with what had seemed undue haste, but he had much on his mind. The poor man was overwhelmed by grief yet had an estate to run.

"And he has many important duties that may have kept him from answering my letter," she explained to Mrs. Jennings, who hastened to agree as they sat together in the morning room on Berkeley Street.

"Just so, pet. He's an important man, and important men have much to occupy them. Could be other reasons too. Always the possibility that he did write, but the letter went astray. Mail coaches can meet with all sorts of accidents. Why, Mrs. Gardiner was telling me the other day of a dreadful one on a bridge up north. Several killed or maimed, she said. And no telling what became of the mail."

That was hardly good news, Charlotte knew, but she found some comfort in it nonetheless. "Or perhaps my *own* letter failed to reach *him*." Not likely, but certainly possible. And dwelling on the possible was far preferable to imagining the worst. Since it was possible her letter *had* been lost, Charlotte set out to pen another. She was determined that they share every minute of their lives apart until they could be together again. Her Thomas would *not* forget her. She'd make certain of it.

> *My dear Mr. Palmer,*
>
> *I hope this letter finds you well. Though I wrote you only Thursday, that letter must have failed to reach you, so I must apologize in case you have been thinking me uncaring. Be assured of my continued devotion. I count the days until I am your bride.*
>
> *Life in London goes on much as always. Mother and I visited the exhibit at the Pall Mall Picture Galleries yesterday. The prince regent himself attended, and Lord Byron! Have you read his* Childe Harold's Pilgrimage? *The melancholy of the title character reminds me a bit of you in your sad state.*
>
> *But I was telling you of the gallery. The paintings were all very modern. Everyone agrees that Mr. Reynolds was a national treasure. If only he were still alive to paint your own portrait, so it could hang next to your father's at Cleveland.*
>
> *How I long to see your face and lend my comfort to you in your time of mourning.*

But Charlotte crossed that last line out, for the memories of the last time she'd offered such comfort still burned.

~*~

Six months of required mourning loomed ahead of Thomas. After sending Charlotte and Mrs. Jennings packing as soon as was feasible, he set about restoring order and control to his life. At night he played chess with his aunt—extended, calculated sessions that required concentration and precision. On off nights, he played piquet with Henry.

"Were you waiting till the clock struck to turn a card?" Henry asked.

"What?"

"Your turn. For God's sake, Tom, you have the elder hand.

You should have twice as many points as I do. Get your head in the game. Unless you're sinking a declaration, you're losing abysmally."

*Sinking.* Thomas mulled over the word as he discarded. "My mind was elsewhere."

"You're never *here* when you're here. You're either staring at your account books or riding hither and yon to canvass for votes. Probably paying for them."

Thomas allowed himself a smile. "Only rarely." And pay he could, for both votes and repairs. He no longer needed to mind every shilling. The marriage settlement he'd signed included a dowry that would cover the loss ten-fold once he was married.

*Married.* Thomas stopped smiling.

As if he could read minds, Henry said, "Any word from your future wife?"

"Several." Mindful of his duty, Thomas had penned a letter a week to Charlotte. Every week a letter, sometimes two, arrived in response. "This week, she writes extensively of her recent purchases on Bond Street."

"Extra point for me. No news of London goings-on?"

"I thought that the period of mourning would keep her from parties and such, but she still seems to talk to a great number of people. And she describes every interaction in detail."

Henry laughed. "Even the second-hand socialization seems too much for you."

Thomas rubbed a hand over his face. "Charlotte means well. She particularly passes on everyone's condolences."

"Will she stay in London for the holidays?" Henry tallied the score. "That's seven tricks for me."

"As you said, my mind is elsewhere. I imagine she and Mrs. Jennings will be off to Barton Park."

"Will you join them?" Henry stretched his long legs.

"The Middletons have extended an invitation to our family. I haven't accepted." Thomas had also failed to respond to Charlotte's repeated hints for him to join *her*, either in Devon or London. "If this weather keeps up, the lanes will be impassable.

The lower pasture is nearly flooded already. I don't see how we could possibly go all the way to Devonshire."

Henry sat up straight. "Not go? I was counting on it. So much better to raise a glass to the new year with cheerful souls than knock about here. Ain't good for you."

"Frankly, the thought of spending the holidays with Mrs. Jennings, Sir John, and those four irritating offspring holds no appeal. You surprise me, Henry. I would have thought you'd be eager to join your friends in town, even if you must skip the parties." In fact, Thomas was surprised that Henry had not already returned to his usual haunts, surrounded by dissolute companions and a few women of uncertain virtue.

"No one worth seeing there. What of Miss Jennings? You wish to avoid her along with her relatives?"

"I'm sure she will understand."

"You don't know females then. Really think you should reconsider, old boy." Henry's attempt to seem casual captured Thomas's attention. "Been writing to Miss Browne, as a matter of fact," Henry continued.

"The intractable Miss Browne? You've maintained a correspondence?"

"Of sorts. A few times a month." Henry shrugged. "Don't look at me like that. She's not like other females."

"Neither is Aunt Georgina."

At that, Henry coughed. "Not what I meant. Miss Browne is — well, she's stimulating."

"You also found that widow in Mayfair stimulating, as I recall."

Henry ignored the jibe. "Miss Browne has opinions. And she's genuinely interested in hearing mine. I've had to form some, just to satisfy her."

Thomas stared at his brother until Henry started to fidget. "By God, you really like her. Of all the women in England, you've picked the prickly Miss Browne. Wait until I tell Aunt Georgina."

Henry's failure to deny was confirmation enough.

At last, Thomas dashed off his own excuses to Sir John

and to Charlotte, citing slippery roads, but accepted for Henry. Charlotte immediately wrote back. Her letter overflowed with loving concern for his safety. She numbered the days until they would be reunited.

Thomas numbered the days he would retain his solitude.

Christmas at Cleveland was a quiet affair, with only his aunt for company. Not even the traditional hanging of the greens brightened the mood still blackened by Sophia Palmer's death. Most evenings, Thomas sat alone before the library fire, alternately remembering his mother's last words and Charlotte's caress. Would that the two could be severed in his mind. The weather mirrored his outlook: by the end of December, a full foot of rain had drenched chilly Somerset without the balm of snow.

"Are you planning to mope about until spring?" Georgina inquired one January morning at breakfast. "Since you've managed to darken what's supposed to be the most joyous season, I'd like to know if there might be an early thaw. I'm getting tired of talking to myself."

"If I felt less, I would talk more. *Curae leves loquuntur ingentes stupent*," Thomas added with a slight smile, the first he'd spared in days. Sparring in Latin always placated Georgina.

"Indulging in grief has its pleasures, I suppose. Was it Ovid who said, '*Est quaedam fiere voluptas*?' And yet, the days are dark and cold enough without adding tears. It has been two months, Thomas. Stop wallowing. Sophia would scold if she could see you now."

He remembered clearly his mother's sharp tongue. "I imagine she'd have a great deal to say if she were here, especially about the inferiority of last night's pudding."

"She would remind you of the family honor. You can't hide away here in the country any longer. Go to town."

"The roads are full of ruts." He returned to reading his paper, which had been delivered from Bath just that morning.

"Nonsense. I see what you're about, Thomas. You can't ignore your responsibilities."

He set his lips in a firm line, swallowing the words

that most readily occurred to him. "You've made your point, Georgina. I admit I've neglected business too long." When she raised her dark brows at him, he sighed with exasperation. "Yes, and her too."

# Chapter Seventeen

The trip to London proved as miserable as Thomas expected it to be. Biting cold turned the muddy roads into sheets of ice. In town, the Thames had frozen over. Near London Bridge, peddlers clogged the way, and careening drunks shouted and passed bottles of rum. How he hated the city. Not even the Frost Fair on the river sparked his smile.

After visiting his solicitor and his banker, Thomas could no longer put off the obligatory call at the Jennings house on Berkeley Street. He contemplated the reunion with mixed feelings. He both wanted to see Charlotte and to avoid her. He'd purposely kept the miles between them so no repeat of his shameful lapse in the library could occur. He was on the brink of being a representative in Parliament. The Palmer name must remain free of scandal.

Miss Jennings, however, might not see the wisdom regarding restraint. When he'd written to say he was coming to London, her response had been practically giddy. He'd reread parts so often he could quote them. *My dearest Mr. Palmer,* she'd written. *At last, we shall be reunited! Already I am counting the hours. Rest assured that you will be welcomed with the openest of arms.*

Charlotte Jennings was partial to superlatives. She also seemed particularly prone to counting — weeks, days, now hours.

He readied himself for an onslaught as he paused in the entry hall of the Jennings' townhouse. On catching sight of him, his future mother-in-law's shrieks of delight and his future wife's trill of welcome resounded off the walls.

Mrs. Jennings bustled forward, arms outstretched. "You're a sight for sore eyes, you are, Mr. Palmer! Why, Lottie, I do believe he's grown taller and handsomer since we saw him last! She's been pining away these months, I'll have you know, but ever since you wrote to say you were coming to visit, she bloomed like a rose! Just look at her!"

Charlotte stood rooted by the stair, so at least in that, she resembled a plant. The look she gave him reminded him of the way his horse perked up when he held out an apple.

He did not deserve that look.

"You've come at last!" she breathed, her entire body practically vibrating with emotion.

Was that a reproach? Thomas squirmed mentally as he removed his black gloves and placed them in his hat. What was he supposed to say to such a greeting? He finally settled on "Good afternoon," then bowed low to retreat from Charlotte's elated countenance.

"Oh, Mr. Palmer, please, let's not stand on ceremony. I've waited ever so long." She stepped toward him and held out her arms.

He hesitated before taking her hands. "Miss Jennings, you look well." She did. Her eyes were startlingly clear, and her cheeks ruddy. Even her curls seemed brighter than he remembered. The fact that she wore light mourning added to her bloom. The lavender gown suited her. He had the uncanny impression of a crocus in a crust of snow. Her hands in his felt both soft and warm.

He defrosted in her presence.

"Now, now, you two," Mrs. Jennings said. "Don't dawdle in the hall. Here, give Manning your coat and hat. Come in, come in. We've a nice fire in the parlor. Lottie, ring for tea. How is your dear brother, Mr. Palmer? And your aunt? I hope they're in good health. Winters can be hard on the constitution."

He assured her all were well at Cleveland, though his brother had only lately returned there from Barton Park. Thomas tried to listen to Mrs. Jennings, but his eyes continually strayed to Charlotte. Whenever he glanced down at her, he found her gazing back at him with abject adoration. She clung to his arm like a stout twist of English ivy. The constraint should have made him uncomfortable, but surprisingly, he felt quite at home.

"Lady Middleton wrote that Mr. Henry Palmer had stayed on for the Twelfth Night celebration," Mrs. Jennings continued. "Quite a few young people gathered for the revels, I understand. I believe your brother and a local lady were lucky enough in their slices of cake to be named king and queen."

"Henry failed to mention that," Thomas murmured, guessing which local lady had been chosen. He wondered how Henry had arranged it. What Henry saw in that stiff-necked martinet was a mystery, one Thomas had no energy to pursue.

Charlotte still hung on his arm, though they were now seated together on a cramped sofa. The sensation of her softness constantly pushing against his arm made him lose track of the conversation.

"I said, was your holiday terribly lonely, Mr. Palmer?" Charlotte asked without pausing for an answer. "I hated to think of you and your aunt all by yourselves at Cleveland when Barton Park was so merry. But next year, we will have our own celebrations and fill the house with revelry. Just think, our first Christmas together. How wonderful it will be!"

Mrs. Jennings chuckled. "Now, ducky, don't go arranging for Christmas with a wedding to plan for first! May will be here before you know it, and you need a trousseau fit for your new position—all new dresses, gloves, hats, shoes! We're already behind before we've begun. Banns will have to be posted by April, you know. Really, there's no time to lose!"

Thomas blinked. The broad swath of time before he and Charlotte were united had shrunk to a scrap.

Charlotte squeezed his arm, which she *still* held on to, as if afraid he might bolt. "It seems too much time to me, Mama." She looked up at him pointedly.

Thomas knew he had to say something. He couldn't count on the females to continue the conversation without him forever. He cleared his throat. "A few months may seem long or short, depending on one's perspective. To a child awaiting a treat, it's an eternity. To a condemned man, all too brief." When Charlotte frowned, he realized he'd failed somehow. Quickly, he added, "Naturally, I eagerly anticipate our being wed."

Thomas did not lie. He very much looked forward to the day when his life was settled and predictable. There had been too much upheaval in the past year. And now that he was sitting next to her, he could not deny how very desirable his Lottie was.

"Oh, Mr. Palmer." The flower was back in bloom. Tea arrived in time to prevent her from making a more effusive response. It also necessitated her relinquishing her hold on his arm. When she turned to pour out, he missed the sensation of her brushing against his side.

Tea at least brought a welcome relief from female chatter, but it was short-lived. "A group of us took a carriage to enjoy the Frost Fair," Charlotte announced. "It's really quite a shame you missed it. There was skating, plus dancing and puppet plays and all manner of food stalls! Can you imagine?"

Thomas silently resolved to stay as far from the Thames as possible during his stay in London.

"My grandfather used to talk about such fairs," Mrs. Jennings said with a sigh. "'Course, there's always the danger that the ice will crack."

Thomas paused with his cup halfway to his mouth. "You will not go again, then, will you?" he asked his future bride.

"Best mind what he says, lovey," Mrs. Jennings said solidly. "Stay on solid ground."

As soon as the cups were passed, an interminable hour unfolded in which Charlotte and Mrs. Jennings recounted every other social occasion each had attended for the past week, bringing him entirely up to date since Charlotte's last letter.

"And you remember that charming colonel, Sir John's friend?" Mrs. Jennings prodded. "I believe you met him at Barton Park. No? Perhaps not. He served in the West Indies, you know."

"We ran into him at a card party," Charlotte added.

Thomas was grateful that only rarely was he required to do more than nod or shake his head. Hearing the London news was even more daunting than scanning Charlotte's pages. He felt thankful he'd missed the actual encounters. Hearing was enough.

At the close of an endless hour, Mrs. Jennings winked. "I believe I'll check with the kitchen about what's planned for supper. Young lovers need to get reacquainted, after all. Come, now, save your blushes. I know how it is with engaged couples."

Thomas was stunned at both the frank statement and the fact that he was alone with Charlotte.

"I've missed you," his fiancée said softly, scooting even closer to him now that they were alone.

Feeling her warm hip pressed against his made forming a response difficult. Thomas inched away. "We've been apart only a matter of weeks."

Up this close, her appeal was undeniable. Alarmed at the embarrassing physical reaction he had to her, he shifted as far toward the arm of the sofa as he could. A rolled pillow blocked his progress, so he found himself squeezed by softness on both sides. "There was much to do regarding the fences at Cleveland," he explained. "I could not leave my duties to follow you. The world would be in a sad state if everyone did only as he pleased and not as he ought."

"Being with me pleases you, Mr. Palmer?" She fluttered her eyelashes at him, making Thomas perspire further.

"Yes." He swallowed. "We're to be married, after all."

She leaned into him. "Did I please you that night in the library?"

"I…I beg your pardon for my behavior that night. I was… distracted." *Distracted* was too mild a word for how he felt now.

~*~

Charlotte wanted to scream. Her beloved was acting so

very proper, despite her best efforts. Where was the man who had held her on his lap and kissed her breathless? This Mr. Palmer wouldn't even flirt. And every time she ventured closer, he froze and moved away.

"I wanted to ease your pain, my love. It's what a wife does, is it not?" Her lips parted. Closing her eyes, she *willed* him to kiss her.

"We are not *yet* married, Miss Jennings. That was the problem."

Her eyes flew open. "Are not couples about to be married allowed some—well, license?" She rested her head on his shoulder so that their mouths were inches apart.

"There's license, and there's folly." But he did not lean away this time.

"Would kissing me be folly or license?"

"Charlotte—."

But he could say no more, for she put her mouth to his and wrapped her arms about his neck.

Charlotte marveled at how different every kiss could be. Their last kiss in the library at Cleveland had been rough, and confusing, and alarming, and—the only other word she could think of was *transforming*. Something about that kiss had *changed* her.

Charlotte wanted more. She'd waited weeks for him to come to her. Now she leaned over Thomas until she was lying on top of him, pushing him into the corner of the sofa, rubbing herself against his chest. Yet he remained maddeningly still, not touching her, not kissing her back.

Until, at last, without warning, he came alive.

*Finally!* His mouth moved beneath hers, and his hands stroked up her sides and back. Beneath her, she felt heat against her breasts and a hardness pressed against her stomach. She startled when she felt his mouth open and—could that be his tongue? She opened her own mouth in surprise, and he used his tongue to touch hers, kissing her thoroughly as he ran his hands over her breasts and pushed that unsettling hardness up against her.

Somehow now it was Thomas pressing *her* down, and she was clasped in his arms, her back against the cushion, every part of her overheated and yearning, heedless of anything but the man she adored and the restless sensations coursing through her. She parted her legs to try to make more space for him, and he surged forward, sending a new shiver through her. Her eyes widened, and her breath caught.

~*~

Above her, Thomas stalled mid-thrust. He'd done it again—pounced on his virginal bride-to-be, this time in the parlor of her own home. He scrambled up. "Please forgive me, Miss Jennings. I forgot myself."

"On the contrary, Mr. Palmer. I believe we find ourselves much where we were the last time we kissed." She still lay on the sofa, cheeks flushed, lips parted, legs spread.

Thomas covered his eyes. "Your mother may return at any instant."

Charlotte pouted prettily but raised herself up and pulled her bodice back in place. "Must you always be so *mindful* of things, Mr. Palmer?"

"I'm mindful of reputation, Miss Jennings."

"And I am mindful of the many weeks we've been apart. I wish you could always be with me." The emphasis she put on *with* encompassed a blush of meaning.

"Be that as it may," he said, readjusting his own clothing, "It's best that I go now."

And so Mr. Palmer retreated to the reassuring order of the cold London streets. Afterwards, every two weeks until the period of mourning ended, he made the journey from Cleveland to London to rein in the wedding plans and reassure Lottie of his continued affections. He was careful not to let stray kisses progress too far and suffered for it. Once they were married, he feared a dam might burst.

Outside concerns—Boney's escape to France, troublesome blockades—these failed to compare to the consternation Thomas felt as his wedding day drew near. Life at Cleveland was about to change in ways he could not imagine.

# Chapter Eighteen

At last, on the appointed day in spring when the lane had turned to dust and lavender spiked the hills, Mrs. Jennings and the eager bride arrived at Cleveland by coach. From the gallery, Thomas anticipated their approach with an uncomfortable mix of ardor and trepidation. With her here all the time, how would he keep his impulses under check? Shortly he would be a married man, with a wife, a helpmeet, by his side. Charlotte. Soon to be Mrs. Thomas Palmer.

Thomas reminded himself of the benefits of his upcoming marriage. The marriage settlement was more than satisfactory. A blessing, really. Those fields that had flooded wouldn't yield much this year, and the money he'd paid out this winter for repairs meant he had very little left in reserve. And he would have Charlotte, though he would have to go through the welcoming ritual before he could be alone with her.

He was spared the need for conversation, however, for the two filled the entry hall with chatter.

"Such interesting coach-companions…."

"The sight of all those fields covered in daisies and cornflowers…."

"Mr. Palmer! I could barely keep the girl in her seat as we

drew near your gates!"

"How I have longed for this day, Thomas!" Charlotte made no attempt to hide her affection, despite the fact that they were surrounded by servants. Thomas shook his head. She genuinely *wanted* to be wed to him. Was looking forward to it, despite the distance he'd kept between them. Pondering the fact occupied him as he saw the ladies settled and then rejoined them for some refreshment.

His intended's cheerful chatter drifted across the yellow drawing room. She and her mother discussed the upcoming nuptials when he would be made the happiest of men. Since they seemed to be content to talk to each other, he settled into a chair and took up the *Bath Chronicle*.

"I do so hope it was the proper choice, Mama."

Mr. Palmer perked up his ear for any hint of dissension regarding completion of the ceremony only days away. Arrangements had been made. He would brook no delay. He'd been tossing and turning half the night just knowing she would be sleeping under his roof. Nothing would keep her from him. Of course, he in no way would let Charlotte see how desperate he was. His grip on the newspaper relaxed when he realized they were once again discussing wedding attire, a topic evidently equal in importance to the Peninsular War.

"Nonsense, Lottie. The dress suits you perfectly. I've always had a fondness for silk. The neckline's quite becoming, and I know how you love puffed sleeves. And my dear, your new yellow bonnet—quite charming the way it frames your sweet face, and the ribbons bring out your eyes." Mr. Palmer wondered if it were too early in the afternoon to pour a glass of Madeira. "Don't you agree, Mr. Palmer?"

Two sets of blue eyes begged him to underscore the compliment. "As I have not yet seen the bonnet, I can offer no reliable opinion on the matter."

"Not even on the sweetness of her dear face and brightness of her eyes?" Mrs. Jennings' sense of fun far outreached her sense of proprieties. Beside her, his Charlotte looked up at him, secure, expectant, and adorable, like a trusting lap dog.

"I hardly think you need any assurances regarding your daughter's unrivaled beauty," he observed, wishing he'd filled that glass. "And since she insists on hiring a second-rate seamstress for her gowns and haberdashery, the fault is hers if they do not suit."

Mr. Palmer adjusted his own well-fitting coat, scrupulously tailored in London. Perhaps there were moments when his boots were dull, but now only Farley would ever see him in such a state.

His intended's laughter might have reminded him of the trill of a brook, were he possessed of a more romantic nature. Since his comments had failed to restore the silence he hoped for, the sound grated like carriage wheels on gravel.

"Oh, Mr. Palmer, you are so comical," Charlotte giggled. "As if I could even consider having anyone but Mme. Roussard to sew my gowns. Why, how would she feed her daughters without our patronage?"

Mr. Palmer's brow contracted into its accustomed groove. "I fail to see what the woman's feeding habits have to do with your choice of fashion. And as for her name, if that woman is French, I'm a rattling mumper."

"She must be French," Mrs. Jennings said stoutly. "No matter where they come from, all dressmakers are from France. They have to be, to get customers."

"As soon as she opens her mouth, it must be obvious she's never been closer to Paris than Cheapside."

Charlotte's only answer was yet another trill.

~*~

At last, the day arrived. Nature cooperated fully in the celebration, for it was May when the mist was light and the breeze merely chilly.

"Oh, Mama, I feel as if my life is about to begin!" Charlotte grasped her mother's hands inside the carriage where they waited, lest the bridegroom catch sight of her and call down bad luck upon the day.

"Oh, the Lord bless you, child. I've never seen you look so happy. You're as pretty a bride as your sister was." With one hand Mrs. Jennings dabbed at her eyes with a damp handkerchief while she fluffed the bow on Charlotte's bonnet until the blue ribbons snuggled nicely on either side of the girl's pointed chin.

Charlotte frowned at the comparison to Mary. Her sister had not said a word to her all morning, and Sir John had said they would be on their way back to Barton Park that afternoon.

"What's the matter, lovey? Nervous?"

"Not a bit. I've dreamed of this day for years. Ever since I first saw him. Oh, Mama, I'm actually marrying Thomas Palmer!" Every plan had finally fallen into place.

As the two exited the carriage and made their way up the stone path, Charlotte resolutely refused to look right or left at the rows of gravestones, one of which marked where the last Mrs. Palmer had been laid to rest. That lady's pearls were clasped about Charlotte's throat, a wedding gift from Thomas. They weighed heavy, but she would not let them remind her of the sad past.

She kept her eyes on the path before her.

Inside the village church, all were glad to stand and thus avoid the clammy pews and musty prayer cushions. Charlotte waited impatiently at the back of the echoing nave in her pale-yellow gown. Its hem was thickly embroidered with daisies, her very favorite flower. At last, she processed down the aisle like a thin ray of sun while her two bridesmaids, distant cousins aged twelve and fourteen, trailed her like clouds. A godfather had been summoned to give her away.

In the front pew, her mother alternately sobbed and laughed, much to Lady Middleton's evident shame. That lady glanced down at the floor as Charlotte passed her, but Charlotte peered from beneath her bonnet at Sir John instead, who looked on benevolently.

At the altar, Thomas stood straight as the stone walls behind him. He was the tallest, most dignified man present. His brother stood up for him, less upright in every way. Her beloved looked ever so handsome in his blue coat, white waistcoat, and buff breeches. His boots shone. Everything about him was— really, just perfect. As his eyes met hers, her heart beat like birds' wings and sang. She thought the tune might be like that of a goldfinch, light and twittery, or perhaps more like the piercingly sweet tune of the wood-thrush, a clear, liquid fluting.

When Thomas took her hand and drew her to his side, Charlotte felt the vows had already been said, and the words of the service were mere window-dressing. *Of course,* they would love and honor each other. Why, they already did! As the vicar read the section of the service explaining the purpose of marriage as "ordained for the procreation of children," however, the import of the moment struck her. Tonight, this very night, *they* would procreate. While the vicar prayed, she glanced over at Thomas, who remained steadfast by her side, his hand firm in hers, his eyes frontward. The ceremony continued through the giving and the taking until at last the final prayers were offered, the blessings cast, and the two were pronounced man and wife.

The blue ribbons on Mrs. Thomas Palmer's new bonnet flapped and waved in joy behind her as she made her way through the ancient churchyard, bells ringing from the tower above her. Over the centuries, tumbled Saxon ruins had been mixed with Elizabethan gables. The church's towering grandeur quite dwarfed Charlotte and her ribbons.

For just a moment, as she looked up at the formidable stone edifice, she felt the heft of centuries on her breast and a cold, wet wind from the north.

But her disposition remained sunny no matter the weather, so Charlotte linked her arm through that of her new husband and thought instead of cake and breakfast. She smiled at the villagers who wished them well and laughed at the rain of coins that Thomas tossed to them.

~*~

The cake had been eaten, the happy couple celebrated, and the guests bid farewell before the rain fell. With some reluctance, Thomas shook his Uncle Tharp's hand and bid him safe travels.

So like Sophia in looks, but warmer in manner, his uncle had long been Thomas's favorite relative on his mother's side. Charlotte seemed equally reluctant to say goodbye to her mother. Thank goodness, Mrs. Jennings, with much exclaiming and weeping, had taken off to visit her friend in Bridgwater soon after the breakfast was over, and the Middletons had departed for Barton Park soon after. Georgina and Henry had discreetly withdrawn to their rooms.

What had been a light mist midmorning blew to a steady deluge as evening wore on. Thomas began to wonder if Charlotte were trying to drown out the pounding rain with the continuing patter of her conversation.

"I am very glad, my love, that we put off a wedding tour. Why, the carriage would have been mired in mud before we left the gates!" Her voice sounded high and hollow in the vast spaces between her and her husband, who felt oddly unsettled now that they were alone. He began steadily draining the bottle of port, whether in celebration or uneasiness, he hadn't quite decided. The heavy wine helped to block images of his mother's burial in the churchyard through which he'd led his bride only hours before. He'd put off the black armband and cravat, but putting off the memory was proving harder.

Still, before him sat a much-needed, much-anticipated distraction from uncomfortable thoughts. The lively lass he'd married could keep such bleak thoughts at bay. "Time to go up, I think," he said and held out a hand. Charlotte hesitated briefly before resting hers on his arm and allowing herself to be led upstairs.

The maid had moved Charlotte's belongings to the adjoining bedroom, but it was to the master's chamber Thomas escorted his bride. As she crossed the carpet, her nervous chatter built like a cloudburst. "My, what a charming room this is. And rendered even more so, I think, by candlelight." She fluttered to the window, where the curtains were drawn. "These draperies are very fine, I must say, and just look at this lovely spread upon the —."

Mr. Palmer watched as her blush spread like the counterpane, stretching up her neck and staining her cheeks. Her eyes darted away from the wide four-poster bed, turned down for their coming together.

*His* gaze drifted back to her and lingered there. Her shyness was unanticipated, given her forwardness in the past. He'd have to proceed slowly. "Should you not ready yourself, my dear?"

Charlotte startled, very much like the rabbit his hound had cornered the other morning. "Let me just ring my maid," she said faintly.

He smiled to relieve her nervousness. "I think we can manage without the maid tonight," he said, reaching out gently to divert her course as she paced about the room. When she opened her mouth to answer, he stopped her with a kiss, a soft, full-mouthed kiss, which quieted her quite satisfactorily.

His second kiss distracted her from his progress at picking the pins from her bodice so he could untie the bow that held the flaps in place. Roused much more quickly than he'd expected, he kissed her yet again as he reached behind to untie the rest of the dress and tug at it until it slipped into a yellow puddle around her, leaving her standing in her petticoat, short stays, and chemise.

"I finally found a way to curb your babble," he murmured. Though two days ago he'd stolen a few moments behind the pilasters to run his hands over her, they'd been necessarily quick and clandestine caresses, just a sample to know that the figure she presented to the world still owed nothing to padding and much to God.

And he silently thanked God for what he was about to receive.

She remained quiet as he skimmed his hands down her bare arms and speechless still as he bent to his knees at her feet and untied her garters. He smiled as he heard the gasp when he slid one hand up the inside of her silken thigh.

He stopped smiling, however, when she squeaked. "Something wrong?"

"No," she whispered, swaying as he ran his hand higher. "On the contrary."

"Good," he said as he leaned down and trailed his lips along the same path as his hand.

Charlotte squeaked again as he moved yet higher. His pulse pounded.

"I'll be back in a moment," she breathed and fled, leaving him kneeling on the floor.

# Chapter Nineteen

With fingers that seemed to have forgotten how to work, Charlotte struggled to compose herself as she shed her petticoat, untied her stays, doffed her stockings, and pulled off her chemise. Looking down at her naked body, she hoped Thomas wouldn't be disappointed. The white cotton nightgown the maid had laid out earlier covered her from neck to toe, and she gratefully pulled it over her head, hoping it would calm the shaking and shield her from a gaze that had proven more than she could handle, despite the months of waiting.

This was the most important night of her life. Her mother had impressed that on her, for the first night together was to set the tone for future happiness. Mrs. Jennings had little to say about the nature of such happiness, but what details she shared had left her daughter both surprised and titillated. Further research in that scandalous novel *The Monk* revealed Ambrosio "rioted in delight" with Matilda, but the specifics of exactly *how* had been left to the imagination.

With a mixture of trepidation and resolution, Charlotte steadied herself, breathing deeply and imagining the years of marital bliss unfolding before her: holidays and balls and trips and children.

And with that last thought, she readied herself for whatever was to come.

His kisses tasted heady and dark, like old casks of wine. That was her first thought after she returned to the room and to her husband's embrace. These touches were vastly different from the furtive strokes they'd shared the few times the opportunity allowed when at any moment they might be discovered. Now his kisses were slower, even more demanding, as were the hands that roamed freely from breast to bottom, calling up quite unsettling tremors.

When he lifted his head, she let out the giggle that had been bubbling up like the fizz of champagne. His dressing gown gaped. Finding herself with only a thin layer of cotton between them increased her nervousness ten-fold. Rarely had she seen a man without a frock coat, much less this, a bare chest dusted with black hair. And she didn't seem to be able to stop looking.

Although Charlotte lacked the strength of character to also look down, she could sense the hardness of his form, lean and insistent, pushing her backward and lower to the waiting bed. His fumbling soon had them both tangled in nightgown and sheets. She almost giggled again, though there was nothing at all funny, really—not the warm lips tickling her neck and moving lower or the hot hands that pushed her night rail higher until it was yanked completely off and tossed aside. And certainly, there was nothing funny about the tense grip of those hands as they ran over her flanks to her hips or the way he covered her, his weight forcing her breath to hitch and her thighs to open. She stopped breathing when she saw the intensity and purpose in his eyes and felt the firm member pressing against her.

His voice was tight and held no trace of the tenderness and adoration she'd dreamed of when she'd imagined this night. "Bend your knees, Lottie."

She did as he asked.

He clasped his hands about her hips and pushed. The suddenness of his movement left her momentarily confused, then shocked by a hot, sharp pain. She'd been warned of this and clenched her teeth to prevent a whimper. She'd barely taken a shaky breath and accustomed herself to the pressure before it was followed by a withdrawal and a second thrust. The sensation was so foreign. Charlotte felt stretched and filled and pinned down like a pattern piece to the sheet.

"All right?" Thomas whispered, his face tense.

She nodded, not trusting her voice.

Then followed a welter of rocking invasions of a force and depth for which she was totally unprepared.

Beneath her, the great bed creaked. To steady herself, she anchored her arms about her husband's waist and held there for the ride. Their rocking settled into a steady pace, one similar to a trot on her mare, a smooth, relentless movement forward and then back, each thrust stretching her further until the sting ebbed. That was better. Almost pleasant, really. Actually, quite pleasant now, as she pulled her husband—husband!—closer, skin upon skin. Gradually, a fine tension built in her as the sweat beaded on Thomas's brow and his breathing grew labored.

After a while, a great, long while, it seemed — much longer than she'd been led to believe the marriage act would last—a strange sort of tingle developed deep inside her, a warmth that spread from her center outward, making her tighten her thigh muscles and press her feet into the mattress to push up and meet his thrusts. The following sensations left her panting and whirling until all she could do was dig her fingers into his damp back and cling. She'd never suspected it would be like this. It was if she were losing a piece of herself.

This was how two became one.

Finally came an odd sense of nothing short of triumph as her Thomas heaved mightily, groaned, and collapsed on top of her. Once.

Then, an hour later, once again.

After, Charlotte lay awake, watching the candles burn low, and then watching the clouds and moon through a crack in the draperies—a moon that had first risen when she was still untouched and was now setting.

So this was marriage.

She turned her head to look at her beloved, relaxed and spent, surely signs that she'd fulfilled her wifely duty and more. She hugged the sheet to her nakedness and wiggled into the curve of her new husband's arm, smiling as she fell asleep to the sound of his snores, rhythmic and soothing, like the breathing of the tide.

~*~

He heard her before he saw her. "Oh, what a day it's going to be, Mr. Palmer! Or should I call you Thomas now? Especially now that—." He felt the stutter. "And just listen to those birds. It's like all of nature is singing." The bed bounced again as if in accompaniment to her trite and tiresome observations.

Thomas opened one eye.

A single sickly ray of sun shot through the heavy drapes, revealing his new wife, catching gold in hair he'd thought was merely blonde. She'd gathered the bed sheet in her lap and clasped it loosely to her breast. The peaks pressed against the thin linen. Surprisingly, he stirred at the sight despite the amount of wine still swirling somewhere deep in his gut.

She had evidently not yet run down. "You're awake, my love! I had rather thought you'd sleep for hours, given the lateness of the hour we retired and the extent of—well, and the vigor with which...." She offered a tentative smile.

That voice. So loud in the midst of the blasted dawn chorus. Homer, wasn't it, who spoke of a dawn chorus? Thomas closed his eyes against the din, head aching and mouth dry. Beneath him, the marriage bed bounced again, making his stomach churn. There were disadvantages to a shared bed.

His head felt like it had been split with an axe, causing him to speak without considering the craters his words might leave upon impact. "Can you not be both conscious and quiet?" Even the act of speaking made his forehead pound and his teeth hurt. The very walls seemed to close in around him. "Have a few paltry moments of release sentenced me to a lifetime of your prattling?"

Even with eyes shut, he felt the sun disappear behind the clouds. "You...find me disappointing?" his bride said. The lilt had faded in her voice. He opened both eyes. She had pulled the sheet higher.

He had made a grave error. He saw that at once. Before she started to cry, he had better pull himself together and say something.

Thomas sighed and dropped one arm over his aching forehead, extending his other hand to pat her rounded thigh. "I had no expectations of our first night together, given your incontrovertible innocence." He meant it as a compliment, a gracious acknowledgment of her sacrificed virginity. Despite the axe cleaving his skull in two, he smiled at the memory of his role in the ritual. And its aftermath. Twice.

Charlotte Palmer inched away, clutching the top sheet to her, leaving exposed the bottom sheet with a loud brown smear of blood marring the white linen. "I see. I'm sorry if I was a disappointment." She didn't look sorry. If he had to define it, he'd say she was furious.

"Lottie—." He was in no way equipped to deal with her at this hour. And he couldn't think straight lying down. He had no skills to navigate this labyrinth of feelings.

"Don't say more. I'll be out of your way in a moment."

This was not the way to begin married life. Gingerly, Thomas struggled to sit up and repair the damage. Every time she bounced the mattress, another wave of nausea rippled through him. "Blast it, Charlotte, stay still." He wiped a hand across his dry mouth. "You are not to go anywhere. No, stay still and listen to me. I didn't mean—." He reached for her, but she drew away. "Dash it, your sister was right. You're more flighty than a bumblebee."

"My sister spoke to you about me?"

"Only out of concern. She simply asked me to look out for you."

"Mary had you watch me?" Charlotte stopped her retreat. The sheet sagged. "When? Why?"

His muddled brain searched for words. "At Barton Park. To keep you from making a cake of yourself. Which you nearly did with Tierney. And with Dysart. And you succeeded with me, I suppose, for here we are." What he wouldn't do for a cup of tea right now.

Charlotte sat absolutely still, sheet pooled in her lap. "I am trying to understand this, Mr. Palmer. Are you saying the only reason you sought me out at Barton Park was because Mary requested it?"

Had he not been distracted by the view, he might have heeded the warning in the question. "She worries about you."

"And you would do anything for Mary."

"She is a woman of inestimable virtue."

"Is that why you married me? Because you hoped I'd be like her?" His wife's lower lip trembled.

Thomas reached out a hand and traced that trembling lip with his thumb. "Lottie, however we got here, we are married now." He leaned forward to kiss her.

She backed across the bed, clutching the sheet to her, practically swaddling herself in it. With the weak sunlight full on her, every nuance of her hurt and indignation was evident.

"What are you doing now?" Thomas was unused to the prick of conscience that had been added to his maladies.

"I can't find my nightgown." She kept her head down, not looking at him as he swung his legs over the side of the bed. "No matter. I'll just go into the dressing room and —."

"Charlotte." Head pounding anew, he fell back on the pillows.

She backed the few remaining feet into his dressing room. He should go after her. He knew that. But he heard no telltale crying. And being closed into a tiny room with a female on the *brink* of crying was more than he could take. He had all day to repair any damage and all of the upcoming night. And his head felt like cannon fodder. He vowed to never consume as much again.

Relieved to have peace and solitude once more, Thomas

pulled the remaining blankets up and willed the wisps of wine-induced fog to return him to the land of Nod far east of the Eden he'd moored himself in. His last thought was to hope his wife would let him sleep.

The slice of sun was high on the curtain when a tap roused him. "Are you ready to rise, sir?" his valet asked from the open door.

"Why don't you just come in, Farley?"

"Your change in status, sir." The valet kept his eyes straight ahead.

"Ah, yes. She's already up."

"Yes, sir." Farley held out the dressing gown. As Thomas tied it, his man moved about the bedroom, picking up discarded breeches and small clothes and laying the missing nightgown on the rumpled bed.

"Riding clothes, I think, Farley. Clear the cobwebs. I expect *Mrs.* Palmer is at breakfast now?"

"Would you like me to check with Mr. Nash, sir?"

"I'll just join her, I think."

"As you wish, sir." Farley's expression remained impassive, even as his eyes swept across the stained sheets.

~*~

Charlotte barely noticed the wet grass as she crossed the lawn, having no destination in mind except away from the house. *Thomas came to my rescue only at the behest of my sister.* Obviously, Mary was the one he cared for. Nothing she'd believed was real. She'd been a fool, a silly, empty-headed ninny. A child.

He'd warned her, hadn't he? "You should expand your acquaintance, Miss Jennings," he'd said the first time they danced. Mary had warned her too. Charlotte thought back to all the times she'd shared with Thomas. He'd never actually spoken of affection. "I offer you a marriage of reason," he'd said. She should have listened. He was nothing if not straightforward. Stupidly, she'd believed his barbed exterior was a shell he showed the world, a shell that hid the warm, generous heart that must beat within.

She'd made a horrible mistake.

Thomas did not love her. Mary's words came back to haunt her. *Marriage is not a guarantee of happiness.* Yet Charlotte had been so sure they'd be happy. She tried to gather her scattered thoughts, but they skittered left and right, circling around and back to one incontrovertible truth. She was not loved. Beneath her feet, the grass turned to gravel, then rock and sand. She found herself at the edge of the sea, with the cold gray waves spread out before her, beckoning.

~*~

The breakfast room was empty—empty, at least, of his bride, though the regular staff stood by.

As Thomas sat down to his roll and tea, he couldn't long ignore the butler's glare. Sighing, he motioned to Nash, who had been butler to his father before him. "I suppose she's already been down and broken her fast?"

Across the room, the maid and footman exchanged looks. After a nod from Mr. Nash, they gathered trays and departed. Mr. Nash cleared his throat noisily before answering. "Mrs. Palmer has not yet eaten, sir."

"Indeed. I expect she was not hungry."

The silence stretched out like Hadrian's Wall between them. "She is not in the house, sir."

"Exploring the grounds, then." Thomas cut the roll precisely in half and spread jam liberally on both halves.

"She took the sea path. Refused the footman."

Mr. Palmer showed no reaction. That did not mean, however, that his body had not gone cold.

"Clouds are moving in, sir." Again, the silence strained. "Perhaps a storm."

Mr. Palmer sipped his tea calmly, refusing to glance out the window to gauge the weather.

"Those rocks by the cove are quite slick in the rain." A pause. "Sir." This pause hung heavy with judgment. "I took the liberty of having your horse saddled."

Thomas threw down the napkin and ran out.

~*~

The wind tossed the yellow bonnet about, sending it tumbling along the shore. As his mount picked its way across the scree, Thomas felt chilled to the bone and deuced uncomfortable because of it. Dismounting, he picked up the bit of silk, its crown sadly dented, gay blue ribbons stained with salt. Somehow, the ruined bonnet intensified the cold and the tang in the wind. He hurried forward to the jutting rocks. There she perched on an outcropping, knees tucked up, hair straggling down her back, hem wet. Thomas slowed to pick his way to her side, dislodging pebbles as he slipped down the shore. She didn't look up, even when he stood above her.

"Charlotte." A single gull hovered above the first line of waves. His wife watched it stall until it plunged into the foam. When she finally met her husband's gaze, her eyes were like bruises.

Shaken and for once fumbling for words, Thomas held out the bonnet. "I found this. Your new bonnet. The one you're so fond of." His tone turned indignant when she still failed to answer. "I discovered it blown against the rocks!" He was still shaken by the fear that he would find her broken body nearby.

She made no move to take the offending bonnet from his outstretched hand. She likewise made no effort to restore order to her locks or to straighten her gown, or to fix anything else about her person. "Yes. The wind caught it."

"What in blazes are you doing out?" Fear sharpened his tone.

She made no attempt to answer.

"Lottie?"

Charlotte stared out at the rush of waves breaking hard upon the rocks. The crash of water on stone nearly drowned out her words. "I thought I might find some shells like I did once when I went to Brighton with Mother. Such a lovely holiday, that was. But…they're all broken. The shells, I mean. I walked up and down the strand and could not find even one that was whole." Her voice wobbled. Thomas didn't need to see the tears to know she was crying.

"The sea is harsh here," he acknowledged.

"Yes." Wind whipped her hair across her face. She did nothing to stop it. "Much here is harsh."

When she made no effort to calm herself, Thomas knew he must speak. "Charlotte, I am sorry if I hurt you."

"Are you?"

Thomas looked out to the bank of clouds, weighty above the whitecaps. "The morning has taken a turn. We should go back."

His wife continued to gaze out to the vast expanse of sea. "I should like to go home, I think."

He relaxed shoulders that had grown stiff as he waited her out. "So we shall. My horse is just this way." He extended a hand.

She refused it. "Not to Cleveland." Instead of rising as she should, she continued to stare out at the waves.

Thomas looked down at her, perplexed and irritated. "You are married now. Cleveland is your home."

"I thought perhaps it would be."

The look in her eyes was like the first cold spatter of rain. He felt unaccountably ashamed, as if he'd just kicked a puppy.

# Chapter Twenty

She did not die of it, after all. The realization came gradually, like the lifting of a fog bank. The pain had dulled to an ache, and a childish urge to rush into the arms of the sea had receded with the tides. Now she could sit calmly, sit and listen to the man who was her husband without rancor, sit perfectly still on her rock and contemplate the future while he pontificated about her duty and her place. He was not, evidently, more than he seemed; his off-putting manner shielded no softer sentiments, and despite their changed status and the night they'd shared, he remained as harsh as the waves that crashed before her. She had been wrong about him. Very, very wrong.

One did not, apparently, die from disillusionment, much as one might wish.

And what of her own deceits? The ruse of a stitch in her side, the feigned distress at being tangled in thorns? Their marriage was founded on lies. She must share some blame, at least.

It was not too late to mend her misstep. Perhaps Mr. Palmer would release her. He would not willingly live with such a disappointment. If she could return home—ostensibly for a visit, an extended visit, perhaps on the pretext of an illness—then something could be quietly arranged. She'd prefer that shame to accepting the hand her husband held out to her.

"You're cold." Mr. Palmer's words were terse as he draped his coat about her, still warm from his body. The sensation took her back to the intimacies of the night and the humiliation of the morning. The coat felt heavy and confining. She wanted none of it.

"I pray you keep your garment for your own use." Charlotte looked from his sandy boots and stained buckskin breeches up past waistcoat and shirt and cravat, indifferent to his state of undress. "Your coat will not ease my chill." She felt a glimmer of satisfaction when she saw a muscle tense in his formidable jaw. Shrugging loose of the wool, she left the coat behind her on the rock, picking her way to higher ground. "I'll be going now," she called over her shoulder before turning her back on him.

She hoped he stood there on the hard, cold rock until the chill seeped into his bones and fused until he became a statue instead of a man—a reverse Pygmalion, perhaps—morphing into his more natural, unbending form. In future years, sailors skirting the cove might remark on the marble figure with hand still extended, gull droppings coating him, waiting forever for her. Waiting in vain. Charlotte smiled her first smile of the day at the thought.

As the day wore on, she sought more reasons to smile, for he could not take that from her. She was not naturally like Mary, always solemn. And so, after wandering about, she smiled at the footman when he opened the door. Upstairs, she smiled at Susan, who exclaimed over the state of her dress and hair. In her own chamber, she smiled when presented with a tray of tea and cold meat and bread and found she had an appetite for them. Dropping the smile, she penned just the right words to convey to Mrs. Jennings her determination to return home without giving away the reason. If there were a great many blots on the missive, she hoped her mother would overlook them.

And then it was the hour for dinner. While it was indeed tempting to dine again from a tray in her room, Charlotte did not want to be thought cowardly. Besides, now that she was certain she had regained her composure and worked out a plan for *future* happiness, there was really no need to hide, was there? She allowed her maid to help her into a dinner gown, choosing an elegant dark green silk with embroidered gold trim instead of the cheerful pastels she usually preferred. The sophisticated gown fully exposed her bodice and arms. She would face Thomas without layers of cloth between them. And she would arm herself also with Mary's brand of coolness. Absentmindedly, she tugged her necklace while Susan twisted her hair into a crown of braids.

Finally ready, Charlotte straightened her shoulders and held her chin up in anticipation of the coming skirmish. The first volley was not long in coming since her husband waited outside her door.

"Allow me, Mrs. Palmer." Thomas, in evening wear, held out an arm, obviously expecting her to accept his escort despite all that lay between them. Had he been listening from his dressing room to manage his timing so perfectly? To refuse him, with servants in proximity, was out of the question. She took his arm.

He commanded the field. "Aunt Georgina and Henry will not be joining us."

No allies to guard her rear, then. She needed the support of the banister as she descended the long staircase ahead of him, sensing him two steps behind her, just beyond her train. *Think of our brave soldiers going into combat at Vitoria,* she thought. *How stalwart. How unflinching. If they can face cannon fire and muskets, surely I can face an evening of soup, fish, game, and cakes.* These considerations sustained her until he seated her to his right, bare inches away from him instead of safely at the far end of the table.

"Some wine, my dear?" Thomas nodded to the footman without waiting for her answer, and she watched as her goblet filled with sweet Madeira, a drink she abhorred.

"Thank you, no," his lady replied, casting an apologetic eye at the footman, who kept his gaze steadily forward.

"Some other drink, perhaps? Claret?" Again he nodded, and the footman poured, leaving the crystal decanter to her right as she accepted the glass. The wine's round, soft taste helped restore her balance.

"A delicious blend," she observed, sipping delicately. Beneath the tablecloth, she crushed her napkin in a fist. If she was to survive the evening, she would have to garner her forces. The wine gave her courage. She schooled her expression into a ladylike mask.

Thomas nodded. "We once had a rather extensive cellar here. My father took great pride in it. Unfortunately, these days, French wine is in short supply, and the stock is difficult to replace. We must savor what there is."

"Mishandled wine can turn bitter, I understand." Her voice remained even and her back as straight as a Baker rifle.

"Cleveland and its cellars offer the very best of conditions, I assure you, conditions under which excellent vintages have been kept for this and, I hope, all future generations." He held her glance. He was the first to blink.

To hide her triumphant smile, she reached again for wine, her hand steady. "You are anticipating future generations, Mr. Palmer?" She lifted her eyebrows in a perfect imitation of her sister's favorite expression. So he still preferred Mary? Let him see how he liked her now. The footman topped her glass.

"It is my dearest wish, Mrs. Palmer." He waved the footman away as he warmed to his topic. "Cleveland is in trust. I take such responsibilities seriously. The care of the lands, the maintenance of the estate and its outbuildings, the status of its inhabitants—all of these concern me." He lowered his voice, although no servants remained in the dining room. "I sincerely hope to secure an heir to fulfill that trust."

"Do you?" Charlotte murmured, feeling the heat climb from beneath her bodice to her face. They'd entered the fray rather sooner than she'd planned. Feigning a Mary-like calm, she reached for the goblet, ignoring the tepid soup. "With whom, I wonder?"

The line was drawn.

# Chapter Twenty-One

Thomas considered his tactics, given the early hour and the number of courses remaining. A lull in the artillery could lure her into a false sense of security. Then he could marshal his arguments, line them up, and shoot them successively, aiming for the greatest impact. A barrage, however, sudden and explosive, could land a decisive victory in this battle of wits. He had the advantage: he'd barely sipped his wine, while Charlotte had downed two glasses of his finest claret and was already sipping the third before the fish was cleared. Time to press on.

"As I've explained, my dear, you are my wife. This is our home. Here is your future. And a fruitful one it will be." When she still didn't answer, he added, "Charlotte, perhaps our union hasn't begun as well as I would have liked, but we have a lifetime to make amends."

"*We*? Mr. Palmer, I'm at a loss as to what fault lies at *my* feet."

Unused to having to justify himself, Thomas spoke slowly. "Every human will frustrate, annoy, madden, and disappoint us. That is human nature." He thought of his own family, fraught with frustration. "And each of us will, without intent, do the same to another." He paused before adding, "I never meant to cause you pain, Lottie."

"Yours is a dark view of the world indeed." Her face showed no feeling—a strange look that sat oddly on her soft features. The ravages of the seaside had been swept away, he noted. Tangled hair had been tamed into plaits and decently put up, with a few fair tendrils escaping to tease her cheeks and forehead. The green of her gown intensified her eyes, darkening them to the hue of the sea at twilight. And the pink of her lips as she put them to the rim—.

But for once, he could not read her reactions. It was as if she'd slipped on a shield. He didn't like it. Not at all. He reached over to clasp her hand, determined to break through. "I pride myself on always remaining rational."

"Always?" Her widened eyes hinted at a memory.

"The world is a hard place. One must be realistic." He felt as if he spoke to himself, for Charlotte merely shook her head and withdrew her hand.

"I know the world is a hard place, Mr. Palmer." She took another sip from her goblet. "Yet I see no point in dwelling on that fact. I'd much rather dwell on the more pleasurable side of life."

"But life is not a succession of pleasures."

Her smile was cold. "That is evident."

Thomas began to feel desperate. "All you lack is experience, Lottie. I trust that, in time, you shall become accustomed to life at Cleveland and to your position here."

"I've written my mother in Bridgwater."

He frowned. "And what did you say?" Was his bride holding to the ridiculous things she'd said on the beach? He'd thought an afternoon of rest would restore her good humor. Where was the Charlotte he knew, the cheerful, amiable, malleable girl who found delight in everything he said? This composed Charlotte was a stranger.

Charlotte kept her eyes firmly on the platter set in front of her. "I've asked her to shorten her stay. When she leaves, I should like to return home with her. For a visit." She took a deep breath. "An extended visit."

Perhaps it was that breath, coupled with the cut of her gown, that decided him. Or perhaps it was the memory of the night he proposed, of her face tilted up to his, her eyes full of — what? He supposed it had been love. That look was gone. He must get it back.

He didn't stop to examine why.

Defeat was not an option. He must win the war, one hard-fought campaign at a time. His new bride would remain here at his side. But he must proceed with caution.

"London is rather dull now that the season is ending," he observed, nodding to the staff as the roast fowl was served. "Everyone will have gone on to Cheltenham or Brighton or Bath." There, a volley successfully launched.

His wife lifted one arched brow, a sophisticated expression totally foreign to her usual open, laughing countenance. "Everyone, indeed? Am I to believe that all carters, chandlers, and porters have fled and left the city wholly deserted?"

The volley had been sadly misdirected. "Everyone that matters left at the close of Parliament." Palmer stabbed his meat with rather more force than necessary to pierce the delicately roasted flesh.

"I believe you'd find London still full of any number of citizens, Mr. Palmer. Bankers, shopkeepers, carters, lamplighters. I imagine workers would 'matter' were you required to do without them. And some of them may perhaps become your constituents."

Behind him, Thomas heard Nash cough. He resisted the urge to turn around. "Your high regard for the working classes is a credit to your sensibilities, my dear," Thomas said, gritting his teeth and scraping fennel from his dish. "You do not, I hope, extend that regard to the laborers rioting in the North." How on earth had they strayed so far from the subject at hand? What the devil did he care how many carters remained in London this time of year? His wife was *not* returning to her mother's London house.

When a footman tried to place a dish in front of her, Charlotte waved him away. "Killing men for breaking machines is hardly a solution. With their livelihoods at stake, how could they hope to provide for their families?"

Thomas Palmer had never had patience with passions. Where was the calm felicity and connubial bliss? He held his tongue and chewed at his irritation, making a prudent tactical retreat. "I can see you feel strongly about this matter," said he, understanding that emotion not a whit. "Perhaps some more claret to calm your nerves?" He looked to Nash, who remained impassive behind him.

"I am all that is calm and collected, I assure you, Mr. Palmer," Charlotte replied, voice high.

Thomas wisely said no more, inviting a lull in the battle. The courses continued, as did the quiet, until dessert. He'd thought perhaps a truce of sorts had been reached, and the nonsense regarding a return to London had been cleared away along with the plates when Charlotte dashed such hopes.

"And I also assure you, despite your fears, life goes on in Portman Square and even on Berkeley Street, whether any member of *society* resides there or no." The rosy hue of Charlotte's cheeks exactly matched the creamy strawberry trifle that was now being brought to the table. Even as he gathered his wits and forces, he could not but note the resemblance and the memories they stirred.

This infuriating, delicious girl was his *wife*. His helpmate. The future mother of his children. The chances of having secured an heir in just one night were slim, though it had been, as he recollected, a quite productive night. The stray thoughts of that night, of her, willing and eager beneath him, cemented the matter. "I prefer we remain at Cleveland for now, Charlotte. In time, we will make our way to London to my townhouse in Hanover Square." That round thudded with the finality of a cannonball.

And yet, the impact apparently remained unfelt. "Perhaps you will be kind enough to call on me on Berkeley Street when you do," the twit replied with all the imperiousness of a duchess.

The first battle had been waged. And Thomas Palmer wanted nothing more than to retreat to his library.

# Chapter Twenty-Two

The drawing room at Cleveland spanned exactly thirty-seven paces from door to far wall and twenty-three from the central bay window to the fireplace. Charlotte measured this space side to side and up and down until she thought she might wear out her slippers. The arrival of the after-dinner tea cart offered a welcome interruption, but once the servants had withdrawn, she stared at the teapot, reluctant to pour with a trembling hand. The flush of the wine and the passion of sparring with Thomas gave way to restlessness.

This agitation felt alien. Were she at home, her *real* home in London, she and her mother would be seated together in their familiar surroundings, reliving the highlights of their morning calls or discussing upcoming lectures and card parties. Charlotte missed the lively shared conjectures of who had set her cap for whom and who was seen blushing when a certain young gentleman entered the room.

No one would ever again speculate so about her, she knew. Not now that she was married. Her restlessness spiraled into despondency.

Only solitary occupations of reading or sewing awaited a newlywed wife who sat alone. As for reading, she soon tossed aside Dr. Gregory of Edinburgh, whose advice to marry only for "proper motives of esteem and affection" chafed her. Rereading Mrs. Radcliffe's novel held her for some while, until the tenth chapter when Charlotte discovered that the heroine's solitary life and melancholy mood too closely mirrored her own. She, too, felt "greatly enervated." And Thomas Palmer bore no resemblance to the novel's hero, the valiant Valancourt. Restless, she picked up her embroidery only to toss it aside, tempted to stab something, anything, with her needle.

Charlotte's mood progressed from restlessness to a more generalized misery. She'd tried to emulate Mary throughout dinner, keeping her temper cool and her voice modulated. Thomas should have been happy with that. Instead, he'd been stubborn and argumentative.

The ploy had failed. Just as well. She'd never have been able to sustain it for long. Nor did she want to. She knew what she wanted. A happy life.

Gazing out the window at the broad, moonlit lawn before her, she saw her own future stretching ahead of her, month by month, a wife and not a wife, her bloom fading with each season. She imagined herself accompanying her mother from country house to country house, only to return to her childhood rooms to fill yet more empty hours: to draw, or take up music, or begin carpet-work, whilst bestowing all her pent-up maternal affections on the children of her sister. Or perhaps a kitten.

In the reflection from the window-glass, Charlotte saw a pale shadow looking back, hollow-eyed—a wan sad-sack of a girl nothing like herself or Mary.

A ghost.

*How very ridiculous.*

The voice in her head sounded like the old Charlotte. What had she been thinking? She was no ghost. She was a living, breathing woman, and where there was breath, there was hope. She could almost hear her mother repeating that adage.

Her misery was all her own doing. She'd gone looking for it, taking molehills of dissatisfaction and heaping them into a mountain of discontent. What wrong had been done her, after all? Perhaps her husband wasn't quite as besotted as she'd hoped, but still, he'd married *her* and no other. Marrying for love was the stuff of novels. It was up to her to make the best of the situation. Her spirits lifted off the floor, at least as high as her knees.

But perhaps staying married was not the most generous decision. Mr. Palmer already regretted his choice. Setting him free would be a kindness. That may be the best, most adult solution. She should shed this bad match the way mallards moult. Her spirits sank to her ankles.

Indecision made her stomach hurt. So many decisions waited, including what to do if her husband visited her room again that night.

Later, in her chamber, Charlotte lay awake, limbs stiff with tension, ears tuned for the sound of footsteps in the hall. Thomas had remained alone long after the tea was cleared, long after she abandoned book and needle, long after her maid had helped her out of her gown and into her nightclothes. Just as she let her eyes close, she thought she heard a faint thump in the dressing-room, but when nothing more followed, she drifted into slumber, uneasy though it was. She did not dream.

Morning came, as it tends to, despite the prayers of those who wish the clock turned back. Sustained by her first cup of tea and a slice of toast, Charlotte had just finished dressing and was seated in the morning room penning a letter to her sister when Mr. Nash appeared at the door.

"You have a visitor, madam."

"What?" Charlotte bumped the writing desk in her haste to rise. "At this hour?" Even in the country, morning calls did not begin until closer to noon.

"It is Mrs. Jennings, madam." The lady sailed past without waiting to be shown in.

"Mama!" Charlotte rushed into her fond parent's arms, forgetting her newfound status and the watchful eye of the butler.

"Oh, la, Lottie, whatever are you about? When I read your letter, I couldn't believe my eyes. I'd only just arrived at Mrs. Simpkins', and here I had to turn right around this morning.

Whatever has come over you? Stand back, now. Let's have a look at you."

"Oh, Mama, I've been such a fool!" At that, Mr. Nash prudently retreated to summon a footman to fetch refreshments since no one had the wherewithal to dismiss him.

Mrs. Jennings patted her daughter and led her to the settee. "Here, now, let's have us a sit, and you can tell me all about it."

It was many more minutes before her daughter could compose herself enough, time enough for the footman to return with refreshments and leave once more. While her mother poured out the tea, which had steeped rather over-long, Charlotte poured out her heart, repeating the main points of the afternoon's letter and adding to them the horrific conversation over dinner the night before. "You must see, Mama, why an annulment may be the best recourse."

Mrs. Jennings coughed, sputtering tea into her napkin. "What? An annulment? Whatever are you about, gel? Never heard of such a thing!"

"Surely, if ever there was a case in which marriage was a sham, this is it."

"Nonsense! Did he not bed you? Thoroughly, I mean? Finishing the act?"

Charlotte felt her cheeks grow hot and refused to look up as she nodded.

"Even if he hadn't done the deed, Lottie, I believe the law requires one to wait years before such a claim can be made. And you'd be examined too," said she with a sharp look. At that, Charlotte reddened all the more. Mrs. Jennings heaved a great sigh. "I doubt Mr. Palmer would appreciate a charge of impotency, and since you two are not related by blood, I can't think of a reason to call the marriage a sham. Given the state of things, you've no recourse whatsoever. You're of age, the banns were read, you've said your vows, and there's nothing amiss in the marriage contract. The only remaining option would be to claim you are insane, and in that matter, I'm beginning to entertain the possibility."

"Then how will I secure any future happiness?" Charlotte's voice cracked as the drama of the moment overcame her.

Mrs. Jennings, for once, did not offer a ready answer. It was not her habit to think before speaking, but her young daughter's prospects very much depended on the words she next uttered, so she made a rusty effort to choose carefully what she would next say. "Men are like dogs, my girl," said she. "They like their lives predictable and easy, with time out of doors aplenty and some rambles about now and again. But when they come home, what they want most is a place by the fire and a loving hand."

"But...Mama, he finds me wanting!" The shame of that moment flooded back to Charlotte like a spring tide, sending two tears coursing down her flushed cheeks.

Mrs. Jennings looked her daughter in the eye. "Did he return to his chamber, or did he stay the night?"

Mrs. Jennings had to lean close to hear the snuffled reply. "We...we stayed all the night in his chamber."

"And did you sleep?"

"After the second time, yes, a bit."

"A second time, you say? All right then, you have nothing at all to worry about. If he went for a second helping, the meat weren't spoiled."

Charlotte's watery eyes grew round with shock at her mother's frankness. She could think of nothing whatsoever to say in response.

"You're a very pretty girl, with all the attractiveness of youth and a gentle heart. I'm quite sure he meant to shower you with testaments of his regard for you."

"He called me paltry," Charlotte whispered.

"I beg your pardon?"

"He said I was a...*paltry release*," she sniffed. "And complained of my *infernal prattling*."

Mrs. Jennings' brow wrinkled with the effort of her thought. "Has your husband said that *he* thinks the marriage was a mistake? Has he made any mention of living apart?"

Charlotte shook her head. "When I told him I wanted to

go back to London, he said we'd go to his house there 'in time.'"

"That doesn't sound like a new husband ready to rid himself of a wife."

"He doesn't want to be rid of me, exactly. He wants me to be different. To not be me. And he said he wished I were more like Mary!" Charlotte had to stop to bring her hitching voice under control. "Last night, at dinner, I tried to act like her. It was awful. Mama, I can't be what I'm not."

Mrs. Jennings sat back in her chair and folded her arms across her breast.

"Then that calls for a different tack. He's married you, not your sister. You must find a way for him to prefer you for who you are. But annulment and divorce are simply out of the question. And you cannot separate after such a short time. Think of your reputation...and his!"

Charlotte looked into her teacup, staring at the leaves floating in the remaining swallow. As girls, she and Mary had played at reading tea leaves, telling their fortunes—fortunes always bright and brimming with handsome suitors and ending in an advantageous marriage. Thus it had been for Lady Middleton, who even in girlhood had one perfect foot poised to climb the social ladder. Charlotte's own future was murky.

"There's something you haven't considered, you know, my pet," Mrs. Jennings added. "Mr. Palmer is set on a seat in Parliament. Any scandal attached to him would ruin his chances."

"What sort of scandal?" Charlotte couldn't imagine Thomas doing anything scandalous.

"You must make every effort to keep up appearances."

Charlotte puzzled through the comment and sighed. "You mean I must stay with him. I cannot ever come home." She felt suddenly older, much older than her years.

Mrs. Jennings leaned forward to pat her younger daughter's arm. "I mean exactly that. Buck up, my dear. Find your backbone. Where's the Lottie I know?"

"He doesn't want the Lottie you know. He wants Mary."

"Hush, now. Enough of that. *You* are the one he married.

That's all that matters. Nothing's broken that can't be fixed with enough persistence. And you have much to be cheerful about."

Charlotte found that hard to believe. "I can't think of much, other than that you are here."

"Come now, find your smile. Why, the sun rose today, the birds are singing, and the flowers are all abloom." Mrs. Jennings' own smile carved a full three chins into the contour of her neck.

Loving her mother as she did, Charlotte made an effort and found that even the slightest of smiles did indeed make her feel better. "I suppose the tides have turned, as well?"

"Things are rarely as grim as you think, and even if they are, it's better to face them with a laugh than with tears. Tears help nothing. They only redden the eyes and make it hard to find your way. Much better to laugh than cry. And that, my dear, is the advice I have for you."

"Laugh?"

"Laughter's best, Charlotte. It masks hurt, disarms barbs, and lightens a heavy heart. We all have our share of sorrows, Lord knows. If we can laugh our way through them, they can't overtake us. Where would I have been when your dear father passed away if it hadn't been for my habit of finding the light in the midst of the heaviness?"

"Surely there was nothing to laugh about at his passing, Mama!"

"Rest his soul, certainly not. I miss him daily. But think how dark all those years since might have been if I'd stayed in my room and cried. Charlotte, it simply will not do!"

"Was there never a time you couldn't laugh?"

Mrs. Jennings stopped smiling. "I can't think of those times."

"There were, then?"

"So many years ago, love. When I do let myself think about them, I still see their precious faces. My poor babies. Little Ann, such a sweet child." Her face hardened. "Scarlet fever. And then William. The typhus. Never thought I'd laugh again. But your father got me through it, and we had Mary. And then you."

"You never speak of the others," Charlotte whispered.

"Sorrow's best forgot. Happiness is largely a choice, you know, not an accident." She folded her arms about her daughter. "Life is for the living. Your life's ahead of you, dearie."

Charlotte gave full voice to her frustration. "I cannot bear to go on like this." Her dramatic tones rivaled Mrs. Siddons' skill.

"Who said you have to go on in the same way?"

"You said I must stay."

"But not like this." Mrs. Jennings lifted Charlotte's chin. "Try good humor. A touch of patience with it. A dash of the snooty elegance your sister employs since Mr. Palmer's expressed a preference. Just a dash, mind you. And perhaps a dose of... willful misunderstanding." At her daughter's blank look, Mrs. Jennings sighed and shook her head. "Did Mr. Palmer see you at breakfast this morning?"

"He has not yet come down. He was up rather late, I gather."

"When he does appear, he will likely be in bad spirits?"

"I cannot imagine he would be cheerful under the present circumstances between us. He's likely to be in a bad temper."

"Ah, nothing's more contagious than a bad temper, they say. You must not let it infect you. Let us imagine that you are he. What might he say when first he greets you?"

"I imagine I would speak first, bidding him a good day."

"And what might you anticipate would be his response?"

Charlotte wrinkled her nose and said, "I suppose he'd ask what was good about it." The thought made her smile.

"To which you will reply as if his observation were the most humorous imaginable. Willful misunderstanding."

"Will this not irritate him?"

"Precisely. But it will give you the edge you need. Keep him on his toes, lovey." Mrs. Jennings gathered her reticule and bonnet, adjusted her shawl about her plump shoulders, and bid her daughter goodbye. "If you act happy for long enough, you'll start to feel happy. Everything will be fine. You'll see," she said and was off.

# Chapter Twenty-Three

Thomas Palmer sensed his wife before he saw her. As he stood at the sideboard contemplating a basket of rolls, he heard her intake of breath and the hushed footfalls that paused, then continued until she took her place at his side.

"Good day, Mr. Palmer."

Her husband said nothing as he tried to decide between marmalade and honey. His eyes felt gritty and seemed to fit too tightly for the size of his sockets. He was in no state to spar with her.

"Such a lovely morning, is it not?"

He glanced out the window. Clouds had gathered with the promise of more rain. "No."

"Why, whatever do you mean? The grass is an especially fine shade of green, and the roses seem in robust good health."

"Thank you for the update on the status of the landscaping."

"Oh, Mr. Palmer, you do make me laugh."

Her forced attempt could hardly be termed a laugh, he thought. Nothing about the day invited laughter. The sky was gray. Even the sheep on the far hill looked sullen. He'd denied himself an escape into the bottle of port and instead stayed awake late into the night until, exhausted, he'd stumbled to his room and slept in his clothes. He should be out canvassing now, but the mere thought of smiling at the masses or shaking hands with them was more than he could bear.

And so he stared at the honey and the marmalade, ignoring how the honey gleamed like Charlotte's curls in the sun, as they had the morning before.

"I had the most delightful visit with my mother this morning," his lady said. "She came straight from Bridgwater once she received my letter."

At this, Thomas turned, aware of the possible implications. Had they already made arrangements to carry his bride back to London, thus making a laughingstock of him and a shambles of his campaign? And leaving him alone? "A delightful visit, you say? That is hard to imagine," he replied, working to keep his voice steady even as he gripped the marmalade spoon.

The smile on Charlotte's face never faltered. "We had a most illuminating chat."

He *would* not betray his interest.

"She's off to Devonshire to see Mary now."

His grip on the silver lessened, and the spoon clattered into the bowl. "Indeed. I expect all Somerset shall go into mourning."

"What a lovely sentiment, Mr. Palmer, from a fond son-in-law! If only Mama were present to hear it!"

"Hear what?" Henry asked as he strode into the dining room. "If Thomas uttered anything even remotely close to 'lovely,' I must hear it too."

"I have no patience for this idle talk." His brother unfolded his napkin with deliberation.

"It may seem like idle talk to you, Mr. Palmer," replied his wife. "But much is accomplished by it, I assure you." Charlotte smiled at Henry, a smile that seemed especially pert to Thomas, who sat and clenched his napkin. "Mr. Palmer was merely expressing esteem for my mother," she explained. "No mother-in-law could ask for a more fond son-in-law."

"Well, they could *ask*," Thomas said darkly, "But I don't know what good it would do."

"I clearly must get up earlier," his brother said as he filled his plate with a sampling from every dish. "I seem to have missed all the fun." He sat opposite his new sister-in-law. "Charlotte, I hope the morning finds you in good spirits."

"I am quite well, thank you. Though I fear Mr. Palmer is a bit under the weather." At that, Thomas frowned, but she continued to speak, uninhibited. "I've had a busy morning. My mother stopped by early on her way from Bridgwater to Barton Park."

The mention of Barton Park caused Henry to pause as he spread a thick layer of butter on his roll. "Had I known she was traveling there, I might have asked if I could join her."

"You just came back from there," Thomas growled. Would his own brother abandon him under these difficult circumstances? Was there no family loyalty?

Henry smiled sweetly. "The Middletons are family now."

Thomas scowled. "And I suppose the fact that a certain acid-tongued lady lives in the neighborhood has nothing to do with your frequent visits?"

Charlotte looked from one brother to the other. "Do you mean Miss Browne? Oh, how delightful! She is by far the most intelligent lady of my acquaintance. And I would like another sister. My congratulations, Henry. To think that both brothers might be married in the same year!"

Both brothers stared at her, mouths agape.

"I'm sure Aunt Georgina would also enjoy having another lady in the house."

At that, Thomas choked, and Henry chuckled. "I'm sure she would," Henry said. "But the truth is that the only bond between Miss Browne and me is a rather thorny friendship."

"But that is the very best way to begin! Future felicity is best secured by shared interests and enjoyment of each other's company. A book my sister gave me says so quite emphatically."

Henry looked from her to Thomas. "Charlotte, I must say, your presence at Cleveland is a welcome change. I look forward to more felicitous mornings like this one."

"Thank you, dear brother. I find *your* company welcome,

as well."

Henry laughed. "Perhaps if Thomas spent less time inspecting the bottom of his glass and more in the enjoyment of your company, he'd be more affable come morning."

Thomas glared. To have his brother, of all people, lecture him on drink was beyond the pale. His mood had nothing to do with drink and everything to do with the contrary female seated to his right. And to add to the unwelcome conversation at his breakfast table, Georgina strode in, nodded to all, filled her plate, and seated herself next to Henry.

"No sense in asking how you slept, Thomas," she greeted him. "I've seen bears in Bankside with more sanguine expressions. Whatever is the matter with you?"

"I'm fine, thank you, Georgina." His glare did nothing to deter her, however.

"You don't look well. Your eyes are squinty."

"Nothing wrong with him that a nice blustery walk wouldn't fix," Henry said. "Isn't that right, dear brother? Always your suggestion when I've been dipping too deep."

Thomas restrained himself from uttering the first response that came to mind, for ladies were present. A walk, however, would be a convenient way to arrange for a very private talk with his new wife and to attempt to soften her hard feelings toward him. He needed to head off any fledgling plot to join her mother. "A walk about the garden is a capital idea," Thomas agreed, much to Henry's surprise. "If you'll join me, Mrs. Palmer?"

Her wide-eyed reaction was all Thomas could hope for.

~*~

Charlotte dawdled as long as she dared while fetching her old straw bonnet and gray shawl from upstairs. She could have sent her maid, but she needed the time to collect herself and prepare for the awkward tête-à-tête to come. Her vow to stay cheerful wavered. Would Thomas lecture her on how she was to behave? Send her packing after all?

Nothing prepared her, however, for his silence once she joined him. The combination of chilly company and a cold wind from the north made her draw her shawl closer. The crunch and scrape of their feet on the gravel ground her nerves. Why did he not speak? If Thomas were determined to have words with her, he might as well get on with it. They'd walked far enough from the house to assure no one would overhear. But her husband kept his eyes on the path before them, his posture and his expression equally unbending. Perhaps the reticence itself was her punishment.

Though, in truth, they'd walked only a few dozen paces, Charlotte could stand the suspense no longer. The few moments of silence became an eternity. She wheeled about in the middle of the path, startling a meadow pipit into flight. "I'd rather you said whatever it is you want to say, Mr. Palmer. Anything is better than this silence. We are away from the house now. Pray, don't keep me waiting." She wrapped her shawl tightly around herself and braced for his reply.

Thomas extended the silence a few seconds longer before answering. "I thought perhaps we could begin again," he finally replied. "Have a fresh start, so to speak."

"A fresh start?" That was not the answer she'd expected. Her emotions tumbled about, each fighting to surface. A spark of hope warred with disbelief.

"Forget yesterday. Forget anything I said at breakfast. Dash it, forget everything since the wedding." With a low bow, Thomas added, "Good morning, Mrs. Palmer. I hope you passed a peaceful night."

"I slept as soundly as you, I expect." Pasting a pleasant smile on her face took a marked effort, but she was intrigued by this new Thomas.

"Sleeping apart leads to restless nights. We are married. And I would like us to go on as married couples do."

Charlotte forced a laugh. "Taking aimless walks on windy mornings?" Perhaps her husband was taking a step onto the path to future happiness, but he needed to offer her more than a good night's sleep. Where were the heartfelt entreaties? The man held onto his words like a dragon guarded gold.

Thomas rubbed his hand across his face. "I am trying to make amends, Mrs. Palmer. Are you determined to thwart me?"

Charlotte marveled at the single vein that stood out of his forehead. "Perhaps if you could explain—." A particularly strong gust tugged her old bonnet and whipped her skirt.

"I was hoping we could converse reasonably." He closed his eyes and drew a breath before continuing. "After some thought, I realize that my words the morning after our wedding might have seemed overly harsh." He held up his hand to prevent her from interrupting. "As you know, I am not accustomed to coating my remarks with sugar. I've apologized before. If I hurt you, I am sorry. I will try not to do so again. But we cannot continue on in this manner."

Charlotte noted the way the stone walls surrounding the formal garden reached higher than her shoulder. She could barely see out to the open meadow beyond. The sweet words she longed for would not come. Her stomach clenched, and her eyes stung. She could not sustain the illusion of cheerfulness any longer. Defiantly, she lifted her chin. "If we are at odds, you are to blame."

When Thomas ran his fingers through his hair, the wind caught at the loose strands and blew them back, setting his face in a fierce, unsoftened profile. The rings below his eyes looked purple in the daylight. Charlotte stomped on the temptation to reach out to him.

"You're right, of course. In this, I am entirely at fault. Domesticity does not come easily for me." For several seconds, he stared off toward the hills. "The Cleveland of my childhood was not a happy place. My parents were ill-matched, I suppose. I had hoped to create a more congenial home for my own family. A place where my children would feel welcomed and cherished." At that, he turned to her. "That is still my wish."

"My mother always says that if wishes were horses, beggars would ride." The wind stung her cheek.

"Charlotte—."

"I, too, wished for a congenial home, Thomas. One where

I was *loved.*" She spared no room in her heart for the boy he had been. Her own heart was too crowded with pain.

Thomas clasped her arms and held her eyes with his. "And what of children?"

Charlotte looked away, remembering the hopes she'd harbored mere days before. "Like you, I dreamed of children."

"To have children, you must act as a wife." His tone was as sharp as the air.

"And you, like a husband." His look of shock failed to quiet her, for she must be heard. "Happy children need loving parents. Mary and I knew our father loved us and loved and esteemed our mother. I was only a girl when Papa died, but the strength of his love stays with me still. I would have that assurance for my children."

"Our children." Thomas pronounced it as if mere words had the power to conceive. "Of course I will love them, Lottie."

"But you do not love *me.*" Her voice broke. "I thought you did. The way you followed me about and rescued me—." She *would not* let him see her cry. "I realize now I was mistaken. Your solicitousness was—" here she swallowed hard— "was mere cordiality, your attention only duty, without passion or devotion." She turned away from him to wipe her eyes with the edge of her shawl. "I used to imagine our life together, rejoicing in each other's joys, ready to weep at each other's sorrows. I see that was a foolish, childish dream." When she glanced over her shoulder, he was watching her.

The rigid lines of Thomas's face relaxed as he reached into his coat, drew out a handkerchief, and gave it to her. "It seems I am still rescuing you."

"I am not a child. It's not rescuing that I need."

While she indecorously blew her nose, he held out a hand and cupped her chin, gently forcing her to look up at him. "I do...care about you, Charlotte. You are my wife. I have promised before God to honor you and comfort you. It troubles me to see you cry." He looked past her to Cleveland's stone face. "I admit I have little experience with the kind of love you describe."

Charlotte sniffed. He cared for her. Was that enough to build on? Her mother had said everything would be fine. *Could he learn to love her as she was?*

He offered her his arm. "Shall we continue our walk? There's something ahead I think you might like to see."

Cautiously, she took his arm again.

They were quiet as they strolled past the wide green park toward the stone outbuildings beyond the stables. The air hung heavy there with the hot scent of horses and damp straw. What of interest could there possibly be in this place, beyond a dung-hill?

Before them lay the poultry yard, where a flutter of brown hens and downy yellow chicks scratched and peeped. Nearby, a lone white chicken pecked beside a red wheelbarrow. At last, Mr. Palmer stopped on a rise overlooking a small pond. "I thought you might enjoy the new additions to the flock," he said, nodding toward a small wooden house with a door at each end. Nestled on the bank were four fat white ducks. "They seem to get on well with the hens," Thomas continued.

Charlotte felt something lighten inside her. "Oh, my!" She climbed a rung of the fence and leaned forward to see them better, caring not a bit that her legs were thus exposed. "Ducks! Four of them! Just look at their sweet pink bills. And you bought them for me? Because you knew I liked them? What a kind and generous thing to do! Wherever did you get them?"

"I had them sent from Aylesbury."

Charlotte balanced on the fence, considering. Aylesbury was nearly as far as London. Thomas must have planned far ahead for this surprise. She turned to find her husband regarding her steadily. "Oh, Thomas!" She threw her arms around his neck, knocking the bonnet from her head.

He hesitated, expression bemused, then bent to plant a soft kiss on her forehead. "I can learn to do better."

"To love?"

Thomas smiled and tugged her bonnet back in place. "You'll find me a willing pupil. Shall we plan for a lesson tonight?" He held out his hand.

Charlotte knew what he was asking. She had a choice. Deliberately, she joined her hand to his. "I also am willing," she replied, reddening at the boldness of her promise. Happiness again seemed within the realm of possibility. She glanced back at the birds. "Have you ever seen anything more adorable?"

Thomas smiled at her. "I have," he said.

# Chapter Twenty-Four

*This time, I will get it right*, Thomas vowed as he added a column of figures for the third time. Much depended upon it. His entire future happiness, in fact, hinged on the evening ahead. The morning had gone better than he'd hoped, though it had started badly. He'd nearly turned back without finishing the walk. But Charlotte's reaction to four mucky fowl had been immensely satisfying.

Tonight, he'd take his time with her. After the wedding, he'd somehow lost control. That could not happen again. From now on, he would remain calm and not let his emotions get an upper hand. He smiled, recalling Henry's ridiculous horse analogy. The comparison may have some validity. Really, the task before him was like settling a skittish colt. He needed a soothing tone, an occasional treat, and a firm but gentle hand. A master's hand. Yet his own hand seemed unsteady as the day wore on.

The rest of the afternoon was taken up with farm matters that required his careful attention. His mind, however, constantly veered away from his ledger to his wife, to the feeling of her soft body in his arms, the way her hair tickled his chin. She'd been sweetly grateful for his gift of the ducks — more grateful, in fact, than she'd seemed when he'd given her his mother's pearl necklace on their wedding day.

But she'd added her uncomfortable insistence on acknowledging his feelings. Thomas Palmer was unaccustomed to such a challenge. He kept his feelings in careful check and disliked discussing them. In social gatherings, though he doled out few words, he always kept appropriate ones at the ready. With his wife, the right words, the ones she demanded, would not come.

That fact was proven as the family sat down to dinner.

"I hope your appetite has returned, Mrs. Palmer," he announced as the first course was served. He meant only a reference to the meal before them, but Charlotte blushed deeply and kept her eyes on her soup.

"It is very fresh mackerel," Georgina stated. "They spawn off the coast in the summer months, you know."

"Are you now an authority on spawning, Aunt?" Henry asked.

"That will do, Henry." Thomas drew his brows together at the unseemly reference, but a glance at Charlotte, looking glowing in a coral-colored gown, reassured him that she was oblivious to it.

"Aristotle says that oviparous fish spawn but once a year," Georgina continued, ignoring Henry. "Fish is said to be a prolific diet too. I imagine more children are born near the coast because of that fact."

Thomas put a portion of mackerel on Charlotte's plate. She glanced at it and then at him. The remaining portion of fish on the serving plate still retained the eye—a flat, opaque eye that made Thomas uneasy.

"Salmon are running in the river," Henry said. "I saw a cluster of villagers fishing by the bridge. They were having a grand time. 'No life so happy and so pleasant as the life of a well governed angler.' Walton," he explained when Charlotte looked puzzled.

"Poachers," Thomas muttered.

"Poachers?" Charlotte asked, fork suspended.

"They steal our fish and put them on their own family's table." Thomas thinned his lips. "I'll alert the gamekeeper."

"Are there so few fish that none can be spared?" Charlotte laid down her fork.

Thomas sighed. "That is not the point. The fish are not theirs."

"All the fish in the river belong to Cleveland?"

"Wherever the river crosses the estate."

"But the same fish, once past your borders, is no longer yours? How can it be both yours and not yours?"

"She has an excellent philosophical point, Thomas." Georgina's amusement irked him, as did Henry's grin.

"And I'll thank you not to get your own *hooks* into the matter." He glared at his aunt. Henry laughed. "Your wit is as sharp as ever."

"I am intimately acquainted with *your* wit, Mr. Palmer," Charlotte replied. "Its hook is sharp indeed." She took a breath and looked about the table. "But I believe there are other virtues than cleverness. Generosity, for instance. Surely you could spare a few fish to feed the hungry."

"Pray do not paint me as a fish hoarder, Mrs. Palmer. I seek only to protect what is ours. If the men were free to take all they pleased, we'd have neither fish nor game on the table. My wit has nothing to do with it." His neckcloth grew tighter as he spoke.

Georgina lifted her glass to Charlotte. "There is much to be said for kindness, as well, dear niece. The world could use more of it. As could we."

It seemed everyone had taken Charlotte's part. Thomas took a knife to his mackerel. When had he lost control? He wasn't an ogre. He treated his tenants fairly, kept their cottages in good repair and their rents reasonable. Was he now supposed to hand out fishing poles to the rabble?

"Have you something against that fish, Thomas? By the way you're attacking it, one would think you held a grudge." Georgina tilted her head to study him. "If you don't want it, send for the next course."

Thomas hated the sense that the conversation had careened away from him. He had thought that the afternoon's talk had banished the animus between his wife and him. Evidently, their conflicts were far from resolved, despite her gratitude. He would have to increase his efforts to smooth out their relationship if he ever hoped to secure some kind of peace within his household. He waved the plate of fish away.

"The Saunders sisters left their card while you were out," Georgina continued. "I expect the morning calls on the new bride will come quickly now."

Charlotte looked up from her plate, her smile restored. "I'm sorry I missed them. How I would love to meet more ladies in the area. I shall repay the call tomorrow! Will you go with me, Aunt?"

Thomas and Henry both turned to watch Georgina's reaction to such an invitation.

"My dear girl, while I quite enjoy your company, I doubt that the Saunders sisters are likely to enjoy mine. Your success in the neighborhood will be greater the *less* I accompany you. And, to tell you the truth, I'd rather crush my foot in a door than set it in the Saunders' parlor."

"Oh." Charlotte's eyes grew round. "Is—are the family not—should I not—?"

Thomas exchanged glances with Henry. "Our neighbors will be happy to welcome you, and by all means, do return the Saunders' call."

Thomas had forgotten that a new bride necessitated an annoying influx of visitors. He resolved to find reasons to be out and about the estate for many afternoons in the future. Charlotte, however, seemed positively gleeful at the prospect. The thought of receiving and returning calls brought an added brightness to his wife's cheek and a sparkle to her eye.

Thomas wanted to bring that look to her face himself. Besides ducks and daisies, what would please her? Perhaps in a few hours, he'd find out.

He had no patience for eating the remaining courses or retreating to the library with Henry. What he wanted was to take his wife by the hand, lead her upstairs, and strip her out of the frock that clung to her in that unsettling manner. And yet, dinner progressed course by course until he and Henry finally took leave of the ladies. In the library, Thomas turned his back on his brother and paced to the window, silently cursing the daylight. The midsummer sun would not set for an hour yet.

Henry sprawled in an armchair, once again without a glass in his hand. "Whatever put the bee up your ass, Tom? You're as fidgety as a parson in a bawd house."

Thomas continued scowling at the sun. "Your similes are ever original."

"Want to ride to the Blue Anchor? New tavern maid. Hair the color of good brandy."

Thomas turned. "Has Miss Browne been so easily replaced, then? You always were a fickle sort. I wonder if you can recall the color of her hair." He watched with interest as Henry twisted in his seat.

"Miss Browne has hair the color of wheat at harvest time." Henry stared out the window. "It shines when the light hits it."

Thomas laughed at his brother's obvious discomfort. "This is a first. I never knew you to wax poetic about a woman without adding at least one *off*-color observation."

"Jane Browne, alas, is beyond reproach." Henry rose to his feet. "She is a paragon. Fiercely, completely, and utterly virtuous." He shrugged. "She possesses every virtue I lack. And if I'm not careful, she'll prove my downfall. As Charlotte has proven yours."

"I beg your pardon?" Thomas's eyebrows shot up.

"You watched her all through dinner."

"What of it?" Thomas resumed his pacing. "Can't a man look at his wife?" The hills to the west still gleamed gold, though the shadow of the cypress had lengthened.

"There's watching, and there's the way you were watching Charlotte."

Thomas opened his mouth to ask what way that was but decided instead to redirect the conversation. "You've done your share of watching Miss Browne. After last Christmas, I imagine you formed an attachment of some sort. Will you make her an offer?"

Henry grimaced. "Exactly what do I have to offer her? Nothing beyond the miserly allowance you give me." He took his turn pacing, stomping across the rug in front of the fire. "She'll marry a better man than I someday."

"Perhaps she doesn't want a better one." Thomas was intrigued by the flash of hope that lightened his brother's face before he shuttered himself again.

"I don't deserve her," Henry said softly.

Thomas felt the stirring of something akin to pity, an emotion he very rarely felt for anyone, but particularly not for Henry. "You could change, you know. Many paths lie open to you. Earn a living. All is not lost. You can have her, if you want her."

"You couldn't have Mary Jennings."

Thomas was taken aback. A year ago, he would have cut his brother down with knife-edged retort, then withdrawn in offense. But now? This night, he had trouble remembering young Mary Jennings' charms. Had her hair been as rich a gold as Lottie's?

"I'm sorry, Tom. Someone should gag me." Henry watched his brother warily.

Thomas clapped him on the shoulder. "The way you argue, Henry, you *should* be a barrister." Beyond them, the sky exploded in red, pink, and purple. The long evening had, at last, come to an end.

~*~

The after-dinner hour passed all too quickly for Charlotte. Sitting in the drawing room calmly sipping tea proved beyond her capacity. She could think only of the night that lay ahead.

"Good Lord, girl," Georgina exclaimed. "If you clutch that teacup any harder, it will shatter in your hand. Between you and

Thomas, I despair of ever again having a decent conversation. Whatever is the matter with *you*?"

Charlotte stared at her cup, wishing herself ten years older. "I beg your pardon, Aunt Georgina. I'm not usually so rude. There's nothing wrong. Truly." She certainly couldn't explain what the problem was, not to Thomas's maiden aunt.

"Nonsense. You're perching on the edge of your seat as if it's full of hot coals, and you've glanced out the window at the sunset every three minutes. I'm aware that we have little in common, but I'd appreciate at least an occasional nod while I talk to myself."

Could she have hurt the lady's feelings by her inattention? That would never do. "It's only the effort of adjusting to a new life that puts me at sixes and sevens. What were you saying?" Charlotte placed her cup and saucer carefully on a nearby table and directed her full attention to the dialogue.

Georgina shook her head. "No sense in trying to have a conversation, with you looking like a criminal on the dock."

Charlotte laughed at the image since it was all too apt.

"It will get better, you know. Once you adjust, you'll find that Cleveland has much to recommend it."

"Cleveland is most welcoming." Absentmindedly, Charlotte plucked at the beading on her skirt until a thread came undone. She was left cupping six tiny pale beads in her hand. Those loose beads, once part of a pretty petal and now scattered and useless, made her sigh.

"Now, now. None of that. Nothing's broken that can't be mended. You *can* tell me, you know. You'll find I'm quite a champion at keeping secrets."

Charlotte tilted her head and regarded her. "I can't imagine you have secrets. You seem very straightforward."

Georgina's laugh burst out with the force of a bellows. "That is my nature, Charlotte. But even I have secrets. Surely you've picked up on them from Henry's jibes. There's a reason I choose not to marry. I find men lack some essential qualities."

"Oh." Charlotte's brows drew together as she balanced

the beads in her palm. "But you *do* like Thomas and Henry. I know you do."

"I love both my nephews. But if I were able to choose a partner in life, it would be a woman." She gazed steadily at her nephew's wife.

Charlotte puzzled for a moment, colored, then smiled. "I can't say I blame you. Women *are* easier to understand. I must admit being married to Thomas is somewhat – confusing."

"I can imagine," Georgina said drily. "I've known Thomas since he was an infant. He was a fussy baby, easily overstimulated. Shy. Nothing like his brother. Sophia always preferred her fair-haired boy. Thomas takes after his father, *my* brother. Oh, not in temperament, but in looks. Sometimes I wonder if Thomas might have been different if he'd had the luxury of being the cossetted second son instead of the responsible eldest. Or if he hadn't been in the carriage that upset on the coast road when he was but a tot." She patted Charlotte's shoulder. "Ah, never mind. He's a good man, deep down. He feels much more than he lets on. But you must stand up to him, or he'll bully you. You have to teach people how to treat you, Charlotte."

Charlotte pondered that advice as she climbed the stairs.

~*~

It would be different this time, wouldn't it? Forewarned was forearmed, so to speak. Charlotte knew what to expect in marital rights. Although her mother's incomplete instructions and her sister's horrifying hints had warned her about the wedding night, the experience itself had added some needed information. She would not be taken by surprise.

And she knew to moderate her expectations. What was to come would be a meeting of bodies, not a melding of souls. They would have marital relations, not true amorous congress. She'd not be drawn into wishing for more.

She would never again be that same Lottie, the one who thought her happiness would continue unabated because she had married the man of her dreams. Sadly, the man she had married bore little resemblance to the man she had believed him to be –

*willfully* believed him to be, against all evidence to the contrary. Thomas Palmer was what he presented himself as: an ambitious, insensitive man who disliked company and was at his best when left alone.

That he was a good man, she did not dispute. That he felt more than he showed, she could not be sure. He'd said he hoped for a peaceful household. She'd seen little peace thus far. And he'd said he could learn to love. She would latch onto that hope, though in the minutes since she'd left Aunt Georgina to retire upstairs, Charlotte wondered if perhaps those were idle words uttered only to secure the desired result: her in his bed.

But he *had* bought her the ducks, ordered specially all the way from Aylesbury. He had remembered her fondness for them and given them to her before any mention of marital rights. That act must prove some level of affection—or at least, of attention, did it not? She wasn't sure.

Charlotte *was* sure that Thomas Palmer wanted what all men wanted: power, position, an heir. One cannot secure an heir by oneself. Would it be right to bring children into a house full of uncertainty?

She smoothed the fine cotton of her night rail. The summer air had cooled as night drew on. Once Thomas arrived, Charlotte would have his warmth. That she remembered well.

The faint knock on the dressing room door was expected, but still, she startled and reached for a wrap, needing another layer between herself and her husband. Then she opened the door to him.

He had removed his cravat and coat. His hair looked mussed as if he'd run his fingers through it—not at all his usual polished appearance. Charlotte lowered her head and stepped back to let him in. Thomas paused just inside the door, looking down at her as she fidgeted with the white ribbons at her neck. Did he expect her to go to him, kiss him? She was at a loss for what to do next.

*You have to teach him how to treat you.*

All right, then. She knew how she wanted to be treated.

Like a wife. And so she straightened her shoulders, dropped the wrap, and held out her arms. But she did not smile at him. The muscles in her face had frozen.

Thomas hesitated only a few seconds before he closed the distance between them and drew her close. "You feel as rigid as a fireplace poker," he whispered in her ear. "Is it as bad as all that?"

He, at least, was smiling. With one finger, he traced her jawline from her ear to her chin, then tilted her chin up. His mouth on hers was gentle, not pushing or pressing at all. Her own lips curved up in pleasure. Kissing was so very nice.

He pulled her closer, close enough that she could feel the heat of him through her thin gown. This sensation, also, was pleasant, comforting. She loved being held, loved the memory of strong arms that rocked her when she was sad or hurt or lonely.

But Thomas was her husband, and his hands were even now stroking her back as he began to kiss her neck, a ticklish and twitchy sensation that made breathing difficult. Now his arms felt more like trusses. She pushed against his chest.

He raised his head. "Something the matter?"

"I like when you hold me," she said.

"I like holding you."

"Could we—could you *just* hold me? For a little while?"

He relaxed his grip. "If you wish."

They stood motionless in her room, a rather anonymous room with nothing of her own to distinguish it save her hairbrushes and garments. Charlotte closed her eyes to her surroundings and let herself lean against the crisp linen of his shirt, feel his warm chest, and listen to the steady beat of his heart. Little by little, her own shoulders relaxed, and she ventured to slip her arms around his back, spreading her fingers wide against the muscles, which tensed as she caressed him.

But Thomas remained still, letting her move her hands at will, over his ribs, down his sides. As she stroked, she gained courage and rubbed herself against him, much like a cat might rub against its owner. The sensation of her chest against his was more than pleasant. When he raised a hand to tug the ribbons at her neck, her breath caught, but she did not move away. Nor did she move away when he dipped his hand inside the gaping neckline or when he bent his head to taste the flesh he'd bared. *This* she welcomed.

Charlotte's heart pounded when he picked her up in his arms and laid her on the bed. And when he came to join her, she clasped him to her and smiled.

~*~

Thomas was about to burst. Never before had his will been so taxed. For eons, he held back, striving with every fiber of his being to woo his skittish wife, calm her and soothe her, trying to undo the damage he'd done a few nights before. He had kissed and caressed until he was afraid he might wear off her tender skin, all the while waiting for some signal from her to proceed.

The effort just might kill him.

She kept running her hands over him, maddeningly close to where he needed them most but always skimming past the critical point. And even though she'd welcomed him into her room and her bed and remained docile enough as he'd doffed his clothes, still, after all the foreplay, she lay with her legs together. There was only so much kissing and petting that a man could bear.

Slowly he raised himself over her, nudging a knee between her thighs. When she finally parted her legs, he sank in with a groan, keeping just enough sense about himself not to crush her. He kept himself on the knife-edge of pain and pleasure, watching her face, noting the flickers of panic, surprise, and budding arousal until he could wait no longer and surrendered to his release.

# Chapter Twenty-Five

Charlotte was careful not to disturb Thomas as she slipped out from under his arm and untangled herself from the twisted sheets. His breathing remained deep and even. Snatching her nightgown from the bedpost, she retreated to the dressing room.

In the early morning light, she filled the washstand basin and dipped a cloth in the cool water, sliding it over her breasts, under her arms, between her legs. As she washed, she looked down, curious to see if the change in herself showed somehow. Slowly she turned and examined her form in the oval mirror by the door. The glass was tilted slightly downward on its stand, so her reflection appeared as if seen by someone gazing at her from a slight height.

Charlotte thought that this must be how Thomas saw her. As she stared, she lifted a hand to trace the pale skin, the swell of a breast, the ribs and hollows, the soft curve of her hip. She saw herself in a new way, not as a form to be dressed up and paraded, but as a woman, complete as she was. Desirable, even. Her lips curved, and she smiled knowingly at her reflection. Thomas may not love her, not yet, but he wanted her. It was a start.

Nights over the next week proved increasingly enlightening and stimulating. Each time she joined with Thomas, she grew bolder, more sure of herself and her wifely status. He'd never called her efforts paltry again. In fact, some nights, she wore him out.

Summer *days* at Cleveland, however, left much to be desired. She contented herself with writing letters, visiting the village, and walking about the estate. During the day, she saw her husband only at meals. At night, they shared a bed, but no conversation.

"Will you be going into the village today, Mr. Palmer?" she asked one morning at breakfast, seeing him in riding clothes.

"Only as far as the farrier." He did not look up from the paper.

"We could take the carriage together. I would like to take some things to the village women."

He looked up long enough to answer. "The other horses are needed in the fields."

"Perhaps an outing later this afternoon?"

He laid his napkin on the table. "I can't go gallivanting about the countryside like a popinjay on holiday, Charlotte. The accounts require my attention. The estate does not run itself. If you need company, can you not visit someone nearby?"

Charlotte struggled with her reply. The standard welcome visits were over. The flood of calls after the wedding had dwindled to a drip. To her dismay, none of her acquaintances had bloomed into friendships. And Thomas steadfastly resisted receiving visitors socially, though a stream of men who spoke of business and politics frequented the library.

"The Saunders sisters visited yesterday. They stayed only a quarter hour and didn't even take off their gloves." She bit her lip. "I'd hoped we could be close, but they seem content with their own set."

"You have your little sketches."

"I do. But it would be pleasant to have someone to talk to."

Thomas rose and planted a kiss on her forehead. "I must be off. Georgina should be back from her morning walk soon. She always has something to say."

After Thomas left, Charlotte gathered her sketchbook and

pencils and strolled outside. The sun had burned off the morning mist, leaving the day clear. Blinking against the glare, she shaded her eyes as she looked about for the stark figure of her husband's aunt. Yet the gardens were deserted save for herself and the kitchen cat. And even the cat kept its distance. She had to creep toward it to get close enough to capture its form.

It was a scrawny thing with huge ears, an unblinking green stare, and patchy tortoiseshell fur. The cook tolerated the beast because tabby cats were supposed to bring good luck. Charlotte reserved judgment on that matter.

This morning, she felt restless as she cast a critical eye at the sketch she'd begun. She'd captured the beast's shape rightly enough and the pert angle of the ears, but its smug expression eluded her. She needed to get this illustration exactly right. The adventures of Catrina the Scullery Cat would be the next set of stories for her nephews.

The cat flicked its tail. Charlotte stirred restlessly on the stone bench. She couldn't fault the day: it was bright but cool, with a steady breeze to rattle the sketch paper. The plantings in the walled garden were at their peak. Red and white roses and spears of blue larkspur bloomed against a rich green backdrop of sculpted yew hedges. She'd painted the flowers, and the purple hills beyond them, and the orchard, and Plucky, Lucky, Plumpy, and Millicent, her delightful ducks. She was running out of subjects, and here it was only June.

Catrina lazily lifted a black and gray paw and washed it thoroughly, ignoring Charlotte entirely. She put pencil to paper and rapidly sketched the pose, but failed to finish before the animal arched its back and stretched, then sauntered down the garden path, tail in the air.

Not even the cat cared to keep her company.

Charlotte laid down her pencil and sighed. Again she squinted at the sun, now high in the brilliant blue sky. It must be nearly noon. Surely Aunt Georgina had returned from her walk by now. Since she was the only other lady in residence, Charlotte had tried to tag along on the elder's morning constitutionals but had been firmly rebuffed. It seemed Aunt Georgina's friends were not interested in expanding their acquaintance either.

With nothing left to draw, Charlotte packed up her papers and pencils and ambled back toward the house, skirting the high hedges that bordered the walled garden on one side. As she passed by the north corner, however, she heard a distinct rustling and breaking of branches. The gardener must be trimming the new shoots, smoothing the top and sides of the hedge so all parts remained perfectly uniform. She was about to shout a greeting to Mr. Jackson, who sometimes paused in his work to tell her the names of the flowers that were new to her.

But she heard the unmistakable sound of ladies' laughter — not giggles but low, throaty sounds from two voices. The laughter came from what seemed to be *inside* the hedge.

Charlotte pressed her face into the foliage, twigs scratching her cheeks and tearing at her hair. A gap extended between the hedgerows. She pushed further, straining to see. Through the tangled greenery, she could see little: only confusing glimpses of a woman's bare legs, a bent arm, a curved back, a braid of hair.

The hair was the dark, rich brown common of the Palmer line.

Charlotte clapped a hand over her mouth to muffle the tiny squeaks that persisted in escaping from her mouth as she backed out of the hedge, heedless of the way the branches snagged her gown. Without looking back, she ran to the terrace. The startling images burned into her memory.

~*~

The drawing room was overly bright, with midday sunlight bouncing off the yellow walls. Charlotte's stomach churned. Not wanting anyone to see her in this state, she hoped to hide there until she calmed herself. Leaning her forearm on the mantle, she buried her face in the crook of her arm, trying to make sense of what she thought she had seen.

"Charlotte."

There was no mistaking the firm voice behind her. Charlotte lifted her head and turned. Aunt Georgina stood between her and the door.

"You left these in the garden." Georgina held up the pencils and sketches. "I quite like the one of the cat."

"Thank you," Charlotte whispered, trying to banish the image of Georgina's own back arched in the same pose the cat had assumed. Hesitantly, without raising her eyes to the aunt's, Charlotte reached for the drawings, keeping as far away from the woman as possible.

"Oh, dear. I take it you saw. I suppose it was inevitable, with you gadding about the garden. I did warn you, you know."

"I beg your pardon?" Charlotte pulled her arms back.

"When we were discussing marriage. I told you I didn't care for men."

"I remember." And she did remember, with painful clarity, all the hints she had failed to fully comprehend. Thomas's disapproving comments, Henry's teasing, even her own mother's relentless interrogation of Aunt Georgina came back to Charlotte, making her cheeks burn. Suspecting and seeing had been entirely different things.

"Ah, well, water under the bridge, so to speak," Georgina sighed. "I don't need to ask you not to repeat anything you saw, I take it?"

Charlotte shook her head. She would not even know what words to use to describe the bits she thought she'd seen. Keeping the settee between herself and this alarming woman, she edged away from the fireplace. "Thank you for returning the pictures. I'll take them up to my room now." Again she reached out.

Georgina continued looking through the sheaf of drawings. "Do you ever draw people?"

Charlotte shook her head again. Imagine drawing those twining limbs! "No. Only animals. Cats, ducks, rabbits. I make up animal stories to entertain my sister's children."

"These are illustrations? Why, I had no idea you possessed a talent."

Should she feel embarrassed or affronted? Unsure, Charlotte remained silent.

"Mr. Nash mentioned you'd been looking for me earlier."

Charlotte nodded, still struggling to find the right thing to say.

"Was there a particular reason?"

She must say something. "Yes—but no, not really. I was merely seeking some company. If you'll excuse me—."

"Dear girl, I really can't let you go when you seem upset."

"I'm quite all right now. The sun was hot, you see, and I had forgotten to bring my bonnet. There is little shade in that part of the garden, at least near the bench where I was sketching, and then I rather lost track of time while I was drawing Catrina, so I'm afraid I became overheated, and then perhaps I moved too quickly in returning to the house...." Charlotte could hear herself chattering on but was unable to stop the rush of words until Aunt Georgina's eyebrows reached a disquieting height.

"You do go on, don't you? A nervous habit, I suspect. Come to think of it, you provide a nice balance to Thomas, who can scarce spare more than a sentence at a time. Come now, sit down before you fall down."

When Georgina seated herself in a delicate carved rosewood side chair, Charlotte reluctantly sank onto the settee, dislodging two yew leaves that drifted onto her lap.

Georgina tilted her head and watched as Charlotte brushed more leaves from her hair. "So, Charlotte, you sought female company today? The Saunders sisters did not deign to include you in their tête-à-têtes?"

"The Misses Saunders returned my call yesterday." Charlotte laced her fingers in her lap. "They stayed only a short time."

"Consider yourself fortunate. They're supercilious, mean-spirited vipers. If they'd stayed long enough to gossip, you would have found your ears filled with poison."

It was Charlotte's turn to sigh. She did not wish to speak ill of her new neighbors, but their slight still stung. If only Cleveland lay closer to Bath, where many of her London friends gathered. If only her sister would come to visit. If only this aunt were more approachable and comprehensible, less severe and odd. "At Barton Park, there are always outings and guests. One is never without a companion. There seems to be little society here."

"Poor Charlotte. While conversing with our neighbors is hardly my ideal pastime, I can see you're lonely. Where is Thomas?"

"In the village."

"And Henry?"

"Out."

"I see. And you've already made the acquaintance of the neighborhood, with no luck in finding companionship. Is there no one you can invite to Cleveland?"

"My sister is entertaining a large number at Barton Park, my friends are with their families at Brighton or Bath, and my mother is staying with my great-aunt Julia, who is ill. She expects to remain with her at New Hill throughout the summer." Charlotte drew her brows together.

"No friends or acquaintances who might come to walk and sketch with you?"

Charlotte brightened at the thought. "There is perhaps one. I shall write to her this afternoon."

"Capital. In the meantime, you really have no option but me. Shall *we* converse?"

Charlotte's eyes widened. Her faint hopes of escaping the awkward conversation faded entirely away.

"There's much news. The London paper arrived this morning. The Corsican Fiend is still loose in France."

"Oh, dear." Charlotte had no idea what she should do with such news. "I'm afraid I do not read the paper."

"That we shall need to remedy. One must strengthen the female mind by enlarging it. You must keep up with what's happening in the world. Do you read anything at all?" From her expression, it seemed Aunt Georgina doubted Charlotte knew how.

"Oh, I very much like to read! When I'm in London, I regularly visit the lending library. I lately read *Waverley*. The descriptions of the Highlands! And Edward—I suppose you might call him the hero—so tragic and romantic. Have you read it, Aunt?"

"I must admit my ignorance. It is a novel?"

"Do you not read novels?"

"I do not. Such works instill false sentiments and mar the reader's taste for loftier prose."

"Oh, no. Quite the contrary." Charlotte forgot her discomfort in her defense of the books she loved. "To truly know the human heart, one has only to read a novel. A novel can transport one to Italy, to Scotland, to any number of wondrous and exciting places with the most perfect of heroes."

"That is precisely the problem, dear girl. The scenes are so highly wrought, the men so improbably dashing, that any reader who loses herself in those pages will be discontented with life as it is. Much better to read Greek."

Charlotte had no interest in Greek. She thought it best not to say so. "Perhaps," she said slowly, puzzling out her thoughts, "Because novels are 'highly wrought' as you say, they are more true than real."

Georgina stared at Charlotte for some seconds without blinking. "There's more to you than meets the eye. Thomas had best watch his step." She rose. "Again, thank you for not mentioning our, ah, meeting this morning. I shall see you at dinner."

Charlotte brushed the drift of yew leaves from her lap and followed her out the door.

# Chapter Twenty-Six

*My dear Miss Browne,*

*I hope this letter finds you well. My sister has written to say that you were lately dining at Barton Park and looked in good health. I was glad to hear it.*

*I very much enjoyed our friendship and often think fondly of the hours we spent sketching together. It would be a great pleasure to renew our acquaintance. Could you perhaps spare some weeks for a visit here at Cleveland? We have paths for walking and views for drawing. The countryside this time of year is lovely indeed, and the gardens are at their peak.*

*Mr. Henry Palmer asks that I send his regards. Please send my own regards to the Reverend Browne and to Mrs. Browne.*

*Yours, &c.*

*Charlotte Palmer*

Miss Jane Browne arrived at Cleveland in time for the celebration of Wellington's triumph at Waterloo. The coach she arrived in flew flags and bore streamers in honor of the victory. Atop the hill above the local village, bonfires blazed. The entire neighborhood was in a state of elation.

All but one. Thomas Palmer hated the disruption to his routine. His married life had only recently settled into a comfortable pattern: a solitary stroll about the estate, then a brief breakfast with his chatty wife, meetings regarding the management of Cleveland or his run for Parliament, perhaps a ride or visit to the village tavern with Henry, dressing for dinner and dining with the family, banter with his brother, then the agreeable effort to beget an heir. Pleasant. Predictable.

But since the arrival of Miss Browne, all was in disarray. His wife planned outings. His brother no longer sought his company. Evening meals were a welter of talk and laughter, and after dinner came cards and music and more talk. The superficial babble had driven his aunt to visit one of her bookish lady acquaintances.

On top of it all, Charlotte seemed set on matchmaking. She teased and giggled and found every opportunity to throw his brother and Miss Browne together. Charlotte had insisted on discussing the couple the night before instead of letting Thomas sleep, as he was wont to do after the climax of the evening.

"Leave off your meddling, Lottie. Henry has no intention of marrying now. Besides, they do not suit," he'd ordered her. "She's as serious and sharp-tongued as Lord Liverpool, and if Henry ever had a serious day in his life, it never lasted past the dinner hour."

"They're perfect together," she'd claimed. "Miss Browne is calm and careful in all she does. And Henry's mind is every bit as quick as hers. They have such delightful rows together."

Not for the first time, Thomas was baffled by his bride. "Why ever would their arguments be a matter of delight?"

She'd laughed at him as if he were two pecks short of a bushel. "Arguments show they care. If they were indifferent, then they would be coldly polite to each other. But they're anything but indifferent! Do you not watch them? They almost glow in their passions, Mr. Palmer! Think what fun they shall have making it up to each other."

The sudden vision of his brother and Miss Browne passionately coupled made Thomas squirm in the bed he shared with his wife. "Even though he's formed an attachment, it is impossible. He has no means, Charlotte. Not until he secures a position."

She'd only smiled. "With the will come the means. Just you wait, Mr. Palmer. You'll see."

This morning, in the stark light of day, he *could* see his brother with Miss Browne on the terrace beyond his office window. They stood very close indeed.

Inside the office, not even the solidity of the estate accounts could lift Thomas's spirits much. He regarded the documents mounded on his desk. The dowry money had been put to good use. More debts had been settled, structures repaired, new fields cleared. But wheat prices were falling. Trade was down. And as soldiers returned home to the countryside, more of his pheasants and rabbits were ending up in a village stew pot. His gamekeeper was at his wits' end. Something had to be done.

Shooting season was nearly upon them, and Parliament would soon come to a close. Within weeks, he expected important political connections to arrive at Cleveland and hunt birds. Mr. Weston, in particular, Thomas counted on to help secure support for his campaign. Josiah Weston was a powerful voice in Parliament. Their association came about from their mutual membership in the Bath and West agricultural society, where they agreed on the importance of fertilizer. They had bonded over manure, a topic that naturally led to politics.

Controlling the loss of game on the estate was paramount to Thomas's election. To that end, he had his gamekeeper regularly patrol Cleveland's perimeter. The walls and fencing must remain intact. Thomas Palmer believed in robust boundaries.

He had already drafted a notice to be posted about the property:

*Game*
*Whereas in former Seasons the Game upon the estate of Cleveland, the property of Thomas Palmer, Esq., have been much harmed by unqualified persons, without the leave of the Proprietor, notice is hereby given that any and all persons who hereafter sport on said estate*

*without leave will be prosecuted as trespassers, as well as under any and all statutes and qualifications requiring a game certificate.*

Yet the notice now waiting on his desk would have little effect on those who could not read. Thomas detested the only solution to the problem. He must confront the miscreants face to face in the village. It was the only way to ensure the poaching would stop.

For weeks he had put off the task. Inspecting cottages was one thing. Bearding the lion in its lair was quite another. Today, however, was the day to act. This morning, the cart waited. His resolve was firm. The problem would be nipped in the bud before it could flower and spread seeds of rebellion throughout Somerset. His woods would be alive with birds to shoot once more.

A noise from the hallway distracted him from his resolution.

"Mr. Palmer? Are you at leisure? I saw the dog-cart out front. Where are you going? And could we tag along?" His wife stood in the doorway to the library, just beneath the *Hoc Age* inscription, as if the family motto might urge him to accept her plea. "It's such a lovely day. I'm sure that Miss Browne would enjoy a ride in the countryside. She's quite keen on nature, you know. And can you believe she has never seen the cliffs in Cheddar?"

Thomas could believe it. He opened his mouth to refuse. The words were ready on his tongue. His resolve was firm. He meant to have this village matter settled promptly. Charlotte's presence would not aid that end.

And yet, the thought of confronting the poachers in their homes made his stomach sour. These were men he'd known all his life. The onerous task could, perhaps, be made easier with Charlotte along. His wife felt at ease in all company. She already knew the names of some of the villagers. And she was still standing at the library door.

Yet he hesitated to extend the invitation. Adding three

people would unnecessarily crowd the vehicle. "I had no plan to tour the countryside, Mrs. Palmer. I am a man of business."

"What business takes you abroad today?" Without waiting to be invited, she swept past him and made herself at home, settling into a deep-seated leather chair that practically swallowed her. He supposed he would have to help her rise before he could evict her.

"I mean to warn the village men against poaching game in the park."

"That again." She shook her head. "So much fuss over a few fish and fowl."

"They are my fish and fowl."

"The men are only trying to feed their families. Mrs. Yates has five little ones now."

Apparently, his wife was now intimately acquainted with not only the names but the personal lives of the villagers. The name *Yates* stirred a dim memory, one that flickered at the edge of his consciousness but would not take shape. "You have visited them too?"

She nodded. "I have visited all the families. Some men are only recently home from the wars, with no pension to show for years of service." Charlotte struggled to sit upright in the massive chair. "Their families are in a bad way."

"There is an easy solution. Let them work. I've expanded our fields." The fact irked him, for the plummet in grain prices made the hope of a fat profit less likely by the day.

"The wage you pay no longer supports them, especially as they have more children."

"Their wages have doubled!"

"But everything costs them three times as much!"

"You've been talking to my aunt." Thomas rubbed his forehead. *Two* women with opinions in the family were entirely too many.

Charlotte nodded. "She used to read the papers to me after dinner while you and Henry smoked. And now I read them myself."

"Could you not sew or something?"

"A woman must be educated if she is to be a proper companion to her husband. And my knowledge of the plight of common people, Aunt Georgina said, is woefully lacking. As Mrs. Palmer of Cleveland, it is my duty to look after those under our care." She lifted her chin in a very un-Charlotte-like gesture. "I take my responsibilities seriously."

Thomas blinked. His wife had a point. The lady of the manor did indeed have an obligation to the lower classes. He was doubly glad, however, that his aunt had recently gone off to visit her "friend" in Halifax and thus would encourage no more uncomfortable opinions. He squirmed under Charlotte's steady regard. "What would you have me do, Lottie?" Sensing his control slipping, he stalked across the room. "I am trying my best to help Cleveland thrive, not only for the present but for generations."

At that, Charlotte blushed. The pointed reference was not enough to dissuade her, though, much to Thomas's annoyance. "Mr. Yates undoubtedly hopes to secure his children's future too," she said. "But they struggle to pay the rent on their cottage, for his leg injury pains him. Could you not lower the rent, given the circumstances?"

"You understand nothing about the management of the estate. If I lower the rent, I lower our income."

Her voice was small. "I don't need very much."

How did a straightforward plan to confront thieving villagers evolve into a debate on the distribution of wealth? His wife somehow turned every conversation sideways. "That is not the point, Mrs. Palmer. If they want more income, they must work more."

"But Mr. Palmer, there are those who have lost arms, legs, eyes. Some have lost their minds. Pray, how are *they* to work?"

The discussion was getting more difficult by the minute. This was a straightforward matter, and one his wife obviously misunderstood. It was a strain to maintain his patience, but Thomas was proud of his calm, well-reasoned response. "You said the Yates family has children. Are there no sons?"

"Yes, but none old enough to work the fields. And some families have no son. What of them?"

Thomas was spared from formulating a reply by the appearance of his brother. Ignoring Thomas, Henry turned to Charlotte. "Did he agree, then? Miss Browne is most eager to see the sights, and I would hate to disappoint her." He turned to grin at Thomas. "I'm sure you will enjoy the company of two such lovely ladies. When can we be off?"

Charlotte bit her lip. "It seems Mr. Palmer is set upon visiting the village to confront the poor, defenseless folk about missing fish and birds. Evidently, he counts them daily."

Henry laughed. "I would not put that past him. Thomas is meticulous in all his accounting. I wager he can tell you to the penny exactly how much he paid for that very pretty new frock you are wearing."

Thomas could, in fact, having looked over the bill. He'd be dashed if he would admit to it, however. "I am merely going to the village to have some words with the men regarding the rise in poaching on the estate." Both his wife and his brother looked at him with such appeal that he hesitated. "If you're determined to come along, then, by all means, join me. It's about time you took some notice of matters regarding Cleveland."

His decision made, Thomas strode toward the door, pausing only long enough to haul Charlotte from her seat.

The road to the village curved about hills and dipped into boggy vales. About him, the ladies exclaimed over clumps of harebell and tansy, the song of the skylark, the warble of the wren, the brilliance of the sky. They noted at length how the downs were dappled over with the shadows of stray clouds. When they passed a thatched windmill, its ragged sails creaking on its circuit, one would have thought they'd found an architectural wonder. After a quarter-hour of their gushing, Thomas began to feel as if he shared a cart with a nest of nattering poets. Thank God the village was around the next bend.

Throughout the trip, Henry had looked only at Miss

Browne, alternately nodding and smiling as she expounded on the blessings of the gentle breeze. When Thomas sniffed, he smelled only grass and a hint of sheep. His brother was utterly besotted. There was no other explanation.

They made a study in contrasts. Her manners were reserved, while Henry's were free and easy. If truth be told, Henry was the prettier of the two, looking much like their mother, with thick, fair hair and regular features. Miss Browne was too sharp, too angular, too intense in every way to be anything as gentle as pretty. But when she turned to look at Henry, Thomas thought, for just that moment, she might be beautiful.

His wife leaned out of the cart in her enthusiasm over a miserable pile of mossy rocks. "Oh, Mr. Palmer, I daresay it's a ruin! There, by that tree! Perhaps it's an altar of old or the remains of an ancient castle wall? How wonderful." She turned her bright face to him, hoping, he supposed, for affirmation.

Henry stifled a laugh.

Thomas glanced at the pile in question. It was but a straggling heap of unhewn stone, a tumbled sheep-fold. He remembered it had once been the favorite resting place for an old shepherd who had lived in these parts. The man and his dog would sit there at the end of the day. Both had been dead for years. Thomas did not correct Charlotte's mistaken fancy, for to do so would have dimmed her smile. "Perhaps we'll explore it another day," he said instead, briefly touching her gloved hand. "We have business to attend to."

They passed the church, crossed over the stone bridge, and entered the village proper. Ahead, a weary-looking woman trudged along the lane shouldering yoked buckets, and a few scraggly boys chased a cat behind a barrel. The smoke from the blacksmith's forge rose thick above the line of thatched and whitewashed cottages. In front of one smoke-stained home in the village center, a girl and her mother sat weaving willow baskets while a grubby toddler played with a puppy in the dust nearby. The puppy appeared to have mange.

Charlotte clasped her hands and beamed. "Why, there is

Mrs. Yates! This is ever so charming, is it not, Miss Browne? Look about you! It is just as the poets expound on. Humble, rustic folk living in harmony with nature!"

To himself, Thomas muttered, "Rather the willful ignorance of country people living disordered lives." To the woman, he said, "Good morning, Mrs. Yates. Is Mr. Yates at home?"

Without stopping her weaving, Mrs. Yates jerked her head at the splintered door to her left. "Aye, that he is, Mr. Palmer. Right inside. And good day to you, Mrs. Palmer. Nice to see you again so soon."

"I'd like a word with him, if I may." Thomas climbed down from the carriage and stood before the door, which appeared to be caked with something he hoped was mud.

"Oh, don't stand on ceremony, Mr. Palmer. Go on in. He's resting up a bit after a morning's fishing."

Thomas straightened his shoulders before he entered. The interior was dark since the cottage windows were small and the walls thick. Central to the room was a stone hearth where a kettle simmered above a low fire. Furnishings were sparse: two benches, a battered sideboard, and, next to the hearth, a wooden armchair upon which the man himself sat. He was a veritable mountain of a man, over six feet, with rust-colored hair and beard, arms like tree limbs, and well-muscled legs — or, one leg. As Thomas walked closer, he saw the other leg was withered.

Indeed, Mr. Yates was resting, and the fruit of his labor lay displayed on the rough-hewn table in the center of the room: what looked to be an eight-pound chub.

"G'day, Mr. Palmer, sir. Lovely day, in't it?" Mr. Yates rose slowly from his chair, favoring the weak leg.

Thomas tried not to stare at it. "Good day, Mr. Yates. I see you've been fishing."

Mr. Yates said nothing, though he did lurch in front of the table, partially obscuring the fish from view. Outside the open door, Thomas could hear the toddler giggling and the girl chatting to his wife about the best places to find willow canes.

Mr. Yates looked him in the eye. "I got me five bairns

what to feed, Mr. Palmer. My lad Jackie, now, he's growing like a weed, he is. Edwin too. And you see Mabel and Tessie outside there. And the newest one in the cradle."

"Fine children," Thomas allowed.

"We hope you and Mrs. Palmer will be blessed yourself right soon. Be good to have young ones at Cleveland again."

Thomas was struck with a clear memory of wading in the creek at Cleveland with Henry and some village boys. Michael Yates had been one of them. He'd been a tall, robust lad, a year or two older than Thomas, strong enough to pull down limbs in the orchard to let the rest pick apples. He'd been a fast runner, too, with his long legs.

Closing his eyes to the still visible fish tail, Thomas bowed slightly. "Thank you for your well-wishes, Michael. I'll be on my way now."

"Thank'ee, Tom," he thought he heard Yates say.

Taking his leave of Mrs. Yates and ushering the group back into the carriage, Thomas turned to the coast road, blocking unpleasant memories of the route. On the side of a cliff overlooking the sea, he recalled, stood a medieval chapel cut into the hillside, walls still standing, though the interior was overgrown and full of rubble. Charlotte would be delighted.

As he rode, he gave up the notion of posting notices on his land.

# Chapter Twenty-Seven

Despite the delights of warm weather and enchanting patches of meadow saffron and sowbread, Charlotte was lonely once Miss Browne returned home. The daylight hours stretched out empty again with only the village women with whom to converse. And while she was happy to pass the time of day with them, provide remedies when they fell ill and share baskets of fruit from the orchards or pies from the kitchen, she missed her family. Mrs. Jennings had left New Hill to visit Mary at Barton Park but seemed to be staying away from Cleveland, perhaps so that Charlotte would not press her to take her back to London.

Not that she would. Not anymore. Her life with Thomas had settled into a comfortable pattern. Perhaps it was not the unparalleled joy and fulfillment she'd once imagined, but it was enough—except for the lack of friends in whom she could confide. Even Aunt Georgina's thorny presence would have been welcome, but that lady was still absent. She had evidently found great amusement with her friend in Yorkshire and showed no signs of returning any time soon—perhaps not until the holidays.

Late summer at Cleveland was a drowsy time. Whenever the weather was fine, after attending to her duties, Charlotte wandered outdoors. There in the open air, she found herself drifting into reverie, thinking back to that original London ball, that first dance with Thomas, and the fateful waltz that had brought her to this place. It was over a year since she had kissed Mr. Palmer at Barton Park. When she looked back at herself then, so hopeful, so woefully inexperienced, she felt that decades had passed instead of months.

Such thoughts made her tired. Most mornings, she found it difficult to rise until she'd had some toast, and even if Thomas had granted her a full night's sleep, she found she must lie down in the afternoon and rest before dinner. And she felt tender in places that had not felt tender before. She'd had to let out her stays, which she attributed to her immense appetite for clotted cream and scones with a liberal helping of strawberry preserves.

The season would begin again come November, and Mr. Palmer's business interests and Parliamentary aspirations would call him to London then, if not sooner. She knew he was anxious to secure a seat in the House of Commons, and in town, he could solicit support and advice from others in his party. Surprisingly, the bustle of London held little attraction for her now.

Despite her solitude, Charlotte had come to love Cleveland and its rolling hills, the roar of the sea through the channel, the salt wind and marshes. A sense of immobility, quite unfamiliar to her, replaced her usual push to join the crowds in assemblies and card parties to hear the latest news. In this in-between time, she was happy to stroll along the footpaths, play with kittens in the barn, scatter cracked corn for her ducks, or sit upon a hillock to watch the flocks grazing on the distant hillside. Town and the season would come soon enough.

August already. She counted the days since her wedding, since her mother's departure, since…could it be? Not since May? She counted back again. Nearly two months. It was what she'd been watching for. Hoping for. With trepidation, she counted forward. It would be in February in London. Then Mama would be nearby. She would not be alone.

Mama — she must write her at once. She would be thrilled to hear that she was to become a grandmama. It did not occur to Charlotte to immediately inform the father. He did not like to be disturbed when he was managing things.

She hurried into the library to fetch paper to write a letter.

From his desk, Mr. Palmer looked up with concern at his flushed wife. "Are you ill, Lottie?"

"I…no…." But the scent of his cigar sent her running from the room.

~*~

Mr. Palmer discovered her, damp and shaking, kneeling in a corner of the dressing-room by the chamber pot. Though the space was tight, he followed her inside and stooped next to her, keeping his eyes on her face instead of the contents of the pot or the too-close walls. "Come, you are ill. Let me help you to your room. I will fetch the doctor at once."

"Thomas, no, wait—it is nothing." She put a hand to her mouth, then turned and retched, thankfully, into the pot instead of onto his shoes.

He took a step back and gave her his handkerchief, looking away as she wiped her face. "I beg to differ, Charlotte; it is most definitely something." Bending forward, he laid a hand on her forehead. Her skin beneath his fingers felt clammy. Thomas frowned. The week before, one of the village wives had fallen ill with a fever. She'd nearly died.

Charlotte took his outstretched hand and held it to her cheek. "Yes, a rather important something, I suppose, but not what you are thinking." She had the temerity to scoff in the face of his fears. "I am not ill. That I promise you. Not in the way you think. A doctor cannot be of service, at least not now."

Mr. Palmer brushed a wet strand from her face. She looked pensive and discomfited, without a giggle left in her. Not like Lottie at all. A chill started in the pit of his stomach. "Just what is this important something?"

Charlotte's cheeks, formerly pale, now flooded with red, making him worry anew about fever. "It's something that's to happen," she said, her voice so low he had to bend lower to hear.

"Oh?" He willed himself to remain still in the tiny room until he heard the particulars. Experience had taught him it was best to wait her out instead of interrupting.

"Or—something that did happen—."

A dozen scenarios raced through his brain in rapid succession, from an extravagant dressmaker's bill to lost ducks to bands of ragged poachers catching her in the wood. He struggled to remain sensible. "Would it be easier if you whispered it in my ear?"

She nodded, and he again stooped beside her to hear. When his legs gave out beneath him, he sat on the floor, hearing the few words that transformed him from husband to father, the head of a family.

~*~

*Barton Park, September*

*My dearest Lottie,*

*I am ever so pleased to hear your news! I'm to be a grandmama once more! Mary's little ones will have a new playmate soon enough! Your happiness, and the happiness of Mr. Palmer, must be complete. Children are what makes a house a home, I always say. It didn't take him long, did it?*

*I hope you are getting your rest and not overtiring yourself. Increasing can be a hard business. Be sure to eat a lowering diet, plenty of fruits and vegetables, and no more tea. And do leave off your stays. Also, get out in the fresh air now and then. A short walk will do you good.*

*It is a great comfort to me to know that you will be in town when your lying-in time comes after the holidays, close to decent physicians and near enough so that I can be available when needed. Not that you aren't entirely capable, love. You will be a wonderful mother.*

*Mary sends her best. Barton Park is full of young people once again, all manner of card games and music, and hunting, of course, for Sir John could not go a day without that, I think. You will be pleased to know that a new family took up residence at the cottage. A Mrs. Dashwood and her daughters are a delightful addition. I met them at dinner the other night, and they were most congenial. The entire family is uncommonly attractive.*

*You might remember that the son from the first marriage*

*inherited when old Mr. Dashwood died, so his second family was forced to leave their home in Sussex and retire to Devonshire. I believe Mr. Palmer was once acquainted with the half-brother's wife, Mrs. Fanny Dashwood.*

*Also at dinner was Colonel Brandon, whom I'm sure you remember, a good friend of Sir John's. I always thought he was too old for you.*

*Miss Marianne Dashwood is very musical; she entertains us at the pianoforte. Colonel Brandon cannot look away. He listens quite attentively when she sings. He is already in love with her. I am perfectly convinced of it. It would be a good match, for he is rich, and the poor Dashwood girls have nothing.*

*Mary remains busy with the children. Annamaria is still not talking much, though she has turned three. She dearly loves to have me read her your little duck stories. Sir John sends his regards. My best to Mr. Palmer.*

Lottie set down the letter, having read it twice. So much of life went on without her. How she wished she could be at Barton with her mother now and meet these new friends — any friends. Her mother's description of the Misses Dashwood, in particular, renewed her loneliness. Miss Marianne and Miss Elinor must be around her own age, though, of course, neither was married. *They* still could flirt and stay late at dances, with a choice in husband still ahead of them.

Charlotte's London friends remained at their country houses, where no doubt they attended local assemblies or visited one another. None had come to visit her, although she'd extended invitations to several.

None but Miss Browne had come.

But it wasn't until November that Charlotte was able to make the Dashwoods' acquaintance. She'd been treated to more letters from Mrs. Jennings touting their virtues. Miss Elinor was as gracious a young lady as ever lived, sensible and calm. The eldest of three, she was an enormous comfort to her mother. Miss Marianne was a beauty, sensitive and energetic, with a love of the romantic. She was soon to be matched with a Mr. Willoughby. The youngest was only thirteen, so her character was yet to be fully formed, though she seemed a good-natured girl.

"I'm quite sure we should be the best of friends if only I could make their acquaintance, Mr. Palmer," Charlotte said one morning, having read him the latest letter from her mother. "Miss Elinor and I could converse about painting, for Mother says she paints. And Miss Marianne and I undoubtedly read the same books and could have cozy chats about them. Oh, I wish they lived in Somerset instead of Devonshire!"

"Have you exhausted the supply of women here, then?" her husband asked. "I had no idea there were so few young ladies in the neighborhood."

"The Saunders sisters have not come to call in an age. Most of the married ladies have no time for me, and many of the unmarried ones are returning to town. All my London friends are thinking of balls and outings."

"And so shall you," Thomas smiled. "How soon can you be packed?"

To Charlotte's delight, Thomas whisked her off on a whirlwind business trip to London with scarcely a day to prepare. He really had no understanding of the efforts required to ready oneself for town. Charlotte despaired of her increasing middle, for her gowns had been let out and now hung awkwardly. She pored over outfits, trying to decide which was least objectionable. Despite the inconvenience of such hasty travel, Charlotte couldn't wait to see her old friends and to visit every shop in Mayfair.

And to see her new London home, of course.

Two days of travel challenged Charlotte's enthusiasm, but did little to dampen it. True, her ankles swelled, and her stomach grew queasy with the constant swaying of the carriage. Thomas had the window blinds rolled back, so the dust from the road made her cough. She did her best to ignore her discomfort. Instead, she pestered her husband for details about his London house. Mr. Palmer's description was meager indeed. She knew the address, size, and number of rooms, but little else. By the time they reached Reading, she was anxious to arrive and inspect the place for herself. Each mile made her more impatient. This was to be her baby's birthplace when they returned after Christmas. She hoped to find it pleasant and inviting.

Mr. Palmer's London residence, however, proved as unwelcoming inside as it was out. The house seemed squeezed between its neighbors in Hanover Square, giving Charlotte the impression it was constantly elbowing them on either side. The white façade and pillared entryway felt more formidable than hospitable, and the wooden butler at the door was no Mr. Nash. Disapproval chipped off him when Charlotte greeted him as warmly as was her wont with Cleveland's butler. She opened her mouth to express her thoughts as she turned to Mr. Palmer but was forestalled by his evident pride in this frigid place.

"Welcome to your London home, my dear. I trust you will find it as comfortable as Cleveland."

She had no doubt that *he* found it comfortable enough. Everything about the house bespoke order and restraint. Even the candle flames did not waver. Charlotte had never felt *less* at home. But it would not do to criticize the building where their child would be born.

Charlotte looked about, trying to find anything that softened her first impressions. Not even a potted plant added life to the rigid Georgian architecture. Bracing herself, she replied, "I shall love it here, Mr. Palmer. Why, look how very high the ceilings are here! And what pretty moldings!" She said nothing about the stark feel of the hall or the chill of the marble floors. "I'm sure that soon, Hanover Square will feel like a home. In time. It only needs to be lived in."

Mr. Palmer already looked *very much* at home. "Will you be making calls now that we are in town?" He seemed less than excited at the prospect of visitors, a fact which Charlotte was determined to ignore.

"To friends. But my mother is still at Barton Park with my sister." Charlotte's mood dipped that much lower, despite her determination to remain cheerful. "It has been an age since I saw her. We have so much to say to each other!"

Mr. Palmer raised an eyebrow. "Of that, I have no doubt."

Charlotte laughed. "You are so very droll, my love. I think Mama and I could chat all day and still not run out of things to say." She rested her hand on her rounded stomach. "I wish I had her to talk to now."

Mr. Palmer said nothing, though he looked at her for some time before turning to the butler.

~*~

Bond Street called Charlotte to stroll along its stone pavements and inspect the windows of various modistes and milliners, and Mr. Palmer was pressed into service to accompany her. They had looked in only eight or nine shops when Charlotte spied a familiar tall figure several paces ahead.

"Colonel Brandon!" she called. "Mr. Palmer, look. It *is* he, is it not? Colonel, do stop!"

Several shoppers turned to stare at the source of the noise.

Thomas looked aghast at her outburst. "I beg of you, Mrs. Palmer, don't shout again. He's already turned back."

Colonel Brandon bowed and greeted them good day. Charlotte thought he looked as stiff and military as ever.

"Indeed it is, Colonel! A lovely day! How lucky to see you. Mr. Palmer was just saying how he wished to renew acquaintances from Barton."

"I said nothing of the sort," Thomas muttered.

"Upon my word," his wife continued, unabated. "Imagine running into someone from Devon all the way down here in London!"

"It is the crossroads of the world," Mr. Palmer stated, looking bored.

"I often come to town, Mrs. Palmer," Colonel Brandon replied. "And what brings you and Mr. Palmer to our great city?"

"Mr. Palmer has business, and he also must keep up with all the latest in the government, for he is to stand for one of the seats in Somerset, did you know?"

The colonel did know.

"Have you lately had occasion to visit Sir John and Lady Middleton? I have not seen them this age."

"When I was last at Barton Park, your family were all well, I'm pleased to say."

"I'm very glad to hear it. I miss them terribly. I understand that a new family has come to Barton Cottage, the Dashwoods. Mama writes that the girls are excessively pretty."

Colonel Brandon allowed that was true.

"And I hear one is to be married to Mr. Willoughby of Combe Magna. Surely you know of him since I believe he is to inherit Allenham."

The colonel said nothing and took his leave soon after.

"How very odd," Charlotte said. "He left in quite a hurry, don't you think, my love?"

"Fast as was polite," her husband replied. "Since you have poked into every shop on this block without a single purchase, I suggest we go home. It would not do for you to get overly tired."

Charlotte's smile was so bright that Mr. Palmer could not help but return it. "You are good to think of me, Thomas," she said. The glow of his attention kept her warm all the way back to the cold townhouse.

The next day, Mr. Palmer surprised her again with a carriage and not a word of where they were going. The second trip in a week was quite astounding since they had only recently arrived in town, and Charlotte knew how he hated travel by carriage. All her cajoling could not make her husband tell her their new destination, at least until they were far into their journey to Devonshire, when Charlotte guessed.

"You are the most thoughtful of men, Mr. Palmer," she told him repeatedly.

They arrived at Barton Park in time for tea, quite late in the day. Charlotte ignored her aching back and ran to greet her family. Mrs. Jennings, especially, was overjoyed at the surprise.

"Why, just look at you, Lottie!" she exclaimed. "Increasing suits you. You're positively blooming with health."

Sir John was as jolly and welcoming as ever, Lady

Middleton was cordial but distant, and the delighted children swarmed about Charlotte like locusts until their nurse took them off to bed.

Charlotte had to wait for the next day to meet the Dashwoods.

# Chapter Twenty-Eight

After a day in a carriage and a night of interrupted sleep, Thomas Palmer was in a testy mood. Charlotte had been so elated at the reunion with her mother and sister that she had chattered on for over an hour after they'd retired, even after he had put the pillow over his head. He was already regretting his decision to bring her from London to Barton Park.

"The Dashwood girls are at the cottage. Isn't it delightful? It was too late to see them tonight. We must visit at the very earliest opportunity in the morning! I've waited ever so long to make their acquaintance. Mama has told me all about them, and I know them to be the most pleasant, polite, and attractive young women I have ever met."

Mr. Palmer set aside his pillow and raised his eyebrow. "How could you possibly know such a thing when you have yet to make their acquaintance?"

"Well, yes, I see your point, but Mama has written so much about them that I feel them to be my dearest friends already. You will come with me to their cottage, won't you, Mr. Palmer?"

"I leave that to you. A houseful of women is best kept that way."

"Hardly a houseful."

Although the teasing and gentle caress to his arm made

him smile, Mr. Palmer shook his head. "With Lady Middleton, Mrs. Jennings, Mrs. Dashwood, and the Misses Dashwood, that's a half-dozen," he replied, kissing her forehead.

When his wife finally blew out the candle, he lay on his back, staring into the dark. He was not eager to meet the half-sisters of the man who had married Fanny, whose adder tongue Thomas remembered with pain. He preferred to avoid awkward connections. And really, Charlotte had more than enough connections already. Why did she need more people in her life? Were not he and their future child enough? Turning on his side, he reached across the bed and pulled her warm, round body to him, clasping a possessive arm about her. He smiled to himself at the sleepy coos she made as she cuddled against him. He fell asleep with his face buried in curls, drifting off to the scent of honeysuckle.

Making a call early the next day instead of fishing with Sir John did nothing to improve Thomas's disposition. His wife's loud enthusiasm for the outing to meet the incomparable Dashwoods was even more off-putting than the visit itself. Charlotte seemed nearly desperate to meet these women. The smile etched on her face was in danger of being permanently fixed there.

Sir John, Lady Middleton, and Mrs. Jennings went on ahead to the cottage, leaving Charlotte and Thomas to follow. "Just think, Mr. Palmer, we shall meet them soon!" his spouse gushed, breathing heavily with the exertion of carrying herself and her increasing bulk. In spite of his efforts to hold her back and prevent her from over-exerting herself, Charlotte forged on to expand her acquaintance. Thomas could not, for the life of him, understand.

Once at the ramshackle rural cottage, Sir John opened a small gate at the entrance to a green court and hurried to an open window, greeting the pretty young woman who looked out of it. Mrs. Jennings soon joined him, hallooing at the casement. "What, Miss Dashwood? All alone? You'll be glad for company to sit with you, then." As Thomas listened, appalled, his mother-in-law related every detail of their arrival at Barton Park, stopping only when Lady Middleton introduced them to the residents.

Mrs. Dashwood, a mature matron not yet in her dotage, eventually opened the door and, along with her youngest daughter, escorted them to the parlor. Thomas bowed to the ladies, scanned the room for the means of egress, and finding none, took up a newspaper from a nearby table and sat down in a convenient armchair at the far side of the room, as far from the rest of the group as he could situate himself.

As the paper was a fairly recent edition, it served to occupy him as he tried his best to tune out the meaningless chatter of his wife. Annoyingly, she seemed determined to draw him into the conversation. Her first attempt he could ignore, for she merely exclaimed at length on the cozy nature of the cottage, which, in fact, was both cramped and damp. At least the number of windows helped the space feel more open.

Charlotte, however, had much to say about the Dashwoods' new home: "Oh, my! What a delightful room this is! I never saw anything so charming!"

Since he would definitely *not* like such a house for himself, he did not answer her question to that effect or raise his eyes from the newspaper, lest he encourage her.

"Mr. Palmer doesn't hear me," his wife said, laughing while looking daggers at him. "It is so ridiculous."

Thomas was content to be thought ridiculous. It saved him from having to converse.

He turned a deaf ear to his mother-in-law's repeated descriptions of their arrival the night before and the extent of her surprise. Why did the tale warrant repetition? He listened intently, however, when Mrs. Jennings pointed out to the company his wife's increasing girth and her concerns about harm to the baby from all the travel.

Charlotte laughed off the concern. "It won't do me any harm," she assured them.

And yet, he worried about her.

He knew any mention of an impending birth to be a gross breach in decorum. Lady Middleton and Miss Dashwood both seemed scandalized at the revelation, although Charlotte's condition must by now be obvious to any who looked lower than her face. Instead of sharing their shock, however, Thomas felt a modicum of pride. Charlotte carried his heir.

That did not mean he desired to be drawn into a conversation about it.

Mrs. Jennings' ill-bred comment had driven Lady Middleton from the rest of the group. Forewarned, Thomas kept his eyes on the summary of Parliamentary debates.

"Mr. Palmer, you seem thoroughly engrossed," she said, leaning over the back of the armchair, closing in on him and adding to his discomfort. "Tell me, is there any news?"

Thomas did not look up from the paper. "No, none at all."

Sir John paid no attention to his wife's desertion. For the first time, Thomas wondered what spurred Lady Middleton to seek him out instead of crossing to her husband. She had married well, gaining a minor title, a large estate, and a genial spouse who had given her four still-living offspring. Sir John was a decent sort. A superb shot. His manners were open and friendly. He'd never been anything but hospitable, although Barton Park lacked a billiard room. His wife enjoyed the benefits of a large income. What more could a lady want?

Thomas lost his train of thought when Sir John announced, "Here comes Marianne." With the emphasis the gentleman put into the announcement, Thomas fully expected royalty. He studied the figure at the door. She was, indeed, as "monstrous pretty" as Sir John had said, tall, with clear skin and dark eyes. She looked two or three years younger than his Charlotte, both of them still young. And though she rivaled his wife in attractiveness, there hung about the girl a nervous intensity plain even to him. Beneath the surface, there could be no greater contrast between Miss Marianne Dashwood and Mrs. Charlotte Palmer.

His regard for Miss Marianne had not escaped his wife, who now flitted about the room commenting on the drawings hanging on the wall.

~*~

The Misses Dashwood proved to be almost everything Charlotte had hoped for. Miss Marianne Dashwood was exceptionally pretty. Even Thomas, who admired nothing, seemed to admire her. Miss Elinor Dashwood was attractive and about her own age, though she appeared much older with her serious looks and careful speech. She said nothing about Charlotte's interesting condition, which was understandable, but she did exchange greetings in the most charming way imaginable. And when Charlotte discovered that they shared a love of sketching, her opinion that they would be firm friends was confirmed.

Miss Elinor's sketches hung all about the room: a blasted tree, an old stone cottage, a quaint church on a hill, a portrait of what Charlotte took to be the youngest Miss Dashwood, Margaret. All were flawlessly executed and quite charming. "How delightful! Do but look, Mama. How sweet!" She thought she could look at them forever, except—there was not a single animal among them. Not a duck, dog, horse, cow, or cat. Charlotte left off remarking on the artistry of the drawings and settled in for a comfortable gossip with the ladies.

Miss Elinor Dashwood proved to be an excellent listener. She made all the right noises. Not so her younger sister, Miss Marianne Dashwood, who seemed put out by Mrs. Jennings' teasing her about her beau visiting in nearby Allenham. Mrs. Jennings had talked at length the night before of the romantic entanglements at the cottage. Both girls seemed on the brink of matrimony.

Charlotte was convinced that the Dashwood girls would be her future closest friends. They would write regularly, and she would invite them to London to visit and take them about, as a married lady should. While at Barton Park, she must get to know them even better. To that end, she joined Sir John in pressing them to join the company for dinner the next night.

The Dashwoods seemed unaccountably reluctant to accept the invitation. That, Charlotte put down to a general shyness and was more than ever determined to bring the sisters out of their shells.

~*~

When at last Lady Middleton moved away from his side, Thomas set down his newspaper shield and stretched, pausing to remark upon how low-pitched and crooked the ceiling was before bowing and following the company back to Barton Park. He had feared his head might crack in two before he could take his leave of the musty cottage. If he never met the Dashwoods again, he'd be content. He could not understand why Charlotte had persisted in pressing them to dine the next day.

She waited for him at the gate. "Were they not the most delightful young ladies, Mr. Palmer? I am vastly pleased with them. And since they are to dine tomorrow at Barton Park, we can further our friendship."

"It's hardly a friendship, Charlotte. You've just met."

"If only we could stay longer here." Her wistful tone warned him that she would not abandon her new quest.

"The Westons come to us next week at Cleveland. There is much to prepare before they arrive." Thomas felt the wedge that threatened to split his skull sink deeper. A great deal was riding on that visit. "Shall we head back?" He winced as another sharp pain shot through his brain.

Charlotte reached up and laid her cool hand on his cheek. "Are you ill, my love?" She looked genuinely disturbed at his discomfort.

He took her hand in his and kissed her palm. "It will pass. The fresh air helps. It was too close inside the cottage. I...dislike crowded rooms." Still holding her hand, he walked away from the cottage into the shaded park. For once, his wife remained quiet for several minutes. Only bird song and the distant bleating of sheep intruded.

Of course, Charlotte could not stay silent for long. "Why is that?"

"Why is what?"

"Why is it that you dislike crowds? You once said you prefer the country because it has fewer people."

"You remember that?"

"Of course. Please, tell me, my love."

*My love.* She used the words so easily. He closed his eyes, willing the pounding in his temples to stop. "Something that happened when I was a boy." His head began to clear as they walked from beneath the arching oaks to the open green.

"Aunt Georgina once mentioned a carriage accident."

"Trust Georgina. It was a very long time ago, Charlotte."

"Not long enough, if it still troubles you. Won't you tell me about it?"

With her hand in his, out under the wide gray sky, Thomas could. "My parents and I and my cousins were riding in my uncle's carriage. The weather was wet, and the roads were pocked with ruts." He paused, seeing the crowded carriage again, with his Uncle Tharp, his aunt, his parents, and three cousins packed in shoulder to shoulder. His mouth went dry, and at the same time, he could feel sweat soaking his shirt. "A wheel caught in the mire, and the carriage was upset. It crashed onto its side, and everything in it was tossed about."

"Were you hurt?"

"No, only banged about." He felt again the weight of all those bodies pressing down and the edges of boxes digging into his side. And he heard the screams. High-pitched, keening on and on. He licked his lips. "But my cousin Alice was thrown onto the rocks. She...died." His eyes pricked at the memory. "It took the driver a long time to get the door open and help everyone out." He smiled ruefully. "I was at the bottom of the pile."

Charlotte gasped. "How awful for you! Oh, Thomas, no wonder you hate crowded places! Why, I'm surprised you could ever ride in a carriage again!"

When she put her arms around him, he felt the swell of her belly. His arms went around her, drawing her to his heart. He no longer heard the screams when he bent his head and kissed her.

The pain behind his eyes was gone.

~*~

Charlotte puzzled over Thomas. He'd been so very different when they walked together after visiting the Dashwoods.

His dreadful story made her heart ache for him as a little boy, crushed under luggage and relatives, when all the while his cousin lay smashed on the rocks. Telling the story had seemed to open something in him. Never had she felt closer to him, not even in his arms at night.

Yet when they'd returned to Barton Park, he'd gone off with Sir John. The closeness they'd shared was as if it had never been. In fact, the distance between them felt as wide as the Bristol Channel. And as cold.

Their marriage seemed like a never-ending game of two steps forward, one step back. It was no wonder she pursued a new friendship with the fervor of a hound baying after a fox.

That evening, she dressed with care. She nearly tripped over the hem of her saffron-colored sarcenet evening dress in her haste to greet the two Dashwood sisters when they entered the drawing-room at Barton Park. Charlotte noted that, while their pale blue gowns were not on the cutting edge of fashion, they were becoming.

"I'm so very glad to see you!" she said, extending a hand to each woman and seating herself between them. "I feared you would not come, and Mr. Palmer tells me we are to leave tomorrow. He is so very amusing. He never tells me anything in advance. I do hope we shall meet in town soon. Perhaps after the holidays?"

Miss Elinor Dashwood did not answer at first. She seemed even more reserved this evening than she had at Barton cottage. "We have no wish to go to town," she finally explained.

"Not come to town? But you must! I shall be ever so disappointed if you do not! You could rent a house right near ours in Hanover Square. Then we could visit every day. And if your mother did not wish to accompany you, *I* could be your chaperone. After all, I am a married woman."

The Misses Dashwood looked somewhat taken aback at the suggestion. "Thank you for the kind offer, Mrs. Palmer," Miss Elinor said. "But we are obliged to remain here at Barton."

Later in the evening, Charlotte tried again to entice her

new friends to visit her.

"You simply must come to Cleveland for Christmas. Oh, yes, you must come! The Westons will be with us. You cannot think how happy your visit would make me. We should have such fun!"

The Dashwood sisters still would not be enticed. They kept looking away while Charlotte spoke until she began to wonder if they had somewhere else to be.

Charlotte was sorely disappointed. No matter how she pressed, Elinor and Marianne refused her invitations. Her dreams of a close friendship wilted like a rose in the frost. Despairing, she turned to Thomas, who had finally entered the room. "My love, you must help me to persuade the Dashwoods to go to town this winter."

He made no answer, though he bowed to the ladies. Charlotte resolved to be patient with him. Knowing his dislike of large groups, she ignored his scowls and complaints about the weather, which had kept him stuck indoors that day, something he also disliked. She also ignored his correction when she miscalculated the distance from Barton to Allenham and his condemnation of that estate as ugly. But when he was so rude as to call her dear mama "ill-bred" for her dining etiquette, Charlotte could not stay quiet, though she clung to the mask of good humor.

"My love," she said, glaring at him, "Do you know that you are quite rude?"

"I did not know I contradicted anybody in calling your mother ill-bred."

Such a remark was beyond the pale. Whatever was the matter with her husband? Charlotte felt her face grow hot.

Her mother, however, easily shrugged off the insult. "You have taken Charlotte off my hands and cannot give her back again. So there I have the whip hand of you."

Had she been such a burden, then? Charlotte forced herself to laugh. What else was she to do? "Mr. Palmer is so droll!" she said to Miss Dashwood. "He is always out of humor." Though she was out of humor herself at her mother's crassness and husband's surliness, she proceeded on her mission. More than ever, she was determined to bring the Dashwoods to Cleveland.

"Now, pray do come spend some time with us this Christmas." For support, she turned once more to Thomas. He owed her that, after his rudeness. "My love, don't you long for the Misses Dashwood to come to Cleveland?"

"I came to Devonshire with no other view."

She ignored his sarcasm as well.

Yet the sisters steadfastly refused the invitation. It was most disappointing. The evening eventually took a turn for the better, however. After dinner, the conversation turned to love, her favorite topic. Charlotte missed the thrill of speculation over who was courting whom and who had found a match. To witness a budding romance firsthand was like dipping into a baked custard. She was thus highly pleased when Miss Elinor asked if Charlotte knew Mr. Willoughby, Miss Marianne's suitor.

"Extremely well," she answered. "Not that I ever met him, but I must have seen him in town. My mother met him at Barton, I think. He's liked by all, though few see him, since he lives so far off." Charlotte sighed. "What a perfect couple they make. Your sister is so handsome and agreeable, and by all reports, Willoughby is also." Miss Marianne and Mr. Willoughby, at least, were a good match. Such matches, love matches, could happen. Charlotte took a breath and thought it very pleasant indeed to be in such congenial company.

Mr. Palmer did not share her sentiments, a fact that was obvious from his disgruntled expression. If he had his way, Charlotte expected he'd whisk her back to Cleveland that very evening.

How vexing that her hopes for friendship must be cut short in the name of duty. Mr. Weston was a man of great importance in Parliament, and Thomas was counting on his advice and support. The next day, Charlotte climbed into the carriage fervently wishing the Dashwoods, instead of the Westons, were to visit.

# Chapter Twenty-Nine

Mr. Weston had been born to privilege. That fact was evident in the way he stood, the way he spoke, and the way he filled the drawing room at Cleveland with his presence. Much about him was larger than life: his white wig, his hooked nose, his jowls, his protruding belly, his booming voice, and his arrogance. Although he was a guest, he directed all about him like a general ordering about recruits. Susan, Charlotte's maid, had confided that Mr. Weston had made a stable boy cry and had whipped his own horse until its haunch was bloodied.

The world considered Mr. Weston a great man, a formidable politician who enjoyed fierce support among his peers. Charlotte did not dislike men with strong personalities. After all, she had married Mr. Palmer and quite admired Sir John. But they were *good* men. She could not abide cruelty, most especially intentional cruelty to those who could not defend themselves.

Mr. Weston was *not* a good man. Apparently, one did not have to be a good man to serve in Parliament. He was, however, a forceful man. At Cleveland, he assumed all he saw was his to dominate. Charlotte grew irritated watching her husband agree with whatever Mr. Weston said and defer to his judgment in all things. Such behavior did not seem at all like her Thomas.

The morning after the guests' arrival, Henry and Mrs.

Weston had not yet come down when Charlotte entered the breakfast room. Aunt Georgina, home in time for the holidays, had retreated to her room soon after their guests' arrival. Thomas and Mr. Weston stood briefly at Charlotte's entrance but barely allowed her a "good morning" before returning to a dull and confusing discussion of political currents in Paris.

She resolved not to feel slighted and instead helped herself to some chocolate, a slice of bread, and a spoonful of preserves, grateful that her digestion had settled down now that she was only three months away from her confinement. She sipped as the men droned on.

Mr. Weston proved himself to be a man of great appetite: the remains of a quantity of plum cake littered his plate. Charlotte resolved to revise the menu. The cook was planning pheasant as one of the items for dinner if the men's hunt this afternoon proved successful. Charlotte had been craving just such a meal. Given Mr. Weston's capacity for food, she should add another two dishes to the first course.

Her cup was nearly empty when her husband rose from the table.

"I have some estate business that needs attention," Thomas said. "It shouldn't take long, sir, and in the meantime, I'm sure the housekeeper or Mrs. Palmer would be happy to show you about the house and gardens."

Charlotte could not be rude and abandon a guest to the housekeeper, who surely had enough to do without leading Mr. Weston up and down stairs. When she had consulted with her and the cook earlier in the day, both women had seemed quite busy. Besides, Thomas had impressed upon her the importance of making a good impression on their visitors. He very much needed Mr. Weston's help if he was to secure the open seat. For her husband's sake, she could endure the odious man's company for an hour without revealing her dislike.

Resigned, Charlotte inclined her head and murmured, "It would be my pleasure to show you Cleveland."

There was nothing pleasurable at all in the tour. Mr. Weston failed to exclaim over the ceiling painting in the sitting room, even when Charlotte pointed out the sweet cupids peeking out from behind the painted foliage. He did not remark over the splendid staircase or the height of the Palladian windows. Charlotte's feet had grown puffy by the time they had inspected all the formal rooms. She saved the most imposing for last. "This is the Grand Hall. It *is* grand, is it not? The ceiling is so very ornate, and the room so very long. I was quite awestruck the first time I saw it. All these portraits are of Palmers from generations past. Here is one of Mrs. Palmer, my husband's mother, who passed only a year ago." But Charlotte was startled to turn around from gazing at her mother-in-law to find that Mr. Weston was standing very close indeed behind her.

"Sophia Tharp, is it not? Granddaughter of the Duke of Somerset. Knew her ages ago," he said, bringing a quizzing glass to his eye. "Must be over twenty years since I saw her last. Dead, you say? Pity."

Charlotte was eager to change the subject, lest Mr. Weston tell her stories of his past with Thomas's mother. Such matters seemed best buried. "Would you care to view the kitchens? They're quite modern." She needed to inform the cook of the menu change.

"I have no interest in below stairs," Mr. Weston replied, dropping his quizzing glass.

Charlotte was at a loss. "Then perhaps you would like to see the garden or the stables?" She truly hoped not. Her swollen feet now puffed over the sides of her slippers. Thankfully, Thomas had concluded his business and was happy to take Mr. Weston off to the woods, leaving Charlotte to face the cook.

Unfortunately, once the menu was settled, there was still Mrs. Weston to entertain. Charlotte's introduction to her the night before had not made her eager to know the lady better. Honoria Weston was a tall, sturdy woman with handsome features that had begun sagging at the edges. Everything about her was fashionable, from her frilled cap to the soles of her silk brocade shoes. Her carriage was ever erect, whether she sat or stood. Charlotte suspected she remained upright in her sleep. Mrs. Weston represented the peak of refinement. She would cast even Charlotte's sister Mary in the shade if the truth be told.

With some nervousness, Charlotte invited the lady to join her in the drawing room.

"My dear Mrs. Palmer," Mrs. Weston began as they both bent over their needlework, "I welcome this opportunity to speak with you. My husband says that Mr. Palmer has a promising career ahead of him in Parliament. It is a great responsibility to serve the Crown as a politician's wife, you know." She appeared as enamored of her position as an important man's spouse as Mr. Weston was of being—well, Mr. Weston.

"I'm very much looking forward to it," Charlotte replied with a hint of cheekiness, for Mrs. Weston was already proving tiresome. "I shall be able to post my letters for free then." She selected a particularly bright shade of yellow for the rose in the center of her embroidery. The screen she was working on would brighten up the dull décor in town when she returned.

"There is more to being a politician's wife than franking the post," the lady admonished. "Your husband will be sacrificing himself on the altar of duty."

Charlotte had to check herself and not laugh at the vision that popped into her head of Thomas, in a Roman toga, spread out on a marble altar with a sword at his throat. She enjoyed the vision rather too much. "I promise you, ma'am, I'm mindful of Mr. Palmer's sacrifice."

Mrs. Weston was unconvinced. "You must do all in your power to support his efforts." She took a great breath. "I have come to a decision. Since Mr. Weston will be sponsoring your husband, I shall take you under my wing and sponsor *you* in society."

Charlotte was confused. "But I've been in society." She next had an unwelcome vision of Mrs. Weston covered in feathers, stretching out her wing, pecking at her and suffocating her under a mound of plumes.

The lady pursed her lips and shook her head. "You had

your coming out, I take it?"

"Yes, three years ago." Charlotte warmed to the memory. "It was absolutely wonderful. Parties nearly every night. And balls! Some nights, I danced until dawn."

"Two seasons, then, before catching a husband."

That observation made Charlotte feel as desirable as a plucked hen. "I had the pleasure of two, yes. And at the end, my husband was fortunate enough to catch *me*." She patted her stomach to reassure the occupant that nothing was amiss.

Mrs. Weston cocked her head. "Be that as it may. I notice your accent isn't from the country."

"No, my family comes from London. Berkeley Street. I spent seven years at a great school in town." Odd, but she didn't think of London as her home any longer.

"A city upbringing! One wouldn't guess."

Charlotte sat up straighter, but she still failed to achieve Mrs. Weston's majestic posture. "Mr. Palmer also has a townhouse. On Hanover Square near St. George's. It's wonderfully close to the shops." She felt no small amount of pride in being able to say that.

"A decent address. Once you are in town, you will be hosting most evenings, I suspect."

"And once Mr. Palmer has been elected, you will have a great many responsibilities. You will be representing Britain. Remember that. Dignity, my dear. Always dignity. No smiling. No laughing. No indiscretion of any kind." She paused only long enough to bite off a thread. "You will need to rise above your parents if you are to do right by your husband. I understand there is the taint of trade?"

Charlotte blinked at the insult. "My father was in trade, ma'am." She thought how inadequate that answer was in describing the merry, affectionate man. In her eyes, he was much more a gentleman than this woman's husband.

"Your sister is married to Sir John Middleton, however. That will help. I will introduce you to the best people," Mrs. Weston replied. "Your husband needs contacts if he is to succeed in Parliament."

"I will help Mr. Palmer in any way that I can," Charlotte vowed, lest Mrs. Weston think she was unwilling to do her part. And she did not smile.

"Good." Mrs. Weston looked Charlotte up and down at great length, now and then shaking her head. "You will need a new seamstress."

Charlotte looked down at her morning gown, one of her favorites, a blue and white striped muslin trimmed in white ribbon. True, it was tight in places, and the laces could not be let out much more. The trip to London had been too short to arrange for new clothes. "I can see the need for some gowns," she said, "But I'm very fond of Mme. Roussard." Charlotte had always enjoyed the *modiste's* familiar ways and her cheerful daughters, who worked as seamstresses. Under Mme. Roussard's ministrations, she didn't feel at all inadequate. When Mrs. Weston looked affronted, Charlotte hastened to add, "I appreciate your advice, Mrs. Weston. I'm sure you know all the best dressmakers." She set aside her sewing and rested one hand on her stomach, where she detected a flutter. Perhaps she wasn't the only one feeling constricted. "Shall we find the gentlemen now? They should have run out of political arguments."

"You will have to become more astute about politics, my dear. Not to voice an opinion, mind you, but to keep an ear open for anything that might advance your husband's position."

That sounded suspiciously like spying to Charlotte. She kept the thought to herself. A politician's wife must be discreet.

When they rejoined the gentlemen, they were discussing the day's hunt. Thomas looked displeased. Henry and Mr. Weston stood side by side, much the same height, but with entirely different demeanors.

"Sad lack of game on this size estate, Palmer," Mr. Weston said. "Expected more of a shoot."

Henry laughed. "I rather thought six brace between us was a good shoot. Enough to fill the larder for the holiday." He exchanged glances with his brother.

"Some of the game has been taken to feed the villagers," Thomas said. "Come spring, we will restock, but the numbers are down a bit just now, I'm sorry to say."

"Poachers." Mr. Weston shook his head. "They're the bane of every landowner. You'll prosecute, then. Can't let that go on."

Henry looked from Weston to Thomas, then to Charlotte, who'd stifled a gasp.

"No." Thomas barely opened his mouth to say the word.

"Good man." Mr. Weston clapped Thomas on the back.

Thomas stepped away. "I meant no, I have no plans to prosecute."

"I beg your pardon?" Mr. Weston's head shot up, and Henry covered his wide smile with his hand.

"I have decided to overlook illicit hunting for now until those in need are on their feet again," Thomas replied.

"Good God, Palmer," Mr. Weston blustered. "One would think you were harboring Whig sympathies! Best keep that under your hat, or you'll be drummed out of the party before you're even elected."

Charlotte moved to her husband's side, took his arm, and looked up at him, proud to be his partner in life. "I think Mr. Palmer will be the very best member of the House of Representatives the nation has ever seen, no matter what party he represents."

"Hear, hear," Henry added.

Thomas smiled down at her. "Thank you, my dear. And what have you and Mrs. Weston been doing all this time?"

Mrs. Weston replied before Charlotte could open her mouth again. "Mrs. Palmer is sorely in need of instruction regarding the proper behavior of a politician's wife. We've been discussing the importance of dignity and discretion in all things."

Thomas nodded and patted Charlotte's hand, which still rested on his arm. "Dignity and discretion are indeed assets in a wife. Mrs. Palmer could benefit from your instruction."

Charlotte felt the blow. He did not defend her. And she needed instruction? She'd had the best teachers in town. She'd studied proper deportment from books. What more must she do to meet these impossible standards? Hiding her hurt, she withdrew her hand from Thomas's arm and schooled her expression into a socially acceptable simper. Being dignified required holding one's tongue. That much she remembered from Mary.

Mrs. Weston, however, had more to say on the matter of Charlotte's transformation. "You do realize, Mr. Palmer, that all of her gowns are woefully inadequate for her new position. She will need an entirely new wardrobe."

Thomas looked his wife over, pausing for a moment at her rounded midsection before raising his eyes to her expectant face. "It is generous of Mrs. Weston to offer to help, my dear," he said. "I'm sure Mrs. Palmer would be grateful for whatever assistance you can offer, ma'am."

If Charlotte had hoped that her husband would protest that, at least in appearance, she was perfect as she was, she was doomed to disappointment. Even now, after months of marriage, he thought she failed to measure up. So many found her wanting. Somerset society ignored her. The Dashwoods rejected her friendship, Aunt Georgina preferred other women, and her own husband would have her made over completely. How hard must she try?

What was it her mother always said? *Better to laugh than cry.* She couldn't laugh now. Mrs. Weston would think it undignified. But.

Charlotte *could* relent and add a layer of polish. A layer of polish need not change her *self.* A table with a layer of beeswax was still a table. She'd still be Charlotte beneath the gloss. If she became the quintessence of quality, then Thomas would be proud of her. And her baby would love her, polished or not. Her spirits lifted.

The next morning, after a fortifying breakfast and a good talking to with her reflection in the mirror, Charlotte submitted to Mrs. Weston's ministrations. That lady's directives made the suggestions from Mary's conduct book seem mild. The fine distinction among Most Honorable, Right Honorable, and Honorable, for example, was apparently of vital importance.

And who knew that a lady should not trick out a squabby Doric-shaped dress with Corinthian finery, lest one create a fashion imbalance?

Charlotte resolved to transform herself yet again. She'd be a perfect politician's wife. Her husband's eyes would shine as he introduced her to members of state. Other matrons would look to her to set styles. These thoughts sustained her through her training ordeal. Day by day, while Thomas canvassed the neighborhood, Charlotte practiced the proper forms of address, the proper posture, the proper expression—which was no expression whatsoever—until she thought every drop of her *self* had been drained and replaced with ice water.

"But how can a compliment be wrong?" she protested during one session. "Everyone loves a compliment. I'm sure I never felt insulted by one!" *Except from Mr. Tierney*, she added to herself.

"Such remarks are impertinent," the lady stated. "And you must speak more slowly, with deliberation. Excessive speed is most disagreeable, even if enunciation is clear. You might practice by reading out loud with extreme slowness several times a day."

The tasks assigned to Charlotte thus dimmed her holiday mood. Merely sitting upright, walking with dignity, and speaking with the right modulation took practice. She dared not hope for a kiss beneath the mistletoe with the Westons about. Carols she could sing, but her form was no longer suited to dancing at the village gatherings. And she certainly could not join in the games of Hoodman's Blind and Snapdragon under the manner dragon's watchful and disapproving eye.

Charlotte found little joy in Christmas that year.

When the holidays drew to a close, at last, the Westons bid farewell and returned to town. And none too soon, for Charlotte's resolve to remake herself had worn thin. Mrs. Weston's tutelage was no longer welcome. As the Palmers, too, were to return to London soon after Christmas, Charlotte silently vowed to avoid any social occasions that included the couple. She'd had enough.

"I have the most shocking impulse to slouch about the Mall in transparent muslin while singing naughty Scottish ballads at the top of my lungs," she confessed to Aunt Georgina, who had resurfaced in the dining room as soon as the Weston carriage pulled away. "Thank goodness they've gone. If Mrs. Weston had stayed through another breakfast, I'd have lobbed a roll at her head."

Georgina pressed her lips together and patted them with her napkin. Charlotte thought she detected a snort.

"Oh, I'd never actually do such a thing," Charlotte reassured her. "She was a guest, after all. And it would reflect badly on Mr. Palmer."

"While I can't condone wasting a good roll, I do understand the impulse. I've often had to restrain myself from flinging things at people." Georgina paused to spread hartshorn jelly on her own roll. "I think, Charlotte, that you pay rather too much attention to my nephew's status and rather too little attention to your own. Thomas can be demanding as well as difficult."

Charlotte twisted her napkin in her lap. "A wife should dwell on her husband's virtues, not his shortcomings."

"Have you been reading that tiresome book again?"

"A new one. It offers practical hints on a wife's duties."

"You've already fulfilled your prime one."

Charlotte rubbed her curved belly. "I'm trying to be a good wife. Truly, I am. It's only that Mrs. Weston made me feel so—so below standard."

"That's your mistake. You bow to all standards but your own."

"Hers have a place. If Mr. Palmer is to succeed, I must meet the mark in his circles."

"At what price?"

Charlotte didn't like to consider the cost. Her nature far preferred to dwell on positives. "Anyway, we agree that it's a relief to see the last of the Westons."

Charlotte Palmer would rather fly afoul than perch beneath Mrs. Weston's suffocating wing. In London, she'd be reunited with her mother. In her childhood home, she could find herself again.

# Chapter Thirty

Thomas Palmer stood knee-deep in mud, surveying the sodden fields of Cleveland. His sheep had liver rot. He'd wisely invested in sheep since five sheep ate as much as one cow, but dead sheep yielded nothing. And how could he plant? He'd read the treatises on drilling and dibbling and crop rotation, knew the difference between local and intrinsic value of hay. But his tenants could not farm in a sea of muck.

He hoped there would be something left to pass on to his heirs. An heir. He wasn't even assured his child would be a boy. Or that it would live.

He shook his head to banish the creeping thought. Charlotte practically bloomed with health. Since the departure of the Westons, she seemed more herself. All would be well. The crops would flourish. His bid for Parliament would triumph. His son would thrive. And his wife? He supposed she would go on as she was wont to do.

It was good that they must soon return to town. In town, she had plenty of distractions. In town, she would not follow him with her eyes, watching, hoping for more than he had to give.

~*~

It was a great fortune that Charlotte's London home was

only a short ride by barouche to Berkeley Street. An even greater
fortune was the news that Mrs. Jennings had pressed the two
older Dashwood girls to join her there in January. Charlotte
anticipated an hour or two of comfortable chat. When she
arrived, she was delighted to find her mother already seated with
the Misses Dashwood. She would be able to show off her newly
acquired social grace. Thanks to Mrs. Weston, she could even
properly address the wives of the eldest sons of marquises or of
Knights of the Thistle, should she encounter them.

"Mama! Miss Elinor! Miss Marianne! I'm so delighted to
see you all. And so surprised that you've decided to visit London,
though it's what I expected all along. But I must scold you for
visiting here when you refused my invitation. But never mind
that. I'd never have forgiven you if you had not come!"

The sisters exchanged glances but said nothing beyond
"good afternoon."

"Ah, my precious girl!" Mrs. Jennings beamed and held out
her arms. "Let me look at you. My, what a fine size you are. And
glowing. Mary looked pale at this stage, but you're in the peak of
good health, lovey. And how is Mr. Palmer? Anxiously awaiting
the big day, is he? And has Miss Palmer made the journey with
you? I'm sorry she could not join us today. Not much for visiting,
is she? I heard from a very reliable source—if you must know,
from Sir John—that Mr. Henry Palmer has an interest in Miss
Jane Browne from Barton. Young love is everywhere. And how
did your visit with the Westons go? They didn't stay long, did
they? And the Gilberts? They were to visit too, were they not?"

After her long afternoons with Mrs. Weston and
comparatively quiet ones with Aunt Georgina, Charlotte found
the difference of truly affable company refreshing and freeing.
She gleefully answered each of her mother's questions, adding
enough details to paint a complete and vivid picture of each
person's health and wherewithal. Anyone who knew the Westons
would be unlikely to recognize them from her whitewashed
account. Throughout the recital, the Misses Dashwood remained
quiet, nodding and smiling stiffly for the hour it took for Charlotte

and Mrs. Jennings to exchange news.

"But we're forgetting your guests, Mama! We must do something to entertain them now that they have come to town! Oh, let us go to Bond Street. I have some purchases I must make." A tour of the shops on Bond Street without the constraining company of Mr. Palmer or Mrs. Weston and her critical eye would be the perfect ending to the afternoon.

"What a delightful idea!" Mrs. Jennings said. "I was hoping to find some ribbon of a particular shade of purple."

"I also have some purchases to make," Miss Elinor Dashwood added, drawing on her gloves. "You'll come, won't you, Marianne?"

"I rather think not," her sister replied. "I'll stay and wait for the post."

"Expecting a *billet-doux*, are you, missy? From a certain gentleman whose name begins with *W*?" Mrs. Jennings teased.

Charlotte laughed gaily, remembering how she used to watch for Mr. Palmer and wait for his letters. "Of course, she must wait! Such a letter is to be cherished — read and reread and tucked under one's pillow at night."

"Be that as it may," Mrs. Jennings continued, "the post doesn't arrive until late, and I'm quite sure we'll be back in time for tea. I've invited Mrs. Tharrington, who lost her husband to the typhus fever, and Miss Phillips. Can you believe it? She's nearly ninety! So far, she's survived five brothers and six sisters."

All agreed that such a feat was truly remarkable.

At last, after much cajoling, Miss Marianne was prevailed upon to accompany the group, and they set off in Charlotte's carriage. Charlotte came to the conclusion that Marianne would have been better off staying behind since her eyes constantly scanned the crowds, and she flatly refused to offer an opinion on any ribbon or length of cloth.

Mindful of Mrs. Weston's advice, Charlotte visited each shop in turn and carefully perused every frippery and furbelow, but the vast quantity of them left her unable to choose any one. Nothing of which Mrs. Weston would approve appealed to her in the least. She wasn't daunted, however, for now that she was back in London. She could wander the shops as often as she pleased, whenever her engagements allowed. There was time enough to purchase suitable gowns. Time enough, also, to add to the growing pile of infant caps and gowns.

With her mother's guests nearby and the prospect of social gatherings, the coming weeks seemed full of promise. That evening, in fact, the Palmers had a full schedule of engagements to help Mr. Palmer on his way to a seat in Parliament.

"Poor Thomas," Charlotte said to her mother as they sat together in the carriage. "All those rooms full of people. All that conversation in closed spaces. He'll be miserable."

"You're out again tonight, then? Be careful you don't tire yourself, lovey. You should stay put now and then to rest."

"I can't, Mama. If I'm with him, I can soften his remarks." She sighed. "The more crowded the room, the sharper his words."

"He'd best watch himself if he's to make a good impression."

"He wants that seat so desperately." Charlotte resolved to double her efforts on his behalf. Surely only some of the upcoming events would include the disagreeable Westons.

She fully intended to make the most of her social opportunities before she was confined in the following month.

~*~

Babies should be born in spring. In spring, the weather was soft, and there was the promise everywhere of new life, with sprouts and buds and singing birds. February in London was not the time to give birth. This Charlotte Palmer knew for a fact. Even her sitting room was cold, while outside, all was bluster and misery. Nowhere could she be comfortable.

In her bedroom, she had been struggling to get out of her seat for at least a minute, first pulling herself up by clutching the chair arms, then launching herself from the cushion. She would get herself partway off, then collapse back onto the chair, more tired and frustrated than when she sat down in the first place. She never went out anymore. Thomas had to attend gatherings alone. *Sit* was all she seemed able to do.

She couldn't eat much, for there seemed to be no room left in her stomach for food. She couldn't sleep, for there was no position she could bear for more than a few minutes. And even if the London weather had been mild instead of brutally cold, she could not take a walk, for her back ached.

The tiresome physician had told her to rest in bed, but she could not find a tolerable position, no matter how she arranged the pillows. Her thoughts kept twirling in such a circle. She wanted an end to it all.

But the thought of actually giving birth was daunting, and then there was the fear of caring for the baby. Too many babies died. Her sister watched over hers constantly. It was a huge responsibility. For now, she kept the babe safely inside her, but what might happen when he was born?

It must be a he, of course. Thomas wanted a son. In a few years, their boy would be toddling about after Wills and John at Barton Park.

Charlotte was distracted from her reverie by the announcement of a visitor. As promised, Lady Middleton had come to call.

With Susan's help, Charlotte hefted herself from her armchair. She managed the stairs one at a time, for her hips felt loose inside of her. Following a series of high-pitched shouts, she found her family in the front parlor. The boys were jumping from chair to chair all about the circumference of the room. Annamaria, thumb in mouth, stood gazing solemnly at a particularly grisly hunting tapestry. Over by the bank of windows facing the courtyard, Mary held the youngest, while the nurse tried in vain to calm John and William.

"Mary! Thank you for coming. How wonderful to see you!" Charlotte waddled forward as fast as she could, arms out.

"Aunt Lottie!" John and William dodged around the nurse and nearly knocked her over with their hugs. "Have you any more Penelope Pond Duck stories for us?" John shouted as William hung on her arm, swinging back and forth.

Annamaria took her thumb out of her mouth to add to the cacophony. "No, Catrina! I want a Catrina Cat story!" Her face turned crimson in her passion.

Charlotte laughed. "After I visit with your mama, I will tell you a new adventure," Charlotte promised, hugging each child in turn. "My goodness, John, soon you'll be as tall as I! And Wills, is that a new tooth coming in? What a pretty frock, Nankin. You'll be the belle of the ball soon enough. Oh, Mary, how they've grown! And the baby must be walking soon?"

Mary handed the baby to the nurse. "I'm in no hurry for her to learn. Three is enough to run after." She smiled fondly. "Both boys have grown prodigiously. I believe William is taller now than Harry Dashwood. Do let's sit down, Charlotte. You look pale. No, John, you cannot go out and play in the fountain. You'll catch your death. William, climb down from there. Stop sniffling, Annamaria. The duck in the hound's mouth isn't a real duck like in Aunt Lottie's stories. That's only a picture."

All finally settled when a tray of cakes was served.

"I'm glad you've come, Mary." Charlotte sighed with relief as she sank into a nearby chair. "We haven't seen each other since we visited Conduit Street. I'm sorry I missed going with you to the party last week. It was quite a rout, was it not? How tiresome it is to be indisposed and miss the fun."

"Hardly fun for all." Mary frowned. "We did not stay long, for Miss Marianne took ill. You heard, no doubt. I was forced to leave in the middle of a rubber."

"That dreadful man, Willoughby. How could he marry another woman after he'd courted Miss Dashwood?"

"His wife came with £50,000."

"Nevertheless, I shall never visit them in Somerset."

"He's hardly a neighbor, Charlotte. Cleveland is nowhere. It would take nearly half a day's travel to reach Willoughby's estate."

"All the more reason not to visit him."

Mary tilted her head to study her sister. "Not long now for you, is it?"

Charlotte rubbed her stomach and grimaced. "Very soon, I think. It...Mary, it will be all right, won't it? You fared well, even with your first?"

"We do not speak of these things." Lady Middleton glanced out the door.

"Please, Mary. I cannot ask Mama. She won't tell me the truth."

Her sister hesitated before she leaned over. "It *is* hard," she said softly, "Especially with the first. The pains come, but not all at once. With John, the birthing took the better part of a day. I thought I couldn't bear it." She gazed steadily at Charlotte. "But I *could* bear it. And so can you. There is no greater joy than holding your newborn babe in your arms."

"What if —?" Charlotte twisted the fabric of her morning gown in her fists.

Mary laid her hands over her sister's. "No 'what-if's.' There's naught to be gained in that." She squeezed Charlotte's hand in hers. "Don't worry. You will have Mr. Donovan. There isn't a finer physician in London."

Charlotte relaxed her grip on her gown and instead held tight to Mary's hand, which felt cold and solid.

# Chapter Thirty-One

Thomas Palmer had the uncomfortable feeling he was being watched. Given that he was seated in his very own library in his own townhouse, he tried to dismiss the notion, but could not. He felt eyeballs drilling into the back of his neck, a most unpleasant sensation. But when he looked up from his paper, he saw no one. Nothing there. He shook his head. It must have been his overwrought imagination. Not surprising: he had recently taken to reading the obituaries in *The Gentleman's Magazine*, as his mother used to. Remarkable how many wives had died — not only widows but young wives: Richard Townsend's wife had been only twenty-six. Wives of the Right Hon. Charles Sutton, Westley Dampier, Esq., Captain Jewell, and Dr. Haygarth had also died young. And then there was the notice of the woman who died in January after her confinement with her fourteenth child.

Fourteen. His mind boggled.

A furtive noise to his left drew his eyes from the magazine. Again, nothing seemed amiss. Perhaps a cinder had fallen from the grate. No sooner had he turned his attention back to his reading, however, than he heard a faint scuffle, followed by a duet of giggles.

He knew *that* sound. He'd seen Sir John's carriage arrive

earlier in the day.

"Come out, boys." From behind the twin columns framing the doorway to his sanctuary came the angel-faced imps. "Well?"

They trained their eyes on him, eyes as bright and clear as Charlotte's but with a hint of deviltry in them. He was struck with the thought that his own sons might look like this someday.

"Do you have any peppermints?" the older one said.

"Is that any way to greet your uncle?"

The boys shifted their feet. "We're hungry," the smaller one said, sticking out his pointed chin.

From the icing smeared on the child's cheek, Thomas doubted the truth of that statement. "You are William. Is that right?" The boy simply stared. "And you are John?" The older one nodded. Thomas set aside his paper, stood, and bowed. "Good day, gentlemen."

The boys looked nervously at each other before John took a step forward. "Good day, Uncle Thomas." He nudged his brother, who inched up to his side.

"H'llo," he mumbled, with a quick bend.

"Now," Thomas said, "regarding the question of peppermints. Will they not spoil your supper?"

William shook his head vigorously.

Thomas clamped down on the smile that twitched at the edge of his mouth. The lad reminded him of Henry at that age. "You're certain?"

Both boys nodded.

"In that case, it happens that I have some twists of peppermint in my pocket." Thomas reached into his coat, where he kept the candy for Charlotte's delicate stomach. He held two sticks out to the boys.

John grinned and darted forward to take them, handing one to William. Both boys immediately stuck the peppermints in their mouths.

"And what do you say, boys?" Thomas could not stop his smile this time.

"Thank you, Uncle Thomas!" they shouted before running

out.

~*~

*"You have proven yourself worthy, Catrina," Penelope Pond Duck declared, and most of the barnyard animals nodded their fuzzy and feathery heads in agreement. The mice, however, abstained, for they chose to keep to their nest in the hayloft. Catrina Scullery Cat was officially accepted into the Order of the Paddock."*

"Tell another, Aunt Lottie," William begged, tugging at her skirt.

"'Nother," echoed Annamaria, who had curled up on the settee next to her.

"We shall have to wait for another day," Charlotte answered, ignoring their groans. "Your mama will collect you soon." She squirmed about, trying to find a comfortable position. The backache that had plagued her since midmorning had grown worse, and no amount of shifting seemed to help. "It's late. Your papa will be waiting for you."

Annamaria pulled herself onto her knees and kissed Charlotte's cheek. Not to be outdone, the boys each hugged their aunt in turn, though they could not get their arms about her middle. The jostling made beads of cold sweat pop on Charlotte's forehead.

"Come home with us, Aunt Lottie," John said, tugging her arm.

"I don't think I can get up right now, sweetings," she said, as a twinge made her catch her breath.

"We'll help you!" John shouted. "Will, get her other arm!" They both began pulling, which made her discomfort ramp into pain. Sharp pain.

"Boys, stop. No, I appreciate your effort, but you need to go and fetch someone if I'm to ever leave this seat. Run, now."

Charlotte closed her eyes against the next twinge as Annamaria gently patted her shoulder.

~*~

"Uncle Thomas! Come quick. Aunt Lottie needs help!" William's shouts echoed through the marble hallway. Thomas was on his feet before the boy entered the room.

"Where is she?" He nearly skidded on the polished floor in his haste to reach the child.

"This way!" The imp turned and ran ahead.

Thomas was not far behind.

~*~

Left alone with his thoughts, Thomas could not redirect them. Even the Book of Common Prayer acknowledged the peril of childbirth: "FORASMUCH as it hath pleased Almighty God, of his goodness, to give you safe deliverance, and to preserve you in the great danger of Child-birth; you shall therefore give hearty thanks unto God." Women died in childbirth with great frequency. The rate in some places was one in five. They died in terrifying ways: hemorrhage, or fits, or childbed fever. No one talked about that horrifying statistic, but the evidence lay in the cemeteries and paraded about in society, where husbands sired children with second and even third wives. Children died too — in parts of London, half before they reached the age of five.

It was best, then, not to get too attached.

But when Charlotte was at last brought to her childbed, Thomas chose instead to remind himself that most women survived the ordeal. If four out of five survived, then eighty of a hundred. Eight hundred thousand out of a million. He repeated the calculations to himself again and again as he waited downstairs, straining to interpret the sounds from above — the rush of feet, the faint cries, and worst, the quiet.

His aunt had asked that she know nothing of the event before it was all done with. Yet the night Charlotte labored, Henry was at his club, and Lady Middleton had taken her children back to Conduit Street. Mrs. Jennings had gone out before notice of the impending birth could reach her in Berkeley Street. Only Georgina remained in Hanover Square to keep the vigil with him in the parlor, directly below the room where Charlotte labored.

Sitting upright as always, Georgina interrupted his mathematical calculations with inadequate comforts. "Women do this every day, Thomas."

"Charlotte is not 'women.'" *How many out of two-hundred-fifty-thousand?*

"To you, yes. But every person in the world got here the same way."

Thomas rubbed his hands over his face. "Death rates are as high as one in five, Georgina. Those are hardly decent odds."

"Charlotte is young and healthy. Her sister had four and survived. Judging by the commotion this afternoon, all of those children thrive."

Thomas thought of the tow-headed devil that had led him back to Charlotte. "They seem a robust lot." He wouldn't mind a son like that. If the child lived.

"Many women have more than four. The Duchess of Leinster had twenty-one." Georgina smiled. "Not that I suggest you follow suit."

"She died last year, didn't she?"

"For heaven's sake, Thomas. She was over eighty. Charlotte will be fine."

His musings were cut short, for the physician hovered in the doorway.

# Chapter Thirty-Two

Charlotte squeezed her eyes shut. The progression was just as Mary had described. Aches became pains, and pains became agony, coming in waves, sharper and closer together. She could bear those. But Mary had not warned her of the gush of fluid, which the attendant had caught in a basin. The waters signaled the onset of unrelenting torment that left Charlotte panting and sobbing.

The attendant repeatedly wiped Charlotte's brow, but the woman's ministrations irritated instead of soothed. When Mr. Donovan, the physician, arrived, he seemed totally unimpressed with Charlotte's suffering. Instead, he merely looked her over as she curled into a ball, watching him through slitted eyes.

"Progressing nicely," he pronounced, and went downstairs.

She'd have slapped him if she could have spared the energy. Charlotte tried to remember that there *was* a reward at the finish. Only an hour or more, perhaps three at the most. Then there would be a baby in her arms, a sweet, warm, tender infant for her to hold and to love. He *must* be healthy. He'd been kicking and rolling about a few days before, so much so that she couldn't finish her tea. But he had been quiet lately, hardly moving at all.

She wrapped her arms around the mound that was her baby and prayed he was sound.

Where was Mama? How could she have gone out when Charlotte was this near her time? She bit her pillow as she felt the next pain start. The pains came closer now, one nearly on top of the other. She could barely catch a breath between them.

"Won't be long, Mrs. Palmer," the attendant said in her irksome, chirpy voice. "Try to rest between the pains."

"There is no end to the pains," Charlotte ground out, ending in a cry.

Mr. Donovan appeared soon after a particularly piercing scream. "Get her on her left side, then," he said coolly, rinsing his hands at the ewer of water on the nightstand. "Take away this petticoat, and let's see where we are."

As the next pain mounted, Charlotte felt a great pressure on her nether regions and succumbed to an uncontrollable urge to bear down.

~*~

"It is finished," Mr. Donavan said.

Thomas leapt to his feet, spilling the brandy clutched in his hand. Nothing about the physician's expression gave any indication of the outcome. Thomas knew terror for the second moment in his twenty-six years. "Is she—?"

"Mrs. Palmer is well. You have a son. A robust, full-sized infant."

The words took their time sinking in. "A boy, you say? An heir? And both are alive?" Thomas's knees wobbled.

"You can go up and see them." The physician held out his hand. "Congratulations, sir."

Thomas took the man's hand in both of his. "Thank you. Thank you." He then turned to his aunt, who stood by his side, and hugged her. "Better than four out of five. Thank God," he whispered. The smile he caught reflected in the mirror by the door rivaled the sun, which was just rising.

~*~

Charlotte's arms shook so that she had to relinquish the

hold on her brand-new son. Her curls, now dark with sweat, were plastered against her forehead and neck. Every muscle ached from the work of birthing, and she was beyond tired but too jittery to settle back against the pillows. There was one more step before she could give in to exhaustion.

Thomas stood at her bedroom door in his shirtsleeves. His hair looked as if he'd been yanking it, his collar lay open, and his cheeks were unshaved. Charlotte's breath caught when his eyes focused, not on his heir, but on her.

"You are well, Mrs. Palmer?" He hesitated by the door frame, then strode across the room to her side as if to see for himself.

Her smile was shaky, but her answer was strong. "Quite well, Mr. Palmer." Merely having him near her sent warmth through to her fingertips.

He glanced behind himself, then turned his back on the nurse and baby on the far side of the room. "You've never looked more beautiful, Lottie," he murmured, then bent to kiss her gently on the lips.

Charlotte's eyes welled with tears, and this time, her voice too trembled. "Come meet your son."

~*~

Thomas Tharp Palmer looked much like an uncooked roast beef. That was his proud father's assessment as he held the infant in his arms. The little red face was somewhat squished, and the tufts of hair on the cone-shaped head stood up like stalks of barley. But when the baby yawned and opened his wide blue eyes, his father was riveted by the gleam in their depths. And when Thomas Tharp Palmer grasped his father's finger and brought it to his tiny mouth, the elder Thomas was bound for life.

All too soon, the news of a Palmer heir spread about town, and a deluge of visitors made siege.

"How can we have so many connections?" Thomas complained to his wife, who was rocking their son in the nursery a week later. "There are sisters by affinity to you, brothers by age and hospitality, distant relatives I haven't seen in years and had no idea were in town. Lord help us. We'll overcome by all the ties of blood and friendship!"

Charlotte laughed. "They've merely come to offer congratulations and pay their respects. You should be happy little Tomkin is universally admired! Just look how he smiles!"

"Gas," his fond father said, stroking the child's cheek and the rounded breast beside it.

"I'm quite sure he was smiling at his papa," Charlotte declared, smoothing the baby's stalks of hair.

"Perhaps," Thomas replied, grinning without realizing it. His contentment was all too soon interrupted, however, by the bustling arrival of Mrs. Jennings, who appeared each morning, every morning. Some days, she also stopped by at tea time. His poor son was thus subjected to women's babbling for hours at a time.

It was high time Thomas joined Henry at his club.

~*~

Spring winds buffeted the trees in the courtyard at Hanover Square, but they could not rival the turmoil in the nursery at the top of the house many weeks later.

"Oh, Mama, thank God you have come. I am quite at my wits' end. Little Tomkin has been crying and fretting since dawn. And look! See here! His poor, sweet face is all over with spots! I fear he has the smallpox! Whatever shall I do?"

Mrs. Jennings bustled over, not even taking the time to remove her pelisse and bonnet. Pulling the fussing baby from her daughter's arms, she drew back the shawl from his puckered face. And laughed.

"Lord, you gave me a scare, you did. Now, now, sweet boy, don't you have a big voice for such a little lad?" She jiggled the baby in her podgy arms while he whimpered. "This isn't the smallpox, dearie. Praise heaven for that. See how he soothes when I rub my finger over his gums here? He has nothing in the world but the red gum. The drooling caused the pimples and that rash about his neck. Once the tooth breaks through, he'll be right as rain, won't you, little man?"

"The nurse said the same." Charlotte wrung her hands. "But I'm sure that cannot be it. He's been crying for hours. Truly, he is most seriously ill. I've sent for Mr. Donavan. My poor baby!"

"There now, love, don't get yourself all worked up into a tizzy. Everything will be fine, I promise."

"He cries so. I can't bear it!"

Mrs. Jennings' stern look took Charlotte by surprise. "There is nothing wrong with this mite but a sore gum, I tell you. The physician will say the same."

They were interrupted by the arrival of Mr. Donavan, who had stopped in sooner than Charlotte had feared. He took thirty seconds to look over the child, then let out a *harrumph*. "Nothing serious at all. Get him a teething coral. And if he's not sleeping, soak a handkerchief in some brandy and let him suck on it." He left soon after, muttering something about "new mothers" under his breath.

"I'm a terrible mother," Charlotte whispered. Her breasts ached, her nipples were chafed, her head throbbed, and all she wanted to do was curl up in her bed and cry.

"Nonsense."

"I'm so tired, Mama. I can't sleep for fear he'll need me. He fusses unless he's eating, and he wants to suck all the time."

"He's spoiled. I told you to hire a wet nurse."

"But he's my baby. He— Mama, he's the only one who truly needs me. I can't abandon the poor little thing to someone else."

"You are a good, gentle-hearted girl," Mrs. Jennings said, patting her cheek.

"I don't want to be only good, Mama. I want to be good for something."

"There's no harm in getting a wet nurse to help. You'll always be his mother."

"I want to be as good a mother as Mary. Hers all lived." Charlotte regretted the words when she saw her mother's face fall. "Oh, Mama, I did not mean to hurt you. I know you loved the babies you lost and did all you could for them."

"I pray you never face that test, Lottie. But you won't be any kind of a mother if you wear yourself out. I'm worried about you. It's high time you left the house. Saw your friends."

Charlotte pressed her lips together and looked away. "My friends have other amusements. It's as if I no longer existed once I moved to Somerset, even though I returned to town. No one comes to me anymore, Mama. Not since the visits to welcome Tomkin. Only you."

Mrs. Jennings cocked her head. "What kind of talk is that, Lottie? That doesn't sound like my cheerful girl. Of course you have friends. What about the Dashwood girls?"

"I try, but they put me off whenever I invite them here. I wonder if they like me at all."

"I'm quite sure their refusals have nothing to do with you. Come on, dearie, perk up. Little Thomas needs you, and your husband would be lost without you. Everyone who knows you loves you. How could they not? You're the dearest girl who ever lived. There, that's better. A smile on the face has a way of bringing a smile to the heart. You'll see. Now I'm going to have a word with Mr. Donavan before he leaves to see if he has any news to share."

# Chapter Thirty-Three

There *had* been news, which traveled within minutes from mother to daughter and on to Thomas Palmer. Mr. Ferrars, who was once linked to Miss Elinor Dashwood, had been engaged to another lady for over a twelvemonth. And Miss Marianne Dashwood still pined for Willoughby, though he was married. The miseries of the Dashwoods did much to put Charlotte's own depression in perspective.

"Oh, poor Elinor!" Charlotte exclaimed to her husband over tea that afternoon. "No wonder she's been so standoffish. Her hopes have been shattered. And here she never let on! And poor Marianne, for *her* heart has been torn apart too. Now that I think of it, she looked positively ill the last time I saw her. Quite pale and trembly. I'm ever so glad that I never made the acquaintance of that dreadful Mr. Willoughby and wish his home were not in Somerset. How miserable Marianne must be! Everyone is talking of it. Dearest, we must have Mother bring the Dashwoods to Cleveland when we leave town. London holds too much sorrow for them now. You must ask them, Mr. Palmer. They think the world of *you*. I know if you ask, they won't say no."

Although Thomas remained unenthusiastic at the thought of guests, Charlotte was far more animated than he'd seen her for weeks. Perhaps company would entirely lift her out of her doldrums. Yet he hesitated to make a call. "Would the invitation not be better coming from you?"

"Oh, no. They are much more likely to accept from you than from me."

His wife's downturned mouth and shadowed eyes were enough to spur Thomas to act. He'd ask every lady she knew to Cleveland if it would bring his cheerful Lottie back. The next morning, he found himself at Berkeley Street, pressing the Misses Dashwood and Mrs. Jennings to come to his home in Somerset. Soon it was arranged: Charlotte would travel with the baby and the nurse, and Mrs. Jennings with the two Misses Dashwood, taking their time on the road and stopping at inns along the way. That left Thomas mercifully free of female chatter, for he was to travel on horseback with Colonel Brandon, whom he'd met in town. That gentleman was surprisingly eager to join the Dashwood sisters.

The men arrived at Cleveland in time for a late dinner. The weather had been beastly since they left Reading. Somerset roads were a sea of mud, as usual, slowing their progress to a walk.

They found the women in the drawing room. "Mr. Palmer! You've come at last." Charlotte launched to her feet and hurried toward him. Since she held their son in her arms, it was fortunate she was able to stop before running into her husband.

"As you see, the colonel and I managed to find our way intact." On the far side of the room, he noticed Mrs. Jennings near the fire and the Dashwood sisters sitting together, far from the rest of the group. "Good evening, Miss Elinor, Miss Marianne. Welcome to Cleveland. I trust your journey was uneventful." He nodded briefly at Mrs. Jennings and his brother, who had already returned to his seat. His aunt, he noticed, was not among the company.

In his wife's arms, little Tom screwed up his face in what might have been a smile or the start of a squall. To forestall the latter, Thomas took the baby from his wife and held the wiggling bundle to his shoulder, muffling the assorted snorts and squeaks.

He then turned to his traveling companion, mindful of his role as host. "Colonel, I believe you know most of the company here. Can I offer you a brandy before dinner?"

The colonel bowed to the ladies and accepted. He then moved to stand beside Miss Marianne. Henry poured from the decanter at his elbow, since Thomas was otherwise occupied dangling his pocket watch in front of the baby. He held onto his son even as the group walked into the dining room, where the nurse waited to fetch little Tom for a bath.

Dinner proved a loud affair. Mrs. Jennings rambled on about the journey, and Charlotte fretted about the hazards to babies from coach rides. Miss Elinor, seated next to Colonel Brandon, spoke at length about a mutual acquaintance, and to his left, Miss Marianne picked at her food in relative silence. Henry and Charlotte conversed about goings-on at Barton Park. Aunt Georgina had elected to have a tray in her room.

Thomas noticed that the Dashwoods had little to say to Charlotte. His hope that the visit would boost his wife's spirits faded.

At last, the meal ended, and Thomas, Henry, and the colonel retired to the billiard room. There, the men could fully enjoy the manly pleasures—a good cigar, fierce competition, and talk of nothing but horses.

Later that night, Thomas came upstairs to find his wife nodding by the fire, the baby nestled at her breast. The firelight burnished Charlotte's curls, and a faint blush warmed her cheeks. In her arms, little Tom stirred and opened his mouth, rooting about even in his sleep. Bemused, Thomas leaned down and kissed each forehead, then gently took the baby from her and laid him in the cradle. Charlotte barely stirred when he lifted her as well and led her off to bed.

Although the miserable rain had finally stopped, Cleveland remained gloomy. A bank of clouds hung over the countryside, and even the air within the walls felt damp. When Charlotte had visited the village with her baskets, she reported that the lane was nearly impassable. Not even the dogs were out and about.

Charlotte and Mrs. Jennings suggested outings to the coast, but their guests seemed reluctant to do much beyond sit by the fire. "I don't know what else to try," Charlotte complained to Thomas one afternoon. "I fear I'm a failure as a hostess. Miss Marianne mopes about the house. No amount of pleading convinces her to join us in any activities. She shuns cards and music and turned up her nose at Spillikins. She wouldn't even play Bridge of Sighs."

"Perhaps a game about thwarted affections was not an appropriate choice, under the circumstances," Thomas observed. "Best leave the girl to her own devices."

The next two nights, as the rest of the household gathered in the drawing room for cards, Marianne ventured outside.

"Whatever is she about?" Mrs. Jennings said to the room at large on the second night.

"My sister is merely enjoying the twilight in solitude," Elinor replied, her gaze on the lone figure who walked along the gravel path beyond the window. "She said she particularly enjoys the wilder sections of the property, where ancient trees grow untrimmed, and the sedge grows high."

"Another poet in our midst," Thomas muttered. The current obsession with wild landscapes and raging storms baffled him.

At last, the subject of their speculation returned to the house. Marianne stood like a wraith emerging from the shadows as if she'd stepped out of one of the tiresome novels his wife read.

"Miss Marianne! You're sopping wet!" Mrs. Jennings bustled to her side. "Why, your lips are blue! We must get you out of these clothes at once. The idea of tramping around in the cold and damp! What were you thinking?"

Charlotte hurried to the bell, nearly tripping in her haste. "I'll ring for a hot toddy," she said.

Miss Marianne said nothing. Her eyes remained fixed on the blue Axminster carpet as if dissecting its pattern of flowers and fruit. Miss Elinor hastened to her sister's side. "I'll tend to her, Mrs. Jennings," she said firmly. She put an arm around

Marianne's quaking shoulders and led her into the hall.

Marianne's sodden shoes left slick footprints on the cold stone.

It was no surprise to anyone that Marianne took sick in the night. Her general malaise had shifted to a full-blown fever by dawn. Her illness was the main topic of conversation the next morning after breakfast.

"Oh, poor, poor Marianne!" Charlotte patted her son with more force than was necessary to dislodge a bubble. "Her sister reports she's very ill indeed. A dreadful cold. And no wonder, as wet as she was. When I visited her this morning, it was evident that a deep cough has settled in her chest." She cleared her throat, then coughed twice herself.

"These things can turn deadly in a matter of hours, you know," Mrs. Jennings declared. "And infections can spread. You must take a care of young Tom, dearie."

Charlotte clutched her son tightly to her chest. "My baby! We must send for the apothecary at once, Mr. Palmer!"

Thomas could not ignore his wife's pleas. Nor could he fail to do what was best for their guest. He set off at once.

The apothecary, upon examining the patient, confirmed the seriousness of Miss Marianne's illness. "Her fever's quite high, sir, and with the pain in her limbs and the rawness of her throat, she's in grave condition indeed. I'd advise against moving her. And I'd keep the rest of the household away."

Thomas suspected this news would further alarm his wife. When he reluctantly relayed the diagnosis, Charlotte turned pale. "We must be off at once, Mr. Palmer. It could be the putrid fever!" She clasped his arm, tugging on it repeatedly. "We cannot expose our son to contagion. Do you know how often infants succumb? Order the carriage, do!" She stumbled as she paced, and Mr. Palmer had to reach out to prevent her from falling.

Gently settling her in a chair, he tried to reason with her. "I can't leave our guests in such a state. What kind of host would I be?"

Charlotte gaped. "You would choose a stranger over your

own child?"

Thomas raised an eyebrow. "Hardly a stranger, Charlotte. Just last week, you called the Dashwoods your dearest friends. I truly think our son is safe. He has not been in the same room with Miss Dashwood since she became ill."

Charlotte's faced flushed. "He is in the same house! Is that not enough? You would risk his *life*? Do you not care about either of us?"

At that, Thomas had to relent. Within the hour, his wife, his child, and the nurse were on their way to his uncle's house on the far side of Bath.

# Chapter Thirty-Four

Thomas spurred his mount the last mile to his uncle's country manor. Hours of travel had allowed him too much time to grow anxious about what might have transpired after he left Cleveland. The memory of Marianne Dashwood's fevered cries echoed in his mind.

At last, he saw a roofline in the distance. His uncle's property, he knew, was in a constant state of construction, having been converted from ancient monastery to hunting box to its current form, a sprawling Georgian manor house. Perfectly symmetrical red brick walls rose three stories past the treetops. Only the cellars retained any remnant of the Gothic arches of the building's religious foundation. As boys, he and Henry had played there. The ancient timbered hall his mother had grown up in was long gone, pulled down and replaced before Thomas was born. Above ground, all was new.

He urged his horse forward. In front of the house, a footman helped him dismount and assured him the beast would be walked, groomed, and fed. Thomas trusted the same welcome had been extended to his wife and son.

He scraped his boots on the steps before handing his heavy wool coat to the servant who opened the door. "Pray inform Mr.

Tharp that his nephew has arrived," he said as he entered.

"Ah, there you are, Thomas," came a voice from the back of the wide central hall. "You made quick time, I see, despite the weather."

His Uncle Tharp stood before him, a gaunt man, slight and graying, but retaining the toothy smile Thomas knew from his younger days. He wondered fleetingly if his uncle was still in the habit of keeping peppermints in his pocket.

"We didn't expect the coach for hours," the gentleman said. "Wonderful to see you. Long time since my sister's funeral. Too long. You look spent. Come in and sit before the fire. Mrs. Tharp remains in town to enjoy the assembly rooms. I'm grateful for your company."

"Thank you, sir." Thomas followed the older man's halting gait to a well-appointed reception room, where a cheerful fire blazed. "I appreciate your taking us in under the circumstances." He looked about but saw no sign of Charlotte. "Is Mrs. Palmer close by?"

"I believe she is resting. Seemed a bit shaky after the trip." His uncle handed him a glass. "Here, boy, drink up. This'll warm you."

The journey the day before must have tired his fretful wife, Thomas reassured himself. That, and the worry over the baby. She fussed over their son morning, noon, and half the night. By the time she'd climbed into the carriage at Cleveland with the baby and the nurse, Charlotte had worked herself into a feverish dither. "I do wish you'd come with us, Mr. Palmer. Whatever would I do if *you* took ill? Please come as soon as you can. Tomkin and I need you."

Hard words to remember. But Thomas had responsibilities to his guests, and he was not a man to shirk his duties. His wife had overreacted. With her now safely ensconced many miles from Cleveland and its dangers, he hoped to find her calmer and more cheerful, more like herself. He would let her rest for the present.

Seeking to reassure himself that the child was also fine,

Thomas climbed the many steps to the old nursery at the top of the house. This part of the building has not yet suffered his Aunt Tharp's passion for redecoration, and the furnishings looked much the same as they had when Thomas, Henry, and their cousins had been children. He dismissed the nursery maid, who looked on the verge of exhaustion herself.

The baby lay swaddled in the old cradle. Curious, Thomas looked down at his son's puckered face and clenched fists. Did infants dream? And if so, what might they dream of? These dreams did not look peaceful. The heir to Cleveland snuffled and whimpered in his sleep. Hesitating at first, Thomas leaned over and picked him up, drawing his blanket more closely about him lest he suffer a chill. In his father's arms, the baby was a solid bundle, fitting neatly in the crook of his arm.

"Now, then, Tom, you've had quite the adventure, haven't you? More travel in a month than most lads have in a year, I'll warrant." The baby slept on, curling snugly against his chest. And so Thomas settled them both into a chair by the nursery fire and stared out the window, seeing nothing, waiting for Charlotte to awaken.

~*~

The hour was late, past country hours for dinner when Charlotte stirred. Despite her long nap, she felt worn out. Even getting out of bed took effort. Mind fuzzy, she wondered if Thomas had left Cleveland. Would he follow her or stay with their guests? It seemed days since she'd arrived at Uncle Tharp's home with Tomkin and the nurse.

*Tomkin!* She must check on him. She vaguely remembered the nurse bringing him to her so that she could feed him, but he must be hungry again by now, for her breasts were full. Fumbling about, Charlotte dragged on her gown and struggled with the laces. The room wavered when she bent to put on her shoes. As she climbed to the third-floor nursery, she had to hold tightly to the banister.

The sight that greeted her upstairs made her pause at the doorsill. Her husband, with rumpled hair and a dark stubble of beard coating his jaw, sat dozing in a great chair. He had come after all. In his arms, he held their son, who slept as peacefully as a cherub.

Charlotte moved hesitantly, reluctant to disturb their slumber. Thomas looked different when he slept. The line that usually creased his brow lay smooth, and his neckcloth was untied.

When the baby stirred and grunted, Thomas opened his eyes. "Ah, you're up," he said, rubbing his neck with his free hand. "They said you were sleeping."

"Tomkin needs his dinner." She eased into a second chair by the fire before her weak legs gave out. "When did you arrive?"

He handed the stirring baby to her and stretched. "Two hours or more now, I suspect. Your trip went well?" He stirred the fire and added a log.

Less dizzy now, Charlotte waited until the baby had latched on before answering. "We arrived in good time. Your uncle has been most generous." She smiled down at her greedy son. "Tomkin seems not to have suffered from another carriage ride."

"And you?"

Charlotte looked up in surprise, for her husband rarely inquired after her own health these days. "I'm a bit tired, but after a good night's sleep, I'll be right as rain. How is Miss Marianne?"

Thomas relayed the seriousness of that lady's condition and explained that Mrs. Jennings had remained behind to help.

"Oh, poor Marianne! Surely Mr. Harris has some potion that can cure her. Mama always swears by poultices in such a case." She held the baby to her shoulder and patted his back until she brought up a burp.

"We shall hope the apothecary and your mother return her to full health soon," Thomas said.

The nurse returned at that moment, and Charlotte handed over her sated son. He was a damp bundle, sorely in need of a change. Looking down at her wrinkled day gown, Charlotte saw that she, too, was in need of a change. If Mrs. Weston could see her, she'd shake her head in dismay. "If you'll excuse me, Mr. Palmer, I'd best dress for dinner before someone else catches me like this."

The room spun a bit as she stood, forcing her to clasp the back of the chair. She must have sat too close to the fire. Her very bones seemed to have melted.

Dressing was an ordeal, and she felt strangely disembodied as conversation floated about her at dinner. She pushed her food about on her plate. Not even the excellent fricando of veal appealed to her. Retiring early, she tossed and turned, restless as strange images flashed before her eyes: Thomas bending over her sister's hand, her son covered with weeping sores, her father dead in his coffin. She woke next to Thomas more tired than when she'd gone to bed and quite unable to rise.

"I'll have the maid fetch tea," her husband said, his face floating over her.

"Thank you." Her answer came out like a croak.

All morning she shook with chills, and her head ached so much she had to ask the maid to close the curtains. She could keep down only a few sips of tea and half a roll. By evening, she called out for her mother, reaching for a figment by the bedside.

~*~

"You should sleep, son. There's no sense in your sitting here." Mr. Tharp rested a crusty hand on his nephew's shoulder. "She's taken a draught the apothecary brought and is resting quietly for now." He cleared his throat. "We've sent for a wet nurse for your son."

Thomas never looked away from his wife's flushed face. "Her fever is climbing. She may wake. I cannot leave her now."

The doctor had bled her twice since the fever's onset. Throughout the treatment, Charlotte had struggled until Thomas was forced to sit on the bed and hold her arm while it drained. He could not bear to watch her lifeblood stream into the bowl.

Now, hours later, he drifted off in the chair by the bedside but was roused by Charlotte's moans. Her fever raged. His own chest hurt when she wheezed and coughed. At times, she seemed out of her mind. Nothing he could do would calm her when she thrashed about. At those times, she could not bear to let the maid touch her, screaming when the girl tried to sponge her hot skin. Only Thomas could wipe his wife's forehead with cool water and pull the soaked shift from her body to replace it with a fresh one. Her skin burned. One minute, she mumbled, and another shouted. She was murmuring now. Thomas leaned close to hear.

"Tomkin?"

"He's fine."

"Thomas."

"I'm here. Thomas. Your husband." He turned cold as her eyelids flickered. Her stare was blank.

"Just the kind of man I like," she whispered. "If only he could love me," she added before sinking again into oblivion.

She could not die. Would not. He simply wouldn't allow it. As Thomas Palmer watched his young wife twist the bedsheets and struggle for each breath, he cursed the fever that wracked her. He cursed the medicine, which did nothing to help. He even came to the brink of cursing poor Marianne Dashwood for bringing sickness into his home. Most of all, he cursed fate, for it was about to take away the one woman he could not do without. Losing her would be like splitting tendon from bone.

And it was his fault.

He should have followed her and their son directly when they quitted their Somerset estate. He should have fetched a better doctor from London instead of summoning one from Bath.

He should have told Charlotte he loved her.

# Chapter Thirty-Five

The fever had broken at last, and the apothecary had promised the worst was over, but Thomas was full of doubt. The pale woman with the tangled hair who lay propped against a mountain of pillows was nothing like his wife. Her face had grown thin, so her haunted eyes overshadowed her other features. Those eyes followed him about the room, not longingly, but with a wariness, entirely unlike the Charlotte Jennings she'd been.

"Won't you come downstairs? My aunt has arrived from Bath."

"Perhaps tomorrow." She turned away from him to gaze blankly at the vase of daisies he'd set on the table beside her bed.

"You've been in this bed for days. The physician says fresh air and company will do you good."

Did she roll her eyes at him? "You can't control everything, much as you try to. I'll come down when I'm ready." Her sweet mouth set itself in a firm, unassailable line.

Outside, a weak sun poked through the clouds, and a bracing breeze blew through the window off the River Avon. Thomas felt the chill. "I miss you by my side, Lottie."

Still, she would not look at him. "You needn't coddle me, Mr. Palmer. I'm a grown woman, not a child. I don't need to hear sweet lies to make me feel better. Words like sugar are sweet, but they dissolve too soon."

"I don't think anyone has ever accused me of being sweet." Charlotte's cough sounded a bit like a laugh.

"Or of lying."

"I meant no insult." She appeared more alert at the thought of having offended.

Thomas tried in vain to control his exasperation. "Charlotte, I have never lied to you. And I do not lie now. Life would be damned cheerless without you."

She shifted in the bed and fixed her eyes up at him as he spoke. "You used a profanity."

"I want my happy, healthy Lottie back again."

She stared at him intently. "You thought your happy Lottie irritating. Hardly a proper future politician's wife."

"Wherever did you get such an idea?"

"From you." She turned her back to him. "You preferred my sister. A 'woman of inestimable virtue' I'd do well to emulate. That's what you said the morning after we were married."

Thomas looked down at his left hand, where his ring glinted in the sunlight. Was it possible he'd said such a thing? His memory of that day was cloudy. "If I said that, I was wrong."

"You wanted Mrs. Weston to make me over." Charlotte's voice was muffled. "I lack dignity and discretion, you said."

He closed his eyes. "I was blind. You need no alterations. You are cut from perfect cloth."

"Yet you prefer silk to muslin." Her words were bitter.

Thomas threw up his hands. "What would you have me do? I cannot make flowery speeches, Charlotte. If I felt less, I might say more." He paced a few feet away from the bed, then turned. "I have no wish to change you. Ours was a dismal family before you came. We want you back. I need you back."

When she turned over, Thomas recoiled at the ire leaking out from her. "You merely need an acceptable wife. You do not need *me*."

She *was* irritating. Why would she not believe him? What

had happened to his sweet, amiable Lottie? "What must I say to convince you?"

"I'm sure you know what I want to hear." She looked away once more. "I'm recovered enough to return to Cleveland. We should leave soon. The election is only a few weeks away. And I *do* know how much *that* matters to you."

~*~

*The election was in two weeks.* Charlotte bit her lip. So much time had been lost — to trying to entertain difficult guests. To her illness. To caring for little Tom. But she would not desert the villagers, who, now more than ever, sorely needed an advocate.

And she would not fail her husband in this mission. He may not be able to admit he loved her. He might never bring himself to say the words. But he needed her. So be it. She knew her duty as his wife. Her future happiness was tied to his. And she desperately wanted to be happy once more.

Thomas wanted a seat in the House of Commons above anything in this world. She would get it for him if she had to muster a guinea for every family in the borough. She'd been saving her pin money for just such a need.

The present plan had evolved gradually as she made friends among the villagers. They'd had such a dim view of Mr. Thomas Palmer before she'd worked to mend it. Of course, the men remained deferential to her. They would never stop to pass the time of day with the lady of the manor. It wouldn't be fitting. Their wives, though, were another matter. And Charlotte knew that the way to husbands was through the wives.

After all, they were the ones who stirred the pot.

"Good morning, Mrs. Yates," she called as she stopped in front of the cottage with her usual basket. "Hello, Tessie. What a pretty dolly you have."

The child proudly held up her rag doll for inspection.

"My, she's a fine dolly indeed. And how is your baby brother today?"

"He cries too much."

Charlotte glanced at Mrs. Yates. "My Tomkin cried too

until his teeth came in."

Mrs. Yates nodded. "It's hard on them, the poor wee mites. Won't you come inside, Mrs. Palmer?"

Charlotte hefted the basket she carried and followed the careworn woman through the door. "I've brought a blanket. And a cold pie, plus some pears and preserves." She had also tucked a coin in the basket, as she'd done on every visit to a village cottage.

"You're good to us, ma'am. Not many would bother the way you do."

"Mr. Palmer very much wants me to see that all the villagers are cared for, especially when the crops aren't doing as well as he hoped."

"Being able to add a rabbit to the stew now and then helps." She held Charlotte's gaze. "It don't go unnoticed."

Charlotte took a deep breath. "You know, he's standing for a seat in the House of Commons. If he could get that seat, he could do even more good, don't you think?"

Mrs. Yates nodded. "I've said as much to my Michael."

"I think Mr. Palmer would be the best representative ever." To herself, she added, *Especially now that he's more sympathetic to the opposition party.* With his understanding of the villagers' plight, Thomas could turn Parliament in the right direction. As she had turned *him.*

"If you don't mind my saying so, he's like to go far with you doing his campaigning."

Charlotte laughed. "Exactly what I thought, Mrs. Yates. I'll be taking my leave now. I have some other stops to make."

And so Charlotte Palmer made her way from doorstep to doorstep, bribing her husband's way into Parliament, not with ale, but with hartshorn jelly.

~*~

At last, election day came.

Thomas Palmer's stomach had tied itself into knots tighter than Gordius had managed at Phrygia. And Thomas feared he was no Alexander the Great this day. He expected to lose. "You needn't come along to hear the votes," he told Charlotte that morning. "The ordeal is likely to last for hours. Georgina and Henry are staying back." The fewer witnesses to his humiliation, the better.

She shook her head. "Nonsense, Mr. Palmer. I wouldn't miss this moment for the world."

Resigned, he escorted her to the waiting carriage and set out. The horses seemed far too swift-paced. The rolling hills sped by. Thomas's stomach rolled with them. By the time they crossed the stone bridge into the village proper, he felt sick.

Upon arrival, he helped his lady down and together, they made their way to the center of the village. Charlotte swiveled left and right, waving and greeting all she met. She stopped to speak at length with a few, including Michael Yates. Thomas remained at a distance and kept his eyes strictly ahead of him. His height gave him a clear view of the tops of scores of heads. Standing amid the crowd of villagers didn't help the cramps in his gut. He kept his arms tightly at his side lest he be jostled.

Her conversations complete, Charlotte stood with him as if nothing devastating were about to occur. In fact, she seemed uncommonly cheerful, much less aloof than she had been of late. "There, there, Mr. Palmer," she said, patting his arm. "You'll be fine. These are all your people. Try to relax."

Thomas leaned down to speak into her ear. "How can I? My defeat will be announced any minute."

She smiled placidly at him. "I'm certain you will win."

Would nothing shake his wife's determination to hope for the best? "You should prepare yourself, Charlotte. I have. There's no chance of victory. The other candidate is far better known. And liked."

Charlotte assessed him with what felt like a gimlet eye. "It's true, Thomas. You *are* hard to like. But actions speak louder than words, my mother always says. And you've been generous to those in need."

He straightened and shrugged. "A few fish and hares."

"A little food means much when someone is hungry. All will turn out as it should. You'll see."

He was amazed at her utter certainty. "How can you be sure?"

"Because I've had the promise of nearly every woman in the village."

Thomas forgot to keep his voice down. "You've *what*?" On all sides, the villagers turned to look at them.

Charlotte grabbed his hand and drew her husband to the edge of the milling crowd. While he shook his head in disbelief, she explained. His mouth dropped open halfway through the narrative.

"While I appreciate the gesture, Mrs. Palmer, it means nothing. The women can't vote. It's the men's votes I need."

"And the men need their women. After a day in the fields or the forge, a soft word and a hot meal go a long way to opening a man's ears, let me tell you!"

As she spoke the words, an official stepped into the center of the square to call for the votes. Thomas closed his eyes. He had to *hear* his defeat. He couldn't bear to also watch it. One by one, the official called on the men of the village. One by one, each man shouted out the name of his candidate.

"Mr. Palmer!"

"Open your eyes, Thomas," Charlotte said. "You will want to remember this day."

He opened them. And opened them wider as the voices rang out. "Mr. Palmer." One vote. "Mr. Palmer." Two. Ten. Dare he hope? Could she have been right? "Mr. Palmer." Twenty.

With each repetition of his name, Thomas Palmer grew more astonished. Thirty. And more.

By the end of the day, his wife had won him the election.

The village elected Thomas Palmer of Cleveland by a remarkable margin. His elation was only partially dampened by the villagers pressing in, cheering and congratulating him. "Thank you. Thank you, good people," he shouted, struggling to stop his throat from closing. "I promise to do my best to serve you."

After much handshaking, he was at leisure to notice

Charlotte still at his side. "I see you were right, Mrs. Palmer." His smile stretched to show every tooth. "The men do need the women."

Charlotte raised her eyebrows. "Any man in particular, Mr. Palmer?"

She deserved his gratitude. "Particularly *this* man. I can never thank you enough."

Her eyes flashed a warning. Charlotte wasn't smiling now. Hands on her hips, she declared, "Your *thanks* isn't what I want."

Thomas frowned. That tone spoke trouble. Nearby, Mrs. Yates grinned at the spectacle. "What, then?" He glanced around him, seeking an escape route, but he was hemmed in on all sides. It was his turn to tug her by the hand, squeezing through the throng, pulling her further from the square toward the bridge, where they might speak in relative privacy.

Once he stopped, Charlotte skewered him further in place with a look. "Do you love me, Mr. Palmer?"

Thomas swallowed. "This is hardly the time to discuss such things, Mrs. Palmer," he said softly, reluctant to be overheard by the few passersby.

"There has never been a better time," she hissed back. "I repeat: *do you love me*?"

He had only to admit it and be done with it? "Of course."

"Of course what?" She narrowed her eyes.

"Of course I love you," he muttered.

"As I am?" She made no effort to quiet her voice this time.

He glanced around. No one loitered within twenty feet. "You're my wife. The mother of my child."

"Those aren't reasons."

She needed specifics. He dug deep to name some. "Your sweet nature. Your care for the tenants. Your loyalty to family. Your acceptance of my aunt. Your unfailing good spirits." When she remained silent, he added, "The light in your smile. Your passion for ducks! Those qualities brightened life at Cleveland."

"What of your own life?" Charlotte crossed her arms, though her smile showed signs of returning.

"Mine particularly." He took a deep breath. "I'm a better man than I was because of you."

"Is that all you have to say to me?"

He gave up any pretense of dignity and declared loud enough to startle a group of men heading to the tavern, "Charlotte, I love you with all my being. And I shall, for all of our days together. I hope and pray that they are many."

Her cheeks flushed. "*All* your being? Truly, Thomas?"

"As I said before, I have never lied to you, and I do not lie now." He had no doubts about his wife's feelings. They were always imprinted on her face.

Later, in the carriage, she lifted her head from his shoulder. "Your heartbeat steadies me." Unshed tears filled her eyes. "My Thomas," she whispered. "I've loved you from the first moment I saw you when you called on Mary. I used to dream you would look up and notice me."

"I did notice. You were always skidding about." He smiled at the memory.

"Did you think I was terribly forward?"

"Terribly? No." He tucked a wayward curl behind her ear.

"Even at the Argyle Room?"

He thought back to the girl he'd seen that night, all pink ribbons and teasing ways. She'd been impossible to ignore. "You were unforgettable."

"In a good way?"

"In the best way."

"And now you love me."

"As I promised you I would. I take my vows seriously, you know." When he looked at his wife's radiant face, Thomas Palmer knew he was, indeed, the most fortunate of men.

# Epilogue

And so, Mrs. Jennings' younger daughter chose to be happy once more.

A year before, Charlotte Jennings had stood in another church to speak her vows. Now Charlotte Palmer stood in St. George's in Hanover Square, the most fashionable church in town. Above her, the white-and-gilt ceiling gleamed, and all about the Flemish glass shot rays of rich color to paint the stone floor and walls. Behind the altar, an ornamental screen portrayed the Last Supper. It seemed to her that the light with which Christ was bathed stretched out to where she stood, warming and transforming her from new bride to seasoned wife and mother.

Much had also changed for the guests gathered for the occasion of Thomas Tharp Palmer's christening.

Since the boy's proud father was now a member of Parliament, courtesy of a by-election, several of that august body were in attendance. Mr. and Mrs. Weston could hardly be missed, for they commanded an entire pew. Lord Dysart sat near them with his new bride, the former Miss Ludford. Also present in numbers were residents of Barton and Somerset and an aunt and uncle from Bath. Sir John Middleton stood as sponsor for the baby, and a more jovial godfather had never lived. And though no one would call Georgina Palmer jovial, she was an attentive and practical godmother.

Lady Middleton's attention was devoted to keeping her offspring in their seats. In that task, she was aided by Miss Browne, who had accompanied the Middletons from Barton Park, much to the delight of Mr. Henry Palmer.

Among the guests, Miss Elinor Dashwood had changed her name to Ferrars. Miss Marianne Dashwood was rumored to soon be affianced to none other than Colonel Brandon. Mrs. Jennings had been all atwitter about the courtship since she had been the first to uncover his *tendre* for the younger Dashwood sister.

"Must you always smile?" her husband said to Charlotte, running his knuckles over her cheek before brushing invisible lint from his exquisitely cut coat.

His wife looked up at him, eyebrows raised in mock surprise. "How could I not, my love? For everything is so very perfect."

Thomas Palmer allowed himself a smile of his own. "I expect you're right, my dear," he replied, and silently added his own prayer of thanksgiving to the service.

THE END

# Acknowledgments

"I could not sit seriously down to write a serious Romance under any other motive than to save my Life, & if it were indispensable for me to keep it up & never relax into laughing at myself or other people, I am sure I should be hung before I had finished the first Chapter. - No - I must keep to my own style & go on in my own Way; And though I may never succeed again in that, I am convinced that I should totally fail in any other."
- Jane Austen, Letter to James Stanier Clarke, 1 April 1816

I'm with Jane Austen on this subject. I owe her a great debt for the inspiration and the subject matter of *Wit and Prattles*. Astute readers will also note nods to *Northanger Abbey, Emma,* and *Pride and Prejudice*. The characters in *Wit and Prattles*, however, are fleshed out by my pen, not Jane's. While Jane gave us the skin of the Palmers, my scalpel carved deeper.

Several primary sources also fueled my writing. The conduct book Lady Mary gives Charlotte is based on a very real volume, *The Mirror of the Graces,* (1811), and some of the quotations are derived from that estimable tome. Another enlightening insight into Regency values that I consulted is Mrs. Taylor's *Practical Hints to Young Females on the Duties of a Wife,*

*Mother, and the Mistress of a Family*, the third edition of which was published in 1815. Thomas Wilson's *An Analysis of Country Dancing*, *Ackermann's Repository* and *The Gentleman's Magazine* are additional informative sources from the Regency period that I perused. Medical practices of the era are partially gleaned from William Buchan's *Domestic Medicine* (1784). Alert readers may also notice some nods to Wordsworth and Williams.

Many postings on the Jane Austen Society site provided reference information. In addition, articles in *Persuasions*, a journal of the Jane Austen Society, also provided insights: " Mrs. Jennings and Mrs. Palmer: The Path to Self-Determination in Austen's *Sense and Sensibility*" by Kathleen Anderson and Jordan Kidd; "'The Bells Rang and Everybody Smiled,': Jane Austen's 'Courtship Novels'" by Gillian Dooley; "Discerning Voice through *Austen Said*: Free Indirect Discourse, Coding, and Interpretive (Un)certainty" by Laura Mooneyham White and Carmen Smith; and "Curious Distinctions in *Sense and Sensibility*" by Ethan Smilie. Other works that also aided my research include Roy and Lesley Adkins' *Jane Austen's England: Daily Life in the Georgian and Regency Periods*, Edward Porritt's *The Unreformed House of Commons: Parliamentary Representation before 1832*, vol. 1, Natalie Tyler's *The Friendly Jane Austen*, and John Russell's *London*. *The Regency House Party*, A PBS series (2004), was both entertaining and informative.

I had a great deal of fun setting *Wit and Prattles* in a specific time period and including actual historical events and weather forecasts from 1814-1816. I'm aware, however, that *Sense and Sensibility* was published in 1811, and also that it was originally an epistolary novel entitled *Elinor and Marianne*, written around 1795. For a detailed timeline of *Sense and Sensibility*, I suggest readers consult Ellen Moody's "A Calendar for *Sense and Sensibility*" in *Philological Quarterly*, 79 (Fall 2000), 233-266.

The research for this novel left me excessively diverted. Did Regency women wear underpants? How was a corpse laid out? When was pheasant in season? What birds sang in Somerset? Would a waltz be danced at a Devonshire country house? How many courses at dinner? Breeches or pantaloons? What were the maternal and infant mortality rates in that period? How far was Conduit Street from Hyde Park? Which were the potwalloper boroughs in Somerset? What role did women play in bribing voters? What hung behind the altar at St. George's?

Now, to address the Janeites who will argue that I took too much liberty with Miss Austen's work. I admit that I strayed. *Mea culpa*. No, she would never have included those sex scenes. No, she would not have delved into Thomas Palmer's point of view. No, she would not have killed off Sophia Palmer. (See Radhika Jones' essay "In Jane Austen's Pages, Death Has No Dominion," 13 July 2017 in the *New York Times* book review.)

Nor would Miss Austen have explored the darker side of childbirth, though her letters do reference it at times. Furthermore, no, her ladies would not discuss the particulars of the war raging in Europe. Their interests would extend almost exclusively to the officers who might appear in dashing uniforms at dances. And no, although Miss Austen's characters could be sympathetic to those less fortunate than they, she would not allow them to dwell on the politics of labor and poverty. And finally, absolutely not, Aunt Georgina's sexual preferences would never have been alluded to, although that character is very loosely based on an actual Regency woman, Anne Lister. But I am writing in 2021, not 1811, and modern readers, I hope, do find such topics pertinent.

Most authors, I think, like a challenge. *Wit and Prattles* offered several. Making a heroine out of a silly chit and a hero out of a rude man were delightful exercises. Crafting Regency language after I'd just finished writing a series of contemporary romantic suspense novels spun a web of new synapses in my brain.

Most taxing in the writing process for *Wit and Prattles* was pairing my made-up tale of Charlotte and Thomas with the plot of *Sense and Sensibility*. And yet, I'm grateful to have had the original novel as a stepping off point for mine. In a few places, I've incorporated Austen's dialogue while adding a new perspective.

Channeling Miss Austen at times was immensely

entertaining. For instance, I sensed her over my shoulder when I wrote, "No wasting disease, gruesome accident, or loathsome act escaped Sophia Palmer's attention. Perhaps had she spent more time in town, she would have discovered a plentiful supply of death, decay, and misery, but life at Cleveland proved disappointing and dull: the tenants were invariably healthy, and accidents exceedingly rare." Austen created a few memorable hypochondriacs like poor Sophia but only hinted at what inspired their maladies. If you doubt that Jane Austen had a snarky streak, read her letters.

My style, then, is my own. I'm a creature of my age, and I write for my contemporaries. Austen's novels can be hard going for a twenty-first century audience. Modern readers prefer concrete sensory description and short paragraphs. Readers may search in vain for the color of Elizabeth Bennet's fine eyes, but Charlotte Palmer's eyes are blue. And while both Austen and I explore dualities in characters' temperaments, I explore the causes underlying personality traits. The four Bennet sisters, Elinor and Marianne Dashwood, and Robert and Edward Ferrars differ dramatically in personalities and behavior. So do Mary and Charlotte Jennings and Henry and Thomas Palmer. *Wit and Prattles*, however, examines the *why* behind their behavior.

I pray that readers will watch for more of my novels, as minor characters from *Wit and Prattles* have their own stories to tell.

Many thanks to all those who helped with this novel, especially to members of my writing groups (Laura Towne, Sharon Kurtzman, Maureen Sherbondy, and Bernie Bro Brown), whose encouragement kept me churning out the chapters, and to Maxine Bringenberg of World Castle and Karin Wiberg of the Jane Austen Society, whose deft editing and thoughtful suggestions added polish to the final draft. Thanks also to my hardworking agent, Renée C. Fountain. And lastly, eternal thanks to my dear husband, who may not be sociable, but who excels at loving.

*Wit and Prattles*, I hope you agree, is a good novel. I'll leave the last words to Miss Austen's Henry Tilney: "The person, be it gentleman or lady, who has not pleasure in a good novel must be intolerably stupid." *-Northanger Abbey*

# Endorsements for
# Wit and Prattles

"Nancy Martin-Young's Wit and Prattles is a delight. With impressive detail, strong voices, clever humor, and just a little bit of naughtiness, this Sense and Sensibility spinoff is perfect for a day at the beach or an afternoon with a cup of tea. Janeites and poets will love the sly literary references, and readers will never look at Mr. and Mrs. Palmer the same way again." **— Karin Wiberg, Jane Austen Society of North America, regional coordinator for North Carolina**

"If you love the world of Jane Austen with some steamy romance, then read this book. The language is spot on for the period and yet the pacing is modern, contemporary even. The secondary characters of Sense and Sensibility come alive in this fun and spicy novel. Charlotte (Lottie), is a young girl in search of a husband and sets her saucy cap on the enigmatic Mr. Palmer. And what Lottie wants, Lottie gets. Or does she? That's the twist in this novel and so true to life. That's all I'm gonna say about the story, so no spoilers, here. The settings are picturesque enough to make me book a ticket to Austen country, rich with description and detail and the characters are real enough to smack upside the head. You'll find yourself rooting for both him and her in this lovely novel." **— L. E. Towne**

"Wit & Prattles is a delightful historical romantic novel by Nancy Martin-Young. Based loosely on Jane Austen's minor characters...I was immersed in cat-and-mouse courtship games of the early 1800's. Surprising updates gave a nod to current conventions. Perfect as a beach read or to curl up with on a rainy afternoon. Fast paced and satisfying. I highly recommend this book. Can't wait for the sequel!" **— Lisa Saari**

**Preview of the next historical romance by Nancy Martin-Young:**

**The Burden of Good Breeding**

# Chapter One

Lady Middleton had secured everything she'd been raised to expect: an elevated standing in society, a reputation for elegance, and healthy children, all courtesy of a husband with a title. Besides these advantages, she had come to her marriage with the gifts of beauty, intelligence, and poise. Nothing rattled Lady Middleton.

Until now.

"No, he's not dead. Don't be ridiculous. He's only sleeping late. He sometimes does that after a quantity of brandy. No, stay away from the window. He wants the shades drawn."

"Madam, we must remove him. He can't remain longer in this state. It isn't sanitary." The physician reached out a hand to her, but let it drop. Even disheveled, Lady Middleton was untouchable.

"He'll wake any minute now," she continued, voice cracking. "You'll see. Look at his color, as red as always." She turned away from her husband's bulging eyes. "He'll be bellowing for his breakfast soon. Calling for his horse. He's never missed a day of hunting when the weather was fine."

A servant hovered by the door of the master's chamber, but advanced no further. "Mrs. Palmer has arrived, ma'am."

"Lottie? All the way from Somerset?" Lady Middleton patted her tumbled hair and glanced at her gown, which was unaccountably rumpled and creased. When had she last changed?

"What is she doing calling at this hour?"

"It's closer to night than morning, Madam." The servant kept his eyes averted and backed up two steps.

"I simply can't receive her like this. And Sir John is indisposed. Tell her to go away."

"Mary." From behind the servant, a plump blonde woman with corkscrew curls pushed her way into the chamber, holding a handkerchief over her nose. "Surely you won't turn out your own sister. Here I've sat in a carriage all day to see you." She moved to Mary's side. "Come, let's order some tea and leave Sir John to the doctor."

Mouth set in a grim line, Charlotte Palmer tugged her sister's arm, persisting with surprising strength until, at last, she dragged Sir John's widow from his bedside to begin the dismal business of mourning.

Widowhood. Mary shook her head. How had she arrived at such an unsettled state in so short a time?

Nancy Martin-Young met Jane Austen's characters when she was eight and remains a devoted Janeite. A former editor, reporter, and college educator, she (writing as Nancy Young) is the author of the Something in the Dark Series: *Seeing Things*, *Hearing Things*, and *Sensing Things*, which was a finalist in the RWA Best Banter Contest. Her romantic suspense series is set in Raleigh's historic Oakwood neighborhood. Nancy's also a prize-winning poet. Other works include a poetry collection and dozens of poems, articles, and short stories that have appeared in journals, magazines, newspapers, and anthologies. For more info, visit her website, nancymyoung.com, and check out her novels' Pinterest pages!